Hippocrene U. S. A. Guide to

ROCKY MOUNTAIN STATES

HENRY WEISSER

HIPPOCRENE BOOKS

New York

A Hippocrene U. S. A. Guide

For information, address:
HIPPOCRENE BOOKS, INC.
171 Madison Avenue
New York, NY 10016

ISBN 0-87052-219-1

Printed in the United States of America

CONTENTS

INTRODUCTION

This is not an ordinary travel guide. It is a book for thoughtful people who may be contemplating either a visit or a move to the Rocky Mountain states. It is written for those who want to read beyond the accomodation and restaurant lists and jumbles of blurbs about attractions that fill most travel books. It is for readers who want to enhance their visit to the region by knowing something about the history, geography, politics, culture, economics, climate and wildlife of these states. It should also help make the relocation of new residents easier.

The booming tourist departments of every state and many municipalities and attractions have inundated prospective visitors with tons of glossy, colorful paper. Every town and every sight seem to come close to exhausting the lexicon of superlatives. What this book seeks to do is sift throught all of that material, select some true highlights and provide sharp criticism for places enjoying more hype than substance.

The chapters have been designed to convey information efficiently. The first two are devoted to travel; the third to special characteristics of the region; the fourth to climate and wildlife; chapters five and six delve into history and chapters seven to eleven take up each individual state included, Wyoming, Montana, Idaho, Utah and Colorado.

This is not a guide for skiers or winter sports. It is primarily for those who will come to the Rocky Mountain states in spring, summer and fall.

The author is a Professor of History at Colorado State University who has lived in the region for over a quarter of a century.

A WORD OF THANKS

I must first of all thank my colleagues in the History Department at Colorado State University who were indulgent when I began to poach on their turf. These professionals who work on the American West include Charles Bayard, Liston Leyendecker, Dan Tyler and David McComb. None of them ever failed to supply information and material, but none of them are in any way responsible for any of the opinions or uncaught errors in this book. Professor James Hansen, who is something of a computer wizard, gently led the author into the new electronic maze while this book was being written.

Countless persons contributed special information for this book, but a few have to be singled out: Debbie Gessaman for topics about Utah; Jeanne LeClerc for information about living in the mountains; Jacques Rieux for broad insights about the whole region; Kim and Linda Hossner for topics about Idaho; Christopher L. Smith, the editor of *The Idaho World* in Idaho City, for information about his location and Linda Waidhofer, an excellent professional photographer based in Telluride for generously letting the author use two of her photographs for this book.

Once again my daughter Jeanette provided editorial help, particularly in the form of those cold, clear criticisms that I have come to rely upon so much. This time my two sons, Steve and Tim, also made a contribution by toning down my critique of the outdoor lifestyles enjoyed in the region. They are, after all, living them.

The Interstate System

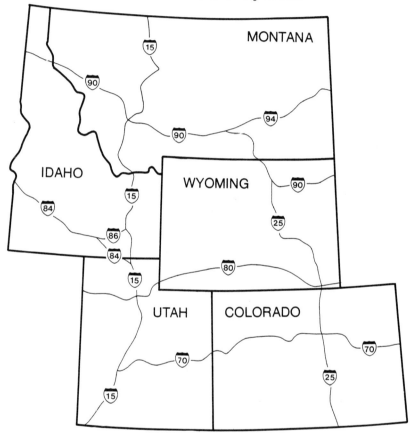

CHAPTER ONE

TRAVEL: SETTING PRIORITIES, GETTING AROUND, AND FACING HAZARDS

An Opening Scene

Those who first see the Rocky Mountains after a long drive over the plains can never forget the sight. Plains stretch for a thousand miles between the old, rounded Appalachian Mountains in the East to the sharp, younger, snow-capped Rockies. After driving for a day through flat, dry, hot western Kansas and eastern Colorado, seeing golden sunflowers waving in vehicular turbulence all along the way, eyes fixed on the flat, monotonous horizon glaze over in boredom. At least a few clouds down near the western horizon serve to add a small note of interest. As the hot August afternoon wears on, the clouds on the horizon begin to build. Clouds that began as little puffs rise a little with each dozen or so miles. Then something peculiar appears. The bottoms of the clouds look quite dark. Wait! They are not clouds! They are sharp little blue triangles that loom larger and larger, with a swirl of bright white clouds building above them. Then bright silver appears glistening on the tops of the dark blue triangles. After a thousand miles of plains, the Rocky Mountains bid welcome to the Rocky Mountain states, promising vistas of natural beauty, the scenes of a romantic history and all sorts of opportunities for adventure and excitement.

Some Suggested Strategies

WHY A STRATEGY IS NEEDED

It is important to work out a strategy before vacationing in the Rocky Mountain States. The region is too vast and has too much to offer for one, two, ten or fifty vacations. It is necessary to sort through what is available, set priorities and sketch out the trip on a road map. Remember that what looks possible for two, three or four weeks of vacation time in Des Moines, Schenectady, Dallas or Birmingham may not be possible when all of the long stretches of road are driven and all of the unexpected opportunities to stop and see things spontaneously present themselves.

Different itineraries work and do not work for different people. Interests vary. A number of people want to concentrate on scenery, particularly in the National Parks. Some want to get as far into the wilderness as possible while others want to enjoy urban amenities and good restaurants, galleries, museums and shopping. Many want to experience what is left of the Old West, or how it is now celebrated. Others want to enjoy sports in the great outdoors, including the summer sports of horseback riding, bicycling, water skiing, golf, river rafting, hiking, tennis, and four wheel driving on old trails. In the winter, downhill skiing, cross country skiing, snowboarding and snowshoeing occupy the time of sports enthusiasts. Fishing and hunting have their own calendars, predicated upon state, locale and species.

Why People May Feel Swamped by Information: People who ask for information to help them plan their trip get too much of it rather than too little. It seems that the Rocky Mountain states have overproduced tourist information. All of these states regard tourism as big and vital business operations, and they have big dispensaries packed with booklets, maps, pamphlets and flyers, most of them free for the asking. Each state also has an 800 number which will bring thick packets in the mail. Hotels, motels, R.V. parks the ubiquitous "trading posts," and all of the state tourist information stations have racks upon racks of this material. Moreover, each major attraction and many towns have information booths, kiosks or offices filled with the same kind of travel information. Picking such stuff up along the way results in the accumulation of several pounds of it in no time at all. Just ask any question at such a place, besides "Where is the restroom, please?", and a helpful person is likely to spring for a flier or map or pamphlet or a combination of them, seeming to deem no answer proper unless it is accompanied by printed material. One senior tourist adviser in Grand Junction, Colorado, admitted that the most daunting question he ever faces is that of the visitors who show up before his racks upon racks of printed material and huge, symbol-laden wall maps only to ask: "What is there to see in Colorado?" The agent must be tempted to reply with one word: "Everything!"

The real problem for visitors is to sift through this mound of printed material to select what may be useful and to discard the rest. Setting priorities becomes a critical undertaking. If a person or family is particularly interested in ghost towns or riding narrow gauge mountain railroads, or white water rafting or soaking in hot springs or enjoying Victorian melodramas in an old mining town, sorting and discarding becomes much easier.

The glossy booklets that each of the Rocky Mountain states furnishes free have major drawbacks. Everything in them, page after page, is depicted as gorgeous, wonderful, breathtaking or miraculous, and the color photography is there to prove it. Every paragraph gushes.

These booklets also chop states into geographically meaningless portions. Idaho, for instance, which has a natural division into three parts, north, central and southern, is cut up into seven parts: north, north central, south western, central, south central, south eastern and eastern. The other states make the same kind of irrational subdivisions in their colorful booklets. Why? Perhaps it is a form of gerrymandering so that the least scenic places are grouped with the most scenic places, or perhaps every location has its own clout in the state legislature and wants to be featured equally in the state booklet. The end result is that many people regard these glossy booklets as having very limited value, which is sad considering the expense that must have gone into producing and distributing them. Many people are so overwhelmed by the surfeit of things to see and do simply everywhere in each section of each state that they just lay the booklets aside. They put potential visitors in a position not unlike that of a diner in a restaurant with a thirty page menu presented by waiters who only say that everything is the very best. The purpose of this book is to act as a helpful waiter who can make some useful suggestions to help bring forth some of the best from a varied Rocky Mountain menu for people who want to see beautiful places and appreciate the region's history and culture.

BEAUTY, THE TOP PRIORITY

Whatever kind of visit or vacation is taken in the Rocky Mountain states, natural beauty must be a top priority. It is simply stunning, whether in the mountains of central Colorado, northwestern Wyoming, western Montana, central Idaho or in the canyons of the arid plateau of Utah, plus a thousand other places. In thin air the colors are wonderful: gray green plains, red plateaus, deep purple canyons, and a variety of colors for mountains: dark blue, purple or golden brown, depending on the light. The highest peaks are crowned with dazzling white patches of snow and ice even in mid-summer. Each season has its delights: in the fall the aspen trees put on a show of bright gold against dark green pines and in the summer thousands of species of wild flowers can make a valley flame in a multitude of bright hues. By day the colors are brilliant in clear air at high altitudes and at night the stars are simply brilliant.

The temptation to go on and on describing Western scenery must be resisted. No matter what word pictures describe, or what photographs reveal, nothing can compare to actually being at a site of natural beauty in the Rocky Mountains where all the senses can combine to take it all in at once. Nothing can compare to actually looking deep down into Colorado's Black Canyon of the Gunnison, or looking across at rugged Long's Peak from Trail Ridge Road going up over the Continental Divide above the timber line in Rocky Mountain National Park, or scanning across the seemingly endless blue and purple rangeland of Wyoming as night falls or seeing the fantastically eroded red rocks of a Utah canyon in the early morning sun. These are overwhelming aesthetic experiences that can engage the whole of one's being.

Nearly all visitors will remember some such scenes of natural beauty as the highlights of their trips to the Rocky Mountain States. Beauty will dominate magnificently, regardless of what activities are undertaken or what itineraries are followed.

THE WIDE OPEN SPACES AND FARAWAY PLACES, ANOTHER PRIORITY

Another fulfilling experience involves the wide open spaces that can still be found in many places in the Rocky Mountain states. Here landscape can still be seen basically as it must have looked to pioneers and explorers generations ago. In this age of multi-million dollar tourist operations, finding unspoiled, uncluttered and virtually uninhabited vistas is becoming more difficult, but there still are many of them left.

Feeling dwarfed and insignificant and alone in a vast, beautiful, ancient landscape can reveal the brief and delicate essence of individual lives. Such experiences should be especially important for people who live in hectic, urban and crowded environments. Problems and conflicts from a busy life shrink into insignificance in the wide open spaces. For many people whose egos convince them of their own great importance, time spent in the wide open spaces may expose them to an important, humbling outlook on their own relative insignificance. Such spiritual experiences can comprise the most important insights gained from a trip to these states.

Much of the rural areas of the Rocky Mountain states are truly faraway places, retaining the look of long ago. Farmsteads and ranches and small towns have the demeanor of splendid isolation. The relatively few people inhabiting rural areas have a look about them indicating that they move at a more normal pace and deal with life mostly on their own terms. The fast paced, more regulated, more driven, mainstream, urban-suburban Americans are not to be found, except as visitors and escapees. Their world seems hundreds of miles away, and indeed it usually is. There can be an enormous amount of space between cities and rural areas in the Rocky Mountain states. For example, the western slope of Colorado is a day away from Denver, and those living in southern Utah are the better part of a day away from Salt Lake City. By contrast, an idyllic village in upstate New York is likely to be flanked by great cities in all directions. Quiet backwaters in New England are not very far from the busy hubs, nor are the most rural of Pennsylvania Dutch settlements. Rural settings in the Rocky Mountain states are not oases or anomalies just over the hill from an urban complex.

Getting Around

DRIVING IN THE ROCKY MOUNTAIN STATES

Why it is Necessary to Drive: The only practical way to see the region is by motor vehicle. While a few Amtrack trains cross these states, airports dot them, and many bus routes still criss-cross them, neither trains nor planes nor buses provide an efficient means of getting around to most places. Of course, those who wish to multiply their risks of an accident can ride motorcycles and those who have time, stamina and a limited number of things to see can ride bicycles. Yet when all things are taken into consideration, the Rocky Mountain region does seem more suited to exploration by motor vehicle than any other part of the United States.

One obvious reason is the sheer size of the area. Two places a visitor might want to see may be hundreds of miles apart and only occasionally served by public transportation or not served at all. Another reason is that many of the most wonderful places are quite remote. Still another reason is the nature of the roads and the driving habits in the region, which are somewhat different from what prevails on either coast.

Roads in the Region—Their Advantages: In general, roads in the Rocky Mountain states are quite good and quite well maintained. They are also comparatively uncrowded. In fact, some of them are almost empty, even at the height of the tourist season. The scenery along them in most places varies from pretty to spectacular.

Several clear and open four-lane Interstate Highways cross the region north to south and east to west, making it possible to cover hundreds of miles per day quite easily. Almost the same rate of progress can be made on many well maintained two-lane highways, where nearly all of the relatively few drivers move along at a fast pace and where engineers provided special passing lanes for ascending hills and mountains.

The aridity of these states gives another advantage to driving. Fog in most places is extremely rare. Motorists from many other parts of the country are well aware of how frightening the sudden onset of thick fog can be, particularly on unfamiliar roads or on high speed multi-lane highways.

Signs along the highways mean exactly what they say in this region. Thirty miles an hour for a curve means just that. Warnings about rough or dangerous conditions, such as steep downward grades, should be heeded literally. It may be a good idea to avoid the third or fourth class roads, which are gravel or in the unimproved category, unless they are known to the driver or the driver is deliberately seeking adventure, hopefully in a rugged four-wheel drive vehicle.

Dealing With Heights: Mountain driving has its own peculiar challenges, even when the highway is a four to six lane Interstate going over a pass. Many people are squeamish about drop offs at the side of the road, particularly if they have a fear of heights and falling. Since there are so many two lane roads going over mountainous terrain, a much smaller percentage of steep drop offs are protected by guard rails than in other parts of the country. This guarantees that breathtaking views will not only come from looking up at snow covered peaks, but that breath will also be taken away by looking straight down a wall of rock for hundreds or even thousands of feet to a stream or boulder pile. Such views can commence just a few feet from the edge of the road on the passenger's side.

Think positively about the situation. The driver is most unlikely to fall asleep and meander off the road in these situations. What is more, bear in mind that nearly every car that traverses the starker stretches continues on. Note how almost no vehicles or parts of them can be seen down at the base of the cliffs. Film makers have overused the sensation of cars bouncing down mountains and exploding. In real life it almost never occurs, at least in the summer.

Winter Driving: In the winter drivers in the Rocky Mountain states expose themselves to considerable risks in taking roads that are steep and snow-packed. Even some snow plow drivers are lost on dangerous roads in the winter. The drivers' best friend in icy weather is actually the cautious police officer who closes the road, something that happens very frequently in the winter.

Since these states have such an economic stake tied up in winter sports, they devote considerable effort to keeping roads safe and passable. Plowing and sanding are carried out with vigorous determination. When the weather is bad, check points will be set up and a chain law will be put into effect for mountain passes. The chain law insists that vehicles going over a pass have snow tires or chains on them.

In general, manpower and machinery are effectively applied in the Rocky Mountain states to handle the severe winter snowstorms that regularly hit the region. Police patrols are stepped up in bad weather to rescue stranded motorists on major highways. When severe storms hit major metropolitan areas, fleets of volunteers with four wheel drive vehicles show up to help keep vital services and personnel operating. Recovery is usually quick.

Motorists must prepare properly for winter travel, because it may mean the difference between freezing to death and survival. Keep the gas tank as close to full as possible. Pack extra warm clothing and blankets somewhere in the vehicle. Include matches, drinking water, canned food along with a can opener and a flashlight. Before departing, call the local weather service and ask about conditions.

Some Hazards of Summer Driving: Summer driving has a few of its own hazards. Mountain passes are found all over the region, promising steep ascents and descents. Going up, slow moving vehicles can become hazards, particularly if there is only one lane ascending. A slow vehicle can accumulate a chain of decreasingly patient drivers behind it very quickly. It is important for the drivers of such vehicles to make use of turn outs or special slow lanes to let those who are stuck behind make an escape.

Going down from a pass is more dangerous than going up. Grades of 6% and higher are common and can go on for miles. Optical illusions about the gradualness of the descent can occur, which are sometimes dispelled by a truly alarming glance at the speedometer. Worse, a truck can have its brakes fail and become a runaway. Sometimes huge trucks plow a path of death and destruction down a mountain pass before they are brought to a halt. That is why there are so many runaway truck escapes in the region, usually in the form of huge, steep inclines of sand sharply jutting off from descents. Some can be seen with their sandy surfaces ominously disturbed by deep tire marks.

When driving down a steep grade, always do what the truck drivers are supposed to do and gear down so that the motor can act as an auxiliary brake. Never coast, which is both foolish and illegal.

On twisting mountain roads with steep dropoffs, many drivers will be tempted to avoid the edge by driving towards the center. This can be disastrous if oncoming traffic suddenly appears, particularly if the driver is momentarily diverted by scenery or wildlife.

Now and then the temptation to pass on a blind curve will arise because a slow vehicle, underpowered for mountain driving, will trundle along up ahead at an annoyingly slow speed. Avoid this temptation, not only because a swift vehicle may be coming the other way, but also because one's own vehicle may be more sluggish than expected on account of the grade and the altitude.

Never stop in a mountain road, no mater how deserted it seems and no matter how lovely the scenic vistas. Always look for a place to pull off entirely out of the way of traffic. The road that looks utterly deserted one minute can have a pickup truck full of high spirited teenagers roar down it the next. Fortunately, most of the major roads in the region have convenient scenic turn out parking areas every so often.

Fallen rocks can be a hazard now and then. They tumble down from above, or are washed down in rainstorms. Zones where they are likely to be found are generally well marked and extra care should be exercised in passing through those places. Do notify authorities of rocks in the road if the opportunity to do so presents itself.

Gas: Obviously, it is important to keep a sharp eye on the gas gauge when driving in those parts of the Rocky Mountain states where the nearest gas pump may be up to eighty miles away. Even on major Interstate Highways, terse announcements that there will be "no services" for the next 50, 60 or 70 miles are ordinary. Take no chances in the wide open spaces. Make an effort to keep the gas gauge towards full.

Any gas will not do because a phenomenon called vapor lock can occur sometimes when cheap gas is overtaxed and vaporizes too early. Vapor lock usually causes a motor to misfire and cough. At worst, it brings the car to a standstill. In most instances, a cooling off period solves the problem.

Vehicles requiring high octane gas may have a problem at many rural gas stations where only regular leaded gas and ordinary, lower octane unleaded gas are available. Therefore it is best to fill up at larger towns where at least some pumps will supply premium gas, usually at premium prices.

Western Drivers: Good drivers and wretched drivers, polite drivers and rude drivers, can be found everywhere, and most individuals can fit into all of these categories at one time or another. Nevertheless it remains true that somewhat different driving patterns can be observed in various parts of the country. Nobody would expect the traffic flow in Brussels, Belgium, to be similar to that of Des Moines, Iowa.

Drivers from the Rocky Mountain states tend to be polite and moderate, more "laid back", in the current slang, than drivers on either coast. They tend not to loom ominously in rear view mirrors, tailgating to push people along or aside so that a destination can be reached a few precious minutes early. Many drivers from the region appear to be in no hurry and have no objections about being passed.

The moderation of Rocky Mountain drivers may be attributed in large measure to comparatively uncrowded conditions on most roads. This is not to say that Rocky Mountain cities and suburbs are without gridlock. Traffic can inch along during rush hour in some cities to emulate the worst highway conditions in California. In fact, it can become worse than southern California when ice and snow further impede traffic or make it more dangerous. But these conditions are not typical of most places in most of these states. There is one kind of driver from outside the region who can be a problem in mountainous areas. He or she is the flatlander, most likely from somewhere in the Midwest, who has never experienced mountain driving. This driver grips the steering wheel with clenched fists as the slightest curves, inclines and declines are slowly and painfully negotiated. Natives who are stuck behind such drivers on twisting roads where there is little room to pass can become very frustrated by them. Often the flatlanders travel at less than the posted speed limit and gather a long column of cars with local plates behind them. The flatlanders should make a point of pulling over at a safe place in order to let those following pass. Otherwise the least patient follower may be tempted to carry out a risky pass that may lead to an accident.

Speed Limits: In the years following the petroleum crunch, the "double nickel" or 55 miles per hour upper speed limit was made mandatory throughout the United States. Citizens of the Rocky Mountain states were bitter about it, regarding it as unfair for their region. While it made sense to put the limit down to 55 m.p.h. for the congested states of the East Coast, it seemed to make little sense to reduce the 65 or 70 m.p.h. limits that had prevailed across the huge and open expanses of the Rocky Mountain states.

A person from a small town in Wyoming would argue that he could travel to another town on good, flat, uncongested roads more safely at 70 m.p.h. than someone driving at 55 m.p.h. on an Interstate near Denver, San Diego, Boston or any such place. For him, slowing down to 55 m.p.h. seemed at once unnatural and unnecessary. It was frequently viewed as another example of how Easterners had used their numbers and power to impose something undesirable on the West.

Westerners solved this problem by ignoring the posted limit and the police generally cooperated by ignoring the drivers doing so, unless they actually exceeded the old higher limits, or if they neglected to at least slow down somewhat when the patrol car was in sight.

One after effect of this 55 m.p.h. era, besides eroding respect for the posted law, is that there is still a 5 m.p.h. slack generally allowed. So 35 m.p.h. on a city street can be safely stretched in most places to 40, and 70 m.p.h. on the highways will be tolerated in general. It is not wise to go above those limits because very well equipped patrol cars can materialize with startling suddenness, even on the most seemingly deserted highways. This is important to keep in mind because several portions of Rocky Mountain highways look like open speedways. Most notorious is the stretch of Interstate 80 west of Salt Lake City which passes near the Bonneville Salt Flats, where cars are raced to test speed. This highway is so straight, so flat and feels so safe that the temptation to speed can become strong.

FLYING

Commercial Flights: Commercial pilots have no problems navigating in the Rocky Mountain region. Sometimes storm systems up over the mountains or coming off the mountains can cause considerable turbulence. Most experienced passengers become used to it. High winds at airports and occasional dangerous erratic wind flows do occur, but the accident rate does not seem to be out of proportion to any part of the nation.

From October to May, flights can be delayed or canceled by blizzards, with the worst storms paralyzing even major airports. Surface traffic around them can be halted or reduced to a slow crawl while the airports' interiors can become vast holding pens for tired, disgruntled masses. The cheery side is that bad snowstorms threaten for less than a fifth of the days on the worst months for snow. Sunshine tends to come back quickly, as does the normal operation of airports. The odds of making travel connections are heavily in favor of the traveler even in the months noted for the most intense snowstorms.

Flying in Private Planes: Odds are much less advantageous for private aircraft, particularly those flown into the region by inexperienced "flatlanders" whose destinations are the ski resorts high in the Rockies. The mountain states are littered with the wreckage of small private planes every year. Grave warnings are given regularly by various aviation groups and authorities, but small, fragile aircraft continue to crash at alarming rates. An old cliché declares that the most dangerous portion of any trip is the ride to or from the airport. Statistics reveal that this cliché is no longer true in the Rocky Mountain states if a small private aircraft is what is waiting on the runway.

It takes experience to fly in the mountains safely. The thin air demands much more performance from airplane engines, to the extent that many planes based in the region are equipped with special fuel injection systems. Air at high altitudes, which is at lower atmospheric pressure, simply does not give as much lifting power. Gaining altitude to get over high places is much more demanding in thin air. Some of the mountain passes are over 12,000 feet, requiring oxygen on board. What is more, turbulent high winds aloft can be expected over the mountains.

Experienced pilots say that there is little or no margin for error in mountain flying. All questionable or marginal weather should be avoided and meticulous planning should be undertaken beforehand.

The existence of these hazards have led to proposals for special mountain flying training and certification on pilots' licenses in the form of a special endorsement for mountain flying. In the meantime, planeloads of skiers will still take off from Des Moines, loaded down with baggage, with a pilot from Iowa at the controls, on their way to a vacation of fun in Aspen or Vail. The pilot needs luck. Colorado is second only to Alaska in having the highest fatality rate for general aviation.

HIKING AROUND

Why You Should Get Out and Hike: A large number of people who visit these Rocky Mountain states never cease to be what National Park officials have called "windshield tourists." They drive here and there and only emerge from their steel cocoons to walk 100 feet or so to centers and exhibits equipped with parking lots. Of course, windshield tourists can see and learn much this way, but to really get a taste of the Rockies it is necessary to park and lock the car, and get away from all vehicular traffic and sounds of civilization by hiking into the interior somewhere.

In the interior, people can escape to what the Rocky Mountains have meant to Native Americans, the Mountain Men, the earliest pioneers and those outdoor types who live in the region. Beauty, serenity, peace and the restoration of a sense of proportion in one's life can all be appreciated on a good hike.

Some basic, practical advice follows for taking short hikes of a few hours' duration at most. This is information primarily for inexperienced vacationers from other regions. Experienced hikers who camp outdoors off the trail overnight and who use sophisticated equipment will want to skip parts of this section because it will be too rudimentary for them. But even experienced hikers, if they are from other parts of the country or world, should look at the special advice concerning hazards of hiking peculiar to the Rocky Mountains. This advice appears in the last section, suitably subtitled for them. See also the section on lightning below.

The Big Fears of Inexperienced Hikers: People from large urban areas may have anxiety attacks on a hiking trail in the great outdoors. The awesome silence of the majestic scenery may lead to these thoughts: If I meet a madman or a thief along the way, how can I call the police from out here? If I fall down and break my leg, how can I be rescued? If a wild animal attacks, how can I defend myself? If I get lost in this wilderness and die in it, how will anybody ever know? Where is the nearest telephone just in case something goes wrong?

Relax. Unwind from city conditioning. This is vacation time! Urban America is a very tense, anxious place nowadays, but on the trail hikers can free themselves from its tensions.

Leave it behind. Stop looking for lighted phone booths, policemen and the safe havens of an urban jungle.

On hiking trails in the Rocky Mountain region hikers run a much greater chance of being struck by a lightning bolt in the sunshine than to become the victim of any kind of assault by a stranger. The author has been hiking in the Rocky Mountain region for a quarter of a century, and during all of that time I never saw a single hostile or threatening person on the trails. Some people may have appeared to me to be foolish or silly, and some of their dogs may have been unfriendly, but nobody ever came along who was obviously suffering from mental illness, neglect, abuse, or deprivation, and who thereby might pose some kind of threat. On the streets of New York City it is difficult to proceed for a few minutes without someone of that description appearing abruptly. Inexperienced hikers from the urban areas need to leave their anxieties about other humans behind when they head up the trail.

A Legitimate Fear—Getting Lost: Getting lost is what all hikers need to worry about, both the inexperienced and the experienced. Attention has to be given to the trail constantly. While most trails are well marked and well worn by traffic, there may be places where the route becomes confusing. It may have a false fork or hard rocks may disguise the path for a stretch, or an intersection of trails may lead the hiker off in an undesired direction. At worst, a sudden snow squall can obscure it.

Being lost off the trail can be an extremely frightening sensation. The situation can come about quite suddenly. In one moment the absent-minded hiker can be confronted by a confusing tangle of trees and rock formations with no way out.

Shouts may bring only empty echoes. Adrenalin begins to pump and the mind races ahead to dire conclusions.

Every hiker has to face the possibility of getting lost. Taking precautions beforehand always minimizes risks. Always carry plenty of water and some light, compact, high energy food. Wear sunscreen and carry an extra supply of it. Always bring matches so that fires can be lit for warmth and to signal one's position. Since dryness prevails in the Rockies so often, extreme care has to be exercised in building fires. Always take along warm clothing, even if it just has to be lugged in a backpack on a bright hot summer day. If you are out on the trail at night it can become bitterly cold at high altitudes in any month.

If possible, let people on the outside know where you are going and approximately how long you plan to be on the trail. Do fill out the information forms that are found at some trailheads. One of the regular tasks of forest rangers is to rescue lost hikers. They are assisted in many places by volunteer search and rescue teams as well as by local law enforcement agencies. Helicopters are used for medical evacuations as well as for searches.

Most people who get lost find their own way out before an official search begins. Here are a few hints on how to do it: If you can hear water running in a stream, go to it and try to follow it down. Trails tend to cross them or go along parallel to them, and further down, people are likely to live along them. If no streams are nearby, try to take a bearing on a large, distant physical object, such as a mountain peak, and try to walk in a straight line towards it. A compass will help to keep a lost hiker going in one direction rather than going in circles, which will waste energy and valuable time before the sun sets. Walking in one direction is likely to lead the lost hiker to something, such as a vista where a road or a house can be seen, a trail or a stream heading down towards habitation.

The fundamental rule in hiking, particularly for children, is never to go where the trail cannot be seen for any purpose. Sometimes parents allow their children to run ahead, out of sight, or to drag behind, also out of sight. Sometimes one parent will stride ahead and the other will fall behind, and their children will spread out in between them or behind them. Many young people simply do not like plodding on at a steady pace. At the outset of a hike their energy levels are likely to make them want to bound ahead. Along the way, and out of the range of parental supervision, all kinds of things can lure them off of the trail, such as a small animal or a butterflies. Once they loose sight of the trail they can become confused and lost easily. A parent on the trail may assume that the other parent has the youngsters in tow, or that they will show up soon if they stop and wait.

Without attempting to be melodramatic or wishing to frighten inexperienced parents from the joys of hiking, it has to be pointed out that tragedies occur every so often in the Rocky Mountains when children are lost off the trails and cannot be discovered before they perish from exposure. See the section on hypothermia in this chapter describing how people can become chilled, confused and die in the Rockies. In fact, some children have never been found, and the remains of other have sometimes been discovered by accident years after they have disappeared.

Let these grim events, few and far between to be sure, serve as a warning to parents to keep their children in sight control when hiking. Under these conditions, parents and children can relax and enjoy the beauty and peace of the trail. Children may also learn the wisdom of the old story about the tortoise and the hare.

Taking Care of Your Body on a Hike: Among those who do not want to remain just windshield tourists are people of all physical conditions. One of the worst experiences is to go forth on a hike, become exhausted, chafed and blistered, and find the return to the vehicle to be a slow torture. Always carry a watch. Often setting goals by time rather than by miles is more sensible since terrain can vary from easy to rugged.

Those who are considerably out of shape should just hike for 15 or 20 minutes in and 15 or 20 minutes back out. Most trails in the Rocky Mountains tend to go up, so the return hike should be ever so much easier. Overweight persons not used to exercise should be careful to gradually increase the amount of time that they spend on trails. Fortunately, in many places a hiker can get the feel of the interior just a few hundred yards from the road.

A slow, steady, plodding pace works best for most hikers. Those who speed ahead can often be found sitting and panting at the side of the trail up ahead. On a long hike, each person should seek a steady rhythm of slow but deliberate steps to maximize the body's endurance. On the Rocky Mountain trails, always bet on the tortoises.

Suffering can come from wearing the wrong kind of shoes. Rocky Mountain trails are usually hard and dry and strewn with stones. Soft shoes will offer little protection and get scuffed easily. Tough hiking shoes or boots are appropriate, but they can become instruments of torture if they are not broken in properly. There are no remedies for blisters that erupt a mile or two up the trail except to hobble back in pain. Limping people can be seen all over the Rockies in the hiking season. So the essential thing to do is to purchase tough, durable, well fitting footgear that is well broken in beforehand.

Inexperienced hikers may be apprehensive about encountering wildlife along the way. Please consult the section on "Living Hazards" below, which deals with ticks, snakes, and spiders. The section on the large mammals of the region in another chapter deals with mountain lions, coyotes and wolves, but they are highly unlikely to make an appearance anywhere near a hiking trail. Do not be overly concerned about these creatures because all of them, except the ticks, do not want to deal with humans and will tend to keep away from trails that are frequently used.

For All Hikers—The Dangers from Dehydration and Hypothermia in The Rockies: The trails get hot and dry in the summer, extremely so on the plateau of Utah, but even at altitudes of over a mile high. Perspiration evaporates quickly, disguising the loss of water from the body. It is absolutely essential to carry large amounts of water on hikes in these areas. Even the most beautiful of mountain streams can be infected with bacteria from wildlife that will make those who drink unboiled water from them acutely ill.

Hypothermia is a killer. It sneaks up on victims and confuses them before finishing them. Hypothermia is, by a medical definition, the "rapid, progressive mental and physical collapse" that comes about when the inner core of the human body is chilled. Hypothermia occurs when the body's temperature drops to 94° or below. Death can occur at 89°.

The way to prevent it is to stay dry. Water against the skin lowers the temperature. If wet, try to stay out of the wind, because the wind steals heat quickly. Be sure to always pack extra warm, dry clothing and raingear, no matter how inappropriate this may seem at the outset of the journey.

The symptoms are uncontrolled shivering, slow, slurred speech, memory lapses, incoherence, fumbling hands, a stumbling, lurching gait, drowsiness and exhaustion. The body goes into a state of shock, and after that death occurs.

Hypothermia can be treated by finding shelter from the weather, removing all wet clothes and building a fire for warmth. Mildly afflicted cases should be given warm drinks and put into dry, warm clothes or a warm sleeping bag. If a person becomes semi-conscious or worse than that, it is necessary to keep the victim awake, stripped and in a warm sleeping bag where skin to skin warming may need to be offered. Above all, professional emergency help needs to be summoned as quickly as possible.

Very often a person who goes on a Rocky Mountain hike does not realize how quickly the weather can turn from hot to cold with the onset of a chilling thunderstorm, hailstorm or snowstorm accompanied by a high wind. A person soaked through is at risk for hypothermia if something is not done. When the newspapers claim that someone died of "exposure," it usually means that hypothermia has claimed another victim.

Another Reason for Staying on the Trails: Besides getting lost, those who leave the trail endanger both it and themselves. Taking shortcuts on switchbacks, those places where the trail weaves from left to right to get up or down a steep incline, causes erosion. Soft stone, such as sandstone, may crumble in locations off of the trail. Rock formations that look sturdy may give way very suddenly, or the quick twist of a loose hard rock may give an equally quick twist to an ankle. It is so much more difficult to get injured on the trail than off of it.

Coping with the Peculiarities of the Environment

ALTITUDE

The sun is fierce at high altitudes in thin air. Plenty of sunscreen is needed because rays that cause skin cancer are particularly potent in the Rocky Mountain States. Dermatologists never cease to warn people to use heavy sunblock, noting that skin cancer is very prevalent in the region. Visitors can look like cooked lobsters on the ski slopes in winter and in the swimming pools in the summer if they do not take precautions.

People who step off of planes in Denver after flying from either coast may suffer from the altitude and take days to adjust to it. Dizziness, giddiness or a feeling of weakness may be the symptoms. The effect is particularly noticeable when alcohol is imbibed. For many people, the potency of the alcohol is doubled by the altitude. Many prominent speakers who are invited to hold forth in Colorado have been seen slumped over and clutching their lecterns because the social libations beforehand were not calculated for a double impact. Noted opera singers who are invited to perform high up in Central City, Colorado, have had difficulty getting through their performances. Athletes who are flown in often take oxygen at sporting events to compensate for what they perceive as a notorious disadvantage for visiting teams.

At these altitudes, the body has to build up more oxygen carrying red corpuscles, which takes a few days for most people. Persons with serious heart conditions should consult their doctors before heading up into the mountains because doctors sometimes set altitude limits for them.

CLIMATIC HAZARDS

Unpredictability: An old saying in the region declares that if you dislike the weather in the Rocky Mountain region, just wait for a short time and it will change. The weather does change rapidly, and it is often hard for even professional meteorologists to predict accurately. From time to time wild weather will come about suddenly, revealing that nature is still a formidable force in the Rockies. The climatic hazards described below might possibly present themselves during a vacation to the region, so it is wise to know something about them, even if their occurrence does not have a high probability on any given day or week.

High Winds: Winds along the Rockies can become ferocious, with gusts of over 90 m.p.h. at their very worst, when flying debris becomes dangerous and boxy vehicles are banned from highways. Local weather forecasters joke about "small dog warnings" on such days.

Strong winds can surge in any season, but windy days tend to cluster in the spring and fall, when the seasons change.

Tornadoes: More tornadoes have been reported everywhere in the United States in recent years, so it is natural that the Rocky Mountain region has its share of increased sightings, aided no doubt by the widespread deployment of amateur and professional video cameras. While the Rocky Mountain region is noted for its strong winds, it is not known for its awesome tornadoes. The plains states to the east are in the region noted for devastation by huge, dark funnel clouds which can dash a town to pieces. There are exceptions. For example, a section of Denver was hard hit a few years ago, and the town of Limon in eastern Colorado was severely damaged recently.

If tornadoes do appear in the Rocky Mountain states they are apt to be small. The reason for this is that the altitude interferes with the build up of great high clouds that spawn tornadoes. Also, some of them may be almost invisible because of the dryness. Swirling air can occur without cloud moisture.

Hailstorms: The Rocky Mountain states have the dubious distinction of being more prone to damaging hailstorms than any other part of the United States. The Front Range region of Colorado extending up to eastern Wyoming above Cheyenne is actually the very worst hail belt in the whole nation, the place that atmospheric scientists use for their research on the subject.

Hailstorms can happen anytime from spring until fall. They strike suddenly, pouring out of high, dark thunder clouds. Part of a town or a farm can be devastated by a bombardment of white pellets while places half a mile away might receive hardly any precipitation. Golf ball size hail is not exceptional. Grapefruit size white cannonballs pouring from heaven are exceptional, fortunately, but they do thunder down now and then. On one recent occasion hail killed several animals tethered outside and one person who was bombarded.

Hailstorms destroy roofs, gardens, car windshields and rear windows, and pit car bodies. Hail piles up in heaps of melting ice during, say, what could have been a pleasant day in July. The cost of repairs to roofs and cars is astronomical, and reflected in the high insurance premiums paid by property owners. After a bad hailstorm, armies of underwriters and roofers flock to the region. Many roofs bear three layers of shingles, evidence of two bad hailstorms. Most local authorities will not allow roofs to carry more than three layers, so everything must be stripped off the next time that white thunder drops from the skies.

It is always wise to put cars away in garages and not leave them out in case a thunderstorm might boil up. There is only one thing to do when heavy rain turns to bouncing ice crystals. Take cover and stay there until it is over.

Lightning: Lightning is often cited as a measuring rod for unlikely occurrences, such as "You are ten times more likely to be hit by lightning than to be eaten by a shark in certain waters." In the Rocky Mountain states the odds tilt somewhat in favor of lightning. Misguided people help these odds by foolishly hiking across exposed ridges or up mountainous trails during thunderstorms. Lightning also kills some die-hard golfers right on the links.

The danger from lightning in the Rocky Mountain states is clearly revealed by electronically tabulated maps of lightning strikes in a given area when there are thunderstorms. High and exposed points serve as the natural lightning rods on a landscape, and these places need to be avoided in storms.

Thunderstorms are very frequent in the Rockies in May and June in particular, when the contrasting warmth and cold collide on account of plentiful sun and high altitude. A build up of clouds usually begins to take place in early afternoon, and the lightning bolts can begin to fly at any time from then until evening. A very good rule for hikers to follow is to head down from whatever heights they have ascended by noon.

Floods: Floods can be killers when they occur in this ordinarily semi-arid region. Floods are rare, but when they do happen they can be devastating. A terrible example was the Big Thompson Flood of 1976, when a wall of water roared down Big Thompson Canyon in Colorado, ripping out a road, destroying homes, pulverizing vehicles, and drowning and mangling over a hundred people caught in its path.

A peculiar climatic condition caused this flood, a coincidence of circumstances said not to be likely to occur in another hundred years in that particular place. Clouds that were supposed to move along and deposit their moisture over a wide area stayed at the headwaters of the Big Thompson River, pouring down on that location for days in a row.

Today there are no physical scars from the tragedy because the road and many of the houses have been replaced. It is a major artery for tourism, U.S. 34 from Loveland to Estes Park.

One aspect has changed, however. Blue and white signs are posted frequently, in Big Thompson Canyon and in other canyons and flood plains. They show people climbing heights to avoid floodwaters.

This is the best advice. When there are indications of a flash flood, particularly in narrow canyons, abandon vehicles, tents, everything, and climb to gain altitude as quickly as possible.

It takes truly exceptional circumstances to produce a flood in the Rocky Mountain states, and nearly all visitors come and go without ever having to face this threat. Nevertheless, peculiar and unexpected circumstances can coincide to bring on a killer flood every so often.

Avalanches: In the summer there is too little snow for avalanches to be a danger. But there is an avalanche season in the Rocky Mountain states, when several lives are snuffed out by nature's process of resettling masses of snow that fall on mountainsides. To unwary, inexperienced skiers or persons on snowshoes, an avalanche can be a wall of white death roaring down on them so suddenly that there is no escape. Victims are buried under the snow so deeply that there is often no chance for survival.

Professionals who work in the mountains know where avalanches are likely to occur and post warnings. Ski resort personnel constantly warn people not to go off skiing in unauthorized areas, but some people always stray, or prefer back country explorations far from resorts.

Potential avalanche sites are sometimes treated with explosives to release them prophylactically. In the past, artillery was fired off at them to start an avalanche.

Rescue efforts now involve electronic beepers, dogs and probing poles.

LIVING HAZARDS

Ticks: Ticks are generally just a nuisance in the Rockies, but a small percentage of them do transmit an illness peculiar to the region, Rocky Mountain spotted fever. Lyme disease, also transmitted by ticks, has only begun to show up in the area so far.

Ticks are particularly active in the spring months of April and May, when they slowly and methodically crawl through the underbrush to seek out animals to burrow into, guided by a strange heat-seeking instinct. In this season, hikers are cautioned to wear substantial clothing so that the whole body is covered, especially the legs.

Close inspection of the body after outdoor adventures is a necessary precaution. These parasites will move towards the warmest parts of the body, so particular attention should be given to the armpits and groin.

If a tick is found still slowly meandering in its relentless, crab-like manner on the body, looking for a place to dig in, it can be brushed off and crushed underfoot. A pair of tweezers and a bottle of salad oil are needed to get rid of a tick that has embedded itself in the flesh. It needs to be removed gingerly. If it is pulled out suddenly the small head, or a portion of it, might break off and be left embedded to become a source of infection. To remove it properly, smother the insect in oil so that it can no longer breathe through its shell. After a while the tick will become so groggy that the burrowing will be abandoned. Then attach the tweezers to the top and bottom of its abdomen and commence a slow, steady pull straight backwards, away from the skin, and soon the host will be free from the parasite.

Spiders: The Rocky Mountain region, like all other regions of the United States, is home to a number of spiders which can inflict painful bites if provoked or threatened. The most feared of them all, the black widow, can show up in suburbia most unexpectedly.

They appear in houses now and then and even in school-yards. They can be identified by the bright red hourglass mark on the bottom of the lower abdomen. Bites are not likely to be fatal, depending, of course, on the victim's body weight and general condition. Nevertheless, seek out professional help immediately if bitten.

Snakes: Many persons are so terrified of snakes that they will flee from any area where a wriggle is sighted. Others will blast away at any snake with the most firepower that can be mustered or mangle them horribly with a shovel or a hoe. Perhaps it has something to do with vestiges of fear from the old struggles between mammals and reptiles, or perhaps it is just an irrational fear nurtured by some in society ever since snakes gained such a bad reputation in folk tales and the Garden of Eden story.

Snakes are very useful for keeping a balance in nature by devouring rodents whose high birth rates would lead them to overpopulate if their numbers were not kept in check by snakes and other predators. Most snakes are absolutely harmless for humans. Only a very few are poisonous.

Snakes are almost invariably as terrified of humans as the most terrified humans are of them. Snakes will want to depart any scene involving humans as fast as possible, which, in all too many cases, is not fast enough

Poisonous rattlesnakes, more than any other kind, have the worst reputations, except among those adventurous gourmets who regard them as tasty. Western rattlesnakes have offered a foolproof method to get rid of any character in a story or a film suddenly. One quick bite and the awkward personage is gone. Rattlesnakes are also useful in providing sinister threats to heroines and children in stories and films and golden opportunities for heroes to display their courage and skill killing them. As the would-be victims are delivered from instant death, the snake gets it instead.

In the Rocky Mountain states, rattlesnakes work on their own agendas, which have nothing to do with human dramas, except for those very rare occasions when human and snake accidentally meet on the snake's own turf, such as its lair or usual feeding location. When so confronted, the snake will either beat a hasty retreat or put on a menacing display by coiling up, ready to strike, and shaking its rattles in its tail as a warning. When they decide to strike, the speed and distance of their lunge is awesome.

Rattlesnake bites are rare in the Rocky Mountain area, considering how many snakes and how many humans come into some proximity. Bites can be treated quite successfully with serum kept at local hospitals. Every now and then, however, a fatal bite does occur, just as they happen in the movies. Sometimes the small stature of the victim accounts for the mortal effect of the venom, but sometimes it is from an unlucky penetration of the hollow, venom shooting fangs right into a vein that goes directly to the heart. In these extremely rare cases, the victim may expire just the way that a movie director would stage it.

Medical advice for visitors about what to do in case of rattlesnake bite is as necessary, supposedly, as airlines' advice on how to use seat cushions for floatation divices on inland domestic flights, but it does no harm to know it.

The key point is to get to a hospital quickly. Forget about cutting around the bite and sucking out the venom because doctors say that this does not do much good. When heading towards the hospital, the victim should move as little as possible. If at a distance from a car, the victim should proceed slowly and deliberately, taking care to keep the heart from pumping rapidly.

For a long time the author was convinced that there was nothing to fear from rattlesnakes. I had hiked through foothill terrain in Colorado noted for a high population of rattlesnakes, both on trails and overland, for over twenty years without any incidents. Once I guided timid visitors from Europe who were warned by anxious relatives to avoid these deadly reptiles. Apparently their relatives had seen too many Westerns where snakes killed people. I had to walk yards ahead of them, while they hurried along as if they were walking through a live mine field. I am sure that these foreign hikers portrayed their walk as a death defying adventure once they were home.

Contempt for others' fear of rattlesnakes ended abruptly for me one fine summer day. I was walking at a fast pace along a well worn, oft traveled, rock-strewn trail, and quite quite noisily. I was late for an appointment and had to get back to town fast. Rounding a bend, I heard a hideous sudden roar, a strange, almost unearthly sound. There before me, coiled up on the ground, absolutely ready to strike, was a rattler vigorously giving me a full ovation with its tail. My retreat was instantaneous.

I breathlessly reported this incident of what is called "menacing" to a park ranger on my way out. He said it was most unusual to have such an incident occur on a well worn stretch of trail that had frequent use. He presumed that the rattler was on its way between a hillside on one side of the trail and a gulch down on the other and just happened to be caught out in the open by me when I was in such a hurry. When asked what the snake had done after menacing me I could give no reply, because my retreat was so precipitous in the other direction, nor could I give an estimate of the size of the snake because under the circumstances which I saw it, the snake was gigantic, filling my whole vision. To my terrified eye, it was the size of a python, its grim, cold, deadly face aimed right at me.

This was a truly shocking incident. There, in the wild, quite suddenly, was the threat of death from another species. But it had taken two decades of regular hiking to encounter one menacing rattlesnake. I had seen a few others and a number of non-poisonous snakes over the years, but they were all getting out of my sight as quickly as possible. I note that I exercise a bit more caution hiking now, but my conviction remains that a *homo sapiens* behind the wheel of a car is a million times more likely to bring about one's sudden demise in the West than rattlesnakes.

Minor Living Hazards: Nature overproduces almost everything, and the voracious gobbling of all living creatures along the food chain destroys most overproduction. In dry areas in the Rocky Mountain states, temporary erratic climatic conditions, such as an abnormally wet spring season, can bring on a temporarily superabundance of some species.

One year it was impossible to drive through the eastern plains of Colorado without smearing windshields with the corpses of thousands of painted lady butterflies, victims smashed out of great clouds of them that migrated across the plains. In another year, armies of crickets crunched their way through farms in Utah and Nevada, resembling the locust swarms of Africa. In other years, millions of grasshoppers have eaten their way through the plains areas of Colorado and Wyoming, devastating the crops of farmers and those gardeners who were in outlying parts of towns. Gardeners deep in suburbia were usually protected from these grasshoppers by the heavy concentrations from insecticides that are regularly sprayed in such places at the cost, perhaps, of greater vulnerability to cancer.

One insect always gets through, at least in eastern Colorado and along the built up Front Range, the miller moth, a dull brown, ugly and harmless creature close to an inch in length. Their larvae develop on the sprawling plains' wheat farms and the moths migrate in masses towards the mountains. They invade houses, garages, public buildings—everything everywhere—in late spring, after which their numbers subside before they disappear. How they get inside is rather mysterious, since smaller insects, such as mosquitoes, are kept outside by screening.

Miller moths flutter around stupidly at night, zooming at lights, and bouncing off of persons and things. At first, most people counterattack with flyswatters and sprays, but the miller moths keep coming. It is pointless to try to kill them chemically, because the next wave will arrive to replace them quickly, and miller moths will only live for a few days inside anyway. Meanwhile the toxic levels of chemicals will build up inside.

Some people get so used to them that they ignore them, as people ignore insects in many tropical parts of the world. Others are ingenious in dispatching them. A sure way is to fill a bucket with soapy water and place a light right above it. The miller moths will zoom at the light and eventually fall into the soapy water and drown. If the water is not soapy they might be able to swim and climb out of it. Miller moths do not eat anything that humans eat, but they fall into everything, including pots on the stove or salads. There is no dish that they can enhance by garnishing it.

A FEW HELPFUL VOCABULARY WORDS AND PRONUNCIATIONS FOR TRAVELERS

Some of the terms and pronunciations used in the Rocky Mountain states may not be familiar to those who are from other regions. Here is a list of words that are most commonly misunderstood or mispronounced. Definitions are underlined and words of sometimes difficult pronunciation are not.

Berthoud is pronounced *Burr*-thud.

Boise is pronounced *Boy*-zee.

Butte is pronounced Beaut.

Coeur d'Alene is pronounced *Coor*-da-lane.

Cheyenne is pronounced Shy-yann.

Ground Blizzard: A ground blizzard consists of wind driven snow.

Hole in fur trader's language meant a sheltered valley, as in Jackson's Hole or Pierre's Hole. It offered water, grass for horses and game for food.

Helena is pronounced *Hell* en-nah.

Hovenweep is pronounced *Hoe*-ven-weep.

Lode: A lode is where precious metals are lodged in rock formations.

Moraine: A moraine is an accumulation of earth and stones deposited by a glacier. Sometimes a moraine appears as a valley full of boulders.

Moab is pronounced *Moe*-ab.

Moroni is pronounced More-*own*-eye.

Ouray is pronounced *OO*-ray.

Park: A park is a level valley between mountains. In the Rocky Mountain states these parks can be at high altitudes.

Placers are the sites for mining where the gold is free from rock formations and can be panned for retrieval. Pronounced Plahsir.

Shoshone is pronounced Show-*show*-nee.

Teton is pronounced Tee-tun.

Ute is pronounced *Yout.*

Vein: A vein is a streak of precious metals in rock, usually in quartz.

Rivers and Mountains

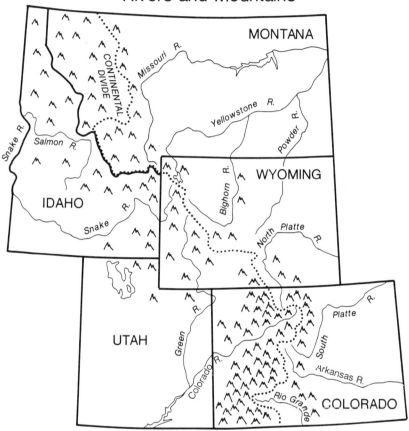

CHAPTER TWO

TRAVEL: WHAT MAKES IT A NICE PLACE TO VISIT AND WOULD IT BE NICE TO LIVE THERE?

Special Travel Highlights of the Region

Every place has certain advantages and disadvantages for the traveler. In the previous chapter the top priorities of scenery and the wide open spaces were stressed. In this chapter the nature of other highlights are considered and in subsequent chapters on specific states details about particular places are given. For example, in this chapter the National Parks are discussed in general, while the chapters on the states will take up each individual park.

This chapter will also consider what crosses the minds of most visitors to the Rockies who ask themselves that classic question: "Would I like to live here or is this just a nice place to visit?" Three different environments in the contemporary Rocky Mountain West, a small mountain town, a prosperous small city and a recreation site are all looked at with this question in mind towards the end of this chapter.

NATIONAL PARKS

Avoiding the Crowds

Originally the national parks were set aside because they were deemed remote and useless parcels of beautiful land which could neither be farmed nor mined. Nevertheless, none of the National Parks became such without first undergoing some changes imposed by humans. Take, for instance, Bryce Canyon National Park in Utah, where land was heavily grazed and deforested for 100 years before it became a National Park. Grizzly bears, wolverines and wolves, all part of the original ecosystem, were long gone before the stars and stripes flew officially over this gorgeous piece of land. At first authorities actually had to recruit people to visit them, but now they are, to quote a popular cliché, "almost loved to death."

With considerable journalistic verve, *Time* magazine declared, (July 23, 1990), that "gridlock" had come to America's National Parks and wilderness areas. "Take a Number to Take a Hike" was the title of the article, and "For a wilderness experience, you have to plan ahead or lose" was the subtitle. The article pointed out that 60 million people would visit 50 national parks in 1990, a situation leading some parks to sell campsites via Ticketron, and to issue permits to only a small percentage of the applicants for biking on certain trails and rafting on certain rivers. Indeed, the baby boomers have arrived in the woods, but the situation is not nearly as grim in the Rocky Mountain states as this article purports. True, bumper to bumper traffic jams do snake along the paved roads of such places as Glacier National Park or Yellowstone National Park during most of the summer and especially on weekends.

Just recently the author found the parking lots of one national park visitor center absolutely full, with cars circling about on the lookout for departing vehicles. This was disconcerting, considering that this lot was high up in Montana but looked like one on Long Island on a hot summer day. Even so, these scenes must be kept in perspective.

Because of their distinctive features and outstanding beauty, the National Parks will always be tremendous magnets for tourists who will go on clogging roads and filling campsites at them forever. National Parks cover much less space than National Forests, which are usually adjacent to them or surround them. These National Forests may have many campsites available, as might state parks or even county parks and municipal parks in neighboring communities. Some of the sites may even be free.

Therefore a good tactic to employ is to establish a base at a campsite some distance from the entrance to a popular National Park, drive into it in the morning, park at an appropriate trailhead or near a path to a significant attraction, enjoy the day and head out of the park to the campsite in the evening. This procedure removes the anxiety of seeking a scarce vacant campsite within the park.

Another alternative is to call the park well in advance and make reservations. The disadvantage of this procedure is that it pins one down to be at a certain place at a certain time, and many people go on vacations just to get away from such constraints.

The Fight to Preserve Them: The ongoing struggle between preservation and development that has marked so much of the history of the West can clearly be seen in the arguments over the National Parks that are going on today. Administrators, who are under pressure from some segments of the public to expand, debate how many concessions, paved roads, parking lots, toilets, water fountains and campsites can be allowed. Some proponents of ecology and nature flatly oppose any more development whatsoever. They do not want one more single mile of new asphalt. They loathe the elaborate hotel accommodations that some National Parks have put up, to say nothing of the gift shops, restaurants and amusement opportunities, most of which are concessions that the United States government has allowed at pathetically low rates of compensation. From the point of view of the opponents of development, the tendency to make National Parks into amusement parks is destructive of their whole purpose, which should be to preserve and display natural beauty and living things. On the other hand, the proponents of development want conveniences, or profit, or job opportunities. Such battles go on throughout the system.

Struggles also go on to designate more wilderness areas, a new category of preservation added in 1964. In them, life is supposed to go on in a pristine world, where humans can only be brief visitors. The problem is that centuries of Native American use, the fur trade, the timber industry and numerous trails criss-crossing the West have permanently altered all areas. Ecology that is altered anywhere is, like Humpty Dumpty, too complex to put back together again in its ancient natural balance, which was itself, to cite another complication, constantly evolving.

No National Park encompasses a whole ecosystem. Water and wildlife always go over park borders where the water is siphoned and the wildlife is slaughtered for one reason or another. For example, Yellowstone would have to expand to almost twice its size to encompass a proper ecosystem. So at best the National Parks display only fragments of nature's old spectacle. Putting more concrete, neon, asphalt and cash registers in them only reduces what they have to offer even more.

DUDE RANCHES

An old stereotype of the dude ranch portrays inept Easterners floundering though cowboy routines while their hosts quietly snicker. Yet spending time on a ranch, arguably the most thoroughly Western enterprise in the West, is an activity that has fascinated individuals from all over the world, including German barons in the 19th century and affluent Japanese adventurers today.

Dude ranches emerged from the depressed days of the cattle industry, when some "paying guests" were accommodated. What began as a sociable supplement to a ranch income has, for some outfits, become a specialty. Furthermore, a variety of experiences are available, from genial and gentle observation to the hands-on hard work of an ongoing ranch. Many people are satisfied with chuckwagon dinners, hayrides and views of the great outdoors. Others want to work like genuine cowboys and cowgirls, at least for their vacation time. Dude ranches cater to each preference and gradations in between. In the early 1990's dude ranches appear to be doing a booming business, which is perhaps another indication of how Americans are dealing with an unsettled economic climate by taking more modest vacations.

One change that has overtaken dude ranches is that more and more people from the Rocky Mountain West are going to them. In a way, this is a reflection of the fact that a highly demanding technical or managerial job in Denver or Salt Lake city can remove an individual from the outdoor opportunities the region offers.

A new popular variation involves taking the dudes out on an adventure trip. For example, a number of covered wagons travel the Bozeman trail from Wyoming up towards Montana through what was the last and best Indian hunting grounds. Gourmet buffalo burgers are standard fare on the junket, which earns the official designation of a "soft adventure vacation."

Each state tourist office has information about dude ranches and will be able to make recommendations to help match the expectations of perspective participants with the varied offerings at the ranches. Booklets from the state tourist office list dude ranches.

FORTS

Commercial operations calling themselves forts, historic forts and places named after forts are scattered throughout the Rocky Mountain states. Historic forts are sometimes reconstructions, and the best of them are very carefully and exactly fashioned from old plans and along the lines of excavated foundations. Some are basically just the site of an old fort, with perhaps a few old excavated foundations on display. The interesting historic forts are now under national or state supervision and their locations are clearly indicated on detailed road maps.

Many early businessmen in the Rocky Mountain region called the shops they set up along pioneer trails "forts." For example, an ex-mountain man names Smith set up a few cabins to trade goods near Bear Lake in what is now Idaho. He dignified his establishment with the name of "Fort Smith." Others grew to become the early 19th century equivalent of a combination of a shopping mall, repair shop, and oasis.

When the Indian wars flared up, some of these so-called forts were actually taken over by the military and became proper forts, serving as bases of operations.

When requisitioned by the United States Army, Western forts came closest to the mythical stereotype of them held by non-Westerners. They became stockaded defensive positions from which the cavalry could be bugled out to ride to the defense of one or another aspect of civilization, including maidens in wagon trains in distress from the threat posed by Indian marauders. In actuality, most of the time Indians were inside the forts, where they either lived or traded. Sometimes large numbers of semi-resident Indians lived right outside of them. What is more, the original entrepreneurs were more than likely to have Indian wives. Concerning forts and so much else, conflict with Native Americans has been sadly overemphasized.

See the chapters on specific states for the best of the Rocky Mountain region's historic forts.

SELLING THE OLD WEST: TRADING POSTS AND BOGUS TOUCHES IN OLD TOWNS AND THE GOODS THAT THEY SELL

Along the major highways of the West, rustic, rough-hewn "trading posts" will appear with some regularity. Some of them are called "forts" as well. Do not be deceived by the exterior, which is usually some form of wooden stockade. Such places can be as contrived as any boutique in a shopping mall. The stock is likely to be acquired and sold by computer and might consist of bits and pieces of curios evoking the Old West: hides, antlers, feathered headdresses, machine washable Western garb, sand paintings, Indian jewelry, dolls and nick knacks.

Great care has to be exercised when purchasing Indian arts and crafts at revervations and at "trading posts" near them. Some "Indian style" arts are actually manufactured in American, Japanese and Hong Kong factories. Some synthetic stones are used in jewelry and some are bathed in oil to gain a temporary lustre. Pottery should be viewed suspiciously also. Some rejects are sold as "genuine" Indian pottery. True Indian pottery is decorated before it is fired, but some of what is sold have paints slapped on after being fired. While some Indian groups still do significant original work in beads, bogus beadwork from Asia have flooded into the United States market.

'Trading post' type outlets reappear in false front frame buildings in old mountain mining towns which have become tourist attractions. The goods for sale reappear again in the "old town" redevelopments in the region's cities. Often they are the same kinds of items that are offered in the shops at the region's airports. Most of the items do look as if they were mass produced somewhere.

Many "movie set" old Western streets have been slapped up rather quickly, with signs that are too cute and with a look that is too new. A smell of freshly cut cheap pinewood lingers about them. Some places have old style wooden sidewalks built right over perfectly useful modern cement sidewalks to give more atmosphere. When questioned about the patent falseness of the wooden sidewalks, merchants along them might respond that this is a touch of the Old West that tourists want and expect.

Some towns come equipped with a "Boot Hill" cemetery whose age might be revealed by the fresh paint on some of the grave markers. The name boot hill comes from the practice of hasty burials for those meeting a violent end, so hasty that they were put under with their boots on.

Another way of getting the tourists out of their cars and spending money is to offer opportunities to pan for gold. Some of these operations are right at the site of old mines.

NEW FESTIVALS CELEBRATING THE OLD WEST

All American states want to impress tourists with the richness of their history. For the Rocky Mountain states, much of their history is new, some of it is thin, and much of it does not have much significance for those not living in the area. Take, for instance, Idaho's zest at touting these landmarks in its Official Idaho State Travel Guide: "1864: Territorial Legislature approves moving capital to Boise; 1920: State Capital Building completed in Boise." Who outside of Idaho could care about these details? All the states send out a blizzard of such details in booklets, pamphlets and on signs and posters.

Whatever history is turned up is celebrated to the maximum extent, in the form of parades, festivals, pageants, fairs, recreations and so on. In most of these clebrations, dressing up in historic costumes becomes a major preoccupation. The aim is to involve the community as much as possible in drawing the interest of dollar laden tourists. Obviously, many of the historic events celebrated have been rather recently rediscovered. Ernest community committees undoubtedly meet many hours to determine how spectacles can be presented attractively to commemorate that which was recently obscure or hardly remembered. The booklets distributed by the respective states all tout a bewildering array of such events based either on an event in history or the celebration of a particular local product.

Nevertheless, there are some classic celebrations, such as Frontier Days in Cheyenne, Wyoming, which have been celebrated for a long time and are very well attended. Details on a few celebrations are in the chapters on the states.

OLD MINING TOWNS

Many old mining towns that did not become ghost towns but limped along boomed once again in the late 20th century as tourist meccas. Some of them only bustle in the summer and shrink in population and activity in the winter, but others can combine their old charms with the lure of nearby ski slopes.

Old mining towns have many charms. There are some old hotels with grand Victorian bars and rooms still filled with huge pieces of Victorian furniture. Saloons still can convey something of the old atmosphere, particularly if many of the locals show up and the music is appropriately Country Western. The starkness of such places, perched in narrow canyons or high up in mountain valleys, adds to the atmosphere. Streets are crooked and homes are quaintly Victorian. Public buildings, such as firehouses and courthouses, may be remarkable architectural achievements, particularly those in Victorian brick with elaborate wooden gables and attachments. Stark slag heaps might surround the town and old wooden mining buildings and steel head frames may be in sight as well. In such environs the imagination can be coaxed to think back to the days of a silver or gold boom rather easily.

Sometimes operas, theater productions and old Victorian melodramas are put on, as well as music festivals for certain specialized kinds of music, such as bluegrass.

Regardless of what is going on, these places are wonderful for walking around. To enhance the experience, seek a room in one of the grand old Victorian hotels. Their rates are considerably less than grand old hotels in Europe.

Gambling in Old Mining Towns: In November of 1990, a large majority of the voters in the State of Colorado decided that limited gambling should be allowed in three historic mining towns, Cripple Creek, Blackhawk and Central City. A new boom will be underway, and places that saw gold pour out in the 19th century will see dollars flow in from gambling that will also enable local businesses to profit.

Undoubtedly the Rocky Mountain states will see more gambling spots open up in the future. The precedents have been many, starting with the dazzling success of Las Vegas and Reno, Nevada, and, most recently, there was a dramatic economic turnaround on account of gambling in Deadwood, South Dakota.

The question remains as to what gambling will do to the charm of these old mining towns. This question was hotly debated by proponents and opponents in Colorado. "History does not pay the bills" was one argument, a declaration that the towns could not live on the revenues from just three months' of summer tourist activity each year. A growing number of rundown buildings and the need for historical preservation were cited, along with assurances that a certain amount of gambling profits would be earmarked for the renovation and preservation of the legacy from the past. Opponents claimed that large crowds, a carnival side show atmosphere, severe parking problems and clogged roads would result. Proponents replied that to an extent most of these conditions already existed in some places during the busiest times of the tourist season. More serious apprehensions were about crime, not just the expected increases in petty theft, but also the appearance of organized crime in the mountains. Proponents retorted that a five dollar limit on bets and close supervision in a limited number of gambling dens would keep gambling out of the clutches of major criminals. Opponents pointed out how speedily a gambler could make multiple five dollar bets.

Clearly, gambling will bring changes to these historic mining towns and other such towns in the future. Already some old wooden structures have been earmarked for destruction in order to make way for expansion. Gambling certainly does resurrect an important aspect of the past, when hapless miners were swiftly bilked of their hard earned money in the gambling casinos. For those who want to see some mining towns in the sweet, soft decay of time, before flashy renovation takes hold, travel to the Rockies soon.

GHOST TOWNS

Because mining was based only on getting precious metals out of the earth as fast as possible, towns sprang up and were abandoned with surprising speed. The tents, lean-tos and shacks of the first prospectors were quickly replaced by hastily constructed frame buildings if a promising vein was being worked. If the vein gave out, the town would be abandoned and its former residents would repeat the process at the site of some other strike.

This pattern has littered the Rocky Mountain states with abandoned towns, some of them in very remote locations. Slag heaps, polluted streams and dangerous mine shafts are other legacies.

Those wishing to visit ghost towns need only go to an old mountain mining town and ask local people where nearby ghost towns are located. For every mountain mining town that has continued to be inhabited there might be over a dozen ghost towns in the vicinity.

Some ghost towns still pulsate weakly with some life, with perhaps a few residents still living on the fringes. Some ghost towns have many streets of deserted and boarded up old buildings that are still owned by someone. Other ghost towns have almost nothing left, just a number of rotting old boards or just some old foundations.

It is often hard to get to ghost towns that are completely dead or nearly dead, and it may even be a chore to ascertain the location of some. Be sure to ask local people for precise directions as close to the presumed site as possible.

Some people enjoy seeking out ghost towns in tough four wheel drive vehicles on rocky roads that may have eroded into traces. Even those who proceed over regular roads to a ghost town may be in for a rough jaunt over dirt roads.

Mine shafts are dangerous. In some ghost towns they have not been properly covered up or not covered up at all. A fall down one of them can be fatal. Sometimes criminals get rid of bodies by chucking them down old mine shafts.

Do not expect to see much in most ghost towns. Just about everything of value has been stripped from them, first by the contemporaries who deserted the towns and then by generations of souvenir hunters have diminished whatever remained. Sometimes people have gone so far as to dismantle the remains of old structures to start fires to warm themselves! Still, the tourist business continues to benefit from passing along the story of an old miner in an undisclosed town who buried a fortune in gold nuggets in a coffee can in his back yard!

For those with rugged four wheel drive vehicles, chasing after ghost towns can become a hobby. Specialized books exist on the subject.

SKI RESORTS IN THEIR OFF SEASON

The ski industry is massive in the Rocky Mountain West, and a highly specialized subject beyond the purview of this book. People who arrive for ski vacations usually go from the airport to the slopes, or they are state residents who drive up to them. This book is written for those who want to vacation in the area outside of the ski season and who want to see more of the Rockies than a ski resort and its immediate locale.

Even so, the ski resorts offer opportunities to enjoy the Rocky Mountains during their off season. The plush rooms, hot tubs, saunas and other amenities may be available at comparatively good rates then. Ski resorts want to keep their occupancy level high throughout the year and may offer attractive vacation packages and maintain a schedule of off season activities to do so. Some solicit conferences of various groups and organizations.

Ski resorts are guaranteed to be located high up, in areas of grand scenery, if the ski lifts going up the swaths cut in the mountainsides are not too much of a distraction. There is bound to be plenty of good unscarred scenery in the vicinity as well.

The big advantage of being up at a ski lodge in the summer is that the nights will be quite cool and the days more moderate in temperature because of the altitude. An additional advantage may be a location near an old, historic mining town or a plush, new, Swiss-style town. In these places various cultural programs can be put on in the summer. The tourist booklets provided by the respective states contain information about these resorts.

HOT SPRINGS

One of the delights of traveling in the Rocky Mountain region is that hot springs are likely to be available to soothe the weary motorist. Hot springs are a visible part of the intense geothermal activity in the region. Yellowstone Park has the most spectacular examples of it, of course, but all of the Rocky Mountain States have many hot springs.

Hot springs vary immensely. Some of them are famous and some of them are little known outside of their immediate localities. Some are in the middle of towns and some can only be reached after a hike through the woods. Some of them are elaborately developed as the main feature of a recreational complex, and others are mere pools, either appearing by the sides of rivers or isolated. Some are frequented by ordinary middle class families and some are enjoyed by throwbacks to the 1960's who regard clothes as something that should be optional. Temperatures vary from the unbearable to the pleasantly warm. Some hot springs offer a variety of pools, each with a different temperature.

Hot springs are therefore not subject to generalizations. The best way to explore the variety of them is to make inquiries about local hot springs from local people wherever one stops.

There are several short guidebooks to hot springs in the Rocky Mountain region, but these slim volumes can prove to be slim on reliable information also. The author remembers an encouraging description of an informal hot spring in Idaho. The directions to reach it were fuzzy and several expeditions up and down roads had to be undertaken and local people were hard to find. The much touted hot spring in the guide book turned out to be a rather dubious little warm pool of muddy greenish water whose volume may have filled one large old fashioned bathtub.

Among the most well known and developed commercial hot springs are Lava Hot Springs in the town of that name in Idaho; the Fountain of Youth in Thermopolis, a city in western Wyoming that literally translates as 'hot city;' Glenwood Hot Springs in Glenwood Springs, Colorado; and Princeton Hot Springs in Colorado; plus a number of hot springs in Ouray, Colorado. These places bear more resemblance to the spas of Europe than do most of the other Rocky Mountain hot springs, which tend to be either in the form of stark swimming pools or undeveloped wild pools.

RODEOS

The rodeo has some similarities to the Mexican bullfight. Both represent the ancient struggle of human against beast, and many writers and commentators have read all sorts of significance and deep psychological meaning into bullfights and rodeos.

Rodeos began as recreational contests among cowboys on ranches, who called early rodeos roundups or stampedes. Rodeo actually comes from the Spanish verb rodear, to ride around.

Rodeo events came to be featured in wild west spectacles, where they began to take on a greater symbolic meaning. Rodeos in a way reenacted the drama of the taming of the West. Contestants stood for the tough, courageous men who overcame the wildness of the wilderness, which was represented by madly thrashing and leaping animals. Bucking broncs specifically represented wild horses that had to be broken by cowboys, called mustangs. In bulldogging, cowboys are required to rope and wrestle steers to the ground by twisting their necks. Bull riding is the most dangerous contest of all, calling upon all the skills of helpers dressed as clowns to divert enraged bulls from impaling and trampling fallen contestants.

It is not a safe sport. Many cowboys care taken from the arenas in ambulances and some of them die from their injuries. Animal rights activists have their own grievances about rodeos. Animals are put in considerable discomfort so that they buck and thrash sufficiently. While it is a myth that the genitalia of animals are afflicted with belts to cause pain, the belts around performing animals are extremely annoying. Therefore, those who are concerned about animal rights may want to omit rodeos from their vacations in the Rocky Mountain states.

Rodeos, grand and small, are held all over the region. The greatest is in Cheyenne, Wyoming, in the summer, and the smallest may be at the fairgrounds of a sparsely populated county. Check with state tourism authorities for details.

OLD RAILROAD RIDES

The Rocky Mountain West is a wonderful place for railroad buffs and everyone else, especially children, who are thrilled by old, huffing, puffing steam locomotives. What makes the region so well suited for nostalgic train rides is the gorgeous scenery which is found along their routes. Their views they offer can be breathtaking.

Good rides are extremely popular, so it is very wise to book tickets in advance in order to avoid disappointment. Making arrangements to be in a certain place at a certain time does limit the freedom of a vacation, but the best of these trains rarely have any extra space on them in the tourist season.

Perhaps the best ride of all is on the Durango and Silverton Narrow Gauge Railroad. The ninety-mile round trip ride originates in Durango and takes eight hours, including a two-hour layover in historic Silverton. Its steam locomotives and 1880's coaches huff and puff through the wild San Juan National Forest, following the course of the Animas river through the canyons and over trestles. Historically, many millions of dollars worth of silver and gold ore were hauled over this route.

This train runs from May until October and is heavily booked. Departures this past season have been at 7:30, 8:30, 9:30 and 10:15 a.m. Fares for adults cost around $40 and children are half price. Reduced one way fares are available. Phone 303-247-2733 for further information, or write to the Durango and Silverton at 479 Main Street, Durango, Colorado, 81301.

The Georgetown Loop is another popular and spectacular ride, but shorter, with only 4½ miles for a round trip. The Colorado Central Railroad reached Silver Plume in the 1880's after laying narrow gave track along steep valley walls, over bridges and round the Loop itself, which was a section of spiraling track on a trestle 100 feet above Clear Creek. In less than two miles, trains rise 600 feet in elevation, which is a remarkable achievement in engineering.

It was abandoned in 1939 and rebuilt in the 1980's by the Colorado Historical Society. Georgetown is a large, well-preserved historic town and Silver Plume, much smaller and wedged into a valley, is also historic nonetheless. The railroad operates regularly from 10 to 4:30 from Memorial Day to Labor Day. Phone 303-670-1686 for more information, or write P.O. Box 217, Georgetown, Colorado, 80444.

Another exciting ride is the Manitou Pike's Peak Cog Railroad in Manitou Springs, Colorado. Although this railroad has been operating since 1891, it has modern Swiss made railcars, which gives something of the ambience of a journey in the Alps rather than in the Rockies. The train crawls up at seven miles per hour on a fantastic 25% grade. It takes one hour and 25 minutes to reach the top. These trains depart regularly in the tourist season from 8:20 a.m. to 5:20 p.m.

Recently the cost for adults was $17 and $8 for children. Call 719-685-5401 for further information, or write the railroad at P.O. Box 1329, Colorado Springs, Colorado, 80901.

Another popular train goes out to Freemont Pass on the Leadville, Colorado and Southern Line. It is standard gauge and has a variety of different cars pulled by a diesel engine. Its round trip takes less than three hours and it runs twice daily in the summer. Recently adults could ride for $16.50 and children for $9.75. Children under three are free. Call 719-486-3936 or write to the railroad at 326 E. 7th Street, Leadville Colorado, 80461.

VISITING INDIAN RESERVATIONS

Of the several hundred parcels of land in the United States that are designated as reservations, many of the largest are in the Rocky Mountain region. Montana has seven; Idaho four; Utah two; and Colorado and Wyoming have one each.

Many reservations invite tourists to visit. In fact, some have multi-million dollar resort complexes, while others just have ordinary campgrounds. The main thing to bear in mind is that reservations are not public parks with Indians present. Also, the very worst thing to do is to treat the reservation as a zoo and gawk at the Indians.

It is essential to obey the regulations that the Indian owners have set forth. Some places are off limits. Some reservations have set parking fees which in effect are really admission fees.

Photography can be a problem. A good rule is to make careful enquiries before taking photos on a reservation. Some

Indians require a fee, graciously called an "honorarium," to have their pictures taken. The money may or may not be split with tribal authorities. Some places on reservations cannot be photographed at all because of customs or religious prohibitions.

Reservations encouraging tourism will usually have a number of "ceremonials" for visitors to enjoy. In actuality most are not really ceremonies but stage shows probably recreating portions of ceremonies. True ceremonies are religious activities involving dancing and song which may last for days. In real ceremonies, relationships with nature and the deity are expressed, including giving thanks and the promotion of fertility for crops and animals. Sometimes tribes will decide to allow some portions of real ceremonials to be open to the public, but there will always be some private and secret portions nonetheless.

Reservations are not the best places to look for Indian arts and crafts because they are being lost in the age of machines and electronics. Museums are actually have the best displays of them, and, interestingly, European anthropological museums have a deep fascination with Native Americans.

Often people who visit reservations are disappointed that they do not find "pure" Indian culture which they somehow associate with "primitive" Indians. Instead they see all sorts of adaptations from non-Indian culture, such as cowboy hats, pick up trucks and jeans. Yet this procilivity to pick items up from another culture has been the way for Native Americans and all other peoples. Tradition and innovation are not mutually exclusive. They go together, as when the Plains Indians began to acquire horses, which were all descended from European stock. There were no horses before the Europeans arrived and there were no pickup trucks either.

THE CONTINENTAL DIVIDE

One of the exciting experiences for visitors to the Rocky Mountain West is to go up and over the Continental Divide, the backbone of the continent. This geographical phenomenon divides the waters of America. To the west of it, rivers and their tributaries drain into the Pacific; to the east of it, rivers and their tributaries drain into the Atlantic, which includes the Gulf of Mexico of the Caribbean Sea.

Approaches to the Continental Divide can be either very dramatic or very ordinary, depending upon just where it is crossed. It is often thought of as a dramatic immaginary line running across the top of snow-capped, jagged peaks. Sometimes it is, and heading to the top of a pass marking the Continental Divide past miles and miles of ever thinning vegetation can be thrilling, especially if it is marked by a big sign in cold thin air at the summit of a high pass.

By contrast, the Continental divide in southwestern Wyoming meanders about confusingly and is anti-climatical to cross and recross. Some claim that there are actually two divides in this particular location.

Glacier National Park in northern Montana along the Canadian border is the site of a unique triple divide. The water in some of its streams goes into the Atlantic, some goes into the Pacific, and some water finds its way north to Hudson's Bay.

The best places for dramatic crossings are in the high country of Colorado, where the highest peaks in the continental United States are found. Another good place is the southern part of the mountainous border between Idaho and Montana, which runs right along the Continental Divide for many miles.

THE FRIENDLY PEOPLE OF THE WEST

All of these attractions are enhanced by the fact that visitors are likely to encounter friendly people all along the way. The spirit of the Old West, where travelers were granted warm hospitality lives on, particularly in the more rural and less developed parts of the region. The very best places to experience Western friendliness are out on the plains and up in the undeveloped mountains. As a rule, people will never be too busy to lend a visitor or a customer a helping hand. Therefore it is an easy area in which to travel. People will give information and guidance readily, in a calm, casual, friendly, unassuming, unpretentious manner.

Increasingly, friendliness is being taught in the cities and suburbs as a business technique, but the perfunctory and automatic nature of such friendliness is often apparent. Naturally, people living in cities and suburbs are more constrained by the pace of their environments, but it can be argued that even the most urban of Western persons tend to display friendliness and a low key approach to strangers as marked characteristics compared to urban persons from other parts of the country. The author remembers being at a Mexican airport and seeing several lines of Americans going home from their vacations. Each line was for a different airplane and different destination in America. The line for Denver was easygoing and jocular. The lines for cities on the Coasts were more intense, if not actually grim by comparison.

Sociologists point out that at a certain population level, people cease to say hello when they encounter other people that they do not know well or at all in public places. There are still hundreds of thousands of square miles in the Rocky

Mountain states where not saying hello would be a surprising breach of local customs.

Such friendliness helps to make a trip to these states a very pleasant experience for persons from distant parts of America. It helps to respond in kind, and to relax and unwind.

OLD FASHIONED WESTERN HUMOR

Here and there in the Rocky Mountain states old-fashioned Western humor can still be savored. Some of it strives to be laconic and blunt, such as the sign that declares: "Open when it is. Closed when it ain't." Other humor depends upon the incongruity of manifestations of a distant civilization in a rural setting. For example, when people wore dinner clothes in early Cheyenne, Wyoming, they were dubbed "Herefords" by cowboys. Herefords are black and white cattle. Something of the same sort of incongruity appears in a recent circular advertising the glories of Laramie, Wyoming. It depicts some raw boned Western youngsters dressed up in 16th century English costumes on a wind-swept hillside advertising a gala "Elizabethan Faire" [*sic*].

Western people can be very ambiguous about how outsiders view their attempts to import and carry on with more polished ways from the outside, something people in the West have made zealous attempts to do from the beginning. Sometimes they want people to be amused at their roughness; at other times they become very angry when outsiders are amused. For example, Buffalo Bill Cody was mad at reporters covering the opening of his hotel in Wyoming because they happily described cowboys in spurs and chaps in the grand ballroom and ignored people in white tie and tails.

Just as stetsons can still be worn even in Rocky Mountain cities without being conspicuous, Western humor can show up just about anywhere, earthy and terse.

In humor and in general, the Old West was not noted for its articulateness. In fact, outsiders have been more inclined to describe the Rocky Mountain West than its natives, starting with its first explorers and continuing with a stream of impressed visitors.

Do You Want to Live There?

DO YOU WANT TO MOVE TO A TOWN IN THE MOUNTAINS?

Many people are contemplating a move to the Rocky Mountains, some who are about to retire and some who want to change their lifestyles. Sometimes a visit inspires such dreams.

Scenery and recreation are the big lures, naturally, but there is also a desire on the part of many to get away from American urban environments, which are increasingly dangerous, difficult, and problem-ridden.

Many people think that the constantly expanding suburban complexes around the main cities of the Rocky Mountain states are becoming reminiscent of the megalopolis on the East or the West Coast or around the Great Lakes region. Therefore they wish to relocate high up and far away, where they can be with snow-capped mountains all year long.

Human expectations and reactions differ so widely that it is quite difficult to offer advice to people in New York, Chicago or Los Angeles who dream of moving to small towns in the Rocky Mountains. Some ex-urbanites find it difficult to adjust to the constraints of small town or small city life. Others adore it. What follows is some advice passed on by some people who have experienced this great leap in environments.

First of all, it is wise to spend some time in a mountain town that looks gorgeous before committing to move to it. Make sure that some time is spent there during all of the seasons. Most of these places have been discovered and developed by the multi-billion dollar ski industry, which means that life in them will vary considerably from season to season.

In the dominant winter, it may be difficult to get into restaurants, bars and shops because of the flood of tourists intent upon skiing and spending. On the other hand, those needing part time work can find it easily in seasonal jobs to serve tourists' needs. Those who come to these mountain towns in the winter to ski are generally pleasant and friendly people who are intent on enjoying the slopes for excitement and exercise.

Springtime is often called the "mud season," because it is subject to intermittent blasts of winter followed by messy melting. It is undoubtedly the most disappointing and least pleasant season of all in mountain towns. Spring is always such a tease, and so subject to obliteration by storms.

By contrast, summer, which takes so long to arrive, is a gem of a season. A common cliché is that "I came to the mountains for the winter, but I stayed here because of the summer." Cool nights and warm, clear, dry, sun-filled days can be expected almost always. Well known mountain towns put on a variety of festivals, institutes, celebrations and performances.

Fall is also a grand season, with days still bright and sunny, but with the nights gaining a sharp chill. The lack of tourists is another feature of the fall, a season which becomes a welcome lull between the end of the summer tourist season and the opening of the ski season in November.

Although tourism provides considerable employment, many residents complain about not having what they call "real" jobs, which can be defined as steady employment not connected to tourism. So instead of "real" jobs, local residents must content themselves with seasonal jobs that are perpetually at the "entry level" when it comes to the pay and the amount of skill required. Many who contemplate relocating to a mountain town might balk at working at such entry level jobs, but there may find nothing available in their professions.

Another negative aspect of moving to a mountain town is that so many needed items will not be available without a long drive to distant outlets. A car may have to be driven hours to get to a dealership, or a missing hardware item will bring a home repair project to a sudden halt and necessitate another long trip. While stores in mountain towns tend to be well stocked with a variety of goods, modern consumerism is so complicated that it is almost inevitable that someday some item will be required which can only be acquired after a long drive, perhaps up to a hundred miles.

All the items in the local stores have to be trucked in, usually in relatively small quantities, and this contributes to the high cost of living which generally prevails in these towns. High real estate prices are another major contributor. Old houses in old mining towns began to soar in value as the recreation boom began in the Rockies. New buildings, often in the form of luxurious condominiums, are astronomical in price. Rent is almost unbearable for those coming in from the outside who have to support themselves on entry level salaries. For example, housing is so tight in posh Aspen, Colorado, that nondescript apartments for seasonal workers rent for over a thousand dollars per month.

Many of these seasonal workers belong to a group that are called "ski bums" in the Rocky Mountains. The "ski bum" is very often a young person who takes a low paying job, without prospects of advancement, in order to indulge their addiction to sport. Many of the younger "ski bums" claim that they are only dropping out for a year or two in order to figure out their priorities. Mountain towns need cheap labor and may supply cheap recreation, rooms, and board in exchange for very low wages. These devotees of recreation get to spend much time on the slopes and the owners can reap good profits from the guests because they need not have a high wage scale to maintain.

Goal-oriented parents tend to express anxiety when their children drop out to become "ski bums." While this is understandable, it must also be pointed out that the "ski bums" support themselves, contribute to the economy and in general stay clear of the drugs, vandalism and violence that scar the lives of less fortunate youth in contemporary America. Besides, they may even get tired of skiing some day.

The relative isolation and small resident populations of mountain towns do not preclude good medical care, at least for emergencies. With so many snow sport enthusiasts at play, medical care has to be on hand to tend to the inevitable accident victims. Complicated medical procedures will usually have to be undertaken at hospitals which might be at a considerable distance from these towns.

Another disadvantage comes from the awkwardness of transportation connections for distant destinations. Small feeder airlines may run irregularly, particularly off season, and local weather conditions can hold them up, which can be extremely frustrating if a distant family emergency is in the offing.

The positive aspects of life in a mountain town are more obvious than these negative considerations. The gorgeous scenery uplifts the spirits and healthy outdoor recreation is close to the doorstep. Crime rates tent to be low to almost non-existent, and law enforcement tends to be efficient and friendly. Local schools and social services can be quite good because of the community's affluence.

After all of the positive and negative features are weighed, whether or not life in a mountain town will suit an individual depends on that person's nature. But it needs to be underlined that even the most enthusiastic potential residents should try living in the mountain town of their dreams during all of the seasons before sending for the moving van.

HOME, HOME ON THE FRONT RANGE: ROCKY MOUNTAIN SUBURBIA

The Joys of the Outdoor Life: The largest concentration of suburbanites in the Rocky Mountain States is along the Front Range of Colorado, stretching from Fort Collins in the north to Pueblo in the south and including the Denver metro area in the middle. Smaller suburban concentrations can be found in all of the other Rocky Mountain states, and most of the people in the area live in them.

What makes the Rocky Mountain suburbanite different from his or her counterpart in Philadelphia or Boston is that the outdoors are readily accessible and an integral part of residents' lifestyles. Nearly everyone in the region has some sort of hobby, pastime or passion connected with the natural and scenic surroundings, including hiking, fishing, hunting, skiing, water skiing, four wheeling, biking or more exotic pursuits such as kyacking or hang gliding. Many combine several activities. All of these opportunities are not far from the suburban driveway, and people have an 80% chance of enjoying them in the sunshine on any given day.

Transplants from other parts of the country who regularly shut off their computers or toss aside their attache cases to head for the mountains are likely to speak rapturously of their new states and be convinced that Americans condemned to living elsewhere envy them. For many, appreciation of the great outdoors becomes a religion and they worship at its shrines as often as possible.

It can be carried too far. Recreation can become a way of life, with jobs being just something to do to make money between recreational junkets. Work becomes just a means to an end, a necessary inconvenience, something to be endured for the sake of those golden hours outdoors.

The Barbecue Lifestyle: Suburbanites in the Rocky Mountain states fancy themselves in the most American part of America. They are supposed to be more optimistic, more individualistic, more mobile and more democratic than elsewhere. They are also supposed to be more friendly and informal, in large measure because they feel less threatened by the pressures of society. Also, they tend to spend more time outdoors and to be more hopeful about an expanding economic base. All of these tendencies are important ingredients of what has been dubbed their "barbecue lifestyle."

People have come to this part of the West for generations after experiencing failure or boredom elsewhere because they wanted to start out where they presumed opportunities were rosier. In actuality, many of them failed once again in their new surroundings, but many did have the American dream come true for them in this new location. Sadly, however, an alarmingly high suicide rate in the region includes the deaths of many persons who have recently relocated.

Mobility is an indisputable feature of Rocky Mountain suburbia. People in these newer, more modern suburban settlements are on wheels. People arrive on wheels and depart quickly on wheels. They also have more vehicles than Amcericans elsewhere, especially recreatonal vehicles.

A society on wheels is a transient society to a considerable extent. People will buy a house and take a job for a brief time, quit and sell out and go somewhere else. All neighborhoods have highly mobile populations. "For Sale" signs sprout like springtime dandelions.

Neighbors, while exhibiting the usual laid back friendliness, tend to maintain only superficial connections with those living around them. People who move in one year may very well be gone the next. For example, the author is atypical because he has lived in the same house in Front Range suburbia for a quarter of a century. But every single house within sight of his has been lived in by from three to ten different families, and that is counting only the houses which changed ownership, not the houses that were rented out and thereby had an even higher number of inhabitants during that time.

How the Attitudes and Composition of Society Differs:
Sociologists who study regional differences by conducting polls
have concluded that people living in the Rocky Mountain states
are more likely to have a live and let live attitude and are
somewhat less likely to attend church. They are inclined to be
slightly more anti-government and much more pro-firearms
than other Americans.

The population in these states is overwhelmingly white, as
overwhelming as Roman Catholics are in the population of the
Republic of Ireland, a percentage in the mid-90's. The population of the United States as a whole is 80% white. Even so,
people in this region are less likely to be troubled about such
things as interracial marriage. Unlike many parts of Europe
and some parts of the United States, society does not have deep
roots, so fewer firmly established social codes prevail and there
is freedom from any hereditary guardians of such codes.
Therefore suburbs and cities in the region tend to freely
tolerate a variety of lifestyles simultaneously.

A Tale of Two Cities' Shopping Malls: There is a certain
ambience about a Rocky Mountain suburbia that makes it
different from suburban areas on the Coasts. It is hard to define
its essence. Perhaps it can be revealed to an extent by compar-
ing scenes at two shopping malls where the outlets and goods
are so similar that they are virtually interchangeable. One of
them is along the Front Range of Colorado and the other is in
suburban Maryland.

A great variety of people will be found at both malls, of
course, but there are some different overall appearances. Those
in the Colorado mall tend to be younger, thinner, taller,
blonder and have fewer members from minorities. More people
in the Maryland mall have darker hair, more rotund bodies and

paler skins, except for those in the larger contingent of people from minorities.

These quick observations at two malls have a basis in sociological statistics. A higher percentage of people in the Colorado mall have northern European ancestry. Overall their educational attainments are higher and they are younger. Greater education and a more youthful median age help to account for the healthier physical appearance of the Colorado crowd.

There is another factor that is more subtle, but quite fundamental. The Maryland crowd tends to be more gloomy and sluggish. The Colorado crowd is more energetic and more animated, so that more conversations break out, where smiles and laughter set the tone. In Maryland, consumers prowl about in a more serious manner, perhaps because they have less disposable income per capita to spend at the mall.

Some years ago a sociologist who was undoubtedly pursuing a thesis topic measured the length and duration of smiles in various parts of the United States. In this study, Colorado won hands down for the longest periods of smiling and the greatest frequency of smiles. By the way, Upstate New York was at the bottom of the list in these categories. (Perhaps the sociologist gathered samples during the bleakness of an Upstate winter.)

Warm Western smiles have been duly noted by students arriving from Africa to study at universities in Colorado. Since warm smiles from females to males have very different connotations in parts of Africa, student advisers have made a point of stressing that such smiles are just a sign of friendliness and not an open invitation for intimacy.

At the Colorado mall salespeople and customers go through the ritual of low key, friendly, smile-brightened exchanges. To be more brusque and businesslike, the way most Marylanders seem to carry on at the mall, might actually be regarded as somewhat rude in Colorado.

Perhaps the Colorado shoppers have much more to smile about. Chances are over ten to one that the sun will be shining when they emerge from the mall. In Maryland humidity is what is as predictable as sunshine is in Colorado. When they leave the Colorado mall, shoppers will see the mountains off on the horizon, reminding them of the good times to come in their vast, ever handy playground. The emerging Maryland crowd sees packed parking lots and ramps leading to packed highways which may remind them of the commuting hours that they are likely to put in going to work. They can see no natural features on their low horizon, but if they could look beyond it they would see the sad urban decay of inner cities.

The Excessive Importance of External Appearances: All environments have their down sides, including those that are largely agreeable. Much emphasis in Rocky Mountain suburbia is put upon outward appearance. It is important to appear friendly, even if the friendliness felt might only be very superficial. The look on the outside is regarded as highly important no matter what feelings may be on the inside. Spiritual and ethical conditions within are downplayed as emphasis focuses on outward appearances of persons and their possessions. Having the right clothes, the right car, in short, the right "look" is the ultimate end for many people. As far as accomplishments are concerned, "having a good time," however defined by these participants, seems to be life's ultimate achievement.

Of course, these tendencies are universal, and every part of the United States strongly manifests them to varying degrees. California is notorious in this regard. Since the Rocky Mountain states have so many people without roots of family and place, they may emphasize external characteristics as a compensation.

Provincialism: One of the clear drawbacks to life in the Rocky Mountain states is provincialism. It is a long way to the East Coast and to California, where a greater number of important events occur and important people live, and where new lifestyles and trends are likely to appear first. People in the Rocky Mountain suburbias catch up with what is new after a delay, whether it is in the form of new clothing styles or new fads. People living in more remote and rural areas in these states may never bother to catch up with some of these things at all.

Provincialism can take many forms. People take the publication of polls about their cities very seriously, despite the fact that the polls are usually hastily gathered and churned out by reporters or editors who are far away, really out of touch and more concerned about deadlines than anything else. Nevertheless, Front Range suburbanites gloat when their town is cited as one of the best places in the country in which to live. They become crestfallen, however, if their town is cited for such things as its amount of pollution, or its high percentage of waste per capita.

Recently Coloradans have suffered great pangs of anxiety over whether major league baseball would come to Denver and remove the stigma of minor league status. Now Denver will overcome some of its provincial feelings by being recognized as a major league city by having a major league team.

Provincialism becomes glaringly obvious when local television stations break into national news or discussion programs in order to warn about threatening weather or describe local plane crashes or fires or some other local disaster. Running a band with announcements on the lower part of the screen is not enough for them, nor is featuring the local stories on the local news. Local stations have to brutally interrupt regular programming to put their own people on the screen, robbing viewers of important national and international news. The problem is exacerbated by the fact that the local people very often have little to say, but they proceed to say it over and over again with minor variations.

A RECREATIONAL SITE IN THE NEW WEST: THE JOYS AND SORROWS OF HORSETOOTH RESERVOIR

Horsetooth Reservoir is a large body of water just to the west of the Front Range city of Fort Collins, Colorado. It can serve as a specific example of what a new, artificial recreation spot is like in the new West. There are many similar places in these states and the people who use it and abuse it are like the people who visit such places all over the Rocky Mountain region.

Horsetooth's water covers a valley that once had farms and a town. The U.S. Army engineers constructed it as part of an elaborate irrigation system and regularly maintain its dams. Mountain water flows down into it at one end and drinking and irrigation water flows out of it at the other end while countless people disport themselves over it and in it.

In the spring and early summer the water level is high because it receives melted mountain snow in those months. Through the hot summer days the reservoir drains down, revealing more and more shoreline and a littering of old rusting beer cans that were thrown out of boats. Every now and then a rusted pistol or bicycle shows up, hinting at evil deeds that may have been done.

Horsetooth Reservoir is in a gorgeous setting. Immediately to the west of the reservoir are the Front Range foothills that rise sharply, stark granite hills heavily covered with brush and pine. Closer to shore red cliffs of sandstone, partly covered by scrub, provide a contrast with the darker foothills. At one point along the distant western ridge of foothills a massive, strange flat rock is deeply notched on both sides, which makes it look like a gigantic horse's tooth, hence the name. The northwestern end of the reservoir joins with Lory State Park, which offers horseback riding, good trails and delightful scenery. There are many coves along the western shore in this park where boats temporarily anchor.

The eastern cliffs overlooking the valley containing the reservoir are also imposing. A partially paved road runs right along its crest, sometimes rising and falling so precipitously that some flatland drivers are brought to a crawl on it. The view from the dirt road portion, at its highest points, is at once spectacular and revealing. Looking east, all of Fort Collins lies below it, as well as all of neighboring Loveland. The Great Plains begin their long march here to the Appalachians a thousand miles away. Looking the other way, to the west, another dramatic view marks the very beginning of the upsurge of the Rockies.

If such a place existed in Europe, special parking lots would have to be built for tour buses and guides would be overwhelmed with throngs. Undoubtedly a collection of legends about drowned maidens and swords stuck in rocks would emerge. But since Horsetooth Reservoir is in the Rocky Mountain states, it is but one small part of this region's unbelievably rich treasure of scenery, a place of no great distinction.

Yet Horsetooth shows, on a very local level, some of the forces struggling over the future for this part of the world. Its waters are troubled by litigation over who will get to use them and how much will be used by each claimant.

Meanwhile the commitment to multiple use means that substantial numbers of people will take advantage of it for recreation in the summer. Water skiing is a very popular activity. On weekends boat traffic can become very heavy. The skiers themselves vary in skill, from those who start and stop repetitiously because they cannot get launched on their skis to those who perform a kind of ballet, twisting, turning and leaping in the boats' wakes. The best time to ski is on early weekday mornings, when there are few boats on the reservoir and the winds are likely to be down. The sport is regulated closely. Patrol boats make sure that the proper number of people, equipment and procedures are involved. Nevertheless, accidents do happen, some of them involving young people drunk from beer consumed in the hot sun.

Recently a plague of single seat jet skis has appeared. They look like sea going snowmobiles and have equally unpleasant sounds. Their sole purpose seems to be to enable the user to enjoy a sense of motion. They bound about in the water, cutting close to the wakes of boats, or go around in circles, all to the accompaniment of an ear splitting, roaring whine. It is no wonder that those seeking to enjoy tranquility along the shore may greet their arrival with expletives.

Whether they come to Horsetooth's shores by boat or whether they descend from the steep slopes, some people are themselves a plague. Their voices, their radios and their clothes are all too loud. Occasionally someone will drive a car off of the road to the very edge of the cliffs, driving right over plant life, so that the car stereo can boom away with bad and monotonous music for a picnic down below. Fortunately, the shoreline is very long, so those not appreciating the concert can hike out of its range.

Anthropologists declare that one of the salient characteristics of homo sapiens is that they mark their presence by litter. Unfortunately, human traces at Horsetooth are all too evident. One of the worst kinds of litter is in the form of shards of glass. Despite all of the prohibitions against bringing glass containers to the reservoir, many people do, and some stupidly smash them. Cuts for swimmers and waders result when changes in the water level make it impossible to see the shards. Aluminum beer and soft drink cans pose little threat, but they look ugly when they are thrown about in clusters. On shore wads of toilet paper litter many clumps of bushes. Even worse are the disposable diapers, often flung ashore from boats.

Some very singular abuses of the environment are worth mentioning: A large family once brought a boat to an empty sandy shore and disgorged all the accoutrements of suburbia. Fearing a problem with ants, they opened a bag of lethal poison and crated a cordon sanitaire around their possessions on three sides. The shoreline provided the fourth side. After a few hours, they put their goods aborad their craft and departed. The poison remained. The next time that a rainstorm washed the shore it washed their poison right down into the reservoir, right down into a delicate ecosystem from which fish are caught and from which town drinking water is eventually drawn.

The cliffs on the eastern side of Horsetooth are right above trails. Many people cannot resist the temptation to toss rocks off of the cliffs, and in some places this can be very dangerous for the people down below. On one occasion a person went out on a high cliff and began to belt golf balls out towards the reservoir. Most fell short, dropping down in the area where the trails passed.

Despite these terrible examples of how some people abuse the environment, most of those who enjoy it are responsible. They pack out their litter and have a live-and-let-live attitude towards other humans, creatures and plants.

Horsetooth for the most part remains wild and free. Except for an occasional ranger along the roadway, there are no signs of officials in control. Hikers regularly see deer start up suddenly. Birds of prey hover in the sky. Rabbits, lizards, and toads populate the underbrush. Spared from the effects of herbicides and pesticides which regularly drench the suburban sprawl of Fort Collins, Horsetooth has an abundance of butterflys, those wonderful creatures which have so sadly diminished in numbers in recent decades. Wildflowers are also abundant, but at some distance from the trails, because some thoughtless people pick them if they have a chance.

As the years go on and Fort Collins grows, more and more use is made of the reservoir. The problem with litter has eased somewhat because the courts dispatch gangs of workers sentenced to community service to clean up the reservoir. On the private land close to the county and state land around the reservoir more and more large expensive houses are constructed to overlook the water. Each new dwelling adds a little more of suburbia and takes away a little more of the wildness of the site. This is, in microcosm, what has been happening all over the new West.

CHAPTER THREE:

THE SPECIAL ENVIRONMENT OF THE ROCKY MOUNTAIN STATES

Scenery Versus Development

A HOMOGENOUS EXTERIOR BUT A SPACIOUS INTERIOR

When these states were first opened for settlement by Easterners, promoters stressed how tame the region was. Now those advertising tourism stress how wild it is and how different it is from the rest of the United States, a task which becomes more difficult to carry out with each passing year.

To a visiting European, America's different climates, topography, time zones, and accents makes it seem more like a continent than a country. Many Americans, on the other hand, perceive a growing uniformity that is making all of the regions more alike. For example, signs on the Interstate Highways are almost universally the same everywhere; a pizza outlet of a well known chain or a hamburger emporium of another chain look alike wherever they are found. Well-known motels are so similar in different parts of the country that blind persons can move in and out of them unhesitatingly. Outlets in shopping malls may or may not change their names from region to region, but their products and setting are virtually identical. The majority of Americans live in relatively affluent suburbs, which can be highly similar in appearance even if the background consists of mountains, deserts, palm trees, oceans or more and more of the same suburbs.

If all of this homogeneity exists, what, then, is different about the Rocky Mountain states? First of all, they comprise one of the least populated parts of the United States. All of these states comprise over 17% of the land area of the 48 contiguous states, but they have just over seven million persons living in them, or just less than 3% of the population of the United States. While the estimated national population density per square mile in 1990 is 69, the most densely populated of these states, Colorado, has just over 31 persons per square mile. Utah has just over 20; Idaho only 12; Montana has just less than five and a half; and Wyoming has the thinnest population of all with just over four and a half persons per square mile. What a contrast this makes with New Jersey's population of just over 1000 per square mile and Rhode Island's 816 or Massachusetts' 715.

Paradoxically, these Rocky Mountain States comprise the most urbanized part of America. As in Australia, nearly everyone lives in urban-suburban oases and very few live on the homesteads and ranches of what Australians call the "outback" and Americans call the "wide open spaces." Unfortunately, the problems of older American cities have reached these states also: pollution, ugly systems of congested arterial roads, and the malaise of "urban decay," which means poverty, neglect, drugs, gangs and crime.

WHY THE REGION IS CLAIMED
BY ALL AMERICANS

These big, block-shaped states do have remarkably extensive stretches of yet unspoiled and undeveloped scenic beauty, as well as extensive wide open spaces that include some of the most barren, desolate and isolated land in the United States.

The natural beauty has led countless Americans to resettle in the region, and yearly millions of tourists come to enjoy it also. Even Americans who have not yet been to the Rockies nonetheless have a vision of its snow-capped mountains, sheer red rock canyons, geysers shooting skyward and purple rangeland stretching open and empty towards a distant mountainous horizon. The author wishes to assure such people that he had visions of palms and beaches in Hawaii long before he ever visited that state.

Having so much natural beauty left is definitely what makes the Rocky Mountain states so special, and it also imparts the feeling that the region really belongs to all Americans. Deep within the American consciousness is a vision of all prehistoric America as a pristine ecological paradise, a wilderness rich with forests and animals and thinly populated by ecologically wise Native Americans who did not disturb the balance of nature. According to this view, settlement brought farms, domestic livestock, villages and towns, and drove the Native Americans and wild animals away. Civilization came to obliterate the green and lovely forested world that once had been.

Since the Rocky Mountain region was so inaccessible, in part too dry and in part too rugged, it was the last to feel the impact of civilization's encroachments. Because there were fewer people scattered over that gigantic area, they have been less able to transform and exploit the region to the extent that the East, South and Midwest have been altered from their natural condition. Therefore, according to this viewpoint, more of the original, untouched, undisturbed America remains in the Rocky Mountain states than anywhere else in the country outside of Alaska.

So the natural beauty and large wild animals evoke the common national memory of the unspoiled American Eden that was supposed to exist before the plow, the horse, the wheel and the gun changed it so drastically in the older states. This is why all Americans everywhere can regard the Rocky Mountain region as part of the national heritage, particularly those famous large portions of it which have been designated for preservation for all time as National Parks and Monuments.

THE LOSS FROM DEVELOPMENT

It is wise to see what is left of this scenic heritage before more of it erodes away. Condominiums are marching across mountainsides relentlessly; suburbs pave over the valleys; the gougings of mining operations go on and on, adding scars to the landscape; more huge concrete structures redirect the precious flow of water from the mountains to flush toilets and irrigate lush green lawns in spreading acres of tract houses; more bad air hangs in malodorous, tinted clouds over cities; and an ever increasing amount of acid rain kills delicate creatures high up in mountain lakes. Meanwhile, formerly untouched remote hillsides and canyons are disturbed by inappropriate new houses, often subject to dangers from fire or flood, which are built by people "getting away from it all" and who always manage to bring much of "it" with them to hitherto undisturbed places.

The more these Rocky Mountain states are plowed under, bulldozed and paved, the more Westerners think it is important to experience and glorify its wildness, at the very time that it is shrinking out of sight in so many places. Development and the much touted "progress" that it brings has been called the "fatal attraction" of the West. It means more money and more jobs, to be sure, but it also means less of what originally brought so many people to move to these states and to visit them.

Resistance to development is strong. Bumper stickers announce: "Unlimited growth is the philosophy of the cancer cell!" Another paraphrases Rhet Butler: "Frankly, my dear, I don't want a dam!" A vintage bumper sticker declared: "Do not Californicate Colorado!" The phrase "malled to death" refers to the relentless gobbling of acres by shopping malls, which are already overbuilt in many places and often detract from the beauty and harmony of locations. In wilder areas, so called "eco-terrorists" threaten all sorts of dire sabotage against mining and timber operations, and in a few places they have actually carried out some of their threats. A more characteristic response is that of a disgruntled Montana rancher who observed hectic construction nearby and said, "Now I know how the Indians felt."

Encroachments upon wild and beautiful places plus the bumper to bumper traffic through the National Parks has led many to conclude that "the West is dead." This phrase has been used many times in the brief history of the region. The Western artist Charles M. Russell may have been the first to say it back in 1917. What the phrase really means is that the West has changed and it is not the same any longer. While more and more of it does resemble the rest of the United States, nature, space and the mountains are still far from disappearing through development. Even so, what has always made these states so attractive—clean air, unobstructed scenic beauty and minimal congestion of open spaces—are all being eroded, at a faster pace in this century than in the last, through the often heedless pursuit of dollars.

The Paradoxical Federal Factor and Its Impact on Western Politics

No other part of the United States has so much Federal ownership and regulation as the West, right up to the Pacific shore. In the Rocky Mountain region, 60.6% of Idaho; 60% of Utah; 46.5% of Wyoming; 29.7% of Colorado and 29.4% of Montana belongs to the United States government. What is more, the federal government has traditionally pumped more money into this area than it has taken out in taxes, leading some to call it a deficit area, a non-self supporting area or a colonial dependency or ward of Washington, D.C.

Therefore it is truly ironic that the West produces so many politicians who pose as rugged individualists and who denounce the Federal government at every opportunity. Republican candidates from the Rocky Mountain states at the national and local levels regularly sweep to victory denouncing the Federal bureaucracy. Even Democrats from these states decry the Federal government's delay, paperwork and double talk. Yet the Western states are more dependent upon this Federal bureaucracy than any other regional group of states. Another irony is that Westerners vigorously defend states' rights at the same time that they zealously pander for as much Federal aid as possible.

In a way, the welfare state exists more fully in the West than anywhere else in the country. Welfare is doled out in the form of military installations, defense contracts, permits to graze on public lands cheaply, permits to cut timber cheaply (called "woodlot welfare"), farm supports and extensive water projects yielding cheap and therefore subsidized water. Money also goes from Washington to National Parks and Indian Reservations. Chronically short of capital and dependent upon government subsidies and investments for the region, the Rocky Mountain states have continued to manifest some of the characteristics of colonies.

Federal support goes far back in Western history. The West was the first region to experience an expanded federal role. For a long time these states were territories, which is usually a status requiring considerable Federal aid. Such aid was forthcoming to quell the Indians and distribute land. The Reclamation Act of 1902 put the Federal government in the position of controlling and developing that most precious of all Western resources, water. More recently, President Roosevelt's New Deal pumped large amounts of money into the region.

Western politicians have been asking for Federal subsidies ever since there have been Western politicians. Senators from the Rocky Mountain states do wield considerable clout since two Senators come from each state regardless of population. The low populations of their home states plus the relatively few basic interests that their constituents have enable Western Senators to operate very effectively when it comes to political vote trading.

Most of the West's successful politicians are Republicans. On the whole, voters tend to associate Democrats with big city problems, big spending and excessive support for both minorities and the poor. In the most recent Presidential elections, all of the electoral votes from the region have gone to the Republican candidates. Nevertheless, a few surprisingly liberal politicians are sent to Washington from the Rocky Mountain states every now and then. Many voters split tickets.

The politics within individual states do often allow the two party system to operate more effectively. Politics in the relatively sparsely populated Rocky Mountain states is a very personal matter. Legislators and governors are not distant figures but local people who are well-known, regularly seen and usually unpretentious.

While the region accepts Federal money enthusiastically, it resists Federal controls fervently. In the late 1970's the so-called "Sagebrush Rebellion" was launched by Western developers, ranchers and other businessmen. They resented government regulations on grazing, mining and the use of water on public lands. They were highly pleased when Ronald Reagan was elected in 1980 and some of the controls on public land were loosened up by his appointees. This was done under the guise of "multiple use."

The conflicts over the use of Federal property in these states will certainly go on regardless of whom is in the White

House. On one extreme, some pressure groups want Congress to give control of Federal land to the states. On the other extreme, environmentalists want to "lock up" large areas free from any exploitation except for recreation.

To a greater extent than elsewhere in the country, the Federal bureaucracy is at the center of the conflicts about Western development and land use. This is because so many agencies and bureaus have extensive jurisdictions in the region. They include the Bureau of Land Management, The Bureau of Reclamation, the National Forest Service, the Bureau of Indian Affairs, the Defense Department, the National Park Service, the Bureau of Mines and the Fish and Wildlife Service. The conflicts about what do with public property occur between agencies and parts of the public, between different agencies and within single agencies. Just one agency, the Forest Service, by the Multiple Purpose Act of 1960, is required to provide for outdoor recreation, range, timber, watershed and wildlife purposes.

As the distinguished historian of the American West, Patricia Nelson Limerick, has pointed out so convincingly in her book, *Legacy of Conquest* (New York, 1987), conflict over resources in the West has been normal since the earliest times and it can be expected to continue without an end in sight.

Where Often Are Heard Discouraging Words: Environmental Issues

THE DELICATE ECOLOGY OF THE REGION

People in all parts of the world should be able to unite in the next century behind the cause of saving the planet from the disaster of ecological damage. The growing number of conflicts in the Rocky Mountain states reflects both the delicate nature of the region's ecology and the ruthlessness of its historic development towards the environment.

Considerable damage was inflicted as far back as the early 19th century, when the mountain men stripped the region of its natural water management teams, the beavers. The miners wanted to get rich as quickly as possible did not have any regard whatsoever for ecological concerns. Once the profits and jobs were gone, they were gone. Poisonous slag heaps were left as a testament to their abuse of the landscape. Some say that the lingering spirit of the frontiersman still influences those who waste and pollute. Frontiersmen, dwarfed in a huge environment, could not conceive of resources being finite and exhaustible.

They were wrong. Resources have been put in jeopardy because in these states the amount of damage that the environment can sustain is quite limited. High in the mountains the air is thin. With less oxygen, it takes less pollution to foul the atmosphere. One of the saddest sights to behold is a cloud of foul, polluted air putting a haze across a view of snow-capped mountains, or creeping along high mountain valleys. Moreover, the region is particularly subject to a phenomenon known as inversion, in which a layer of warm air clamps down over stable cold air, trapping pollutants near the ground. In many places restrictions on burning wood have gone into effect and car pooling is strongly encouraged by municipal authorities.

Water is also in shorter supply in this region because of the natural aridity prevailing over most of the surfaces of these states. Therefore a given amount of pollutants discharged in Rocky Mountain streams will do relatively more damage than elsewhere. In the plains parts of these states ground water has been depleted for irrigation. Nevertheless, the normal prairie and grazing lands that have been plowed up for crops have still dried out and to an extent they have blown away.

Debates about how to preserve the environment rage throughout the Rocky Mountain states. Should more places be set aside as sacrosanct wilderness areas forever, without any development, so that people can get inside of them on horseback and foot and just tarry there briefly as visitors? Should the way of life of ranching be preserved by continuing cheap Federal fees for grazing? Should the market demands of the winter tourist industry be followed, especially if this means more ski slopes and lodges on Federal land? Is the plight of endangered species, on the one hand, more important than jobs or being less dependent upon foreign sources of oil or having a better balance of trade on the other?

Environmentalists have exerted their influence on a wide variety of very specific concerns and projects. They have insisted that forests should not be treated as crops, but that they should be wild. They see clear cutting, or cutting a whole section of forest right down instead of taking trees here and there as the ruthless intrusion of industrialism into the forest. They declare that whenever an official says that a species of tree needs "treatment," he or she is using a euphemism for cutting. They decry the creation of new ski areas, wondering how much of the national forests will have to be destroyed so that skiers will not have to wait long in lift lines. Some want to end grazing on public land, using the slogan: "Livestock free by '93." Some of their other concerns are more particular: They want to protect wild horses, tortoises and certain rare fish. They also want to prevent dams interfering with water life, especially salmon on their way to spawning areas.

Environmentalists have received some sharp criticism. They are often portrayed as the enemies of jobs, since the cutting of timber and the smelting of ores employ many people, despite what it does to the environment. Environmentalists have also been criticized for adopting "no growth" policies as a way of preserving the West as a playground for the East.

A CASE STUDY ON WATER QUALITY

Since ecological issues are so complex, an examination of just one situation may be a useful way to assess the seriousness of environmental damage in the Rocky Mountain states.

For generations, Westerners have been worried about the quantity of water available to them, but their concerns are now shifting to the quality of water as well.

Along the Continental Divide, high in the subalpine valleys of Colorado, from 9,000 to 10,000 feet up, most of the water for the Southwest originates. The watersheds of four major rivers are located in this specific area, that of the Arkansas, the Platte, the Colorado and the Rio Grande. Agriculture in ten states downstream depend on this runoff, and at least ten million people drink from it, including one million in Denver and other millions in places as far away as Los Angeles, Phoenix and El Paso.

A massive geological accident of 70 million years ago guaranteed that Colorado's chief water source would be found in close proximity to huge deposits of metals. Continental plates collided and thrust their edges three miles up into the air, forming the Rocky Mountains. Molten gold, lead and zinc and other metals were released from the earth's core and flowed upwards, where these metals hardened into rich veins embedded in granite and other rock formations. Deep valleys were carved into the landscape as a result of millions of years of snow, rain and wind. In ice ages, continuous snowfall built up great moving packs of ice called glaciers. Over time these rivers of ice gouged away granite walls and widened valley floors. Finally, around 15,000 years ago, the glaciers retreated, leaving rocks and debris all over .

Water ran down off of the mountains in streams, and, below the surface, aquifers formed when running water eroded the rock to get down to a permeable layer of gravel and sand. These aquifers were actually natural filtration systems to purify water as well as an underground reservoir of flowing water.

Aquifers below and streams above soon allowed a ribbon of life to establish itself in the high, cold, rugged mountains. Beavers came to play an important role by making dams which slowed down erosion and enriched the aquifers. These healthy subalpine watersheds with their high alpine aquifers were crucial for this otherwise dry Rocky Mountain region because they provided a steady flow of pure water.

This delicate ecosystem was rudely disrupted, first by the depredations of the mountain men, and then, more massively, by the sudden advent of mining. Miners with gold fever are caught up by a ferocious gamblers' urge to go through as much material as quickly as possible. They felt like transients in the Rockies, which struck most of them as a cold and inhospitable region. They had the right to mine any public land without the hindrance of any environmental protection laws. So they took profitable ores out as fast as possible and left waste and byproducts. Tailings, or sand like remains from the milling process, were dumped anywhere that was convenient. Considerable quantities of water was used to dislodge gold in placer mining, necessitating canals and ditches in many cases, with the result that aquifers were ripped up and streambeds were dislodged.

Deep hard rock miners did the most damage, because they moved rapidly from claim to claim, abandoning mine shafts that soon filled with groundwater. The reaction between this groundwater and exposed sulfide minerals and oxygen was disastrous. Sulfuric acid was produced, which ate away at exposed metals in the mineshaft walls. The result was acidic water containing large doses of heavy metals. This evil flow would then go down through the damaged aquifers and streams to disrupt the delicate balance of mountain ecosystems. These heavy discharges of chemicals went into a system of high aquifers that has a very low tolerance for such substances.

In some places yellowish orange water can be clearly seen joining mountain streams. This means that it contains a mixture of iron and manganese. Dissolved lead, cadmium, zinc, and aluminum cannot be seen.

Recently the Colorado Health Department declared that 1,300 miles of streams were biologically damaged by acid drainage from mines. There are an estimated 15,000 abandoned metal mines in Colorado.

Leadville, Colorado, was at the heart and center of the Colorado mining industry, and today it is designated as a prime recipient for a Superfund clean up project. There are good reasons for designating Leadville. The town environs exudes a flow of water laden with heavy metals which follows a course right down into the Pueblo, Colorado, reservoir, which is the source of water for that city as well as Colorado Springs, Colorado.

Tailings are the major source of pollution for Leadville. These ugly sandy piles and hillocks contain tons of metals long exposed to the air, metals which were not removed because of the inefficiency of the processing then carried on. The chemicals in such piles of tailings are unstable and constantly reacting to the environment. The result is poisoned waters, as revealed by sick and misshapen fish downstream. Alarming studies have also shown that children in Leadville have dangerously high levels of lead in their blood.

Leadville is not the only place where the first hundred years of mining in the Rockies has left acres of ugly, exposed tailings. Eleven million tons of tailings loom over the beautiful and rapidly expanding ski industry town of Telluride, Colorado. In Aspen, Colorado, another old mining town, expensive condominiums have been built over tailings contaminated with lead. Idaho Springs and Central City, two more old Colorado mining towns that famous now on account of their tourist trade, are plagued with a similar legacy from unregulated mining.

The decades of the 1970's and 1980's marked a new era of environmental regulation. For example, clean water acts required mining operations to treat waste water and get permits before discharging it. Nevertheless, the scale of contemporary mining has made the operations of the 19th century small by comparison. Today whole mountains are moved and pulverized by great multi-national corporations.

The gigantic molybdenum mine at Climax, Colorado, just outside of Leadville, is a case in point. At full production it employs over 3,000 people who can process over 50,000 tons of ore per day. Molybdenum, known as "moly" to the miners, is a key alloy used to harden steel. While the mining company at Climax is one of the most environmentally sensitive in the country, the sheer size of its operations creates daunting problems. Its tailings cover a grand total of over 1,600 acres. The snowpack covering the tailings for eight months out of the year sometimes reaches as high as 15 feet. Snowmelt goes right through the tailings and despite ernest efforts to treat the water, toxic metals continue to flow downstream into Dillon reservoir, which holds drinking water for the city of Denver.

The magnitude of this particular problem highlights the fact that the regulation of mining in the Rocky Mountain West is still in its infancy. At least citizens and companies are working to apply new knowledge and new safeguards for the environment.

Mining operations do not pose the only threat of pollution for Rocky Mountain water. For some time Europe and eastern North America have been alarmed over damage from the controversial and warmly debated phenomenon of the effects of acid rain. Now its effects have been discovered in the Rockies as well, where the situation is compounded by the phenomenon of acid snowmelt.

Since the Rocky Mountain region has been one of the fastest growing regions in the United States, the production of sulfur dioxide and nitrogen oxides that escape into the atmosphere can be expected to continue to increase at a disturbing rate. In addition, coal powered energy production for California's millions at the western edges of the region results in polluted air being blown eastwards into the mountains, where it washes down as acid rain or acid snow. Already its effects have been sighted in ponds and lakes in the form of fish eggs that do not develop properly and swiftly decreasing numbers of salamanders and frogs.

In contemplating the damage that will ensue from mining and power production, natives of the Rocky Mountain states might reflect on the fact that their beautiful environment is far more valuable to them in dollars than the ores and fuels that are extracted. "You can't eat scenery," is an old cry from those who want to reap profits from resources. As the mayor of a mountain town recently countered, "We do eat scenery because we sell it." Recently tourism generated over five and a half billion dollars per year in Colorado alone. Mining in the same state during a given year was worth only one billion.

Many things need to be done to save the environment of these states: Specific basic research on the ecology of subalpine valleys needs to be undertaken. Contamination from acid rain can be fought by national legislation. Funding needs to be increased to enforce existing environmental laws. Restrictions have to be put on emissions, even down to ordinary citizens' wood burning stoves. Above all, national efforts to recycle metals of all kinds must be undertaken.

THE REGION'S UNIQUE GEOLOGY

The Rocky Mountains, the high, sharp backbone of America, are unique geologically. Altitude provides several life zones: desert and semi-arid plains rising to about 6,000 feet; a foothill zone from 6,000 to 8,000 feet; a montane zone from 8,000 to 10,000 feet; a subalpine zone from 10,000 to 11,500 feet; and a small amount of surface above 11,500 feet in an alpine zone. The highest peak in the Rockies, Mount Elbert in Colorado, reaches 14,431 feet above sea level.

These changes in altitude actually mean that a person in Colorado can contemplate blooming cactus plants baking in 90 degree heat on an unirrigated plain on a sunny morning and see delicate flowers of alpine tundra surviving in cold wind high on a mountainside in Rocky Mountain National Park in the afternoon. Just climbing a high pass in a car can reveal changing life zones to the most inexperienced eye.

The Rocky Mountains are sharper and higher than the Appalachian Mountains in the East because they are younger. The geology of the region is fascinating to geologists and amateur "rock hounds." How these mountains got to be the way they are, in terms of geological history, is best treated by experts. Its proper relation requires grasping a different, an infinitely slower, concept of time.

Suffice it to say that the area was a vast sea bed hundreds of millions of years ago. Heat and pressure produced a geological revolution which thrust upwards sea bed rocks, such as sandstone and limestone. These were the ancestral Rockies, which mostly eroded away into swampy, tropical lowlands where dinosaurs roamed. Then another period of violent up-heaval occurred, lasting from 160 million years ago to 60 million years ago, a time when the earth's crust gave way and folded, a process that thrust mountains upwards. Other mo-untains were blasted upwards by volcanic upheavals and their consequent lava flows. Then came a series of ice ages and the combined effects of advancing and retreating glaciers, whose ice flows shaped mountains by their tremendous scraping, leaving their residue of rocks and earth in places called moraines.

Glaciers made their last retreat 12,000 to 15,000 years ago. Today there are only a few spots where small glaciers remain in the Rocky mountain states. The Tetons have one, so does the high country of Colorado, but the place with the most of them outside of Alaska and Canada is appropriately named Glacier National Park, which has about sixty of them. Moraines are much more common, and are classified into several categories. Their strewing of rocks and boulders, some of enormous size, testifies to the force of glacial impact.

Despite all of these upheavals in the geological past, the area is relatively stable today. Earthquakes are highly unlikely and volcanic activity is no longer dangerous. There are no mountains like Mount Saint Helen's in Washington which exploded in an eruption a few years ago.

Volcanic activity continues in the Rockies today, however, in the form of hot, subterranean activity. When rainwater seeps underground and passes over superheated rocks it can often return in the form of hot springs and geysers. Yellowstone National Park, which is basically a plateau resting over molten lava, is the best place to see this phenomenon, although many other places in the Rocky Mountain West are subject to such activity. That is why recreational hot springs are so prevalent.

Old volcanic activity created the Craters of the Moon National Monument in Idaho and the Devil's Tower National Monument in Wyoming, and the San Juan range in Colorado.

Other ranges can be discerned by a trained eye to have emerged from another process, the folding of the earth's crust. They include the Front Range in Colorado, the Wasatch and the Uinta mountains in Utah; the Teton, Wind River and Big Horn Mountains in Wyoming; and many, many more throughout the region.

THE REGION'S UNIQUE ARIDITY

Aridity is a special condition for these states and for their neighboring states in the Southwest. This condition makes them different from the rest of the United States.

If ten inches or less of precipitation per year classifies deserts, these Rocky Mountain states fall into the category of semi-arid because they average only ten to eighteen inches of precipitation annually, depending upon the locations within them. The temperate zones to the east and in the Northwest receive at least double the average of most locations in the Rocky Mountain states.

What is more, precipitation is not spread out evenly throughout the year. As in many arid African regions, precipitation is heavier seasonally. For the Rocky Mountain states, the spring months of March and April are noted for the greatest amounts of snowfall, and heavy rains can be expected for some of the days in May and June. Occasionally torrential downpours will unleash sheets of rain to account for 10% or 20% of the annual rainfall in a fairly short period of time.

If left alone, many places in the Rocky Mountain region, particularly on the eastern plains, would be a high semi-desert, bright green in the late spring, fading green in the summer and tawny in the fall as well as in the winter when free of snow, which is the case most of the time out on the plains.

Obviously, much of the region is not now in its natural state. It is irrigated so that lawns, flowers, gardens and farms can flourish. But if ditches dried and pipes and hoses were shut off, suburbs in the Rocky Mountains would come to resemble the dusty brown towns of the poorer parts of New Mexico.

Without the complex system of dams, reservoirs and ditches, many of the farms in the Rocky Mountain states would be out of business. "Dry farming," or farming without irrigation, has always been a risky business. An ironic old saying is that dry farming can only succeed in wet years. Those who practice it need more than luck. They also have to know the land and use it with great care or topsoil will blow away as dust.

All of this means that now water, not gold or silver, is the real treasure of the Rocky Mountains. The economic salvation of the region rests upon the storage of spring runoff from the melting snow of the mountains. The problem is to gather moving water from the few places that have a surplus of moisture and to distribute it to the many places that have a water shortage. Some portions of the mountains comprise the only part of the region where annual precipitation exceeds evaporation and the transpiration of plants. Indeed, a very few places along the spine of the Rockies actually exceed the national average for precipitation.

The reason why moisture comes to the higher elevations of these states is due to the fact that moisture laden clouds from the Pacific must rise to get over them. At higher altitudes their moisture condenses and much of it spills. Forests down below act as key watersheds to hold this moisture.

The depth of the winter snowpack in mountainous forests is always a critical measurement for distant farms and homes. A further complication comes from the dryness of Rocky Mountain snow. While its powdery nature may bring smiles to skiers, a gallon of it only yields 1/30 of a gallon of water compared to the yield of 1/10 of a gallon from wet snow.

Warm weather melts the mountains' hoard of winter snow. All of the region's great waterways begin in the wet belts along the Continental Divide, which includes Yellowstone and Glacier National Parks and Colorado's high alpine meadows. While these rivers may be quite long, none of them are navigable. They include the Rio Grande and the Arkansas flowing eastwards and the Snake and the Colorado flowing westwards. Neither the Arkansas nor the Rio Grande carries much water away from their drainage area. The Columbia does, engorged by a great flow from the Snake River.

Perhaps the Colorado River is the most interesting of them all. Its relatively modest flow is carried 1,360 miles from high in the Rocky Mountain National Park to the Gulf of California in Mexico. Part of the flow runs at over two miles above sea level and, along with its tributary, the 730 mile long Green River, it flows through gorgeous uninhabited canyonlands. One of its gorges begins at Moab, Utah, and passes 70 miles through Canyonlands National Park. Then it is backed up to create the over 200 square miles of Lake Powell.

The Colorado has been called a bankrupt river because it owes more along the way than it carries. Its water was divided up by a multi-state compact in 1922 which was based upon an exceptionally high water flow. Suburbanites as far away as California make claims on it. Nevertheless, confident engineers have boasted that they can control the Colorado's flow "like a garden hose."

Controlling and diverting all of the rivers originating in the Rocky Mountains has been a crucial subject since settlement by Euro-Americans began. The Mormons were the first to irrigate when they tapped creeks in Salt Lake City. They were followed thereafter by miners who used great quantities of water to in the various processes of separating out the metals they sought.

Since water flows across state boundaries, states came to make delicate compacts over water use the way that nations make treaties. States, corporations and individuals have constantly resorted to expensive litigation to gain and maintain water rights. In fact, a whole highly specialized subdivision of the practice of law in the region specifically deals with water laws. These laws were not the same as water laws in the eastern United States where the supply of water was not a problem. For instance, in the Rocky Mountains, the doctrine of prior appropriation declares that the first party to use river water has the first right to it. In most of the East, all property owners on a river have an equal right to use it.

Legal complexities are matched by engineering complexities. An elaborate system of dams provides irrigation water, flood control, domestic water supplies, power and recreation. Diversions involve reservoirs, canals and giant syphons as well as dams. For example, the complex Big Thompson project in Colorado draws water from the more sparsely populated Western Slope, which is the name for the western part of the state, and feeds it to the thirsty suburbs along the Front Range, where the plains meet the mountains and where most of the people in Colorado live. The Big Thompson project even includes a thirteen mile long tunnel under Rocky Mountain National Park.

Another major diversion moves water from the Wasatch Mountains in Utah westwards to supply the thirsty cities on the plain to the west of the mountains. Various other diversions supply irrigation water to farms on what would have otherwise been the very dry plains of these states.

To the delight of environmentalists, heavy industry has been curtailed in the region because of a lack of water. There are only two steel mills in the Rocky Mountain states, one in Pueblo, Colorado, which is now shut down, and another in Provo, Utah. the lack of cheap water has impeded projects such as the development of the oil shale industry and coal fired steam power plants. Nevertheless, the water shortage has not kept a major beer company from establishing a gigantic new brewery in, of all places, Fort Collins, Colorado.

As new developments make increasing demands on finite mountain water supplies, disputes over water are bound to escalate. How much water should go to corporate agriculture, to small farms, to ranches, to the urban areas, to the power companies, to industry, to the Indians and how much should be set aside so that recreational users can enjoy themselves without finding the levels too shallow for whatever they are doing? Right now industrialists and cities are buying up ranch and farm water rights and scheming to build new diversion projects, thereby alarming environmental and residential groups. As mentioned above, the fights are now over the quality of water as well as the quantity. This has become a Rocky Mountain gold mine for lawyers.

CHAPTER FOUR

THE SPECIAL CLIMATE AND WILDLIFE OF THE ROCKY MOUNTAIN STATES

Where the Skies Are Usually Not Cloudy All Day: The Climate

UNIQUE CLIMATIC FEATURES

Denver newspapers have been known to boast of the Front Range as the "climate capital of the world." This statement becomes hard to believe on cold late April days when spring flowers are inundated with a heavy, wet snow or when an October Denver Bronco football game has to be played on a white field in the midst of a blizzard. Another saying about the regional weather is that if it frustrates you, just wait a little bit and it will change. There is truth in this saying. Even professional meteorologists in the region have considerable difficulty assessing changes.

Since the Rocky Mountain climate has always been the subject of both praise and condemnation, it is necessary to have a close look at its outstanding characteristics and then at its seasonal patterns.

Everyone knows that mountainous regions are cold because of elevation. A common estimate is that the temperature drops three degrees Fahrenheit for each 1,000 feet of elevation. If snow can stay all year on the top of Mt. Kilimanjaro, which is close to the equator, it will surely stay on the slopes of the Rockies.

Most of the people in the region, however, do not live on the slopes of mountains or in high mountain valleys. Most live in the cities and towns on the flat plains close to the mountains. Nevertheless, these plains are properly called the High Plains. Flat Denver is, after all, accurately called the Mile High City because it is at an an elevation of 5,280 feet.

At high altitudes there are usually remarkable swings between high and low temperatures on any given day. It can be up to 50° cooler at night than during the day. On a 90° July day, for example, it may be necessary to don a sweater to ward off a 60° chill in the evening or a 50° chill before dawn. The reason for the temperature swing is that the sun becomes so hot in the dry, thin air. Moving from a sunny spot to a shady spot reveals a surprising difference in temperature, much more in the Rockies than elsewhere, leading some visitors to declare that it is too hot in the sun and too cool in the shade. Because the high plains semi-desert or the mountain valleys cool off swiftly and dramatically at night, wonderful sleeping conditions are guaranteed. It is one of the outstanding advantages of this climate. The Rockies are free from the hot, humid, muggy mid-summer nights that plague other parts of the country, nights which result in either discomfort or a higher electric bill from air conditioning.

Another considerable climatic advantage is the abundance of sunshine every season of the year. Up to three hundred days of it can be anticipated every year. If psychologists' studies indicating that brightness gives people a lift while heavy overcast can contribute to depression, sunshine is a definite plus for the region.

While there may be bleak stretches of a few overcast, rainy or snowy days, particularly around the time of the seasons' changes, the sun prevails for the rest of the time in every season. Even most days that have showers of rain or snow are dominated by sunshine. In fact, there are as many sunny days in these states as in southern California. The coldness from altitude and the existence of distinct seasons are what make the Rocky Mountain states' climate different from that of sunny but smoggy southern California.

ROCKY MOUNTAIN SEASONS

Like the temperate parts of the United States, the Rockies have four seasons, but their characteristics differ somewhat. The subject is more complex because the seasons can vary considerably within the states of the region because of elevation.

The Rocky Mountain seasons impress different people in different ways, depending upon where they lived previously. One man who moved to the High Plains from New Orleans complained that he had left an area with three months of winter to come to a place with nine months of winter. Relocated refugees from the white world of Minnesota or Upstate New York, on the other hand, have little but praise for the warm, sunny winters of the High Plains. Those who enjoy warmth will appreciate the region from mid-May to the end of October.

Winter: For the mountains, winter is king. It arrives early, in late October or early November, and it can hang on until April or early May, when skiers can be seen swooshing down the slopes in bathing suits in the hot sun. Sudden attacks of winter in the form of snow squalls can occur at the higher elevations in June, July and September. Mountains can impose their own local weather systems that induce gusty storms at the summits while the valleys below can remain calm.

Winter's dominance is appreciated by those who like snow sports and the contrasting warmth at gregarious lodges and resorts. Those who want to live in the mountains are, like Alaskans, reconciled to winter's dominance, which means frosty nights occuring into the summer and starting very early in the fall, which allows a growing season so short that only high pasture and gorgeous flowers can flourish up high. Some of the lowest temperature readings in the Continental United States come from places high up in the Rockies, with -40° or -50° not uncommon. Yet severe cold is only temporary, and the sun brings a quick rebound to even the coldest places.

Some of those who enjoy winter's dominance in the Rockies are very worried about the phenomenon of global warming. They fear that it will diminish the amount of annual snow, and that recent seasons short in snow might be an indication of what is coming. News of recent bad seasons in Europe also concern them. A remedy in bad seasons, the manufacture of artificial snow with equipment, is time consuming and very costly.

Winter is far less dominant on the High Plains below. While the peaks may wring January moisture out of the clouds in the form of a snowstorm, the plains below may be basking in bright sunlight at 60°. Furthermore, the winter chill is usually a dry cold, not the moist cold that seems to penetrate the very bones in places like England when it might be only 35° Fahrenheit. On sunny January and February days on the High Plains people can pop outdoors in shirtsleves.

Mild winter days can be damaging for many non-native trees that get their seasonal signals wrong and prepare for spring too early. "Winter kill" can result when the temperature plummets again, freezing sap that should not have been running. Young and delicate trees are often bound and wrapped to protect them from premature winter warming.

In general, winter is a time of quiet weather on the plains. Many storms that rage in the mountains never carry over to the plains, which remain bare of snow for a considerable part of the winter. This is not to say that the High Plains are free from severe winter storms that drop several feet of snow in blizzard conditions. These can occur all winter, and when they do they can paralyze airports and commuter traffic and cause a rash of minor accidents. Yet the mathematical probability of such a storm occurring on any given day from November until February are low. Even when one does strike, the effects usually will be ferocious for only a short term. In a day or a few days, much of the snow will melt away, except in a cold spell.

Local agencies are well equipped to handle snow emergencies and in extremely severe circumstances they have enlisted volunteers with four wheel drive vehicles to help out. Such preparedness is even more striking in the mountains, not only because more snow falls but also because economic prosperity depends upon keeping the roads to resorts open and safe.

Spring: The noted poet T.S. Eliot declared that April was the cruelest month of all. Any April in the Rocky Mountain region will prove his contention beyond a doubt. March and May are cruel months as well.

The cruelty of spring in this region stems from its sudden reversibility. Springlike manifestations can be snowed under by another burst of winter right up until the middle of May. In more temperate climes, each week of springtime is a week of progress, manifested in more greenness, more buds, more flowers, more insects and more singing birds. Warmth increases, gradually and steadily. Not so in the Rocky Mountain states! The author has had to wade through two feet of snow in his back yard in mid-May in two different years to see whether or not any of his tart cherry blossoms survived.

While this is an extreme example, not likely to happen in most years, it is recorded fact that the greatest amount of snow falls along the Front Range plains in each of the months of March and April, considerably more snow than in the quieter months of December, January and February. Much of the March and April snow is of the heavy, wet kind, destined to melt in a day or so, but some of the snowstorms create days so bleak and cold that they seem to be in mid-winter.

Spring does not cheat only with snowstorms. Days of harsh wind occur regularly, spoiling plans for outdoor activities. Cold winds from the north can roar across green suburbia as late as May, after the trees are full. Chilled parents can be seen watching their offspring play at sports. On these days it is wise to wear heavy winter coats and forget about the calendar and the green surroundings.

National weather maps are not comforting when it is springtime in the Rockies. On many days, darkly colored circles of cold center on the region while the rest of the country is likely to be basking in gentle spring temperatures. The Rocky Mountain states are often the coldest places in the continental United States in this season. It is indeed frustrating to note on some spring days that Denver or Cheyenne are colder than Buffalo or Anchorage.

In the midst of bad spring weather there are stretches of warm, bright weather, days when spring seems like spring in temperate climates. On these days temperatures can soar to the high 70s and 80s, lulling the inexperienced to believe that warm weather has come to stay. Then everything is reversed by another blast of winter.

Summer: Warm weather finally comes to stay generally in the last two weeks of May on the plains. Milder temperatures at night also arrive, although a frost may come as late as June 1. The advantage of the occasional cold night is that mosquitoes dos not appear until mid-June.

Late spring and early summer are the greenest times in the Rocky Mountain states because the heavier precipitation of March and April pay their dividends then in plant growth. May and June are months with a fair amount of precipitation of their own, often in the form of afternoon thunderstorms.

Midsummer is a wonderful season in the Rockies. The jet stream high above curves far to the north, allowing warm air from the south to go up into the Rockies. While the East, South and Midwest swelter, the Rocky Mountain states are guaranteed nighttime coolness regardless of how hot the day might have been. People who live close to the Atlantic or Pacific shores can ordinarily take 20° or more off of the thermometer on hot summer days by going to the ocean shore. The same effect can be had by those living on the Rocky Mountain plains when they head up into the mountains, where pleasant temperatures prevail during the days and sweaters are likely to be needed for July and August evenings.

In the summer, the forecasts have a glorious monotony: "Sunny and hot with possible scattered afternoon thundershowers." The heat is in the 80s and 90s with occasional days of 100°. A few places on the eastern plains of some of these states have 100° days more regularly in the summer. It is all wonderfully dry heat in this semi-arid region.

Skies in the summer are beautiful and fascinating. A thunderstorm might occupy only a part of it, while sunshine will play in the rest of it. These storms, which appear and disappear so quickly, can be very refreshing on a hot day and crucial for the survival of plants on non-irrigated land. Another feature of summer skies is that clouds will often discharge moisture but the dryness of the atmosphere will absorb all of it before it hits the ground. Great purple clouds can be seen racing across the plains with ragged edges that hang below them like tentacles. The tentacles are streams of rain that never make it to the ground.

Skies are usually blue and calm in the morning, but by the mid or late afternoon on a hot day, moisture-laden clouds will tend to boil up in populated plains regions along the foothills of mountain ranges. They usually clear by sunset, which can be absolutely spectacular. High clouds can display bright red, deep purple or brilliant orange. If the mountains are to the west of the observer, the sun will sink behind them but leave a golden afterglow that will slowly fade as the skies become progressively dark blue, purple and black. These may very well be the most beautiful skies in the whole world.

Western skies have been called "big." Montana in particular capitalizes on this phrase, but it can be used all over the Rockies. Skies do seem higher and much wider than they do elsewhere. Many authors have said that the great drama of the West has always been between the sky and the land.

July is the hottest month of all, and very dry. African students at regional schools who often suffer terribly in the winter do enjoy the summers. In fact, a Kenyan once wrote home from Colorado to declare his amazement that "it gets just as hot as Mombassa here!" August is a hot month also, but frequently around the third week of August there is a break in the temperature when cool breezes act as a harbinger of the coming of fall.

August's warm days and cool nights are particularly exciting in the mountains, where hundreds of species of plants flower splendidly in order to complete their life cycles in the brief time allotted to them by the short mountain growing season. Mountain meadows and hillsides take on a dazzling radiance of color. Viewed up close, the intricate, multi-colored beauty of any square yard of a rich Rocky Mountain meadow in August is spectacular.

September is a grand month in the Rockies, with sharp, clear, sunny days and cooler nights that mark the transition to fall. Yet cold snaps can whistle down from Canada suddenly in September, bringing actual winter conditions for a brief period of time. Frost can actually arrive as early as September 1.

Fall: The media delight in focusing on a freak early blizzard in the Rockies, and this can indeed happen in September or October. Someone passing through Denver on a bad day in these months can get the impression that the severity of winter arrives very early. The truth is that nearly all of the days of September, October and frequently even the early part of November are simply glorious. Ordinarily the air is crisp, the sun is warm and the skies have an intense, bright blue. It seems that one bad storm is likely to come through in October, but recovery follows quickly.

For many people, fall is the very best season of all in the Rockies because the heavy pressure from summer and winter tourism fades. The State and National Parks are not crowded.

The autumnal change of color in the Rockies is widely appreciated. Aspen trees turn a bright, shimmering yellow in the high country, set off grandly by the perpetual dark green of the pines. It starts as early as early September closest to the timberline and usually reaches its peak in the mountains in late September. The local media are keen to report and advise about the best times and places for viewing.

One group of visitors to the Rockies in the late summer or early fall are not as impressed as the rest. New Englanders miss the bursts of red and orange that join with the yellow and dark green in their region. Not even the Rocky Mountains can claim a scenic superiority to New England or Upstate New York on a hazy, precious, warm Indian summer day in October.

Colors on the Western plains are pleasant but much less intense than in the mountains. Heavy, severe frosts usually do not occur until much later on the plains than they do in New England or up in the Rocky Mountains. By mid-November the leaves are down, the grass becomes tawny and the chances of having a heavy snowstorm increase. December can be either surprisingly mild or bitterly cold or both. There is always a chance for a white Christmas or a warm Christmas, but there is also always a chance for a white Thanksgiving or a warm Thanksgiving and a white Easter or a warm Easter as well.

Where the Deer and the Antelope and Many Other Large Mammals Play: The Large Animals of the Rocky Mountain Region

PARADOXES ABOUT WESTERN WILDLIFE

The topic of wildlife in the Rocky Mountain states is beset with paradoxes. Wildlife is treasured for its own sake and for tourism at the same time that it is annihilated if it threatens profits from ranching and farming. Moreover, sportsmen want to preserve it so that they can kill it.

The Rocky Mountain states have some of the last great herds of large hoofed and horned animals, but these are but the remnants of what once was, pushed into a few locations, usually National Parks, where they are protected at least until they stray over the borders where ranchers or hunters may await them eagerly, guns in hand.

Yellowstone is a case in point. The only large species that remains in great numbers are the elk, numbering over 20,000. The rest of the large animals number in the hundreds except for the bison, which are a few thousand strong.

Before Euro-Americans settled in the region, it resembled the few remaining open ranges of wild animals on the plains of East Africa. It is hard to imagine the present day Western plains of farms, cattle and barbed wire fences covered with bison, elk, and antelope.

The West was romantic and exciting in the 19th century in part because it had these great mammals. The ferocious grizzly bear and the massive bison, called the buffalo, came to symbolize the region. Ironically, they became revered symbols at the very time they were almost destroyed by rifles.

MANAGED WILDLIFE

Today wildlife is managed to a much greater extent than casual visitors might imagine. Animals are studied, tagged, followed electronically, moved from place to place to avoid people, introduced or reintroduced, and, as best as possible, protected. In some places, hunters provide a useful culling of overpopulated animals.

Before management was applied, the nation ran the risk of seeing its great mammals disappear. At wildlife's ebb, around 1900, it is estimated that only 2,000 elk, 7,000 deer and 1,000 pronghorn antelope remained in the State of Colorado. Now there are over 200,000 elk, 700,000 deer and 50,000 to 60,000 pronghorn antelope.

A very specific kind of management, called "genetic management" is applied to various populations of wildlife, including grizzly bears in Yellowstone Park. Since Yellowstone's grizzlies are isolated from other places where the species ranges, the Wildlife Service feels it is necessary to import a new bear every so often to provide for genetic diversity.

Proposing to reintroduce species to areas where they have become extinct can elicit firestorms of controversy. Cases in point involve reintroducing wolves to Yellowstone and Rocky Mountain National Parks. Wolves, the "missing link" of the ecosystems of these parks, would help reduce the numbers of overpopulated elk, particularly by culling the old, sick, and weak specimens. Livestock ranchers have been livid about these proposals, believing that the wolves will leave the park and attack their sheep and cattle as they used to do before they were driven to extinction in those places.

Ordinarily, human habitation has had a negative impact on wildlife by drastically reducing their numbers. Sometimes just the opposite situation results, with the numbers of certain kinds of wildlife going up because of human habitation. The bald eagle, the national symbol, is a case in point. More eagles live in northern Colorado than ever before. Their numbers have increased because their prey, waterfowl and fish, are now in greater abundance because humans have impounded water in many reservoirs. Public education favorable to eagles and strict laws protecting them from shooting and poisoning from agricultural pesticides have all contributed to this happy result.

Canada geese have also taken advantage of the large number of reservoirs in the region, but the results have not been as happy. Take the experience of Fort Collins, Colorado, for example. Today Canada geese are on the city's symbol, flying high against a mountainous background. Thousands of geese live in town all year and thousands more fly in and stay a while during migrations. Originally no Canada geese lived in the city, but some flew over it on their north-south migrations. To gain a permanent population, wildlife officials brought some trapped young Canada geese from the north and transplanted them in the city, and even built floating nesting structures to give them increased opportunities for reproductive success.

The success turned out to be beyond the imagination of the wildlife managers. Flying geese dropped out of their migrations to join a burgeoning Fort Collins population until places in the city were overrun with squawking geese whose penchant to excrete copiously on pavement was nothing short of remarkable. Complaints from citizens led the wildlife officials to introduce a "goose management plan." Now the birds are being trapped and removed, the safe nesting sites have been removed and hunters have been given the opportunity to bag some of them.

WHERE TO SEE ROCKY MOUNTAIN WILDLIFE AND WHERE TO AVOID IT

African students from urban areas delight in telling Americans that the only place where they have seen lions or elephants has been in zoos. For some Rocky Mountain animals, such as the mountain lion, the zoo is the best bet for seeing them. But many other large animals and many birds will be easy to observe.

National Parks and Monuments, free from hunters, have the largest concentrations of animals. Look for an assortment of cars with out of state license plates lined up on the sides of the road and on the shoulders in unlikely places. This usually means that some large wild animals are being observed and photographed with an almost Japanese intensity.

There are also specialized animal preserves in certain parts of the Rocky Mountain West. Montana has a National Bison Range within the Flathead Indian reservation. There is also a million acre C.M. Russell National Wildlife Refuge where large numbers of elk graze on their native prairie in east central Montana. Small herds of bison are located in various places, fenced in like cattle. The author lives within a half hour's drive of a herd of bison which have been brought in to decorate the surroundings of an otherwise drab power plant.

It is wise to get into the habit of regularly scanning the skies in wild areas. It is quite common to see predatory birds soaring dramatically. It is also wise to always have binoculars handy. Rangers and local people give the best information about where to see wildlife.

One place not to see it is as a sudden apparition immediately in front of one's vehicle. Roadkills are frequent in the region. One of the most dangerous places to run the risk of crashing into an animal is Wyoming, where people drive fast and the fastest of local mammals, the pronghorn antelopes, race across highways.

Because the region is generally arid, it takes more space to support animals than it does in temperate regions. This holds true for either wild animals or domestic livestock. Therefore campsite marauders may not be as prevalent as they are in parks in the Appalachians.

Bears will forage near mountain campers in the East or West. Bears are said to have minds as complex as those of dogs, but their behavior is unpredictable and potentially dangerous. Fools who seek to hand feed them or pose with them can suddenly become victims of an attack. Above all, bears do not like to be startled, so when in the vicinity of bears, make a great deal of noise so they can be forewarned that humans are about. Otherwise they may strike out in a furious, defensive rage.

The best way to discourage the attentions of bears or other unwanted visitors to campsites is to keep food securely away from them. This means keeping it locked in a hard topped car, preferably in the trunk. Backcountry campers need to suspend their food supplies on poles or cables. Never leave food on tables or stored in a tent because it will act like a magnet for foragers.

People are constantly admonished that wild animals must be allowed to be wild. That means not trying to feed them, not touching them or not molesting them in any other way. The danger to the animals is that they may become so dependent upon humans that when the tourist season is over they starve. The danger to humans is in the form of scratches and bites. Even a seemingly peaceful deer can be dangerous. In a National Park in Utah a youngster was seriously injured when a deer butted him and punctured his rib cage.

KILL THE VARMINTS

A varmint is defined in the dictionary as an obnoxious or pestiferous animal, and varmint can be an alternative word for vermin. From the time that Euro-Americans entered the Rocky Mountain region, varmints have been warred upon and blasted away joyfully. In practice, a varmint was redefined as any creature that stood in the way of profit. Since livestock was introduced, varmints came to include mountain lions and bobcats. Coyotes became varmints also, despite the fact that most of the coyote's diet consists of rodents. Grizzly bears were varmints until they disappeared from most places. To some, buffalo and elk became varmints too, because they ate up the grass that could be eaten up by cattle and sheep. Less surprisingly, so were prairie dogs because they disrupted grazing grass and dug holes that might be hazardous for cattle or sheep. Snakes qualified easily, and for trigger happy people that meant any kind of snake, even the most beneficial kinds that fed on rodents and were non-poisonous. Even eagles became varmints because they might swoop down on an occasional unprotected lamb.

Faced with a multitude of threatening varmints, ranchers and gun enthusiasts have developed ingenious ways to kill them. State legislatures under the influence of politically powerful ranching elements have cooperated by paying bounties for dead mountain lions and coyotes. Vacationers in mountain states have been invited to hunt some varmints all through the year, even at night. Ranchers have lured eagles with poisoned dead animals as bait, and some have gone so far as to shoot them out of the skies from helicopters.

Eagles are a treasured and protected species and killing them is absolutely illegal, but it goes on surreptitiously. Since destroying prairie dogs and coyotes is legal, it goes on blatantly. Recently stockmen announced a "coyote challenge" to see who could kill the most of them in a given period. Colorado has hosted the Top Dog World Championship Prairie Dog Shoot, when over a hundred hunters shot over a thousand of them for prize money. When twenty or so animal rights activists protested loudly, the police issued citations to them for trespassing.

THE GREAT ANIMALS
OF THE ROCKY MOUNTAINS

What follows is a consideration of some of the great animals that are unique in the Rocky Mountains. Smaller animals or animals that appear in large numbers in other parts of the United States have been omitted from consideration below.

Grizzly bears: For a long time, grizzly bears were just as symbolic for the wildness of the Rockies as lions were for the wildness of Africa. Grizzlies were depicted as powerful, strange and dangerous. Both symbols have vanished from most of their old terrain.

Grizzly bears today can be found in only a few locations in the Rocky Mountain states. Some are in Yellowstone Park, and some are in remote parts of Idaho and Montana. There is debate over whether any still inhabit Colorado. The occasional sightings of them may be misapplied to black bears who are large and in an off color phase. Debate aside, some Coloradans want them reintroduced. A recent estimate puts their number in the Continental United States at 1,000. They are in more ample numbers in western Canada and Alaska.

Once there were so many grizzlies that mountain men said they could spot over fifty in a single day. Heroic and desperate combats with grizzlies made up part of the legendary activities of these frontiersmen, some of whom tended to attribute any deep scar on their bodies to these bears, as well as record any hostile encounter with any bear as a desperate fight with a grizzly.

Grizzlies threatened mountain men because their single shot guns might only wound and enrage a grizzly who would be likely to charge and grapple before the gun could be reloaded. When the repeating rifle was developed hunters gained a great advantage over these utterly fearless bears who once suffered from the Latin name, *Ursus Horribilis*, the "horrible bear." They are now *Ursus Arctos.*

"Hungry bear" might be a better name for them because grizzlies are omnivorous, consuming vegetation, small animals, anything sick or young that they can catch, fish and even carrion. They eat ravenously, and most of their waking hours consists of a search for food. A fully grown male can weigh from 500 to 800 pounds and be six or seven feet long, standing 3 to 3½ feet at the shoulder. A female weighs about 400 pounds. It takes eight to ten years to grow to this size, which is about half of the grizzly's lifetime. They have one to three cubs, rarely four, born during hibernation.

It is not always easy to distinguish grizzlies from black bears. Grizzlies are dark brown in color, but some of the color phases of the black bear match the grizzly's hue. To identify grizzlies, look for a distinctive hump on their backs and a silver tinge to their fur, which gives them their popular name. They have rather concave faces compared to the more rounded faces of the black bears.

Sometimes grizzlies have lived up to their old name of horrible bear. There are a very few isolated incidents on record when grizzlies have attacked backpackers in sleeping bags. The best advice about dealing with grizzlies and other bears is to keep as much distance between them and yourself as possible and be noisy when in their vicinity.

Park rangers take no chances at some campgrounds that have what they call "high bear frequency." They close such areas to tents, tent trailers, pop up vans and sleeping on the ground.

Black Bears: Black bears are much more numerous, smaller and more diffused across the United States. While not nearly as dangerous as grizzlies, black bear mothers with cubs can be ferocious defending them. When a bear becomes a problem to campers, rangers call them "trouble bears" and try to move them to remote places. In many cases, if they come back three times they are "controlled," which is a euphemism for destroying them.

Black bears, too, are omnivorous, eating small animals, fish, eggs, berries, fruit, some insects and honey. They will rumble over areas of many square miles to satisfy their appetites. A full grown male black bear will weigh 300 pounds, and a few will carry as much as 500 pounds. Black bears will grow from 4½ feet to 6½ feet long.

Bears sleep through most of the winter, but hibernation is broken by a few forays every so often. Bears give birth during this winter sleep. From one to three cubs will emerge in the springtime and the mother will devote a whole year to raising them. She will only mate every second year, during the late spring and summer, and this is the time that male bears temporarily abandon their solitary lives.

The Bison: No other animal comes close to the American bison as a symbol not only of the West but also of the closing of the frontier. The bison also demonstrates how the profit motive can drive an animal close to extinction.

Today the bison is preserved on some ranges here and there, tiny pieces of the domain that once ranged from Pennsylvania and Tennessee to Oregon and from Canada to Mexico. Some people raise them for food, others keep them about as a decoration. Yellowstone National Park has the only continuously wild herd of buffalo, which is augmented by domestically raised animals.

Recently a furor has erupted about the shooting of buffalo when they stray from the park on account of the fact that they carry brucellosis, a germ that attacks domestic cattle. Stockgrowers want to keep their cattle free from this disease and insist that buffalo be slaughtered when they emerge from Yellowstone's confines. When protesters ask that the animals be treated for the germ, the response from authorities is that Yellowstone Park is not a zoo, and the wild animals need to be untended. So outside of the park, buffaloes have become varmints again.

Buffalo is their popular name. They have weak eyes but have compensation from a sharp sense of hearing and a keen nose. A full grown male may weigh a ton and be ten or eleven feet long. At the shoulders such a specimen would be 5½ or 6 feet tall. They live up to 40 years.

When Spanish explorers described them as large, humped cattle with lions' manes, there may have been up to sixty million of them in existence, and some estimates go much higher than that. The Western plains were certainly thick with them, scenes fortunately recorded by early 19th century artists. For many tribes of Native Americans, they were the most important natural resource, providing food, clothes, and shelter in the form of tepees, and fuel, in the form of dried droppings called buffalo chips by settlers. Although some of the methods Native Americans employed to hunt them were wasteful, they never killed bison for the joy of killing.

Native Americans began to exchange larger and larger numbers of buffalo robes with traders from the 1840's on. Buffalo meat fed those who crossed the Continent on the trails and those who built the railroads. Meanwhile, pickled buffalo tongues became a delicacy on the East Coast, tough strips of buffalo hide were used as industrial belts and tanned buffalo leather was used as buffing cloths. Even buffalo bones had their uses. Fresh bones were utilized in sugar refining and old bones were ground into fertilizer. At the time of the worst slaughter of buffaloes, bone piles rested on the prairie as large as twelve feet high and half a mile long.

The buffalo had to go to drive the Native Americans away and give the grasslands to cattle. Professional hunters, ranchers, sportsmen and cowboys dispatched them in a great rush, littering the plains with carcasses. Some people even took shots from passing trains. Just one British hunting party in the Rockies in the late 19th century slaughtered 3,000 of them. Buffalo Bill Cody killed thousands to feed railroad builders.

Shooting buffalo is not necessarily an exciting experience. When one of a group of buffalo goes down wounded and kicking, the other buffaloes circle around the victim, probably trying to support it. That makes it easy to shoot down the others. As professional hunters advised, "Always shoot to just wound your first buffalo."

The slaughter almost made them extinct. By 1890 fewer than 1000 were left; by 1900 the number was down to a few hundred at most. Buffalo Bill Cody exhibited a few survivors in his Wild West show, where buffalo hunts were reenacted and cowboys tried to ride them.

When they were down to their lowest numbers, the buffalo began to be revered. The buffalo nickel was minted in 1913, at a time when prized stuffed buffalo heads were hung in railroad stations, restaurants and saloons. The bison appeared on a state flag and on the seal of the United States Department of the Interior. Finally, laws were passed making the shooting of buffalo a crime.

The animal made a comeback. There may be over 50,000 of them now, mostly in private herds. Hundreds can be seen in the National Bison Range in western Montana, near Missoula, which was established by the American Bison Society.

Buffaloes are unique in that they are the only wild animal that is put out to pasture like a domestic animal. Buffalo meat is a lucrative product today because it contains little fat and has a taste similar to beef. Some restaurants and vacation tours have buffalo steaks and buffalo burgers on their menus, items which can surely be advertised as a genuine taste of the Old West.

Mountain Lions: Mountain lions dwell throughout the Rockies, but they are so secretive and elusive that ordinarily they are hardly ever seen in the wild. It is possible to live a lifetime in these states and never observe one of these large, graceful cats outside of a zoo.

One jogger running just outside of Idaho Springs, Colorado, in January of 1991 saw one in the wild but briefly before it killed him. This was an extremely rare event. He was the first adult killed in 100 years, although there are one or two attacks on children every year. All told, only seven human deaths from mountain lions have been recorded in history in the past 100 years.

Humans walking upright do not conform to what' mountain lions think of prey. Children crawling about or on tricycles, as one recent victim was doing, come closer to their concept of what the shape of prey should look like. Ordinarily mountain lions avoid dogs, but recently a French poodle named Fifi from the outskirts of Boulder, Colorado, was last seen securely held in the mouth of a fast moving mountain lion. Apparently the mountain lion did not think that this French poodle looked very much like a dog.

Because of these incidents, something of an hysteria about mountain lions has developed in the populated areas of the foothills of Colorado in the past few months. Some claim that mountain lions have gone crazy, showing up in places where they should not be found, appearing to humans when they are supposed to be very shy of the human presence.

The real problem is that humans have put more and more houses into the foothills, in the ordinary habitat of mountain lions. Since mountain lions and humans are competing for the same territory, they have more accidental contact, and as they do, the lions loose their fear of humans. Humans who try to feed the mountain lions' natural prey, raccoons and deer, when they show up at their foothills homes only make the situation worse, because the lions follow the game. Some people even put salt licks in their back yards so that they can observe wildlife better.

As protected game continues to grow in numbers, mountain lions continue to increase their population also. In Colorado many of them live along the Front Range foothills in the winter and follow deer back into the mountains in the summer. Some make occasional forays into livestock pens in addition to new housing subdivisions. Sometimes they will kill colts, calves or sheep, a penchant which made them varmints to ranchers, who traditionally shot them on sight. Some even live at the infamous Rocky Flats nuclear weapons plant near Denver, which is supposed to be a wildlife refuge as well. It would be unfortunate if Colorado became the home of the world's only great cats suffering from nuclear radiation.

In the unlikely circumstance—that old airlines' preface—of confronting a mountain lion in the Rockies, do not run away. Try to raise your arms and shout in a loud voice—prayers, if so inclined. If this does not ward off an attack, the experts advise doubling up and putting hands over the back of the neck, since that is where they bite to break animals' necks. Since they have claws up to 1½ inches long to hold animals and two inch fangs to break their necks, one is not really very secure in this position.

Yet the point is that attacks do not come readily. Children in foothills locations, which are far into the cat's habitat, are in the most danger, but even for them the statistics for avoiding contact with mountain lions are remarkably favorable. Mountain lions simply do not like being near people, and the only reason why there are contacts is that the cats will not give up their Front Range habitat just because people have moved into it. Their aversion to humans means that they will avoid campsites and frequently used trails. In the wilder parts of the Rocky Mountain states, they are almost never seen. They like to live in the most rugged and inaccessible places ordinarily. There they continue to play an important predator's role in maintaining the balance of nature. Each of these animals will roam over a vast area in which they come to kill the slowest and weakest specimens of their game. In these remote areas deer would overpopulate and strip resources if it were not for the mountain lions.

Controlled hunting of these animals is still allowed. A popular way to hunt them is for mounted hunters to give chase with packs of dogs, often at night. The dogs are at risk of being killed or clawed before they can get the mountain lion up a tree. Once aloft, it can be shot easily.

Mountain lions are also called pumas or cougars or panthers. Their original range was from northern Canada down to the southernmost part of South America, but today they are found only in the more remote parts of their former range, with the conditions along the Colorado Front Range excepted.

Adults weigh from 100 to over 200 pounds. They can grow from six to 9½ feet long, which includes a tail up to 36 inches long. Mountain lions reproduce at a modest rate. Females mate only every two or three years, bearing from one to four kits every third or fourth year. Males are usually driven away from the kits to forestall their tendency to eat them. A female will care for young for as long as two years, teaching them the skills of survival.

Elk: Visitors to National Parks in the region are likely to see many large, stately elk because they now exist rather abundantly in those sanctuaries. They weigh from 400 to 1,000 pounds, males usually around 800 pounds and females around 500. They are from seven to nine feet long and four and a half to five feet tall. Both males and females have maned necks but only males have huge braces of antlers which extend backwards. In the mating season in the fall, males will bugle at one another and then fight ferociously, using their antlers. The reproductive stakes in these contests are high because the victors acquire harems of five to fifteen cow elk.

Their proper name, first given by Native Americans and rarely used today, is Wapiti. Confusingly, in other parts of the world the word "elk" means what Americans call "moose." "American elk" might be a less confusing designation.

American elk once roamed widely from the Atlantic to the Pacific and from Canada to the south and southwest. Today fair sized remnants of their once great numbers can be found in the Rocky Mountain region from Colorado to Canada. The largest herds of them are in the northwest corner of Wyoming and in the White River National Forest in west central Colorado.

The fate of elk in Colorado's Rocky Mountain National Park is illustrative of the pressures on wildlife over the last century. Elk vanished from the area as sportsmen slaughtered them, especially one English earl with an obsessive lust for hunting. Many were slain, like rhinos in Africa today, just for their horns. When the National Park was founded in 1915, elk had to be reintroduced. Freed from their natural predators, the wolves, who had been blasted into extinction in the area, elk multiplied rapidly. They followed the old migratory pattern of going up to the mountain meadows in the summer and down to the valleys in the winter where they eat the grasses beneath the snow on the margins of streams, places that become winter oases because the running water never freezes.

Hunting was reintroduced in the 1940's to keep their numbers in check and as the last decade of this century began, the encroachment of roads, houses and fenced lots surrounding the park cramped their movements considerably and exposed them to many more dangers, cars and vicious dogs in particular.

Recently an odd alliance of wildlife enthusiasts, boy scouts, hunters and homeowners began to work together around the town of Estes Park to replace barbed wire fences with smooth wire fences so that elk which crashed into these barriers would not be torn up at the impact.

"Slow elk," by the way, is a term referring to cows that are mistakenly shot by hunters.

Pronghorns: The pronghorn is not a true antelope, but that is what most people call them. They are the only split toed animals to survive from distant geological ages. They almost did not survive, however, when the rifle came to the plains. Their numbers went from 120 million or more to a few thousand by the turn of the century. Now their numbers have gone up to several hundred thousand and they have been reintroduced to many places, such as Colorado, where they became extinct previously.

Pronghorns have slender horns and a white rump patch used to signal other animals of danger. Up close they are surprisingly small. The larger males will weigh 130 pounds and be only three feet tall at the shoulder. They have extremely sharp senses, especially eyesight, and can go 30 to 40 m.p.h. for long distances and up to 50 m.p.h. in short, intense bursts.

Pronghorns gather in herds of 50 to 100, in which bucks may have up to 15 does in a harem. Females give birth yearly, often bearing twins. Fencing of the range and continued hunting have continued to be problems for this species.

Southern Wyoming is the best place to see these wonderfully swift animals. They do play, as the song "Home on the Range" proclaims, and they are curious animals as well. In Wyoming they can easily be seen bounding and leaping across undulating tawny plains in much the same way that antelope appear on African plains. Sometimes it takes a sharp eye to spot them at a distance.

Moose: Moose are huge, ungainly and sometimes oddly comical animals. They like to feed on aquatic plants, and can consume 40 to 50 pounds of this fare daily. A bull moose can weigh from 900 to 1,400 pounds and have antlers as much as six feet across.

Sometimes they join a herd of elk or even domestic cattle. They are known to appear at odd moments at campsites or along trails in the woods. In the fall the males fight so ferociously to see who will mate with the cows that the losers are often so badly wounded that they die.

Idaho, Montana, Wyoming and Alaska have populations of them. Every now and then a stray moose will wander into Colorado and some have been reintroduced.

Bighorn Sheep: Bighorn sheep are closely associated with the Rocky Mountains, where these agile, bounding, big horned creatures gambol over the snowy peaks. Originally they, too, had a much wider range, and they still exist in distant deserts. Because of their magnificent horns, they became one of the greatest prizes for big game hunters and their numbers suffered accordingly. The estimated population of two million two centuries ago has been reduced to perhaps 20,000 in the Rocky Mountain states.

Mature males stand around three feet high at the shoulder and weigh around 400 pounds. Females are five inches shorter and weigh around 150 pounds. What makes the large, hollow, curly horns so magnificent is that they grow all through the animal's life, adding sections each year.

Mating takes place in the late fall and tends to be somewhat tumultuous. When a female comes into heat, several males will seek to mate with her. Butting contests occur, and the head on crashing of horns can be heard for a great distance. Lambs are born from May through July.

Bighorn sheep use their keen vision and agility to stay away from people and competing grazing animals. This means that they confine themselves to the higher reaches of the Rocky Mountains. Helping them survive is a serious task of wildlife management personnel. Some poachers kill them, as well as mountain lions, and coyotes attack their lambs when they can.

The worst danger comes from disease, often carried by domestic sheep. When foraging opportunities are poor, malnutrition makes bighorn sheep more susceptible to disease. Because of their beauty and playfulness, the survival of these living symbols of the wild Rocky Mountains will continue to be given top priority by conservationists.

Rocky Mountain Goats: Rocky Mountain goats are found in Montana and Idaho. They are not actually goats, but related to the antelope family. Unlike the bounding bighorn sheep, Rocky Mountain goats are much more clumsy and plodding on high slopes. Nevertheless, they manage to get to mountaintops much more readily than bighorn sheep. They have white, shaggy coats and short black horns.

Bears, mountain lions and lynxes prey upon them. They have a 10 to 12 year life span if they avoid these predators and disease.

Wild Horses: Wild horses are called mustangs by Americans, from the Spanish word for them, mesteños. Bands of them still survive in remote corners of the West, particularly in Nevada and Wyoming. Ranchers do not like them because they consume grasses useful for livestock. Dog food companies have made considerable use of wild horses, much to the outrage of their advocates. To ease the situation, the Bureau of Land Management has operated an "adopt a horse program" to transfer wild horses to private owners willing to break and use them or at least give them pasture.

Wild Burros: Some pack burros, slaves to the early mining industry, managed to get away. A number of their descendants are still found in remote areas, where they bray hideously. Hence they are called "Rocky Mountain Canaries" or "Colorado Mocking Birds" or "Arizona Nightingales."

Mule Deer: The mule deer is one species still abundant in the Rocky Mountain region. Visitors to any kind of wildlife habitat are likely to encounter them. They can be found from the foothills up to the high mountains' timberline, at least in the summer.

In some places they are unabashedly tame and in other areas startled deer will bound high out of the bush and gallop away with high prancing steps.

They are less than half the size of the American elk, with bucks weighing approximately 250 pounds and does from 100 to 150 pounds. They are tan colored to grayish, with the latter color predominating in the winter. Mule deer are a Western species, ranging from the Great Plains to the Pacific Coast and from Canada to Mexico. They are distinguished from their near relatives, the white-tailed deer, sometimes called the .Virginia white-tailed deer, by a narrow tail, a bright rump patch, prominent ears and antlers in two similar Y shaped parts. They feed mostly at night and tend to spend the day in heavy cover. Their sense of smell and hearing are acute and their sight is keen for objects at great distances. Yet they might miss a quiet observer up close and downwind from them.

Mountain lions, coyotes and bobcats prey on them, especially on the young and weak or those snow and ice bound. Bears will eat fawns if they come upon their lairs by luck. Car traffic and hunters take a heavy toll, but not to the extent that unlimited hunting did in the last half of the 19th century. In the early 20th century even these now abundant creatures were becoming scarce.

Gray Wolves: Although wolves are terrifying creatures in European folklore, there are no well documented accounts of wolves killing people. On the other hand, profuse documentation exists on people killing wolves, including professional "wolfers" who went to work to slaughter them under a law of 1915 calling for the termination of wolves on federal lands. They used guns, traps and poison. Yet it was probably the rapid disappearance of the American elk and bison that sharply curtailed their numbers initially. When wolves turned to sheep and calves instead of their usual prey, stockmen warred upon them relentlessly until whole regions were clear of them. Today they can be found in fair numbers only in Alaska and parts of Canada. Some remain in remote corners of Idaho, Montana and Wyoming.

Wolves were successfully reintroduced into Glacier National Park where they coexist naturally with grizzlies. Some wildlife proponents want to reintroduce them to other National Parks. The controversy over wolves being brought back to Yellowstone has already been mentioned.

Ironically, after great efforts have been made to make them extinct, they have now been listed as an endangered species and are the subject of various recovery plans.

Wolves are very interesting creatures, hunting in packs, mating for life and maintaining close family ties. They are close to the size of a large German shepherd. Their scarcity and remoteness makes it highly unlikely that anyone visiting the Rocky Mountains will come anywhere near them.

Coyotes: Native American legends proclaim that the coyote will be the last animal on earth. In the last century and a half they have survived persistent attempts to poison or shoot them out of existence. To Mexicans, a person who is "muy coyote" is regard as clever and crafty, traits that may account for this animal's persistence despite the wrath of sheep and cattle ranchers who regard coyotes as dire threats to calves and lambs.

Coyotes do kill stock from time to time, usually when their ordinary food supplies are short. Their diet is broad, including rabbits and all other kinds of rodents, ground nesting birds and even snakes and skunks. When they get a chance, coyotes will try to kill deer. In the winter carrion is an important part of their diet also.

Ordinarily coyotes will hunt in pairs on regular trails, many miles in length. Packs of them, sometimes more than a dozen together, will run together. Although they are usually quite skillful in avoiding humans, the author has observed them on several occasions bounding along on a hunt. They will pair off for mating, at least for a few years. Female coyotes will prepare dens for their pups and the males will forage for their families.

Their range is enormous and they have been able to maintain most of it despite the inroads of civilization. They can be found from Arctic Alaska to northern Costa Rica and from the Pacific Coast to the Great Lakes. Obviously, they are adaptable in a great variety of habitats.

Coyotes look and to a considerable extent act like their biological kin, dogs. They can be recognized by their black tipped tail which is directed downwards while they run. They grow about as large as a medium sized German shepherd. Like dogs, they can suffer from rabies, fleas and internal parasites.

Coyotes provide the Rocky Mountain region with wonderful calls of the wild, consisting of several yaps followed by a long, high howl. It is a sound reaffirming that there is still some wildness in the West. Even so, it is a bit eerie to hear these howls while walking down a mountain trail, perhaps first to the left, then to the right, then from behind, as if the coyotes are stalking the hiker. Do not be alarmed. Coyotes are animals too clever to bother with people.

CHAPTER FIVE

THE MYTHS AND REALITIES OF WESTERN HISTORY

Getting Historical Bearings

WHY A GRASP OF THIS REGION'S HISTORY IS HELPFUL

Nothing can enhance a visit to an area more than having a grasp of the region's history. Scenes and locations gain meaning when something is known of the people and situations associated with them.

There can be too much of a good thing. Sometimes quaint details from the history of the Rocky Mountain West are given an importance that they do not deserve by local boosters. The mind can be numbed by too many details that do not seem to have much significance.

Legends and myths can be another problem. Legends grow from tall tales and myths are often ways of explaining what people really want to believe. Behind legends and myths there are usually at least some historical realities. Separating one from the other is always a problem. Professional historians are always at work at finding the truth in myths and legends.

Points of view can alter an understanding of history also. Victors and losers, victims and perpetrators, active participants and passive participants, main actors and those with other roles will all tend to view events differently. To understand something which is as complex as the history of one of America's regions, taking several points of view rather than just one can be quite rewarding.

What follows is an overview of the history of the Rocky Mountain states, citing the main patterns in broad brush strokes. There is also emphasis on pioneer trails and the developments that came from mining. The current lively disputes and issues over Western History are also examined, taking note of different interpretations of such things as the frontier. It is followed by a section on the economic history of the region. The next chapter takes up three legendary types in detail, mountain men, Native Americans and cowboys. Furthermore, the chapters on specific states contain historical details pertaining to specific locations.

Both of these chapters strive to present the big picture of Western history, and establish a basic framework. This should help visitors handle the masses of details encountered along the way by placing them in some sort of perspective. It should therefore be easier for them to appreciate the more important facts and to dismiss the more trivial bits of information that inevitably will be encountered while traveling.

THE TEXTURES OF THE HISTORY OF THE OLD WEST

The New West is easy to find. It is everywhere the bulldozers, building contractors, strip miners, real estate developers and corporate executives have been at work, and that means nearly all of the inhabited locations in these states. Steel, glass, suburbia, and landfills are all over the New West.

The Old West is harder to find, although the tourist industry does all that it can to promote its myths. The real Old West was much more ordinary, and workaday, and much less violent and heroic than the romantic legends, tall tales and myths that have gathered about it.

Those willing to look carefully can find traces and remains of it here and there, amid the noise and ballyhoo of the mythical Old West that has been seized upon with such vigor by those who seek to commercialize it.

The real Old West did not have a thick history compared to the East Coast. All of it involving English speakers took place during the short span of one quite long lifetime, calculating from the Lewis and Clark expedition of 1804 to the presumed end of the frontier in 1890. For most places, settlement occurred only between 80 and 150 years ago, which, for most historians, is just yesterday.

By comparison, an English speaking population lived on the East Coast for nearly four hundred years, and for much of that time it was thicker in numbers than the English speaking population in the West ever was. Compared to the rich and complex textures of European history, the history of English speakers in the West is even thinner.

Archaeologically, the region is one of the oldest in the United States. Native American experience in the region is truly ancient, and Hispanic civilization has had its influence in the West since the 16th century. In most of the states considered in this book, both the Native American and Hispanic populations tended to be relatively thin and scattered. Moreover, the more important centers of Hispanic civilization were to the south of the Rocky Mountain region. So while it may be one of the oldest parts of America for human habitation, it was still one of the newest for English speaking Americans.

No one would expect the last part of the Continental United States to be settled to have a deep and complex history. To some sophisticated Europeans and some Americans from the East Coast, Western history can be laughable in its shallowness. For example, when a local building is touted as "the oldest in the region," and it turns out to be a sad affair of logs and plaster dating back only to 1900, or when the claim to fame of a leading local personality comes only from the fact that he owned a modest store, called it a trading post, charged the highest prices he could get and used this business as his base to gain local elected offices.

The crude, petty and mundane nature of so much of local history in the region should not obscure its great strengths, namely its immediacy, its democracy, and the fact that it occurred at the outermost Western edges of a civilization whose centers were always to the east, in Eastern America and in northwestern Europe.

The history of the Old West in Rocky Mountain states is immediate because it is in the living memory of older residents. They still incorporate the stories and tales of some of the very first settlers in some places as the stories were told to them in childhood. The grandparents and great-grandparents of many older residents were actually engaged in making the history of new settlements. So the humble first buildings of plaster and logs gain a significance because there was absolutely nothing constructed before them by English speaking civilization. By comparison, Europe would have layers upon layers of settlement going back literally thousands of years, and there would be no sense of immediacy for nearly everything.

While they may have been laconic by outside standards, most of these early settlers were literate, and some of them saved letters and wrote diaries. Moreover, once towns were established, it was not long before a local newspaper appeared, since the press was so dominant in 19th century communications. Therefore, those who explore the real history of the Old West have rich immediate sources, some of them from oral history, some from humble written records, and some from early newspapers.

These verbal and written sources are highly democratic, meaning that they were by rather ordinary people or about rather ordinary people who toiled away most of the time. Most of the physical remains left behind from the Old West are also democratic in this sense, crude buildings, furniture and all sorts of wooden and metal tools and devices designed to enable survival in difficult conditions. Most of these dwellings and artifacts are those of ordinary people, whose names are unimportant and unrecognized for the most part.

While modern revisionist historians like to point out the high incidence of failure in the Old West, most of these people arrived hoping to fulfill an early version of the American dream. They may have failed in the Midwest or East, or they may have faced limited or dreary prospects back there. They came to the Rocky Mountains to make better lives for themselves in a newer region. While some succeeded and some failed, during their struggles for a happier future they engaged in a remarkably active form of participatory democracy. Their local churches, local governments, and local organizations of all sorts came to be supported by highly involved citizens, who were known and who counted as individuals.

These considerations, taken together, should lead observers of the more simple and crude artifacts and dwellings of the Old West to view them with respect rather than derision.

An Overview of the History of the Rocky Mountain West

THE ROMANTIC PATINA AND THE REALITY OF CONQUEST

Since most of the history of the conquest of the West by Americans took place in the 19th century, it is highly colored by romanticism, which was the dominant cultural expression of the Victorian era. Romantics treasured the remote and exotic, the heroic and the overwhelming grandeur and power of nature. Aspects of the Old West were made to order for the romantics. Artists could paint the mountains with exaggerations of size and color. At the hands of artists and writers, Native Americans became exotic noble savages. Cowboys became heroic figures dressed in exotic attire. Pioneers became larger than life, stalwart, heroic, handsome and noble in the very simplicity of their lives. The landscape, its plants and its animals were all depicted as strange and unique, appealing to the great desire of the public for scenes which were distant, exotic and colorful. Mountain passes had to be virtually insurmountable, rivers had to rush along in torrents, and grizzly bears had to appear frequently and ferociously to satisfy a romantic audience. All of these scenes and figures were swept into what became a colorful cavalcade of the history of the Old West.

Science and capitalism were the true driving realities of the 19th century, providing a sharp counterpoint to its romanticism. Science and capitalism opened up the world to the dominance of Europeans and Euro-Americans and enabled them to dominate it until they wasted their power and lost much of their prestige and credibility in the horrible wars of the 20th century. Only a few places in the world remained free of their control in the 19th century, as vast European empires circled the globe. Like Russia, America's expansion in the 19th century was largely overland. Its imperial conquests were not overseas in Africa and Asia but to the West, in the name of Manifest Destiny, or the belief that it was the will of God that these vast lands be developed by these energetic white people. Europeans and Americans in the 19th century were quite assured that their civilization as well as their ethnicity were superior to that of all "lesser breeds," and that included what were then universally called American Indians. See the next chapter under "Some Broad Perspectives on the Conquest of the Indians" for an elaboration of this theme.

In the West as in so many other places in the 19th century, conquest came when capital combined with science and technology to produce the tools of empire: the telegraph, the railroad, the steamship, and accurate, mass-produced, rapid-firing weapons. So armed and equipped, relatively small numbers of whites could first penetrate and then control and then exploit vast territories. In the case of the American West, there was a further step not accorded to European empires established over salt water: permanent assimilation.

EXPLORATION AND ACQUISITION

Americans first explored the West before the steam engine was available to them. The first explorers in Utah and Colorado were Spanish and the first in Montana and Wyoming were

French. The 18th century was the time when these Europeans first saw large portions of the area.

Captain Meriweather Lewis and Lieutenant William Clark were the first Americans to embark on a heroic expedition from the Missouri, across the Rockies, and over to the Pacific. They took forty or so explorers with them from 1803 to 1805 on what became a 6,000 mile trip. Their best guide was a young Shoshone Indian girl named Sacajawea. Only one person perished along the way, from an illness. Congress supported this and later expeditions. In the case of Lewis and Clark, Congress appropriated what was then a considerable sum: $2,500. Expeditions went out as late as the 1870's, when Major John Wesley Powell led a group who were the first to see some very remote portions of the West, particularly the spectacular canyons of Utah.

Zebulon Pike explored the central Rocky Mountains a few years later. He had a famous peak that he could not scale named after him. He also circulated a myth that gained wide acceptance back East. He described the West as the "great American desert" because of the treeless plains and rocky expanses he observed. Other explorers echoed his views, declaring that it was a region hopelessly dry and barren. In the minds of many, America had come to possess a wasteland.

They came to possess it by treaty and by war and by the threat of war. The Rocky Mountain states were originally claimed by Spain, France and Britain, the same powers who had claimed other parts of North America, claims that completely ignored the territorial possessions of hundreds of Native American tribes. These European claims were based upon the wanderings of various explorers and missionaries. The Louisiana Purchase of 1803 bought out the French and added 828,000 square miles to the young United States at the paltry price of $15,000,000. Its expanse covered the western watershed of the

Mississippi and ran along the Continental Divide. Nevertheless, Britain claimed Montana, Wyoming, Idaho and Western Montana. The flow of American trappers and then American settlers into this contested area and the resolution of the American government in the 1840's to fight Britain over them in a new Anglo-American war caused that nation to back down in the famous Oregon controversy. Its resolution involved drawing that long straight line across North America to separate the United States and Canada. Western Colorado and Utah along with the Southwest were gained from Mexico, Spain's heir, in a short and easy war that broke out in 1846.

TRAPPERS AND TRAILS

From the 1820's to the 1840's, the fur trade was active in the Rocky Mountains. It was the first of many examples of the West's natural resources being exploited by distant companies empowered by capitalism. The legendary mountain men who ranged far and wide to almost eliminate the beaver were sponsored by companies headquartered as far away as St. Louis and New York. When the fur trade went flat, ex-trappers became tradesmen and guides for the flow of settlers heading through the region. See the section on the mountain men in the next chapter for much more about these colorful figures.

Settlements of Euro-Americans simply did not spread from the East Coast until they reached the shores of the Pacific. For the most part, except for a few forts here and there and a group of Mormons who settled at Salt Lake City, the Rocky Mountain region was skipped over until 1859, when gold was struck in the Rockies. This was just two years before the outbreak of the American Civil War in 1861.

During this time, the Rockies were seen as an obstacle blocking the path to the fabled rich lands of Oregon and California. The region had to be traversed through hardship and perseverance on the Oregon Trail and its offshoots. Some of the most celebrated sites in the region are along the trails of those who were trying to get through the region as quickly as possible from 1840 to 1860.

Great historic trails crisscross the Rocky Mountain states. During the decades before the Civil War and the transcontinental railroads, hundreds of thousands of people migrated West, usually in animal-drawn wagon trains, but also on foot, often with carts that were pushed by hand.

Small groups went across the Rockies to the West Coast area in the 1830's, but between 1840 and 1870, 300,000 made the trip. In each of the peak years, 1850 and 1851, over 50,000 settlers moved through.

What prompted this vast migration at a time when the total population of the United States ranged between seventeen and thirty-nine million? There were several reasons: There was a push from panics and depressions on the East Coast and Midwest and a pull from tales of gorgeous free farmland in Oregon and California. The United States, although huge in comparison to European countries, was still overwhelmingly agrarian, so there were always restless people hungry for good land that was cheap and easy to farm.

"Oregon fever" and "California fever" swept the settled parts of America, bringing pioneers to Independence, Missouri, the traditional jumping off point for the westward trek to the Pacific slope. What became the Rocky Mountain states were just spacious obstacles in the way of these travelers.

Settlers knew where to go. Indians and mountain men had traversed the region successfully for decades, and no wagon train went out without a scout in advance. The pioneers followed the course of the Platte river, which presented wide variations in depth, unlike Eastern rivers. Many saw it when it was "a mile wide and six inches deep." Fording it was difficult because it was filled with quicksand and its shallowness prevented boats from floating in most places. In Wyoming settlers left the Platte and followed the Platte's tributary, the Sweetwater River. The trail went up and over the Continental Divide at South Pass, Wyoming, the most unspectacular and low pass in all of the Rockies, measuring only 7,550 feet high and twenty miles wide.

Thereafter the trails split, with the Oregon trail going on along the Snake River in Idaho, the Mormon trail forking south at Fort Bridger to Salt Lake City and the California trails heading further westward along complicated routes. Later there would be a mail and stage route a bit further south through a portion of Colorado, Wyoming and Utah called the Overland trail. Of all the states, Wyoming is outstanding for having the most visible and unspoiled portions of these trails. There is much more about them in the chapter devoted to Wyoming.

While the Oregon trail, or as it was known, the Platte River Road, missed some of the most spectacular Rocky Mountain scenery, it offered over 600 miles of mostly smooth and mostly mud free road from the Missouri to central Wyoming. Ox drawn wagons could make ten, fifteen or up to twenty miles per day. Water and grass for forage and game for food was available in abundance at first.

Native Americans who lived in the region observed the first trickle of settlers with interest and wanted to trade with them. When the trickle became a flood they became upset because game was driven off and riverside grass was destroyed from overuse and watering places were polluted. The pioneers also brought disease and caused prairie fires. As time went on, growing Indian harassment was added to the perils of the trek.

Lookouts, rifle pits and the circling of the wagons at campsites became necessary.

Without the lure of good farmland or, until 1859, gold and silver, passage through the Rocky Mountain region was regarded as a sheer ordeal. The large number of human grave sites and animal skeletons deposited along the way attest to its severity.

The pilot or guide of the wagon trains roamed far out in front. He marked the obstacles and fording places and chose the campsites. The wagon train was divided up into sections and the sections were switched about regularly so that every section would have its turn to choke in the dust at the rear of the column.

A rough and ready democracy prevailed. Usually captains were elected and there were councils to enact regulations, settle disputes, punish wrongdoers and maintain security.

This great American trek westwards became an epic adventure for countless ordinary Americans. Fortunately their experiences can still be appreciated and to some extent relived today by following some portions of the trail through Wyoming. See the section "Along the Oregon Trail" in the chapter on Wyoming.

THE IMPACT OF MINING

The settlement of the Rocky Mountain states began suddenly, in a great rush to places where precious metals were discovered, starting in Colorado in 1859. Gold was discovered in various locations in Idaho a year later and in Montana a few years afterwards.

With mining, there was no frontier that was a line of civilization moving westward. Towns simply mushroomed haphazardly here and there, depending only on proximity to precious metals. Some locations were in the most remote, cold and inhospitable places. They might be separated by vast expanses of unsettled land from other English speaking locations. There was indeed some truth to the exaggeration of the old verse:

> A good silver mine
> Is above the timber line
> Ten times out of nine!

Many places in the Rocky Mountain states were actually settled from the West rather than from the East because prospectors and farmers flocked from recently settled parts of California and Oregon back to the Rockies where they hoped to participate in a bonanza. Many old Forty-niners from California became Fifty-niners in the Rockies. Others came from the Midwest.

Because miners had to be fed and supplied, farms and businesses developed in the new towns close to the mines. After a time enough people had arrived for the area to apply for territorial status. Without the population explosion that came with mining, the region would never have gone down the road to statehood. Ordinarily it took 60,000 inhabitants to qualify for admission as a state.

In the process of opening the area to mining operations, Native American tribes were goaded to war by the massive intrusions on their territories mining necessitated. Again and again, solemn treaties became mere scraps of paper when silver or gold was discovered on Indian land.

Many mining settlements were abandoned just as quickly as they were established once the ore ran out, littering the Rocky Mountains with old wooden structures and slag heaps. The motto was: "Get in, get rich and get out."

The first prospectors were not unlike addicted gamblers. They had such a fever for gold or silver that they would search unceasingly. When they heard of a strike they would rush to the vicinity, hoping to cash in on it.

The first stages of a mining operation in the Rocky Mountain states were largely carried out by these poor but hopeful prospectors who looked for "free gold" in the form of nuggets and dust, gold that got its name from being uncombined with other minerals or rock formations. Free gold was usually found in stream beds or banks. Prospectors used pans for the simple process of retrieving free gold, relying upon gold's heaviness to sink it to the bottom while mud, dirt, stones and debris could be washed away. This was called "placer" mining, pronounced with an "a" as in "placid." The sites where free gold was found were called placers.

Placer mining was a backbreaking and slow process when carried on day after day. To speed things up, wooden contraptions, such as a sluice box, were rigged up to wash greater quantities of dirt bearing free gold. Flowing water was absolutely essential, so when streams were at a distance from a site, primitive ditches and dams were constructed.

Gold or silver strikes brought tens of thousands of the poor but hopeful to the vicinity in a surprisingly short time. The phrase, "Pike's Peak or Bust," comes from the miners who headed for Colorado's gold strikes in the early 1860's. Thousands were disappointed and turned back, perhaps grumbling, in Mark Twain's words, that a mine was "a hole in the ground owned by a liar."

Many poor prospectors who struck it rich could not handle their success and indulged themselves in various excesses which, one way or another, led them to sell off their claims to hard-eyed men who came upon the scene later and who had the capital behind them to apply expensive technology to get much more gold and silver out than placer mining could accomplish.

Free gold or silver in a rock formation is called a lode. Lodes have streaks of ore in rocks called veins. It took much more than pans and sluice boxes to get at embedded gold and silver. When veins disappeared into the earth, shafts and tunnels had to be constructed to get at it. When ore bearing precious metals were extracted, it had to be crushed mechanically so that gold could be separated from rocks. Smelting processes, that is, melting metals out of ore, were also required.

Who were the people with capital to carry on such massive operations? Some were Easterners who already had huge corporations to manage. Some were clever lawyers who took out their fees in shares or who invested in promising sites whose secrets were known to them from litigation. Some were successful businessmen who made their money from supplying the miners in the area. There were even a few very prudent prospectors who were able to join this group of determined capitalists.

Individuals who had gone to the gold and silver strikes to be independent entrepreneurs found that they became dependent upon on wages. Their employers were powerful corporations which had great influence in the territorial legislatures and owned local newspapers. Foreign workers, particularly from southern and eastern Europe, were recruited in large numbers and joined the poor Americans working in the mines. When strikes occurred, the miners were put down quickly and sometimes violently because close collaboration between the

owners, legislators and governors usually prevailed. Work in
the mines, mills and smelters was dirty and dangerous. Air and
water pollution led to various illnesses, including dysentery.

Mining Towns: Although they grew quickly, mining towns
did go through several stages of evolution. At first they consisted of a slum of tents, lean-tos, shacks and crude log cabins.
Then frame buildings with false fronts appeared and, finally,
brick and some stone construction was put up.

No matter how much the surviving and still inhabited old
mining towns have been spruced up for the tourist industry,
they were ugly and nasty when they first appeared. Their
unpaved streets were either dusty or muddy or frozen in ruts,
depending on the season. Litter was everywhere and the stench
of sewage filled the air. Slag heaps, junk yards for broken
machinery, hillsides denuded for wood and streams colored by
mine tailings replaced what may have been been a lovely
natural landscape shortly before. When smelters were erected,
vile fumes were added to poison the thin air.

Historians estimate that for every miner five other persons
flocked to the region. Those who came first, saloon keepers,
provision sellers, prostitutes and gamblers, were out to mine
the miners. Prices for everything were simply outrageous at
first. After a time, whole families arrived, along with the school
teachers and preachers that they supported. The drive for
permanence and respectability was manifested by the opening
of schools and the building of churches and the appearance of
a temperance movement.

Culture was sought by many newcomers earnestly, no
matter how rude the surroundings, which resulted in the
erection of music halls, libraries, theaters and even opera
houses in places where mines continued to be productive. Some
towns took pride in their first class hotels, some of which

offered excellent European cuisine. Rich men built elaborate Victorian houses and filled them with the furniture and bric a brac that had to be imported from the East at great cost. Today, many of these houses are on display, restored to their late Victorian splendor.

In the early stages of these places, considerable self-government was practiced because claims had to be defined and protected and order had to be maintained. Mining districts were formed, officials were elected and meetings took place to organize the affairs of the community. All of this served to counteract tendencies towards chaos and disorder in the minefields and mining towns.

The extractive industries have gone from boom to bust many times in the Rocky Mountain West. Many mining towns died when their booms collapsed. For example, Silver City in Idaho, now mostly boarded up, once had 4,000 inhabitants. Elkhorn, Montana, now an almost dead collection of weather-worn and sagging old wooden buildings, was the place where 14 million dollars worth of silver had been extracted.

Other towns have hung on and some have prospered by mining droves of tourists. Many celebrated Colorado towns are in this category, plus a few in Montana and Idaho. See the chapters on individual states for details.

THE REGION AND THE CIVIL WAR

Only one campaign of the Civil War involved the Rocky Mountain region. Confederates acquired New Mexico and General Henry Sibley began to move north towards Colorado with the intention of seizing Denver and the gold mines nearby. Colorado's governor rapidly put together a force of volunteers that managed to defeat the Confederates at La Glorietta Pass near Santa Fe, New Mexico, in March, 1862.

The Civil War did deprive the region of the services of the regular army for a time. It had functioned as something of a police force on the plains, and in addition the army carried on explorations, built roads and protected settlers and communications. Local recruits replaced them when the went off East to fight against the Confederacy. Simultaneously, the Indian wars broke out, a subject treated in the next chapter.

THE ERA OF THE CATTLE BARONS, PONY EXPRESS, AND THE RAILROADS

Shortly after the beginning of mining in the Rockies, the open range cattle industry boomed in the high plains areas of what became the Rocky Mountain states. The era of the cattle barons only lasted for a few decades, from the 1870's to the late 1880's. Overstocking the range, a disastrous winter in 1886-1887, the use of barbed wire, first by farmers and then by cattlemen, divided up the open range into holdings. The railroads and the homesteaders further cut into it. The topic of the open range and the era of the cattle barons is treated in great detail in the next chapter in the section on cowboys.

The rapid evolution of communication conincided with the conquest of the West. Mail on stage coaches outpaced the plodding wagon trains, and the celebrated Pony Express could get a letter from Missouri to the Pacific in ten days by changing horses every ten miles and riders every 50 to 100 miles. The service lasted only eighteen months before it became obsolete and was replaced by the telegraph in 1861.

The railroads truly amalgamated the Rocky Mountain region with the rest of the United States, at the same time that railroads incorporated parts of Asia and Africa into European empires. Building the Transcontinental Railroad was a truly heroic achievement, involving hard, dangerous, hand labor. One railway extended eastwards from California and another extended westward across Wyoming. They met just west of Salt Lake City, where the symbolic golden spike was driven to unite the whole country by rail. Without railroads, the massive exploitation of minerals could not have been accomplished. The railroads that went up into the Rocky Mountains often required heroic feats of engineering to build them. Some chug on today as narrow guage adventures for tourists.

The owners of the railroads, the open range cattle industry and the mines were generally located outside of the region. This circumstance led to a feeling of almost colonial dependency in the West towards the East. Eastern culture, fashions and styles were zealously imported and imitated. Any historic and opulent Victorian building restored to its original condition is a testament to this phenomenon. The Federal Government fostered the interests of the outsiders by granting land to railroads and rights to use public land to the cattle barons and the great mining companies. In effect, the government in Washington granted massive subsidies to encourage the development of the region by operations which were usually headquartered outside of the region.

A FEW HIGHLIGHTS
OF REGIONAL HISTORY AND
ECONOMICS IN THE 20th CENTURY

Tourists started to arrive in numbers before the end of the 19th century. Even well-to-do ladies were arriving by the late 1880's. Tourism continued to grow with each passing decade. A big boost to the region was given by President Theeodore Roosevelt who had lived in it with great enjoyment when he was a young man. He put millions of acres of forest and mineral lands into reserves and put the Federal Government into the business of building dams on the basis of the Reclamation Act of 1902. In a timely manner, National Parks and National Monuments were established to preserve some of the most interesting and remote parts of the region.

Many middle-class Americans migrated to the Rocky Mountain states in the 1920's. During the Depression of the 1930's, great Federal projects were carried out by the alphabet soup of administrative bodies that Franklin Delano Roosevelt organized. Huge dams were constructed to control floods, supply irrigation water and generate electric power.

World War Two brought further immigration as people headed towards employment booms in many places. In the post war era the trend has continued in some places while other locations have gone through boom and bust cycles resulting in little or no net population growth. The location of many defense industries and installations and the establishment of many new, light industries in some parts of the Rocky Mountain states has accounted for much of the recent growth. So has the lure of the Sun Belt and the many opportunities to pursue varied lifestyles with an emphasis on the outdoors.

The West was traditionally the supplier of raw materials and foodstuffs that the rest of the nation wanted, starting with furs and continuing on with minerals, timber, oil, gas, and ranch and farm products. Since the processing of raw materials adds considerable value, it was unfortunate that so much of the processing of its products has been carried on outside of the region.

Freight rates were chronically high due to the vastness and remoteness of the region, the absence of navigable rivers, the presence of mountain barriers, and the sparse population. For example, it ordinarily cost more to ship goods from Montana to Chicago than from Los Angeles to Chicago.

Agriculturalists in general have not been enjoying good times in the region. Many farmers struggle to pay high interest rates on their large debts while receiving low prices for their crops. Although they sell at wholesale prices, they must buy most things at retail prices. The old saying still applies for many farmers: "Their three crops are grain, freight and interest."

A few farmers manage to strike it rich when a city expands close to their land. They become millionaires just by being there and waiting for development to engulf their acres. Thereafter what was their farmland produces only one crop: tract houses.

Ranching also has its economic difficulties. While there may be twenty times as many cattle and sheep in the area than humans, the owners may be financiers in New York, Chicago or Houston, perhaps doctors, lawyers, executives or corporations who may find tax advantages in running unprofitable ranches. While some ranches are larger than 40,000 acres, it must be borne in mind that grazing can be so poor that only two head of cattle can find sustenance on each square mile. The federal subsidy in the form of cheap grazing on public land is absolutely critical to many operations. Just recently a furor has erupted over proposed hikes in federal grazing fees.

Recently some Eastern academics raised another furor by suggesting that the dry High Plains be allowed to revert to nature and become a vast National Park where the buffalo could roam once again. They pointed out how uneconomical farming and ranching had become in that part of the world. The constant emigration of the young and able from the dying towns of the flat, agricultural High Plains does give some support to their arguments.

These states have always yielded their natural resources according to the unsteady demands of the larger national and international economies. The result has been cycles of boom and bust from the beginning of outside exploitation to the present. Tens of billions of dollars worth of ore have been gouged out of these states, and millions more continue to be dug out every week. There have been gold and silver rushes, a copper rush after telephones were developed, a uranium rush, and an oil rush. Each rush has produced a rapid but vulnerable local development dependent upon the exploitation of one natural resource.

The most recent rush, shale oil production, has become the most recent of many busts that have disrupted the economies of the Rocky Mountain states periodically. Colorado, Wyoming and Utah have literally mountains of it in the Green River Formation, which comprises what may be the largest mineral deposit on the surface of the globe. It locks up over three times the world's known reserves of petroleum, and has been described as the Saudi Arabia of the 21st century.

When petroleum prices soared in the 1970's, investments in oil shale by the big oil companies produced rapid development. Yet cost effective technology for powdering the rocks and heating the powder to release the oil proved elusive. There was also opposition from environmentalists who resented exploitation of federal land as well as the need to divert large amounts of water for the project, to say nothing of the question of the disposal of waste.

The Rocky Mountain states continue to be a storehouse of energy resources, including oil in its liquid form, natural gas and coal. Oil is extremely important to the economies of Colorado, Wyoming, Montana and Utah. Coal was important from the beginning because so many new locations, like Denver, were short of timber. Coal was used to fuel the mining industries' smelters and mills as well as the railroads that transformed the region. In the future, coal is likely to be extracted in parts of the West by huge surface mining or strip mining operations.

These states have worked hard to attract new high tech industries in order to establish a more balanced economy that would not be so dependent upon the extraction of raw materials and its attendant and uncontrollable boom and bust cycles. Another plus for high tech industry is that the output of such industries has a small bulk which thereby mitigates the effects of the region's disadvantageous freight rates. High tech industries have been lured by the Rocky Mountain states through promises of cheap labor, cheap land and the prospect of scenic, outdoor lifestyles for corporate executives. Fast growing "industrial parks" on the outskirts of Western cities have been the key competitors for these modern, clean and hopefully permanent high tech corporations.

In what are now the more affluent parts of the region, large, well-landscaped high tech factories have been established by these efforts. Nevertheless, it became clear that layoffs and overproduction can hit the high tech industries also, and something as marvelous as the production of computers can have busts also.

The Federal Government has helped the region in many ways, including substantial investments in defense production in electronics and missiles. The other forms of investment by the Federal Government, in agencies, defense installations, and subsidies for extractive and agricultural pursuits have been considered elsewhere in this book. See the section entitled "The Federal Factor" in chapter three.

As part of a worldwide phenomenon, tourism continues to grow as an important sector of the economy. Calculated by the number of dollars it draws, it has surpassed both agriculture and mining in importance.

Although the economy of the Rocky Mountain states may continue to be erratic from one location to another or not follow national trends in such vital matters as unemployment percentages, the time honored Western tradition of pulling up stakes and moving on to brighter prospects elsewhere continues to prevail. So if jobs are short in Wyoming because the oil industry has too much slack, rental trucks crammed with household goods will roll along the highways to new locations where there are jobs or rumors of jobs. As always, optimism and mobility continue to be hallmarks of life in this region.

The Great Debates over the History of the Old West

History is constantly rewritten. Each generation brings new concerns and new questions, and historians busy themselves by refocusing on the past to provide fresh interpretations and answers to satisfy the intellectual demands of the living generation. A case in point is the new outlook on American history that has been developing since the war in Vietnam. Part of it has come to bear upon the history of the Old West, triggering an emotional verbal shootout among many professional historians engaged in the field.

Professional disputes can mystify and confuse non-professionals quite easily. When historians carry on such debates, accusations of exaggeration omission, overemphasis and underemphasis are common, which serve to bewilder ordinary readers who may not have grasped the basic facts of the situation yet. What follows is an attempt to simplify the ongoing conflict over the history of the Old West for non-professionals. Whenever significant new historical concepts emerge, they collide with old, established opinions. Sometimes they overthrow them and sometimes they merely modify them to some degree. At present the degree of modification that will come about from the post-Vietnam revised interpretations is unclear, but their impact will undoubtedly be substantial.

For the sake of what historians may see as drastic oversimplification, those espousing established opinions are called "traditionalists" and those pushing new views are called "revisionists" for the purpose of this brief summary. In actuality, all historians are to some degree both, and their positions can shift over time. When those who are in large measure on the revisionist side make an attack, those who are positioned mostly towards the traditional position are quite likely to respond that they recognized and incorporated the substance of the revisionists' thrust long ago.

The Turner Frontier Thesis of 1893 is the battered bastion of the history of the Old West which has served as the topic of countless debates, students' papers and examination questions. Turner celebrated the frontier as the forge that turned Europeans into Americans and he traced its grand march from the very first settlements on the East Coast until its demise in the

1890's. Free land to the West made the frontier possible, and it produced Americans who had to be adaptable, innovative and democratic on account of the demands it put upon them.

In Turner's view, the frontier was a moving line, along which heroic Americans wrested the West from savagery, barbarism and wild nature. They "won" the West and guaranteed its future prosperity and peace under a system of freedom and justice. In terms that Freud would have found interesting, some followers of Turner wrote of how the seeds of civilization were brought to a virgin land. In all of this, the dominant Victorian notes of progress and improvement are trumpeted. It was a triumph when windmills, silos, wooden towns, barbed wire, telegraphs and railroads replaced what was called a wilderness.

All sorts of romantic images of heroic pioneers struggling with treacherous Indians and violent outlaws emerged from this outlook. In the hands of film makers and novelists, the traditional views were puffed into a mythical Old West where John Wayne types fitted in easily. It became a conservative form of the American dream, stressing rugged individualism, stern, unyielding justice, conflict with other ethnic groups, and an eagerness to exploit natural resources because that is what they were deemed to be for. Above all, this was the manifest destiny of America, as ordained by God.

A less mythical and more sober rendition of this outlook is the stock in trade of traditional historians of the Old West and the very stuff that appears in standard American history textbooks. It is also the focal point for demolition by revisionist historians.

Revisionists do not see the frontier as a moving line in the American West. They see spots of settlement appearing and often disappearing in various places, such as mining boom towns. They deem Turner's yardstick of two persons per square mile to determine when the frontier was over as unworkable.

They point out that Turner measured places with small farms rather than the ranching and mining settlements of the Rocky Mountain West.

More significantly, revisionists question the whole concept of the frontier. They see the area that traditionalists call the frontier as already occupied by shifting populations of Native Americans and Hispanics long before the Anglo-Americans arrived. It is their aim to bring these people and other participants into the history of the Old West to a much greater extent than has been done previously. Revisionists accuse traditionalists of concentrating almost exclusively on the role of white, English speaking males. They want to emphasize the roles of Hispanics, Native Americans, African Americans, Asians and women, all of whom are just on the fringes of traditional accounts. They ask how the conquest of the West looked from the perspectives of these hitherto neglected participants. What emerges from their studies is a highlighting of social prejudice, class prejudice and brutal industrial strife.

The hardship endured by women is strongly underlined in revisionist research, which reveals that they were overworked and extremely vulnerable to male power in the Old West. Fertile women were usually pregnant, and they could only expect to keep on working hard until very late in their pregnancies. They also had to witness their children going to work as early as they could be put to tasks. On a psychological level the loneliness and isolation many women faced sapped their spirit.

Through utilizing neglected sources, revisionists have come to see the West as a meeting place where diverse people and diverse cultures interact and struggle. They push this concept right into the present by showing how conflicts over cultural dominance continue, for example in the disputes over bilingualism in the schools, immigration from Mexico and the assimilation of Native Americans. They find conquest of the region to be the keynote of its history, just as slavery has been the keynote of the history of the South. For the surviving Native American and Hispanic populations, American culture was almost unconditionally imposed upon them by the victors.

What made this conquest different from the conquest of other parts of the United States was that it was accomplished with speed and brutality during the high tide of romantic American nationalism. Therefore it was destined to be portrayed in a grand, noble and heroic manner. American nationalists did not call it a conquest. They said the West was "won."

In their general assault on the myth of "how the West was won," revisionists demolish some minor myths and cherished stereotypes along the way. For example, revisionists point out that many ordinary Americans seeking a life of independence in the West became part of wage dependent populations in the mining and ranching industries. Moreover, many who fled from failure and corruption in the East found it again in the West. Revisionists have cut down to size some hitherto heroic developers of the Old West. For example, some railway builders actually mismanaged and fleeced their enterprises, tolerated cheap, poor construction and exploited their workers heartlessly.

Instead of heroes in white hats and villains in black hats, revisionists depict most white Western men in grey hats, preying upon each other avariciously. Perhaps one of the most treasured stereotypes to go is that of the showdown with gunplay to determine land ownership. The revisionists point out that then, as now, lawyers in courtrooms performed these functions.

Historical controversies are healthy. While they may send people into squalls of doubt and confusion, they stimulate thought about the past and reflections on the present. This particular controversy serves to keep the Old West from becoming a faded romantic saga. It freshens it and keeps it alive, linking the Old West with the New.

CHAPTER SIX

THREE TYPES FROM THE OLD WEST IN MYTH AND REALITY: NATIVE AMERICANS, MOUNTAIN MEN AND COWBOYS

Why These Figures Have Been Chosen

Wherever visitors go in the Rocky Mountain states they will be reminded of the history of the Native Americans, the mountain men and the cowboys. Whether at state or national historical sites, where everything is carefully presented, or at commercial operations where hoopla and exaggeration tend to obliterate historical reality, it is impossible to avoid being exposed to something about the history of these figures. They appear on signs, posters, and every conceivable form of advertising. They are the inspiration for countless festivals and celebrations. More than anybody else, they stand for what the Old West was all about in the romantic imagination. Therefore knowing something about their lives and the myths about their lives will enhance any visit to this area.

What follows below is an attempt to explore both the myths surrounding them as well as the hard realities of their existence in the romantic 19th century. In the case of the cowboys and the Native Americans, there is also a brief assessment of their circumstances today.

Native Americans, Alias Indians

WHERE ARE THEY NOW?

Not only did the Rocky Mountain region belong to Native Americans, but so much of its scenery prompts anyone with an imagination to think that the Indians belong to the landscape. The question nowadays is: where are they? Weeks can be spent in the West without seeing a single Indian anywhere, or without at least being able to identify one. The answer is complex. They are everywhere inconspicuously in the form of descendants from intermarriage; they have joined the polyglot mix of populations in the West's large cities; some have become the West's best cowboys, a cultural type erroneously thought to be their cultural nemesis; and some are tucked away here and there on remote reservations, particularly in the states of Montana and Idaho. The states with the largest Native American populations are California, Oklahoma, Arizona, New Mexico and North Carolina, in that order, but since the Western states have such low populations generally, some of them have up to ten and twelve times the percentage of Native Americans nationally, which is only ½ of 1% of the total population.

Meanwhile all the rest of the people who have pushed into the West and built over Indian hunting grounds and village sites have honored the defeated and uprooted by naming all sorts of places after them, including cities, towns, roads, schools, forests, and grasslands. For example, consider Native American names in Colorado: Across the eastern approaches to the state the visitor will drive through the Pawnee National Grasslands. Continuing into the mountains, he or she will drive through the Arapahoe National Forest. In Denver, a major thoroughfare is named Arapahoe. So is a county. Where are the Arapahoe now? They were shipped either to Oklahoma, along with the Pawnee, or to the Wind River Reservation in northwestern Wyoming, which they share with the Shoshone tribe. Colorado's only Indian reservation is in the southwestern corner, which is for the Ute Indians and not for the Arapahoe or Pawnee or for the Cheyenne, all of whom once enjoyed life in eastern Colorado. Any left in the state are likely to be in the urban tribal mix in Denver.

Did guilt over the conquest of the Native Americans prompt such lavish commemoration? Clearly their history in the Rocky Mountain West is an emotional and controversial subject. It can call into question differing interpretations of American history and raise troublesome issues about right and wrong, justice and injustice. Even the name "Indian" causes difficulties for some who prefer "Native American" to be used exclusively. The people who are the recipients of these designations are divided over which one they prefer. Most actually prefer a third, the name of their own tribe. The controversy about names goes all the way back to Columbus, who named them "Indios." Traditionally this Italian word was supposed to indicate Columbus' mistaken notion that he had arrived on the outskirts of Asia or India. Now some historians claim that it means 'native' in the Italian of his day. Regardless of the controversial nature of this designation, both names are used interchangeably in this book.

EARLY RELATIONS IN THE ROCKY MOUNTAIN WEST

The Native Americans in the Rocky Mountain region in the 19th century were what many have come to regard as "real" Indians: They wore feathers and skins, lived in tepees, rode horses and hunted buffalo. All of the other varieties of Native Americans' lifestyles, from the swamps of Florida to the fishing grounds of the Northwest, have never made as deep an impression in the public mind as those who rode and hunted in and near the Rocky Mountains.

With closer scrutiny, Native American life in this region becomes more complex. First, the Indians of the Great Basin west of the Continental Divide were seen as poorer and less advanced by the Plains Indians themselves. Second, Indians were always disunited and owed their primary allegiance to their tribes, which were constantly under pressure to move into or out of territory because of tribal warfare. At one level tribal wars were dangerous games of stealing horses and bravely confronting enemies and at another level they were life and death struggles for lands which held the resources for survival. Third, each tribe had its allies and its enemies. For example, the Sioux were usually allied to the Cheyenne and Arapahoe and were bitter enemies of the Shoshoni and Crow. The

Shoshoni were pushed westward by their enemies and the Crow had to take refuge in the Big Horn Mountains.

The original High Plains and Rocky Mountain tribes were encroached upon when the horse revolutionized the Native American way of life in the region during the 18th century. Unresolved struggles were going on when the first Euro-Americans intruded. Some Indians saw them as potential allies or at least as suppliers of war material. The Shoshoni, Crow and Flathead tended to seek the whites out as allies while the Blackfeet tended to attack them. In general, Indians were quite friendly as well as curious towards whites when the first few penetrated the area. The friendliness generally lasted through the 1840's and the 1850's, most notably demonstrated by the helpfulness of Indian guides.

It took a while before the white intruders were feared and distrusted. At first Indians were not alarmed because the number of whites in the region remained low. As time went on, their numbers grew alarmingly at the same time that they made an increasingly devastating impact upon the environment. At first the coveted beaver was almost driven to extinction. Then whites in the wagon trains depleted grass, timber and game along their increasing number of trails. Finally, the economic base of Indian life was destroyed when the buffalo were slaughtered. By the 1870's, there were actually more whites in the region than all the tribes put together.

All the while, Indians were becoming as hooked on the whites' trade goods as contemporary Americans are hooked on the electronic goods of the Far East. Alcohol and guns were the most notorious trade items, but Indians also wanted such mundane products as rice, sugar, coffee, flour, candy, shawls, bright cloths, ribbons, knives, tobacco, brass nails and glass beads. In exchange, Indians bartered skins or whatever else the whites would take. Sometimes Indians themselves participated in the slaughter of buffalos so that they could swap buffalo robes for trade goods.

Another connection between the Indians and the white intruders was marriage. Indian wives bridged both societies, serving as interpreters, keeping whites informed of tribal affairs and promoting trade. They also were a source of labor for their white husbands.

It was always best for a white to marry the daughter of a chief. The marriage transaction had a commercial element, similar to the paying of a bride price in Europe. In fact, Horace Greeley, a famous newspaperman and Western booster, reported that the price for Indian girls in Wyoming was between $40 and $80, which was roughly comparable to the price of a good horse at that time. White husbands often had another wife or wives elsewhere. As it might be expected, such marriages sometimes lasted only for a few years, when it might be terminated by either of the parties.

Very different reactions occurred when white women were abducted by Indian males. These women, in the Victorian rhetoric of the day, suffered "a fate worse than death." Romantic tales of heroism centered around rescuing these fair captives from the grips of "savage barbarians." Those who did settle into tribal life, cohabiting with Indian men, were regarded quite differently from white men who lived with squaws. There was a Victorian double standard for whites and Indians plus a double standard for men and women at play in these situations.

SOME BROAD PERSPECTIVES ON THE CONQUEST OF THE INDIANS

The Native Americans in the Rocky Mountains and Great Plains were seen as a barrier to the expansion of a higher civilization until they were pushed aside in colorful struggles that few in America or Europe can fail to depict in bright images. Almost everyone has an image of Custer at Little Big Horn, Indians riding around a circle of covered wagons or chasing a stage coach, or the cavalry riding to the rescue, flags flying and bugles blowing. It is truly remarkable that in the film versions large numbers of howling Indians fall to the earth dead while their horses almost always keep on running. Along with the slaughter of horses, merciless massacres by both sides, rape and the mutilation of corpses are also rarely depicted.

According to patriotic versions of American history, this was the time when Indians had to be defeated and "tamed" so that American ranchers and settlers could move in and peacefully "unlock" the land's great resources and use them much more productively than the Indians had ever done. In this version of history, the more energetic, hardworking, progressive, Christian, white Americans had a right to occupy these lands that their heroism had freed from primitive barbarism.

These views are woven into the tapestry of the "winning of the West," a nationalistic and ethnocentric view of history that allows mainstream Americans to justify their conquest of territories belonging to Indians and also of lands that had been settled by Hispanics. Long enshrined in films and textbooks, these themes of the "winning of the West" are now under close scrutiny and attack by revisionist historians, some writers and some film makers. Hispanics and Native Americans, of course, have always had difficulty subscribing to these themes.

Like other urbanized and industrialized peoples in the 19th century, Americans' outlook included elements of racism, some of it inspired by misapplications of Darwin's theories about biology to society. From this perspective, all groups had begun in savagery, but some groups, notably the Europeans and their American descendants, had been able to evolve towards a higher civilization. While savagery did lead to some noble behavior at a primitive level, it was obvious that agriculture and industry were better than hunting and gathering; that Christianity was better than Indian superstitions; that literacy was better than picture writing and that private property was a higher form than communal tribal property. Above all, Euro-Americans applied reason to life, not savage emotions.

Americans with these viewpoints could justify "freeing" the Indians from their chains of savagery, even if this meant warring upon the tribes and taking away their lands. Greed could be rationalized very easily this way.

The conquest of Native Americans actually fits into a much broader framework than American history. In the 19th century nearly all of the world was conquered by Europeans or transplanted Europeans. Never before or since were there so many white people, and never before or since did they hold sway over so large a portion of the globe. While Britain, France and Germany expanded over salt water, The United States and Russia expanded overland. "Manifest Destiny" was the famous cry of American imperialists, meaning that they followed a Divine command to drive west until they reached the shores of the Pacific.

Very few countries remained free from conquest by imperial powers, only a small group that included Japan, Ethiopia, Liberia, Siam (Thailand) and the Ottoman Empire. (Latin America is considered here as a part of transplanted European civilization because of its languages and religion, if not its dominant ethnicity.) The history of the 20th century has featured the reversal of this process, in which Asian, African, Oceanic and Middle Eastern peoples have, for the most part, thrown off white rule. Native Americans, however, were too few and too weak to resist in both the 19th and 20th centuries.

Just like Africans and Asians, Native Americans in the 19th century did not have a chance against the superior weapons of their conquerors. Better guns that fired more accurately and more rapidly, canons, the steam engine in shallow draft gunboats, trains bearing troops and supplies, improved medicine and hygiene and various forms of sophisticated all terrain equipment ensured defeat for the whites' enemies. So did the telegraph, known as the "singing wires" to the Indians, which made it so much more efficient and easy to muster and direct forces against indigenous peoples. Conquest was also helped by the ravages of disease brought in by white forces, including smallpox, venereal ailments and alcoholism.

Conquerors everywhere were aided by divisions among those being conquered. Just as the British could play off Hindu against Moslem in India and Hausa against Ibo in Nigeria, conquering Americans could count on some Indian tribes to supply warriors, spies and scouts against whatever tribes they were fighting.

There was conquest by paper as well as with guns. Treaties were the scraps of paper that legitimized wholesale land acquisition. Usually native peoples had different concepts of land ownership, which ordinarily held the land in perpetual trust from the dead to the living to the yet unborn. Land rights could be rented out or partially alienated, according to the laws of many indigenous groups, but the idea of forever forsaking ancestral ground was an anathema. Whites, by contrast, had the concept of absolute legal ownership of property through titles and deeds. Everywhere, in Asia, Africa and Oceania as well as in North America, illiterate or semi-literate natives were persuaded to sign away what they felt they could never sign away. Desired goods, particularly alcohol, served as inducements.

AFTER THE CONQUEST: PAST POLICIES AND PRESENT REACTION

The height of Native American resistance was reached after the American Civil War of 1861-1865 broke out, and it continued intensely long after the South surrendered. Little Big Horn, otherwise known as Custer's Last Stand, was in 1876, and the last upsurge and slaughter was at Wounded Knee in 1890. The period of vigorous resistance was brought on by deep encroachments into Indian territory, actually violations of solemn treaties, as well as by the notorious Sand Creek Massacre of peaceful Indians in eastern Colorado in 1864. The fact that regular troops had been sent to the East to fight in the Civil War gave Indians hope that their uprisings would be successful. Details of the Indian Wars are taken up in the chapters on specific states where the sites of particular major encounters are located. See in particular the chapters on Wyoming and Montana.

There was always an ambiguity in how the United States dealt with Native Americans. For a time the United States made treaties with individual tribes as if they were sovereign states, although the United States claimed sovereignty over them. Relations with Indians were always something of an anomaly. Indians received special services, special land and were more or less held in a kind of trust by the government. The United States was hardly consistent in dealing with this special relationship. Some administrations wanted to end the Indians' special status and other administrations wanted to strengthen and preserve it

Right after Indian resistance was broken, the remnants of defeated tribes were forced onto reservations which were often hundreds of miles from their ancestral grounds. The government attempted to break the tribes by such measures as the General Allotment Act of 1877, known as the Dawes Act, which granted plots of reservation land to individual Indians who could sell them off if they wished. Before this act land had been owned communally by the tribe. The net result was to reduce the Indian land holdings from 140 million acres to 50 million acres by the late 1930's.

Policies to break the tribal structure were reversed in 1934 with the passage of the Indian Reorganization act. It fostered Indian self-government under written tribal constitutions and the recovery of tribal land. Social services, particularly health and education, were also guaranteed to those Indians who remained on the reservations. So was the continuation of tax exempt status.

A shift occurred the other way, towards assimilation, after World War II. Indians were encouraged to migrate to urban areas so that the reservation system could be terminated. In the words of the Eisenhower Administration, the aim was to "free the Indians from the reservations."

This policy stood until Indian protests came forth in the 1970's. The current policy is to let the Indians control their own property and make their own decisions about the future. This policy, which seems so enlightened, has been hampered by severe budget cuts for social services on the reservation.

A new factor is the skill of Native American lawyers and their legal allies who have revived the struggles for Indian territories and rights, only now the battlefields are in the courtrooms rather than on the plains of buffalo grass.

Non-Indians who have been using Indian properties and rights have been subject to legal challenges. Often courts allow the non-Indians to continue their use after the Indians have been paid off. There are many claims because many treaties were ignored. Indian lands have been used by non-Indians to fish, hunt, and graze, and minerals, timber and oil have been exploited on them. There seems to be no end in sight for ongoing litigation.

A striking example of the new Indian resistance in the courtrooms has been provided by the Shoshone and Arapahoe Indians of the Wind River Reservation in Wyoming. A U.S. Supreme Court ruling in 1989 gave them rights to half a million acre-feet of water from the Wind River annually. (An acre foot is the amount of water it takes to cover an acre to the depth of one foot.) The reservation has cut water allocations to non-Indian irrigators, some of whom have farmed in the region for generations. Rumors abound that the Indians want to drive them off of their farms. The Indians have denied this, declaring that they are trying to keep water levels high so that they can stock a section of the Wind River going through their reservation with fish to entice tourists. They cite a 70% unemployment rate, high welfare dependency and a number of teen-age suicides to underscore their need for economic development.

The terrible scourge of alcoholism and the large number of deaths from vehicular accidents can also be cited as chronic problems that make reservation life so painful. On the other hand, Indian ways of community cooperation and community consensus continue to exert a positive influence.

THREE PERSPECTIVES ON NATIVE AMERICANS TODAY

Americans have held a traditional view of Indians for centuries. In it they are savages, a barrier to opening lands to civilization. They were the raiders, the pillagers, the dangerous killers who might attack with cunning and stealth or in a howling mob. This view was embedded in popular consciousness by a host of novels, short stories, and movies, nearly all of which indulged in historical inaccuracies. In countless films Indians were wrongly dressed, had improper haircuts, had the wrong blankets, and slept in the wrong kinds of shelter. Tribal differences were for the most part brushed aside. Since the Indians only played simple villains who had to die at the hands of white heroes, their inaccurate depiction did not seem to bother most people. Undoubtedly many more Indians were killed in films than were ever killed in Indian wars. Of course, there were the occasional "Tontos," or friendly, helpful Indian allies, who were as likely as not to be played by white actors since one of the Holywood prejudices was that Indians could not act.

This traditional view of Indians may have been started by Buffalo Bill Cody in his famous Wild West Show. Although he hired real Indians, some of them actual survivors of Custer's Last Stand, and despite the fact that they appeared to be proud and courageous in these performances, they always went down to defeat every afternoon and every evening that the show operated.

Militant, revisionist views are put forth by a substantial number of Native Americans and non-Indians who oppose the traditional depiction with anger, bitterness and uncompromising vehemence. From this perspective, whites are brutal, greedy and unprincipled, stealing Indian property and lying to get what they want. The "Tontos" who help them are merely "Uncle Tomahawks." Indians, from this perspective, lived with nature and had good sense about ecological matters. Sometimes it seems that the old European concept of the "noble savage" has been reborn as the saintly and wise Native American ecological hero. Therefore his defeat and displacement by Euro-Americans can be seen as a disaster. Those who carry this point of view to an extreme regard the five hundredth anniversary of the arrival of Columbus as the celebration of the beginning of a "Western hemisphere holocaust" in which countless Indians were killed and their remnants forced into concentration camps called reservations. Similarly, militants have declared that to have a "Custer Battlefield National Monument" in Indian land is tantamount to having a Hitler monument in Israel.

Those who wince at the passion of these extreme statements need to reflect upon the anti-Indian prejudices that were so firmly held at the very time that they were being remorselessly defeated. The saying that "the only good Indian is a dead Indian" was repeated often, most notably by General Phil Sheridan, who was a hero of the Civil War and a key figure in the so-called "pacification" of the West.

The militant Native American outlook seems to bear some similarities to "nativist" reactions to European culture that took place in what were then colonies. After imperial conquest, the dignity and self-respect of native ways suffer as foreign ways of life are imitated. Defeat brings degeneration or dissoluteness to many of the conquered. In time counter-movements arise, "nativist" movements which aim to promote the old indigenous culture as morally superior to that of their conquerors. In a way, Native Americans' militant attempts to reinterpret the history of their relations with the dominant culture fits into this larger picture.

A third perspective comes from the anthropologists and historians who take great pains to avoid any ethnocentrism while seeking to view issues from all sides. They apply cultural relativism, which regards ideals, values, behavior and outlook as relative to the culture under consideration rather than matters of universal application. For example, the importance of consensus to Native American organizations and the emphasis put on cooperation rather than individual competition will be understood.

The hope is that non-Indian historians and anthropologists with this perspective will treat Indian culture fairly and objectively. That means seeing Indian culture form an Indian point of view, which means recognizing Native Americans as many peoples having many varied customs, languages and traditions. After all, between 50 and 100 Indian languages have survived north of Mexico, and two of them, Navajo and Siouan, are widely spoken. Appreciation of this diversity among Native Americans is a key strength of this third perspective.

CONTEMPORARY NATIVE AMERICANS

Indians as Cowboys: One of the myths of Western history is the heroic struggle of cowboys against Indians, which was a favorite children's game for a long time. In actuality, cowboys and Indians usually just passed each other by without hostilities. Sometimes they traded small items or passed on information.

The relationship between cowboys and Indians was complicated from the outset because Indians very quickly became cowboys, and the cowboys' lifestyle gained them the nickname of "white Indians."

Native Americans are perhaps the most visible and the most natural cowboys in the Rocky Mountain states today. Nothing could be more normal than to see Indians wearing stetsons, jeans, cowboy boots and Western cut shirts as they ride the range on horseback or drive their pickup trucks through Western towns. Their traditional Indian costumes may be laid aside for use only at festivals or ceremonials. Some own ranches. Some regularly participate in rodeos. Some even show up on stage as country Western musicians.

Urban Indians: Only a small percentage of Naive Americans have become cowboys. Like other Americans, many have moved to the cities where they have intermarried with people from other tribes and other ethnic backgrounds. Reservations have lamented a "brain drain" of talented, ambitious youngsters who depart for the bright lights and greater opportunities of the cities. Denver, Cheyenne, Boise, Billings and Great Falls have all received large numbers of them.

Urban Indians face obstacles in maintaining their culture in modern cities, where it is much more difficult for them to think of themselves as belonging to a particular tribe than it is on the reservation. The positive side of this situation is that a pan-Indian movement has been strengthened, despite centuries of identification with a tribal nation first and an Indian nation second.

Determined efforts are underway to keep the "old ways" alive. For example, the Denver Indian Center has urban powwows to invigorate Indian culture and to bring young urban Indian males and females together. The Center fosters inter-tribal programs, adult education, senior citizens' gatherings, an Indian radio station and Indian low cost housing for seniors.

The Mountain Men

Cowboys and Indians have been popular in stories, films and childrens' games all over the United States for generations. Except for some popularity for Davy Crockett several decades ago, less attention has been given to the first white hunters and trappers to exploit the West. In the West they are called "mountain men" and in the Rocky Mountain region they attract considerable attention. Just as history buffs like to dress up in Civil War costumes east of the Mississippi, in the Rocky Mountain region they like to dress up in costumes from the era of the fur trade, the 1820's to the early 1840's. They also delight in putting on recreations of "rendezvous," or annual gatherings of mountain men, Indians and tradesmen to buy, sell, celebrate and have a raucous time. Although what they engage in is just dressed up role playing, many modern urbanites and suburbanites love to don buckskins, change their language and habits, and revert to an idealized time when the West was wild and those who plunged into its recesses to trap could roam free from most of the trammels of civilization.

Several places host these rendezvous, including Bent's Old Fort in southeastern Colorado, Fort Bridger in southwestern Wyoming, and the Green River rendezvous site outside of Pinedale, Wyoming, on U.S. Route 187, where there is also a museum on mountain men. For a description of just what goes

High above Horsetooth Reservoir, Fort Collins, Colorado.

Bent's Old Fort in southeastern Colorado. (Photo courtesy of Bent's Old Fort National Historic Park)

Deep ruts of the Oregon Trail near Guernsey, Wyoming.

Along the Oregon Trail in central Wyoming.

Split Rock in southwestern Wyoming.

Ancient Indian ruins in eastern Utah.

The wide open spaces in central Utah.

The approaches to the ghost town of Elkhorn, Montana.

A scene at Fort Laramie, Wyoming.

A view of South Pass in Wyoming.

Real cowboys at work.

An early settler's home in Capitol Reef National Park, Utah.

A late Victorian Mormon tabernacle in Paris, Idaho.

The Main street of Idaho City, Idaho.

Recreated mining town, Hell Roarin' Gulch, at World Museum of Mining, Butte, Montana.

Near the mining town of Cripple Creek, Colorado.

Crowded parking lot at Glacier National Park.

Overlooking the White Bird Canyon Battlefield in Idaho.

Zion National Park, Idaho.

Arches National Park, Utah.

Buffalo Bill Historical Center, Cody, Wyoming.

C.M. Russell Museum Complex, Great Falls, Montana.

The interstate in central Utah.

Deserted buildings in the ghost town of Elkhorn, Montana.

on at a modern rendezvous, see the section on Fort Bridger in the chapter on Wyoming.

Just how free and wonderful were the lives of the mountain men? A romantic outlook colors all reflections on the century in which they appeared. Daily life in the trapping season could be hard. Trudging about with considerable equipment, including six or eight five-pound traps, must have been difficult. So was wading in ice cold water so that traps could be set at a proper depth, ensuring that an animal would drown before it could chew off one of its feet. Mountain men had to go on spring hunts up the mountains before the beaver began shedding in June. They also had to go on fall hunts but then they started out at high altitudes and worked downwards, because a cold environment produced better pelts. In the winter they might live in Indian settlements with Indian wives, or they might set up lonely camps.

Mountain Men were noted for being taciturn and stoic about death. Mostlikely they had to be. Sudden death could come from hostile Indians, grizzly bears or a freak accident in new or known terrain. When they learned that one of their kind had died in one of these ways, they were more than likely to just shrug without comment. Some of them had a few old books with them, but others could not read. While they were men of few words, a few phrases in English are attributed to them, namely "to make tracks" and to be "rubbed out."

When a mountain man traded his beaver pelts, or "hairy banknotes," he usually had to pay outrageous prices for goods imported from cities to the east. He was also likely to drink and gamble away his earnings in wild rendezvous celebrations, indulgences which undoubtedly compensated him briefly for what was undoubtedly a physically demanding, hard and lonely life.

Even so, the freedom in their lives has wondrous appeal for those chained to desks and computer screens today. Some anthropologists take the view that hunting and gathering was always the desired occupation of prehistoric humans. Farming was taken up reluctantly, out of necessity when populations in certain areas grew so large that hunting and gathering could no longer supply the population. These assumptions seem to be corroborated somewhat by the willingness of so many young men to abandon more settled lives and go West to wander the Rocky Mountains in search of furs, masters of their own destinies for the most part.

Yet it was the profit motive of fur companies, headquartered at great distances from the Rockies, that gave them the impetus to pursue this way of life. The fur trade marks the first major remorseless exploitation of Western resources by companies based outside of the region. It would happen again many times in the future. The British headquarters were Fort Vancouver on the Columbia and Montreal in Canada; Taos, in New Mexico, was a Mexican center; and the American Fur Company was located in St. Louis. The American Fur Company was operated with ruthless competitiveness by John Jacob Astor, who was born in Germany and who lived and managed the company in New York City.

For a time these smooth, rich beaver pelts were in great demand for fashionable fur top hats in America and Europe. When the fashion flopped, the fur trade flopped also. It would have had to cease anyway, because the beaver were being driven close to extinction. There were simply hardly any untrapped streams left. It took only two decades, from the 1820's to the 1840's, to bring about this depletion. Considering how ecologically useful the beaver is in helping to conserve water supplies in the region, the slaughter of these clever animals was a disaster for the environment.

Mountain men did not plunge into an unknown wilderness. The Indians knew it all rather well, and without their help the mountain men could not have carried on they way they did. Their relations with Indians were ambiguous. They used Indians as guides and married Indians after virtually buying squaws from tribes with gifts. Like Mormons, mountain men fancied having several Indian wives, but for different reasons. Several wives, if each belonged to a different and strategically located tribe, might mean that the mountain man could range widely in his quest for pelts under the tolerance of Indians to whom he was related by marriage. Tolerance could also be arranged by offering alcohol, the deadly firewater that fur companies liberally supplied to encourage trade or alliances against uncooperative tribes.

The Blackfeet tribe was uncooperative to the point of killing some mountain men. The Sioux could be dangerous also. With most of the rest of the Indian tribes, however, the mountain men gambled, drank and traded, contributing thereby to the breakdown of the Indians' self sufficiency as well as their growing dependence on the white men's goods. Worse, the mountain men brought venereal diseases and the dreaded scourge of smallpox, which simply ravaged Indian populations.

While some distant observers declared that mountain men reverted to savagery in the Rockies, the fact was that mountain men learned and used the skills and help of Indians to survive. Some, like the aptly named Jim Bridger, came to act as a bridge between white and red cultures.

Although the fur trade at its height involved probably no more than 500 mountain men, their impact on the history of the Rocky Mountain region was profound. They were the pathfinders for the English speakers who came after them. All subsequent immigrants, settlers and miners benefitted from the knowledge of trails, Indians, geography, plants and animals that they accumulated. They knew where the fertile valleys and mountain passes were. In fact, when the fur trade died out many of them stayed on as guides on pioneer trails as or proprietors of trading posts along the way.

Mountain men have a romantic mystique. They have been called "knights in greasy buckskins" and "true American originals." According to this view, they were men who were tested by the frontier, survivors who were bolder and braver than those who never confronted the wild West. On the other hand, if the romantic gloss is removed they can be seen as ruthless and relentless exploiters of a natural resource, animal fur, without any thought for the future. They responded to the specific demands of people in the fur business, and when that business slackened they were out of work. Many of them actually became mountain men by answering advertisements for trappers in St. Louis newspapers! Even in the wildest part of the Rockies they were still dependent upon urban made or processed goods, such as knives, guns, coffee, sugar and tobacco.

Nevertheless, they did have an exotic appearance, one that the *avant garde* of the 1960's could appreciate: beads, long hair down to the shoulders, deep tans, fringed buckskin shirts, sometimes decorated with colored porcupine quills, leather pantaloons, moccasins of deer or buffalo leather, often adorned with beadwork, and the whole regalia topped by a cap of skins. When moving along fully equipped, they would be likely to carry a hatchet, knife, pistols, bullet pouch, powder horn and musket.

Their diet was truly remarkable. They were as omnivorous as grizzly bears, consuming, among other things, roasted beaver tail, lynx, puppy dogs, roots, berries, buffalo blood, buffalo liver, raw legs of unborn calves, which was regarded as a great delicacy, soup of buffalo leg bone marrow and blood, fat from buffalo hide, roasted buffalo intestines, buffalo hump, cougar meat, horse blood and some insects.

Tall tales have expanded on these gross appetites to include the ears of mules and the bodies of victims they scalped. Other tall tales involve combat with Indians and grizzly bears. Just about every mountain man had a story about a deadly struggle with a grizzly bear. One suspects that many black bears were transformed into the larger, fiercer grizzlies for their stories. There are also tales about how they laid clothes across anthills so that lice would be eaten off.

It seems that mountain men reacted to the accusation of reverting to savagery by feeding the accusation with their own exaggerations. History buffs who dress up as mountain men are likely to keep up the tradition. Coarse conversation, gross descriptions and rough humor can be expected from these imitators. Mountain men were at their worst at the rendezvous, which were really places where goods packed in from distant cities were exchanged for pelts. The location varied from year to year, but Jackson's Hole and Pierre's Hole in Wyoming were popular places to hold them. The rendezvous was also a summer festival, lasting a week or two, normally in June or July. The largest would bring 1,200 to 1,500 people together, including mountain men, friendly Indians, traders from the east, some Mexicans from the south, as well as some French Canadians from the north.

For many mountain men, the rendezvous became a wild and grand debauch, a time of heavy drinking and dangerous frontier sporting contests, such as tomahawk catching bouts that often sliced off fingers. Mountain men could spend the proceeds of a whole year's worth of effort on drink and gambling. Sometimes furious fights broke out, leading to murders. The bloodiest rendezvous on record was that at Pierre's Hole in

1832, when 38 died, largely because Blackfeet Indians arrived and clashed with rival tribesmen.

For fur company traders, the rendezvous was first and foremost a business venture. They took pelts for coffee, sugar, tobacco, traps, alcohol, powder, lead, knives, beads and cooking utensils. All of these goods were necessary for the mountain men, either directly or indirectly for trade with the Indians.

Not all of the mountain men stayed on as guides or proprietors when the beaver fur trade died. Some went on to Oregon or California to settle and others went back East to pursue ordinary careers. Some left a lasting impression with their names, such as Jacques La Ramie, a shadowy figure who was killed by Indians around 1820. His pleasant sounding name was given to a city, a county, some rivers, and a mountain range and an individual mountain. Another obscure person, David E. Jackson, gave his name to Jackson Hole, Jackson Lake and the city of Jackson. One mountain man was certainly living testimony to the diversity in background that is a feature of the history of the West: Edward Rose, a guide and trapper in Wyoming, was part white, part Cherokee Indian and part black, and eventually he was adopted into the Crow tribe.

Some other mountain men were much better known, such as Jim Bridger, who was a shrewd trader and outdoorsman who married three Indian women from three different tribes. Tales about this illiterate, tough six-footer with a keen sense of humor border upon legend. John Colter was another well-known mountain man. He traveled with Louis and Clark, and later explored and traded in the Montana and Wyoming region. When he told about the wonders of gushing, bubbling terrain and spouting geysers that he found in what became Yellowstone National Park people thought he was only telling more mountain men's tall tales. In fact, Yellowstone bore the name of "Colter's Hell" for a time.

The Cowboys

JUST WHO IS A COWBOY?

Cowboys are as important to the image of the Rocky Mountain states as the snow-capped peaks. Cowboys are symbols not just for the region but for some idealized aspects of American character. At the same time, cowboys have been commercialized from the beginning, appearing in dime novels, films, before microphones as country singers, in commercials for such diverse products as tobacco and savings and loans, and even as urbanites who can react against their environment by buying and wearing cowboy clothes. In the process, the cowboy has been transformed so often that today it is difficult to define just who is a cowboy.

"Pure" Cowboys: Consider first the purest form of contemporary cowboy, those who ride horses and work with cattle. Their actual number has decreased so drastically that a shortage of cowboys exists. Recently the immigration authorities have made exceptions to their rules by issuing extra work permits to potential cowboys from Mexico and Latin America so that they can come to work on the ranches of the Rocky Mountain states.

Ranching is much more prosaic now than when Texas longhorns were driven long distances to railheads in clouds of dust. Freeways and fences prevent cattle drives now. Today most cattle are tended and mechanically fed in fenced and malodorous feedlots, where the only mountains that must be surmounted are mountains of manure. Cowboys who still tend cattle on the range may use a pickup truck or a three wheeled

Japanese vehicle or even a small plane to check on the cattle. The essence of stock tending might consist of dropping bales of hay from trucks. Other duties are likely to include digging ditches, hauling rocks and fixing fences. While calves still have to be dehorned, branded, inoculated and castrated, most suffer these attentions nowadays in a mechanical contrivance.

Cowboys who are still fortunate to work the land on horseback still come up against the old hard realities of their craft: It is an isolated, lonely, arduous, low paid occupation. Room and board are supposed to compensate for low wages, but living conditions tend to be stark on many ranches, prompting many cowboys to follow their old tradition of moving on after a while.

These "pure" cowboys, riding horses and tending cattle, cannot be seen readily. A recent national network program questioned whether or not the cowboys were becoming a "vanishing species" in the most cowboy oriented of all the states, Wyoming, where cowboys adorn signs and license plates, are extensively used in tourist literature, and give their name to athletic teams. Wyoming is, after all, the "Cowboy State," that even has an eyeglasses emporium named "Quick Draw Optical."

It is indeed possible to drive hundreds of miles in the Rocky Mountain states without seeing a single cowboy on a horse tending cattle, although cattle, sheep and even antelope scattered across landscapes are common sights. But "pure" cowboys can suddenly appear every so often in fields along the highway, complete with stetsons, chaps, horses and cattle.

Some of them are still there, and they continue to recruit romantic and footloose individuals from other parts of the world who have been steeped in the lore of film and fiction about the wide-open spaces. A few years ago Wyoming newspapers featured stories about a former East German dockworker who was so inspired about the world of John Wayne that he was inspired to escape from his country and head for the Rockies. Another poignant story is that of a woebegone would-be cowboy from New Jersey. He and his wife arrived in a Rocky Mountain state completely dressed in Western gear. His stride was bow-legged and exaggerated, a self-conscious affectation of how he thought a cowboy should walk, and his arms swung wide. His remarks were suitably clipped and terse, but in an undeniable New Jersey accent. On one occasion soon after his arrival he whipped his guns from their holsters and blazed a lowly field mouse into oblivion.

He remained an amusing caricature of a cowboy until he started to do the real work: tending stock, riding along fences, helping to deliver calves in terrible terrain, enduring the heat, cold, rain and snow. Slowly but surely the man became what he had at first imitated, a real cowboy. The stance, the walk, the expression all became less self-conscious and more natural as he was hardened by the demands of a cowboy's job. As in the past, this work can transform young men and women from whatever background or ethnicity who are willing to take on backbreaking, exhausting and monotonous labor for long hours at very low pay. The cowboy from New Jersey provides yet another example of the human capacity to become what one does.

Other Cowboys: Various kinds of people have tried to take up the cowboy image, with varying success. Urban and suburban cowboys only need the minimum equipment of Western style clothes, including stetson and boots. A pick up truck with a gun rack would help shape the image immensely. Some would say that strongly conservative or, in the eyes of their critics, reactionary viewpoints on social issues go along with the garb. Drugstore cowboys and the now mercifully extinct disco cowboys are variations of urban-suburban cowboys.

In the Vietnam War era student bodies of Western high schools often divided into self-styled "cowboys" and "hippies," two bitterly antagonistic groups who actually came from identical or close socio-economic groups but had sharply different political orientations.

A further complication in defining who is a cowboy came from the cult of "Western chic" that sold tons of clothes in the 1970's, which were followed by urban cowboy fashion statements in the 1980's.

Besides urban and suburban cowboys, many truck drivers, construction workers, welders, oil field roughnecks and garage mechanics either consider themselves to be, or pretend to be, latter day cowboys. For horses they have trailer rigs or pick up trucks and for bunkhouses they might have mobile homes or motel rooms. These are men whose jobs are, for the most part, hard, dirty, tough and physically demanding. Often this is the only work immediately available to them.

Another kind of cowboy is the country music cowboy. Appalachian country musicians were purveyors of what was called "hillbilly music" until some of them took a conscious decision in the 1920's to show up on stage wearing big stetsons and brightly spangled pseudo-cowboy regalia. Since then hillbilly music has become country western music, carried on today by Willie Nelson and a bevy of his imitators.

Cowboy Pitchmen: The cowboy as pitchman has been around ever since advertisers realized that the public has an image of the cowboy as honest and straightforward. For a time, an elderly, folksy cowboy in a stetson appeared regularly on television urging viewers in a homespun manner to put their funds in a safe, secure savings and loan. When it sank ingloriously and suddenly, it revealed a scandalous management whose image was totally at variance with that of the kindly old cowboy.

Of course, the most famous use of cowboys in advertising is by the tobacco industry. Cowboys are shown in gorgeous settings, polluting some of the best air left in America with tobacco smoke and running the risk that their opportunity to enjoy such lovely surroundings will be curtailed by a ghastly disease.

The epitome of the convincing cowboy style may have been presented by President Ronald Reagan, who was, after all, most at home when on horseback at his ranch. His rhetoric urged America to be proud, courageous and self-reliant, the very virtues extolled by the cowboys he played so often in the movies.

Why Not 'Horseboys'? For some observers of Western life, having boots and stetson are not enough to make a man or woman into a cowboy or cowgirl. They think that a real cowboy must have a horse, even if cows to tend are not mandatory. Yet cows will always serve to enhance the intelligence of any horse in their vicinity. Since cowboys and horses can become very close when they work together, and since cattle will always be at a great spiritual distance, would it not have been more appropriate to use the term "horseboy" or "horseman?" Incidentally, the English prefer the name "drover."

Cowboys have been notorious for sentimentality over their horses to the extent that they have sung sad lamentations about their deaths. Individual horses have become famous in their own right. "High Ho Silver: Away!" was the Lone Ranger's famous cry, and faithful Tonto had his faithful "Scout." Gene Autry had "Champion" and Roy Rogers was so attached to "Trigger" that when he went to the great pasture up yonder his owner had him stuffed so that he could stay in a heroic pose for all time. (He prefers the term 'mounted.')

With perhaps one exception, there are no cows who can vie for fame with these heroic steeds. The exception is a milk producing monster named "Momma" who broke all the records for lactation at Colorado State University. When she died she was slowly lowered into a special large grave by a block and tackle at a spot marked by a headstone today.

Cowboys' horses are unbelievably cooperative in films and stories, standing around most of the time while waiting to be mounted. They are very infrequently shown being tended or excreting, circumstances that are extremely common around real horses.

On a collaborating horse, an experienced cowboy becomes a magnificent, dramatic centaur, the mythical creature that was half man and half horse. On the ground, stomping about in awkward and jangling high heeled boots, he is likely to shrink in stature.

THE ORIGIN OF THE COWBOY

While the legendary cowboy has become an all-American hero, the true origin of the cowboy is Hispanic. Although his name is English, derived from a name for cattle thieves, just about everything else concerning him is Hispanic in origin. Even the horse and the cow first came to the New World from Spain, shortly after Columbus' discoveries. The famous Texas longhorns were descendants of Spanish cattle that escaped and multiplied in the wild.

Cowboys began as an American version of the Mexican cattle drover called the *vaquero*. Their clothes and equipment are adaptations from the *vaqueros* who started work in the New

World three hundred years ago. The Spanish origin of many words that cowboys use daily reveals the link: *Las reatas,* "tie ropes," became lariats; *lazo,* or slip knot, became lasso; *chaparejos* became chaps; *rodear* is a word for roundup that became rodeo; bronc comes from *bronco,* Spanish for a rough or crude horse; mustang comes from *mesteño,* meaning wild horse; and stampede comes from *estampida.* The cowboy's broad-brimmed hat, saddle and style all have Spanish origins. So does the social status of the job. *Vaqueros* had a variety of origins and ethnicities: some were slaves; some were Indians and some were lower class European immigrants. Cowboys had a similarly varied origin: many were black; many were all or part Indian; some were Hispanic; some were drifters from the East and some were Civil War veterans from the North or from the South. All started out as poor young men, mostly vagabonds, who were willing to take up hard, dangerous work for low pay. There was nothing mystical, glamorous, symbolic or profound about their origins. They were just ordinary people, cowhands in Mexican dress.

Cowboys branched off from *vaqueros* first in Texas and New Mexico. They spread northward during the great drives of half-wild Texas longhorn cattle to the railheads in the two decades or so following the end of the American Civil War. Perhaps ten million longhorns were driven up during these decades. Some went to the northern plains and to valleys in the Rocky Mountains where the cattle business boomed. Tens of thousands of cowboys were employed in driving and tending this livestock which inherited all of the feeding grounds of the slaughtered buffalo.

Despite all of the romantic images of the cowboy as a strong individualist, or a "loner," cowboys worked in gangs, and they were ordinarily the employees of rich and powerful owners, who might be capitalists as far away as England or

Scotland. The era of the cattle barons saw many foreign and American owners carve huge grazing domains in the West, most of it on public land.

The cowboys had the task of making the land safe for the cattle barons' livestock for very little pay. To earn it, they had to do such things as fight rattlesnakes, endure hailstorms and snowstorms, halt stampedes, guard against rustlers, break wild horses and tend to equipment and animals. At one time or another Indians, sheepherders and small farmers were all perceived as threats to the profits of the cattle business and cowboys were sent forth in many instances to confront them.

Cowboys worked in isolated groups and often had to carry out lonely tasks by themselves. Their loneliness was punctuated by short periods of raucous gregariousness and wild celebrations in town. Most of the time they endured their hard life quietly. They did sing or play harmonicas as they rode around their cattle, believing that music served to keep the beasts settled down. Their music was filled with unabashed sentimentality, often maudlin and self-pitying.

The cowboy diet consisted of plain food. Steak was a staple, but it was fried well done, not broiled as it is so often prepared today. Other staples were flour, beans and coffee. Dried fruit and syrup was a simple desert. A good chuckwagon cook could make light biscuits and remarkably strong coffee.

THE ORIGIN
OF THE MYTHICAL COWBOY

It is not easy to separate the actual, historic cowboys from their mythical roles as symbolic Western heroes. The mythical cowboy probably originated in Buffalo Bill's Wild West Show which played when romanticism was so much in vogue in Europe and America. Romanticism was a complex movement, but one of its clear indicators is a heightened appreciation for the exotic. People from far away places doing strange things entranced romantic audiences. Cowboys and Indians joined mysterious Africans, Asians and Arabs as objects of romantic interest.

Buffalo Bill himself was not a cowboy, but he had excellent credentials as a Western adventurer. He had been a wagon train scout, a messenger for the cavalry and a Pony Express rider who had many close shaves. He killed a small number of Indians and a large number of buffalo. He claimed that nearly all of the buffalo that he dropped were taken for meat for pioneers and railroad builders who were moving westward.

His Wild West Show featured Indians and buffalos, but the real heroes were the cowboys, who led the parades, performed stunt riding and successfully fought with Indians in a melodrama about how the West was won.

The show ran for 30 years, enthralled Europeans, inspired a flood of tourists to visit the West, and led to the beginning of what would become the enormous pulp Western fiction industry. It also elevated the stature of the cowboy to that of the great heroic symbol of civilization in a savage environment.

Over time, he became the most American of Americans. He was a frontiersman who was courageous; he was kind, capable, plain spoken, honest, a hard worker, an achiever without pretensions, a man of action who was fearless and willing to use force skillfully for righteous causes. He was also a free wanderer, always likely to ride off into the sunset after setting things right. Against a background of natural grandeur, the cowboy tamed the wilderness and made it safe, battling with bad men, wild horses, and nature's perils.

Seen thus, the cowboy was the last noble and heroic figure of the frontier, living where civilization ended and the wild began and facing challenges with capability, boldness, strength and virtue. After him, the West was tame and peaceful and the frontier was no more. Such is the myth.

The transformation of the wrangler to the mythical hero was only started by the Wild West Show. Dime novels carried it on. A milestone was reached by the publication of Owen Wister's *Virginian* in 1902, the first full length heroic cowboy novel. His stoic wanderer inspired hundreds of other authors, and thereby thousands of other novels and short stories.

A vast number of them were transferred to the screen. Most middle aged Americans came to appreciate the mythical cowboy from movies. In the 1920's, 30's and 40's film cowboys were usually courageous, soft spoken, often bashful but above all extraordinarily good fellows. While being quite chaste, they were able to deliver a number of women from the jaws of deadly peril. Some of them were singing cowboys who wore flashy clothes. Then John Wayne towered on the screen and created a classic cowboy who could do naughty, earthy things but was solidly good inside. There were other classic images: What heroes could have been more noble than Gary Cooper in "High Noon," or "Shane," either in the novel or the film?

Classic old-fashioned Western films had their own odd conventions. The hero had to be handsome and win over the prettiest girl. The wicked inevitably got shot and died remarkably antiseptic, quick, neat deaths. No worthwhile cowboy ever shot a horse or a bystander by accident and no matter how lengthy their fist fights, cowboy heroes recovered very quickly without suffering broken jaws, broken noses, lost teeth or badly cut faces. Usually only their hair was mussed and their fallen hats might have gotten dusty. While horses were everywhere in these films, the cows with which cowboys were supposed to be occupied are nowhere to be seen. Above all, the good and the bad were boldly displayed in these classic films, without ambiguity, clear and unmistakable.

A theme that emerged from these films was that cowboys had to be on the move. Cowboy heroes acted out the American urge to wander when they appeared as mysterious figures "just passing through." Many of them were capable loners who would use violence when properly provoked. When the gunsmoke cleared and the situations were set to right, the mysterious cowboy would ride away. Where? Towards the sunset, of course. Cowboy heroes and the traditional frontier both moved towards the sunset, further West where new adventures and opportunities beckon.

Classic Western films reached their peak of popularity in the 1940's and 1950's, although people suffering through the depression in the 1930's enjoyed them also. In recent years there have been a number of rather melancholy films dealing with the difficulties faced by cowboy loners in a West with its frontier and wildness gone who have been appropriately amoral, bitter and troubled. Meanwhile, classic Western films have been eclipsed by action films emphasizing policemen and urban criminals instead of cowboys and frontier villains.

Most recently a new image of the cowboy has emerged that is shorn of all of its mythical characteristics. The cowboy is seen by militant environmentalists as an ecological threat, the agent of overgrazing, who causes wildlife to disappear and grassland to turn to desert. What is more, his commercial operation is subsidized by the Federal Government because public land is rented out to grazing concerns at a much cheaper rate than the rate offered by private owners.

COWBOYS AND WOMEN
AND WOMEN AS COWHANDS

Actual, historic cowboys usually encountered two distinct kinds of Victorian women. One kind was the women of easy access, prostitutes who doubled as or who were euphemistically called dance hall girls. Most of these women were drifters like the cowboys themselves. Romantic writers would have their readers believe that some of them had hearts of gold, but in reality most were hardened and brutalized by what usually was a rough and dangerous profession in the West or anywhere. Cowboys would drink and cavort with these women during their sporadic "blowouts" in town, ignoring the classic admonitions of old hands that hard liquor, cards and such women were all dangerous for the lonely cowhand.

The other kind of Victorian women cowboys encountered were on pedestals, like Southern belles, but different from the idle and idealized Southern women in that they had to work hard in the West, taking on many responsibilities that men would claim elsewhere. These Western women were the wives, mothers and daughters of settlers, ranchers and townspeople who were raised to be virgin brides and chaste homemakers in conformity with the strict Victorian standards of sexual morality. In a region where men traditionally outnumbered women, this kind of Victorian female was especially prized and admired by cowboys. Their presence was likely to alter cowboys' behavior and curtail their discourse considerably. Films made much of how cowboys were shy and awkward around such proper women, although cowboys would always be willing to risk their lives for them when something or someone threatened them.

Western women in the era of the cowboy have tended to project capable, plain spoken, blunt, no frills, no nonsense personalities who savored ironic humor. They have not disappeared in the West today. Ranches all over the region have women who do everything on them. Some are daughters who have inherited spreads and who want to keep them going.

Western heroines were modeled on the capable, confident, skilled women that the region was noted for producing. One of the first of the Western heroines was Pheoebe Ann Moses, alias Annie Oakley, who appeared in Buffalo Bill's Wild West Show, delighting audiences with her spectacular marksmanship and striking Western garb. Alas, she was from Ohio!

For a long time "cowgirls" fully participated in all events in rodeos, including roping and bulldogging, which is the sport of wrestling a steer to the ground by twisting its neck. It seems that some male promoters feared that the cowgirls' performances detracted from the rough and tough image of the cowboys, and so women were relegated to the tamer events, such as barrel riding contests and flag bearing in fancy costume parades. Cowgirls also appeared as rodeo queens and queen's attendants, whose occupation seems to consist only of riding around the arena waving and smiling at the audience.

Myths also developed about cowgirls. They became chaste glamour girls in the 1920 to 1940 period, after which they became more sexual. Any standard Western film had the convention that good men are better shots than bad men and good men get the girl in the end. Yet it should be noted that major confrontations in Western films are not between men and women, as they are in so many romantic movies. In Westerns men confront each other while women usually wait patiently for the outcome of their struggles, a pattern similar to the mating rituals of many large mammals.

OUTLAWS AND VIOLENCE

Cowboys as Gunslingers: Anthropologists point out that literate and preliterate cultures have myths about themselves that explain who they are and justify what they have done. In many ways, the mythical cowboy allows Americans to glorify the fast and furious conquest of Mexican and Indian territory. Mythical cowboys have also set an ideal of masculinity, just as the samurai have set an ideal for the Japanese and the medieval knight has for Western Europeans.

All of these mythical ideal figures are adept at using their own specialized form of violent behavior when challenged by evil. The mythical cowboy reinforces the American conviction that they must be willing to fight for peace, something they have taken up all over the globe in this century. It is interesting to note that when foreigners fear that an American leader is rash and trigger happy they are likely to call him a "cowboy."

Of course, films have exaggerated the cowboy's need for guns. In the actual circumstances of ranch work, guns were likely to be used very rarely, perhaps to make a distant signal or to put a crippled animal out of its misery, uses which did not require any expert marksmanship.

Perhaps one of the least beneficial aspects of the mythical cowboy is that he has glorified guns and gunplay. A number of gun magazines in the United States feature the heroic mythical cowboy. Fast draw competitions and reenactments of gunfights are popular attractions in the region. Consider the "Gunslinger Gunfights" put on in Cheyenne, Wyoming, from early June through mid-August at 6 p.m. weekdays and at high noon on weekends and some celebration days. "Get Them Hombres!!!!" the advertisements declare before pointing out that the "Gunslingers" are an organization dedicated to "fun" whose "excess funds" will go to charity. They admit that they are not "entirely authentic" but that they do "provide entertainment." They encourage tourists to "live the Old West" by rubbing "elbows with gunfighters and cowboys," and guarantee that the bad fellows will always lose in their reenactments.

Laughter, shouts, cheers and clapping go on while grown men play as children and shoot blanks. The antiseptic deaths of the bad guys in the recreations are similar to those on television and in the older, classic films. The ghastly business that bullets do on viscera and bone and the bloody, ugly, painful realities of violent death by gunshot are omitted, naturally. Undoubtedly the gleeful audience at these reenactments would be horrified at the modern equivalent of a Western shootout, a drive by shooting in Los Angeles or Washington, D.C.

Recent historical research shows that gunplay in the West has been highly overemphasized and romanticized. Most real gunplay took place on what people would call the "wrong side of the tracks" and only about a third of those who were shot to death ever returned fire. In fact, many were not even carrying arms when they were gunned down. On the right side of the tracks disputes were handled by those gunslingers of words, lawyers, who settled most matters in the West in their time honored manner which is almost invariably slow and expensive on the draw. Also, when dealing with disputes over land, mining claims, fences, water rights or horses, it is often very hard to tell the good guys from the bad guys, then or now.

There is much more violence in American cities today than there ever was in the Old West, including some of the cities of the New West. Murders, shootings, stabbings, rapes and beatings go on at alarming rates. Of all the major industrialized nations, the United States has the worst statistics on violence. The extent to which the highly exaggerated and romantic treatment of the gunplay and violence of the Old West has contributed to these appalling circumstances will never be known.

Western Outlaws, Vigilantes and Lawmen: Romantic myths have so heavily disguised Western outlaws that they appear as dashing and witty as Robert Redford playing the Sundance Kid. Outlaws' hangouts, such as Robbers' Roost in Montana and the Hole in the Wall in central Wyoming, attract great interest. Books on outlaws sell remarkably well.

At best, the outlaws of the Old West were ill-educated, impulsively violent bullies and at worst they might have been sociopaths and psychotic killers who inflicted pain and suffering on innocent people.

Contemporaries felt that they knew what to do with outlaws. When possible, they rooted them out like varmints and hung or shot them as quickly as possible. In doing so, they resorted to "taking the law into their own hands." Vigilante groups, bands of armed citizens, hung many persons who did not conform to the expected norms of behavior in frontier society, including many despicable criminals. Yet the problem with vigilante justice is that it is likely to be too hasty, pushed along as it is by popular passions. When applied, their justice was absolute. Vigilantes in the saddle, with guns and ropes at the ready, were hardly prone to presume anyone innocent until proven guilty, or apply any other constitutional safeguards for criminal justice. Their mistakes or indulgence in excesses could never be reversed.

The sheriff and the posse are two of the most outstanding transfers from the old Anglo-Saxon frontier in England to the American West. If they were honest, sheriffs worked to ensure that violent people who had or who could hire those with the best hand and eye coordination did not have their own way. If they were dishonest, they became the tools of local power brokers.

It is extremely difficult for Americans to abandon their heroic images of the cowboys who wore the tin stars and contributed to the traditional "winning of the West." These were the brave men who were supposed to put themselves at the edge between civilization and savagery. Can Gary Cooper, a quiet, civil man who puts on the star in "High Noon" be dismissed? Think of him striding down main street in stark black and white, all alone against a group of ruthless outlaws who arrive when both the little hand and the big hand point straight up. His only help came from Grace Kelly, who shot one of the outlaws in the back, a remarkable feat for the Quaker lady she played.

Wyoming: Places Mentioned in the Text

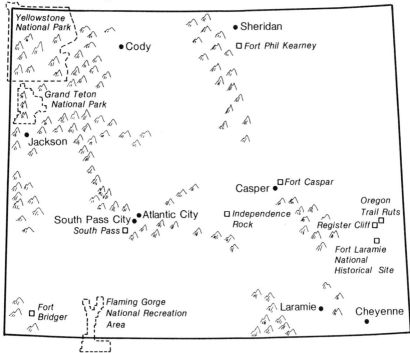

CHAPTER SEVEN

WONDERFUL WYOMING

What is Special About Wyoming

Wyoming is a large, raw, windy slab of high plateau graced by gorgeous mountains in the northwest. It is the least populated and the least industrialized state in the union. There are far more cattle and sheep than humans, and, as the state tourist industry boasts, Wyoming has plenty of real cowboys, Indians, ranches, wide open spaces, and rich wildlife, much of it in magnificent National Parks.

Wyoming's statistics confirm some of these generalizations: It is the eighth largest state in the country, with 97,809 square miles, but it has only approximately 450,000 people, which yields a density of only 4.6 per square mile. Its largest city, Cheyenne, has 49,000 people; its next largest, Casper, 44,700. Other cities which are prominent on state maps have populations which would only yield the status of town elsewhere. Also, 52% of Wyoming is owned and controlled by the federal government. Another interesting statistic is that only 3% of Wyomingites are employed in manufacturing.

All of this means that Wyoming has much to offer visitors from the more crowded and more industrialized parts of the country. Indeed, the classic phrase: "It's a nice place to visit but I wouldn't want to live there" fits Wyoming exactly, judging by the number of people who show up yearly compared to the number that stay. Most people have found Wyoming too high, dry, windy and cold for year round residence. Although hundreds of thousands of people went through Wyoming on pioneer trails, worked in Wyoming on building railroads, highways, and exploiting natural resources, very few sank roots. Most people who came to Wyoming were either on their way to a more promising land or ready to leave when their jobs terminated. Now millions of tourists arrive and depart, with few having plans to relocate to this vacationland.

Nearly all of Wyoming is better suited for grazing than for plowing. The soil is thin and the mean elevation of 6,700 feet, higher than any state except Colorado, guarantees a cool climate. Snow falls from November until May, but overall precipitation is so light that the state is semi-arid, except for the high mountain ranges at the upper corners of the state. Unfortunately, some of the precipitation that falls annually along an eastern section of Wyoming is in the form of destructive hail. For all of these reasons, gray-green grass continues to cover most of the state, as it has for ages.

Wyoming features a number of rodeos and pageants in the summer, has first-class skiing in some locations in the winter, offers exceptional fishing most of the year and has outstanding hunting in the fall. Its numerous dude ranches vary from plush resorts to ordinary working ranches. Wyoming boasts of a "real Western welcome where no man (and one may presume woman also) is a stranger."

Wyoming calls itself "the Cowboy State," uses the image of a cowboy on a bucking bronco on its license plates, billboards and advertisements. As might be expected, the University of Wyoming's football team goes by the name of "Cowboys." Yet ironically, there is such a shortage of real cowboys that ranchers must advertise for them outside of the state and outside of the country. To promote the image of the Cowboy State, chambers of commerce have been known to urge citizens to wear western clothes regularly, and one town insisted upon nailing down old style wooden sidewalk planks over a perfectly good concrete sidewalk. Regardless of such aberrations, Wyoming's appeal as a rural cowboy state is quite genuine.

Wyoming is conservative in politics and lifestyles. The easiest way to get into a hot argument anywhere in the state is to suggest any measure of gun control. Wyoming legislators are noted for preaching the benefits of simple government, balanced budgets, the work ethic and self reliance. They are also so enamored with development that they are traditionally highly reluctant to impose restrictions on the developers. The population is quite homogenous also, with less than 1% of the population black and only 5.2% Hispanic. The census also lists 2.9% as 'other,' and in Western states this usually encompasses a large number of Native Americans. Whites make up over 96% of Wyoming's population.

Ironically, Wyomingites view the federal government with great suspicion and exercise this view by regularly sending conservatives to Congress. This is ironic, since over half of the state is owned by the federal government and federal money is pumped into it regularly for such things as maintaining the national parks, monuments and forests, reclamation projects, and defense installations. Indeed, the largest international ballistic missile base in the world is located in the desolate area around Cheyenne, and manned by personnel from nearby Warren Air Force Base. While these grim silos are reminders of the Cold War, they also serve to mark some of the vast outpouring of federal funds into this sparsely populated region.

Powerful local interest groups have dominated the Wyoming legislature over the years, thereby insuring its conservatism and its hostility to most of the operations of the federal government not pertaining to putting money into the state.

The Wyoming Stock Growers' Association and various oil, railroad and mining companies have all asserted powerful influence over legislators historically. So it is no wonder that it has been very difficult to tax the extraction of natural resources. Although Wyoming has one of the highest per capita tax burdens in the nation, there are no state income or corporation taxes.

Despite the infusion of federal funds, Wyoming has, like many other Western states, a feeling that it is a colony of the distant power and population centers of America, whose banks and corporations draw out Wyoming's raw materials in the form of meat, wool, coal, natural gas, oil and uranium ore with considerable profit to them and with little profit for Wyoming's inhabitants. Some feel that this state of affairs is responsible for the drain of Wyoming's youth out of the state in all but boom times.

Wyoming's economy has never been diversified sufficiently to hold them when the extractive industries have sagged. Booms and busts have always tended to alternate in that important sector of the Western economy. Just recently, from the late 1960's to 1980, Wyoming had a spectacular boom resulting from the demand for energy. Cheaper foreign oil brought a bust in the eighties. In the boom years, Wyoming had a growth rate that was temporarily steeper than that of Florida, but since 1980 the population has declined, unemployment has risen and the use of food stamps has gone up. If oil prices soar again and oil shale is heavily exploited, Wyoming may see a boom that will match or exceed any previous boom. Yet the question remains open about how much of the new wealth will stay in Wyoming and how much will be drawn out of the state to the centers of corporate America.

Highlights of Wyoming History

Wyoming's earliest history, like that of the other states in the region, involved the struggles of various Indian tribes for territory. Indians regarded Wyoming as an excellent hunting ground for buffalo, elk and antelope. French speaking and then English speaking fur trappers explored and exploited the region. They were followed by pioneers who used Wyoming as a thoroughfare to more promising locations, namely Oregon and California. The Mormons also passed through on their way to Utah. Wyoming is exceptional for having more historic trails than any other state, and many substantial portions of them are highly visible, unspoiled and sometimes quite dramatic. See the section "Along the Oregon Trail" in this chapter for details.

Perhaps only Montana can rival Wyoming for having dramatic episodes of the Indian wars. See the section on "Battle Sites of the Indian Wars." There was also a gold rush. The section on South Pass and its ghost towns has details.

Wyoming, name and all, was created arbitrarily by people outside the area. The Wyoming Territory was hacked off from other Western territories, Dakota, Utah and Idaho, and its few residents had to organize themselves in what was a leftover region. While its name was indeed of Indian origin, the tribe that provided it was the Delaware Indians, and their reference to "where the plains end" or "at the big plains" was originally given to a stretch of northeastern Pennsylvania. United States Senators thought it sounded nice and applied it without consulting the few non-Indians resident in the new territory.

Eventually, these people were able to choose the official nickname, "the Equality State" in recognition of their truly remarkable achievement of being the first place in America to grant women the right to vote in all elections, hold office and sit on juries.

This advance in democracy came first to a distant, wind-swept part of America because of peculiar local circumstances. The root problem was a shortage of women. Women's right to vote was passed in 1869, when women in the territory were outnumbered six to one. By 1890 the ratio had dropped to three to one, but even as late as 1930 there were seven men for every five women. Women's suffrage was actually promoted to lure more women into the territory so that a better balance between the sexes and therefore a greater number of families would be fostered, which would eventually raise the population sufficiently to allow the territory to become a state. At the time there was a surplus of women on the East Coast and a shortage of women throughout the West. So, in granting the right to vote and hold office to women for the first time in the United States, the Wyoming territorial legislators were boosting Wyoming's prospects for statehood in a place where there was no risk of losing male dominance.

It was easier to take this advanced step in a territory than in a state because it needed only a majority of the legislature to vote to enfranchise women. By contrast, a state would need a constitutional amendment, and this required a two-thirds majority.

Today a statue of Wyoming's first female office holder, Esther Morris, graces the U.S. Capitol's Statuary Hall as Wyoming's most outstanding deceased citizen. Called the "mother of women's suffrage," she was elected Justice of the Peace for South Pass City, and had brought some influence to bear on the legislature to pass women's suffrage. Wyoming is also distinguished for having elected the first woman state legislator and the first woman governor, who must share that honor of 1924 with a woman governor of Texas. Wyoming's female governor was what some call an "Evita," meaning that she was elected to fill out her deceased husband's term.

Despite these initial breakthroughs, the subsequent record for gender equality in Wyoming has not been exceptional. After appearing on juries in 1870 and 1871, women were not called again until 1950, except for cases where women were to be tried. Also, a smaller percentage of women have been elected to serve in the state legislature than in many other states.

The building of the transcontinental railroad through Wyoming was a unique circumstance because it was the first time that the construction of a railway preceded rather than followed the creation of a new territory. The railroad provided a decisive turning point in Wyoming history as it built up a series of communities along the southern tier of what became the state; fostered coal mining to supply its fuel; brought in diverse people from Europe and Asia and made cattle ranching profitable. Once the trains were running, cattle could be shipped from Wyoming grassland to distant markets much more cheaply than the old way, which was to drive them to faraway railheads.

Not all of the markets were far. The army posts, Indian reservations, railroad towns and Colorado mines all bought Wyoming beef. From 1870 to 1890, massive open range cattle ranching took over, with cattle eating the nutritious grass that used to feed great herds of buffalo. Each head of cattle took a minimum of 20 acres of the better grazing land and 130 acres of the poorest. As large operations came to cover thousands of acres, a group of powerful cattle barons emerged, some of whom were absentees, living as far away as the East Coast or in Great Britain. Others lived in towns like Cheyenne and patronized exclusive clubs where cowboys were not welcome.

Cattle barons overstocked the open range and in a series of fierce winters the cattle industry suffered severe losses.

Homesteaders and small ranchers who fenced lands roused the cattle barons' wrath and some violent struggles broke out, including the notorious "Johnson County War." The famous Western novel and film, "Shane," is based upon such a conflict.

As the sheep raising developed, herdsmen ran sheep up into mountainous areas in the summer and down into the valleys in the winter. Some cattlemen loathed sheep, claiming that they, unlike cattle, pulled up and destroyed the grass they grazed upon and fouled water holes used by both species of animals. Sometimes cattlemen clubbed sheep to death and sometimes the sheepherders were killed also. To this day lamb and mutton are scorned in some cattle raising areas. On the other hand, some ranchers run both animals on their spreads.

Once these range wars were over, violence broke out in industrial relations. When strikes occurred on the Union Pacific, the railroad fired the striking workers, imported cheap help and called for federal troops to put down the discontented.

When Chinese workers who would take lower pay and shun union membership were imported in large numbers, hostility towards them became ferocious, culminating in the notorious "Rock Springs Massacre" of 1885 when 28 Chinese workers were killed. The situation was resolved only when the federal government suspended Chinese immigration.

Regardless of ethnic origin, when workers were killed or maimed in accidents in Wyoming, there was no compensation from either the company or the state until 1908, and even then only paltry sums were paid. The workers' cynical conclusion was that the Union Pacific valued a mule more than a man.

Oil and gas companies were also not known for their compassion or for their civic concerns. Oil originally oozed from the ground in a few places and was used by pioneers to lubricate their wagons' axle joints. Up to the 1950's, natural gas was treated like a hindrance to pumping oil and was simply

burned off in a wasteful process called "flaring." It was extremely difficult to compel companies to pay even a small severance
tax on the oil and gas they extracted for the profit of mostly
distant corporations. Many stockmen with influence in the state
legislature were the recipients of royalties from these same
companies for pumping oil and gas on their lands.

Although oil and gas operations in Wyoming were capital
intensive rather than labor intensive, gangs of a new kind of
Western type appeared, the roustabouts, who were the heirs of
the cowboys and free trappers. Like their colorful earlier
counterparts, these Wyoming roustabouts worked at hard,
dangerous jobs for comparatively low pay in the oilfields while
distant, powerful organizations profited from the fruits of their
labor.

Some Scenic Highlights

NATIONAL PARKS

Wyoming has two kinds of scenery: wide open windy
spaces and beautiful mountain ranges. The wide open spaces
predominate in the southern part of the state and the best of
the mountain scenery is in the upper western corner, the
location of Yellowstone and Grand Teton National Parks. In
fact, this area possesses two of the most beautiful views in the
United States: the magnificent Teton Mountains viewed from
across Jackson Lake or Jenny Lake, and the lower falls of the
Yellowstone River with the Grand Canyon of the Yellowstone
in the foreground.

Yellowstone is an amazing, almost surrealistic, National
Park. The molten interior of the earth is so close to the surface

in this place that it spawns two-thirds of all of the geysers in the world, mud volcanoes, and 10,000 hot springs. Most of the park consists of a high volcanic plateau rimmed by mountain ranges. The park encompasses 3,472 square miles and draws several million visitors each year. An elaborate system of paved two-lane highways goes all through the park, making it possible for "windshield tourists" to see many of the sights through the glass or on short walks from a convenient parking lots.

Lodges and campsites are liberally scattered throughout the park, but in the peak season they are almost guaranteed to be full to overflowing. Arrangements need to be made in advance with the National Park Service at 307-344-7381.

Wildlife is abundant. Binoculars are very helpful for gazing upon substantial numbers of elk, bison and antelope. Unfortunately, binoculars are not needed to see the bears most of the time. They come too close sometimes, looking for handouts. As pointed out in the section on wildlife, feeding wild animals is foolish.

Controversies about the use and abuse of Yellowstone National Park abound. One group wants to limit access in order to cut the number of visitors down, while another wants to provide more amenities and lodging. Already famous Old Faithful geyser seems to be in an urban setting, surrounded at each blast by throngs of visitors, and behind them rises a backdrop of buildings to cater to them. A recent flap has concerned the degree to which snowmobiles can be accommodated. People who have truly appreciated the silent, snow-laden mountains of Yellowstone have little difficulty in finding their stand on this issue. A few years ago Yellowstone's burning issue, literally, was whether or not to allow forest fires to renew areas of the park naturally or to intervene, terminating them before too much damage was done. Most recently a plan to reintroduce wolves in order to keep the numbers of hoofed animals in check had fearful neighboring stockmen up in arms.

Grand Teton National Park, just below Yellowstone, is quite different. It has only 485 square miles, but its mountains soar to 13,770 feet. They are truly spectacular, so spectacular that they inspired French trappers to name three of them the three breasts, *les trois tetons*. Can there be a higher Gallic accolade for scenery than that?

Unlike Yellowstone, thermal features are not prominent. Instead there are a dozen glaciers and many beautiful lakes, all providing gorgeous settings for abundant wildlife.

Jackson Hole, an old fur trappers' rendezvous, is a 400 square mile valley right by the park. It has become the base of a fabulous ski area. The town of Jackson, a few miles to the south of the park, is like other glitzy tourist centers to be found on the edges of several national parks. It tries, like other places, to evoke an old West atmosphere with log buildings and false fronts.

WYOMING'S TRULY WIDE OPEN SPACES

Wyoming is one of the best states for experiencing the wide open spaces of the American West. With ranches often 50 to 100 miles apart, and real estate developers nowhere in sight, at least in many places, Wyoming is the place to capture the feeling of openness and loneliness that the pioneers must have felt. In fact, Wyoming has often been called a lonesome land. Just scan part of the high, empty, blue green plateau in a chill wind to capture this feeling.

The national parks and the scenic roads are not the places to sense the big emptiness of Wyoming. Instead, go across the plateau on such roads as U.S. 26 or State Route 220, or U.S. 287 and State Route 28. The main Interstate Highways, 80 going east-west, and Interstate 25 going north-south, have too much traffic to give much of a sense of lonely isolation, although by the standards of the East Coast they are remarkably scenic and lightly traveled.

OTHER SCENIC AREAS

Wyoming has been called a state where mountains are never out of view. Actually, Wyoming has no spine or backbone of mountains such as that which goes through Colorado. Instead the middle and eastern part of the state is a high plateau, which is almost constantly subjected to strong winds because systems from the Pacific and Arctic find less resistance moving across it than over mountains to the north and south of it.

The scenic Medicine Bow Mountains are in the southeast and can be traversed on State Route 130. The Bighorn Mountains are in the north-central part of the state. Both U.S. Route 14 and U.S. 16 reveal some of the beauty of the Bighorn Range.

Flaming Gorge: Flaming Gorge National Recreation Area is typical of so much in the new West, a combination of gorgeous scenery and artificial water management. Originally it was a brilliant red gorge of the Green River. Today a 500 foot dam has backed up water to form a 90 mile lake with 375 miles of shoreline, all surrounded by the great multi-colored rocky cliffs that soar skyward for up to 1,500 feet.

The area is well supplied with campgrounds and boat ramps, most reached on a 160 mile loop drive around the 200,000 acre area. It is best reached from Route 530 south from Green River, Wyoming. Since part of the area extends into Utah, fishermen need a special use stamp if they wish to fish in both states.

The Visitor Center at the Red Canyon Vista is well worth a visit, especially for the view, which is guaranteed to exhaust the superlatives in one's vocabulary quickly.

Flaming Gorge was completed rather recently. The dam was begun in 1957 and the recreation area was set aside in 1968, serving as another example of how federal dollars have transformed the West.

Some Special Places in Wyoming

BATTLE SITES OF THE INDIAN WARS

Everybody knows about Custer's last stand at the battle of Little Big Horn in Montana. The scene of this hopelessly outnumbered and surrounded force bravely fighting on until death at the hands of swarms of fast moving Indians has been etched on the national consciousness. What is often not known is that there were several similar occurrences, one of which was Wyoming's Fetterman Massacre.

Indians in what later became several Rocky Mountain states were aroused by the ghastly massacre of Cheyennes and some Arapahos at Sand Creek, Colorado, in 1864, under the leadership of the unstable Colonel Chivington. Thereafter these Plains Indians, along with the Sioux, harassed emigrants, robbed and destroyed installations such as the new telegraph stations and launched full scale attacks on small emigrant wagon trains. When they could, they wiped out small detachments of U.S. troops but generally fled from large forces.

The Fetterman Massacre took place close to Fort Phil Kearney, the remains of which are just south of Sheridan, Wyoming. This fort and two others were built to protect the infamous Bozeman Trail, a shortcut to the gold fields of Virginia City, Montana, established in 1863, when the American Civil War was raging. It departed from the North Platte at Douglas, Wyoming, and stretched 500 miles northwest to Virginia City, Montana, skirting the Bighorn Mountains on the way. The Bozeman Trail cut right through the last and best of the Sioux and Cheyenne hunting grounds, land guaranteed to the Indians by treaty. Incidentally, the Sioux and Cheyenne had wrested these lands from the Crow Indians not long before, at a time when the Crow thought that the best way to preserve their hold in the region was to ally with the white intruders.

The Indians decided to fight for their guaranteed hunting grounds by attacking traffic along the Bozeman Trail. As wagon trains were attacked, soldiers from the new forts made efforts to protect them and were in turn attacked when it was tactically advantageous for the Indians to do so.

Historians estimate that the Indian wars were fought more fiercely in this part of northern Wyoming than anyplace else in the West. As a result, the Bozeman trail and the forts guarding it were abandoned because it was just too costly to maintain, particularly after the Montana boom slackened.

The best place to investigate some of these battle scenes is from the site of Fort Phil Kearney where the Wyoming State Historical Society operates an informative Visitor Center in the summer months. Not a building of the fort remains, so imagination is required, both at the fort and at the Fetterman and

Wagon Box battlefields nearby. Good directions are readily supplied.

Like Custer, Fetterman was rash and overconfident. When woodcutters near the fort were besieged by a band of Indians in December, 1866, Fetterman marched forth with eighty one mixed cavalry and infantry to relieve the woodcutters. When the Indians retreated, Fetterman pressed on in pursuit, against the orders of his commanding officer which had been issued to him when he left the fort.

Fetterman had been decoyed by legendary chief Crazy Horse of the Oglala Sioux, who was then a young and brilliant warrior. Soon Fetterman blundered into a vast number of Sioux, Cheyenne and Arapaho warriors who wiped out his whole force and then stripped and mutilated the corpses. Just ten years later Custer would also charge right into an over-whelming number of Indians. Unfortunately, Custer did not learn from Fetterman's fate.

One hero emerged from the disaster. Those left at Fort Kearney, including many women and children, feared that their stronghold would be overwhelmed by the victorious Indians. "Portugee" Phillips volunteered to carry news of the massacre and the dangerous situation to distant Fort Laramie, where reinforcements could be mustered. His desperate four-day ride of 236 miles, mostly through hostile territory and in fierce winter weather, became an epic of courage and endurance, one of the most heroic rides in American history.

Indians were less successful a year later when they attacked a train of wood hauling wagons whose civilian crew was protected by a force of 32 troops. The soldiers circled the wagons, just as they do in the movies, and knocked off the wheels. They fired at attacking Indians from behind the circled wagons for three hours after which the Indians retreated. These tactics and new fast-firing Springfield breechloading rifles saved them. They killed a substantial number of Indians while losing very few of their own men.

Eventually, the massacred Captain Fetterman gave his name to another Wyoming fort, which is located to the south, on the Platte River, eleven miles northwest of Douglas, Wyoming. Fort Fetterman was built in 1867 and abandoned in 1882. Today two original buildings remain, and one of them houses a museum. Because of its exposed position to raw weather, Fort Fetterman was regarded as a hardship post by soldiers. The fort's desertion rate broke records. Fort Fetterman is open from May 15 until Labor Day, 9:00 a.m. to 6:00 p.m.

CODY AND THE BUFFALO BILL HISTORICAL CENTER

Cody is due east of Yellowstone National Park on Highway 14, which goes through beautiful stretches of the Shoshone National Forest. Cody's chief attraction is the Buffalo Bill Historical Center, which has much more to offer than the Buffalo Bill Museum, which is primarily a collection of the photographs, trophies, guns, saddles, stuffed buffaloes and other memorabilia and accoutrements of the great Western showman and self-advertised adventurer. The Center also houses the Whitney Gallery of Western Art, exhibiting works of famous artists of the American West, such as Bierstadt and Remington and the works of many lesser known artists as well. There is also a Plains Indian Museum where the culture of the Sioux, Cheyenne, Shoshone, Crow, Arapaho and Blackfeet is exhibited through extensive displays of costumes, tools and weapons. Most recently the Winchester Gun Museum has been added, a display of literally thousands of guns.

Taken together, these four major museums and galleries comprise what has been called the most comprehensive collection dealing with the West. Visitors can spend hours in the modern, spacious, attractive corridors of the Center and learn a great deal about the historical West in the process. The Buffalo Bill Historical Center is open daily and has extended hours from June to August, 7 a.m. to 10 p.m. During the rest of the year hours are more restricted. Call 307-587-4711 for further information.

The economic life of this town of less than 8,000 is geared to the constant flow of tourists heading to and from Yellowstone in the summer months. Cody is the "gateway to Yellowstone" because any visitor using the east entrance has to pass through Cody. This was actually the original purpose of the area's development in the 1890's, when Buffalo Bill himself was brought to inspect it by its developers. He was enthusiastic, and gladly lent his already famous name to the new town. He also built his Irma Hotel, which still retains some of its turn of the century atmosphere for its guests.

One mile west of Cody is Old Trail Town, consisting of a collection of largely unimproved historic buildings brought from various places on the Wyoming frontier, including a cabin from the infamous "Hole in the Wall" outlaw hideout.

SHERIDAN AND THE TRAIL END HISTORIC CENTER

Sheridan, now a town of just over 14,000, was founded in the late 1870's on what was up until then Indian land. From the beginning it was a peaceful, spacious, ranch oriented community. When the railroad arrived in 1892, a large hotel with many gables, the Sheridan Inn, was built to resemble a large Scottish country inn. Among the famous guests who have stayed in it have been Theodore Roosevelt, Will Rogers and Buffalo Bill Cody. Cody was remembered for recruiting cowboys and Indians for his famous Wild West Show while sitting on its front porch.

Another famous historic building in Sheridan is now the property of the Wyoming State Historical Society. Its name now is the Trail End Historic Center, but it was long known as the mansion of John B. Kendrick, who was both rich and famous by the turn of the century. Kendrick's career is the epitome of the Western version of the American dream. He began as a cowpuncher, driving a herd of cattle from Texas to Wyoming in the late 1870's. While his cohorts drank, gambled and caroused, Kendrick doggedly educated himself. When he became a ranch foreman he not only built up his own private herd, but married the rancher's daughter. Accumulation continued, until Kendrick had hundreds of thousands of acres and millions of dollars. Politics was next: Kendrick became governor of Wyoming in 1913 and three-time senator from the state thereafter. It was he who called for an investigation of the Teapot Dome oil field operation, which lead to an expose of one of the worst scandals of the 1920's.

His mansion is a prime example of a great display of imported opulence, the kind of display characteristic of the very rich around the turn of the century on the East Coast and in Europe, but extremely ostentatious in the West since so many items were entirely new to the region, often requiring importation and assembly at premium cost. For example, dozens of boxcars were filled just with paneling for the house. Other boxcars brought in decorations and fixtures for the house, so that eight bathrooms, a paneled library and a third floor ballroom could be outfitted. The exterior was built in an architectural style that was absolutely unique in the area: Flemish! It even has a red tile roof. The house was completed in 1913, one year before World War One began. Its name derived from the owner's wish to have it be the end of his long and romantic trail from the life of a cowboy to that of a rich and famous political leader.

Trail End Historic Center is well worth a visit for its rich atmosphere. The staff is very pleasant and helpful. It is open in the afternoons from Labor Day to Memorial Day and from 9a.m. to 5 p.m. in the summer season. The phone is 307-674-4589 or 307-777-7014.

WYOMING'S MAJOR CITIES: CHEYENNE, LARAMIE AND CASPER

Some say that Wyoming would be much better off if the attributes of its three largest cities, Cheyenne, at 49,000, Laramie, at 26,400, and Casper, at 44,700, were all combined. Cheyenne is the capital, housing state and federal bureaucracies; Laramie is something of a cultural center, since it has the only state university; and Casper is a business and industrial center, so crucially important to the oil industry that it has been called the Tulsa of Wyoming. All three cities have low skylines and spacious but somewhat depressed looking core areas.

None of these cities gives the impression of being anything more than a large provincial town. Their old-fashioned appearance, wide streets, slow pace and ample parking would qualify all of them as worthy movie sets for films shot in the early 20th century.

The Union Pacific Railroad gave birth to Cheyenne as a rough and rowdy town, a place where the notorious "hell on

wheels" railroaders drank, gambled and cavorted with prostitutes. A few "cowboy bars" with swinging doors, antler decorations and stetson-wearing customers still exist in Cheyenne, but
it is generally a tame, quiet place now, so peaceful that carloads
of Wyomingites regularly head south across the Colorado
border to visit the shopping malls and bright lights of Colorado's Front Range cities.

Nowhere in the United States is a State Capital in such a
quiet setting. Across the street from it is the Wyoming State
Museum, which displays Wyoming history chronologically. Two
other museums in Cheyenne are noteworthy: The National
First Day Cover Museum (307-634-5911) and the Cheyenne
Frontier Days Old West Museum (307-778-7290). Another
significant place in Cheyenne is the Union Pacific Depot, a late
Victorian building of considerable size and charm, which is in
effect a memorial to the importance of the railway to the town.

There are a few other sizeable Victorian buildings, but
most of the center of Cheyenne consists of rather small and
unimpressive single family houses built earlier in this century.
The newer, more fashionable sections of town are in the
suburban growth areas built at some distance from the old core
of the city.

West of the center of town is the F.E. Warren Air Force
Base, hub of the great intercontinental missile deployment on
the plains surrounding the city. The base was established as an
army post in 1867 to protect the Union Pacific from Indians
and was kept open long after the Indian threat subsided. The
Air Force took it over in 1947, utilizing many handsome
buildings built from 1855 to 1911. The base has a museum and
the Air Force extends a friendly welcome to visitors, which
sometimes includes tours of a missile installation.

Laramie began as another wild railroad town, and it is to this day a rather gaunt place with some seedy old streets that exude their own peculiar charm. The southern approach to the city, from Colorado on U.S. 287 goes past a stark and ugly industrial plant that seems to loom over the highway.

The university has a geology and an anthropology museum open to the public, and the Laramie Plains Museum (307-742-4448) has exhibits from pioneer days. Laramie struggles to bring programs and performances from the cultural heritage of the East and Europe to windswept Wyoming on a regular basis. The city also has ambitious plans to build a Western history theme park in the future.

Casper is a rather sprawling, nondescript place, like Rawlins and Rock Springs. All of these places rapidly expanded in the energy boom of the 1970's in a rather desultory fashion, complete with parking lots, shopping malls and fast-built suburbs. Casper's most notable physical feature is the prominence of huge oil tanks. When the energy business booms, Casper booms. When it slumps, the rental trucks leave town loaded with families' household goods.

See the section on the Oregon Trail for Casper's Fort Caspar, which is spelled differently from the city.

Cheyenne's Frontier Days: For one celebrated week in the year, Cheyenne is so jam packed with people that the best chance to find a motel room for those who have not reserved a place in advance may be 50 to 100 miles away. Nevertheless, this is hardly a daunting distance in Wyoming, Colorado or Nebraska.

The Cheyenne Frontier Days are billed as the "Daddy of 'em All," meaning that it is the original big Western rodeo and frontier celebration. Although places all over the Rocky

Mountain West have put on rodeos, festivals and pageants to pull in the tourists, no town does it as well as Cheyenne in late July. For a week, excited, celebrating people come from all over, crowd the city, fill the stands, and make Cheyenne into a Western carnival town, a New Orleans near the Rockies.

The rodeos have been the centerpiece of the festival, but big evening shows by bigtime country Western entertainers have become increasingly important. The big parades are also featured, where it seems that everyone in Wyoming and all of the horses in the state must take part. Some wear formal Western garb, others put on patriotic displays that would warm the hearts of the Reagans, and some play Western saloon buffoons or gunfighters. The air is filled with band music and the noise of pistols firing blanks. Children of all ages are delighted by these Frontier Days parades.

For many professional rodeo cowboys, Cheyenne's Frontier Days rank with the World Series for baseball players because the crowds, pay and prestige are all big time. A wide variety of events are scheduled, including bareback riding, steer wrestling, steer roping and wild horse races. Over a thousand professional cowboys compete, along with over a thousand more or less terrified animals.

Next to the rodeo arena is a carnival, featuring rides of all sorts and shops where Western goods, near Western goods, and far-eastern goods are sold. The carnival allows some opportunities to see craftsmen at work and to dress up in Western costumes for souvenir photographs.

During Frontier Days Cheyenne's civic resources are taxed to the limit, so do not expect all members of the police force, undoubtedly working many overtime hours, to be in the laid back Western mode. Also, parking may be a problem, so be prepared to walk some distance to events.

Along the Oregon Trail in Wyoming

FOLLOWING THE TRAIL BY CAR

One of the best ways to appreciate the dogged determination of the early settlers of the West is to follow the Oregon trail through Wyoming. Pioneers did not get to see the spectacular scenery of the northern part of the state because they had to follow rivers along the central plateau. Instead of passing the magnificent Tetons, they went up and over the Continental Divide at its most gentle and unspectacular pass.

While the Oregon Trail and its offshoots start in Missouri and go all the way to the Pacific, they are preserved closest to their original condition and environment in Wyoming. This is because so much of Wyoming has not been developed and is as open, empty, lonely and windy as it was when those hardy souls creaked along in covered wagons to cross it from the 1830's up to 1870, the decades before the railroads were established.

Modern highways follow most of the old route rather closely. Starting from the Nebraska border, follow Route 26 until it joins Interstate 25. Leave the Interstate at Casper and take Route 220. At Muddy Gap pick up Route 287 and follow it until in joins Route 28 below Lander. Take Route 28 down to Atlantic City and South Pass City. After that, the highways depart from the trail, but by going down Route 187, Interstate 80 can be reached at Rock Springs, which can be taken down to Fort Bridger historic site in the far southwestern corner of Wyoming.

The principal attractions along this most unspoiled and historic segment of the Oregon Trail are, moving from east to west, Fort Laramie, Register Cliff, Oregon Trail Ruts, Fort Caspar, Independence Rock, South Pass and Fort Bridger. There are also a number of more minor attractions along the way, most of them indicated by detailed signs. Each one of the major attractions is worth describing in some detail.

FORT LARAMIE, THE WILLIAMSBURG OF THE WEST

Fort Laramie National Historic Site is one of the most outstanding historical attractions in the whole Rocky Mountain region. Because of its costumed interpreters, demonstrations, carefully reconstructed buildings and richly detailed interiors, it can claim to be something of a Western version of Virginia's famous historical reconstruction of colonial Williamsburg.

Like many forts in the West, Fort Laramie began as a fur trading post and later became a United States army fort. It was established in 1834 at the confluence of the Platte and Laramie rivers. A considerable trade for fur was carried on for some years. Traders based at the fort fanned out with their merchandise to the rendezvous points of mountain men in order to acquire beaver pelts and to the Indian villages to barter for buffalo robes. Fort Laramie became something of an economic and social center for Indians. Often bands of Indians camped outside of the fort while they bargained robes for such items as blankets, tobacco, powder and beads.

Fort Laramie was the principal station for repairs and resupply for the flow of emigrants heading westward in their covered wagons and for those walking with hand carts. All types of people stopped there: Mormons on their way to their New Jerusalem in the rugged landscape of Utah; Midwestern farmers lured by the tales of the land of milk and honey on the Pacific coast; miners gambling everything they had on striking it rich in distant goldfields; people escaping from something or someone back East.

The fort marked the end of the first third of their journey and the first contact with civilization for 300 miles. It was here that equipment was refurbished, draft animals were replaced or exchanged, food supplies replenished, and travellers refreshed before continuing their arduous journey.

The Indians had viewed the arrival of the first white travelers with interest, but when the trickle became a flood and the flood swept away grassland and game, the Indians began to harass the wagon trains. Calls for government protection rose, and in response the army bought Fort Laramie in 1849 and made it a strategic center for operations against hostile Indians until the end of the Indian wars near the close of the century.

In general, combat was a very rare event for the soldiers at Fort Laramie, who spent most of their time drilling and maintaining the place. The only Indian 'attack' the fort ever suffered was a raid of no more than three dozen Indians whose only purpose was to dash in and steal horses.

The fort was the scene of a grand assemblage of over 10,000 Indians in 1851, who were gathered to parlay about the settlers crossing their land in what were now numbers of over 50,000 per year. The Indians agreed to guarantee the safety of the settlers on the trail and promised to give up intertribal warfare. In exchange for these agreements, Indians were granted annuities, or yearly allowances, and were to be protected by U.S. troops against provocation by the settlers. The agreement broke down quickly as further encroachments and retaliations against them took place.

The small detachment of professional soldiers at Fort Laramie always served to maintain communication and transportation links across the continent. The Oregon Trail, the Bozeman Trail to Montana and the trail from Cheyenne to Deadwood, South Dakota, were all protected by the fort. So was the Pony Express route and, later, the telegraph lines.

Fort Laramie had a high desertion rate, which was a reflection of its isolation, its relentless winds, and the high percentage of foreign recruits who were easily disenchanted by their duties at such a place.

A number of impressive buildings have been restored from the days that Fort Laramie served as an army base. The earlier buildings from its days as a fur trading fort have been completely destroyed. While the trading post fort had a wooden stockade around it and blockhouses, the army's fort did not have this essential configuration of the popular concept of a frontier fort. Instead, Fort Laramie looked more like a town, with a scattering of buildings thrown across stark, treeless flat land by a bend in the Laramie River. The most important buildings flank a large open parade ground. Close to a dozen buildings have been painstakingly restored to their appearance during the 1850 to 1880 period. Restoration was aided by the fact that after the fort was abandoned by the army in 1890 its buildings were sold at a public auction. For a time some of these structures housed businesses and homesteaders and some even sheltered livestock. While some buildings were stripped of timber and allowed to decay, others could be acquired by the government intact and fit for exacting restoration.

The most impressive building is "Old Bedlam," former quarters for bachelor officers who supposedly gave parties so wild that the building gained the name of the famous insane asylum. There are also other officers' quarters, a military prison called a guardhouse, a bakery, a traders' store and the surgeon's quarters all restored to their prime condition. The fort also has ruins or foundations of many other structures that failed the test of time.

The "living history" programs enhance visits. The park staff dress up as troopers, traders, bakers and laundresses, among other roles, and function at the fort in these capacities, paying strict attention to historical accuracy. In fact, one laundress assured the author that she was dressed accurately to the skin by allowing him a discreet peek at her Victorian underwear!

Be sure to note the wind at Fort Laramie. It is called the wind that never stops, or the wind that drives people mad. Imagine its effect on lonely troopers far from their homes.

The staff explain the history of the fort extremely well. There is as twenty minute audio-visual presentation at the Visitor Center and there are interpretive talks at 10 a.m., 11:45 a.m. and 2 p.m. daily as well as ranger conducted tours at 10:30 a.m. and 3 p.m.

It is important to bear in mind that Fort Laramie is quite distant from the city of Laramie. It is off of Route 26, three miles southwest of the town of Fort Laramie on Route 160.

Fort Laramie is open year round, but much more goes on from June 1 to August 31, when the hours of the Visitor Center are 8 a.m. to 7 p.m. From September to May the hours are 8 a.m. to 4:30 p.m. Check details by phoning 307-387-2221

REGISTER CLIFF AND THE OREGON TRAIL RUTS

South of the extremely friendly small town of Guernsey, Wyoming, are two dramatic reminders of all those who passed through on the Oregon Trail. First, just south of the town are ruts cut deep into soft sandstone. Rough terrain in the immediate vicinity forced the wagons to follow one set of tracks, which, over time, dug deep ruts. The site is now a National Historical Monument.

Register Cliff, three miles south of the town, is a 100 foot high sandstone and limestone formation. Names, hometowns, dates and sundry notations cover it. The most significant inscriptions, numbering over 700, date from the 1820's to the 1860's. Pioneers recorded their passage at two other places in Wyoming, Independence Rock, 180 miles west of Register Cliff, and Names Hill, 175 miles further west beyond it.

Near Guernsey is a remarkable rest stop that has a group of posts overlooking a panorama of Oregon Trail scenery. Each post is keyed to an inscription about an aspect of the trail and has a peep hole which enables an observer to ascertain easily the exact location of a described feature.

FORT CASPAR

Both the fort and the town are named for a young Lieutenant Caspar Collins who died in battle against some Indians nearby. A typographical error somehow changed the name of the town to Casper. Both arose at an important crossing of the Platte River, the site of a ferry run for some time by Mormons and later the site of a toll bridge. Part of the old toll bridge is exhibited today at the fort.

Fort Caspar was established to deal with hostile Indians and then served to protect a Pony Express station and a telegraph station. It has been reconstructed and furnished by Wyoming's historical association as the log fortification of 1862.

Part of the helpful and friendly staff dress in period costumes and give informative talks.

Fort Caspar on the Fort Caspar Road is easily reached from the Rancho Road exit of I-25 in Casper. The city itself is Wyoming's major industrial city where oil refineries abound.

Fort Caspar is open from 9 a.m. to 6 p.m. from mid-May to mid-September. For the rest of the year, the fort is open from 9 a.m. to 5 p.m. Monday through Friday and from 2 p.m. to 5 p.m. Sunday.

ALONG THE TRAIL WEST OF FORT CASPAR

West of Fort Caspar the landscape looks much as it must have to those who made the crossing in covered wagons. It is a bleak, windswept, quiet panorama, free from most signs of the modern era. The uncrowded, open stretches of the access highways, routes 220, 287 and 28, do not detract from the lonesomeness of the setting. Plaques all along the way indicate what the pioneers experienced.

The trail follows the rivers because of the need for water and pasture grass. Campsites were used by group after group, some guarded by rifle pits dug into the hillsides. A gorge near the trail called Devil's Gate is completely devoid of development and therefore must look exactly as it did in the 19th century.

Split Rock is a massive cliff well-known to Indians and trappers before the pioneers arrived. It was near here that Buffalo Bill Cody was chased by Indians when he was a Pony Express rider. Its vicinity too, is free from any indications of the 20th century.

Independence Rock is now right by a new rest stop, 50 miles southwest of Casper, but a brief hike is required to get close to its thousands of inscriptions. This large granite monolith, a word meaning 'one stone,' rises up to 190 feet, and has a base that covers 27 acres. It got its name from a group of mountain men who celebrated the 4th of July there in 1830. It was one of the best known landmarks on the whole Oregon Trail.

SOUTH PASS AND ITS GHOST TOWNS

The Continental Divide, an awesome obstacle elsewhere, meanders unimpressively in southwestern Wyoming. South Pass was the easiest way to get over the spine of the Rockies to where the streams and rivers flowed forth into the Pacific Ocean. An estimated 350,000 to 400,000 emigrants crossed this 7,550 feet high and 20 miles wide pass between 1840 and 1868.

The pass looks today much as it did then, with tawny grass stretching as far as the eye can see and low blue mountains gently sloping in the distance. It is a place to spot scampering antelope.

Close to South Pass are the ghost towns of South Pass City and Atlantic City, which were once gold mining boom towns. Today Atlantic City is still alive but South Pass City is now a carefully reconstructed and maintained State Historic Site. Both can be reached by turning off of highway 28 at the clearly marked signs. Getting to them requires a brief ride on a dirt road, but it is well maintained and safe. Campgrounds exist along the way.

These ghost towns had little to do with the Oregon Trail because they were mining boom towns that mushroomed in the late 1860's, after the main flow on the Oregon Trail had passed through. Nevertheless, their proximity to the trail makes them a worthwhile stop and adds a change of pace to a trip through southern Wyoming.

Atlantic City tries to make the most of its raucous past, which began with a gold mining boom in 1868. While A-frames, pickup trucks and satellite dishes may seem incongruous with the wooden log buildings and wooden sidewalks that predominate in the town, they do indicate that contemporary folk dwell in this old, rough, windblown town. There is a "T n' T" Cafe, and a colorful old "Red Cloud Saloon." A sign on an emporium called the "Atlantic City Mercantile" offers something for everyone: "Museum, Gals, Steaks, Cabins." The sounds of Western music come from bars that have old wood, Victorian flourishes and racks of animal horns. In a word, Atlantic City, remote and off the beaten path, still has some of the old atmosphere and is well worth a visit.

South Pass City, by contrast, is more antiseptic today. This is a dead ghost town, embalmed by restoration and preservation by the State of Wyoming. In its boom year of 1867-1868, the population soared up to 2,000. South Pass City in its peak years boasted of dozens of nearby mines, hundreds of placer mining claims and a main street half a mile long that had all kinds of shops, several saloons, hotels and what were called "sporting houses."

South Pass City was the unlikely source of advances in equal rights for women. A local saloon keeper, William Bright, served in Wyoming's territorial legislature and introduced the bill to give women the right to vote and hold office. One year after its passage, Esther Morris was appointed as South Pass City's Justice of the Peace, the nation's first female judge.

Despite such progressive advances, the town was entirely dependent upon mining. When boom turned to bust, people rapidly drifted away, so that by 1875 less than one hundred people remained in the area. There were other rushes in the locality later on, as new technologies unlocked more minerals, the latest of these occurring in the 1960's. Today there are still a few hardy prospectors about who pan and dig for minerals.

Numerous buildings and a Visitor Center are open for inspection in the restored town. Exhibits at the Visitor Center include information about the Oregon Trail and mining technology as well as about life in the town during its booming years. Hotels, saloons and shops are on exhibit and there is a statue honoring Esther Morris. For further information call 307-332-3684.

FORT BRIDGER

The last major stop on the Oregon Trail in what became Wyoming is Fort Bridger. It is just off of Interstate 80 at exit 34, quite close to gorgeous Flaming Gorge National Recreation Area.

Its founder, Jim Bridger, was a legendary figure, mountain man, explorer, guide, trader, businessman and story teller. He lived from 1804 to 1881, came from St. Louis, and, over the years, developed an uncanny knowledge of Western landscapes, Native Americans, and wildlife which he mixed liberally with outlandish tall tales. He shrewdly noted that as the fortunes from trapping dwindled, money could be made from the flow of settlers westward over the Oregon Trail. Therefore Bridger and a partner established a trading post at a fork of the Green River in 1843, a crude affair of log buildings surrounded by a stockade.

Among the early emigrants to stop off at the trading post were Mormons, at first a trickle of them and then a flood as they fled persecution in the East and sought their New Jerusalem in the West. The Mormons soon built their own post, Fort Supply, twelve miles from Bridger's fort. By 1855 they bought him out, but only occupied the site for two years because tension between the Mormons in what is now Utah and the Federal Government became so intense that U.S. troops were sent to the region. As these troops advanced, the Mormons burned their forts and fell back on Salt Lake City.

Eventually the army rebuilt and expanded Fort Bridger and made it a station on the Pony Express and Overland Stage routes. When the Civil War broke out volunteer units staffed the fort as regular troops were called to the battlefields to the East. Fort Bridger served as a supply base in the subsequent Indian wars and protected work crews building the Union Pacific Railroad.

Because the region around Fort Bridger was peaceful by 1890, the last garrison departed in that year and thereafter some parts of the fort were sold off at public auction. The State of Wyoming bought back what was left in the late 1920's. Today Fort Bridger is an interesting cluster of restored and reconstructed buildings. The State of Wyoming maintains a number of exhibits and programs on the site.

The original trading post built by Jim Bridger stands reconstructed and fittingly is a commercial operation that sells goods to tourists. The restored army buildings display their Victorian coziness, especially the large, white, two-storied commanding officer's quarters. Wyoming's first schoolhouse is also here, completely restored. The barracks building contains a large museum which displays not only the history of the fort but something about all of the people who made the region so exciting in the 19th century, the mountain men, the Native

Americans, the emigrants, the pony express riders and the cowboys.

During the summer, costumed historical interpreters enhance the experience of visitors. Also, for nearly two decades there has been a mountain man rendezvous over Labor Day weekend. It features competitive black powder shoots, and displays of 1840's trade goods, such as beads, blankets, traps and buckskin clothing. There are dangerous knife and toma-hawk throwing contests, Indian dances, cooking contests and contests over the authenticity of clothing and paraphernalia. While all of this is going on, those playing the roles of moun-tain men are established in a village of tepees at the fort, just as real mountain would have camped in the 1840's. The announcement for the rendezvous invites the public and "free trappers, buckskinners, mountain men, traders, squaws, hunters, wives and pilgrims!"

Fort Bridger is open from mid-April to mid-October from 9 a.m. to 5 p.m. daily. From mid-October through mid-April it is open from 9 a.m. to 4:30 p.m. Admission is free. Telephone 307-782-3842 for further information.

CHAPTER EIGHT

MAGNIFICENT MONTANA

What is Special About Montana

Montana is the largest state in the region and one of the largest in the country. Its 147,138 square miles is only topped in size by Alaska, Texas and California. It is slightly larger than Japan which has 145,856 square miles and considerably larger than either the United Kingdom at 94,226 square miles and Italy, possessing 116,303 square miles. It is three times the size of Pennsylvania. Montana's northern border is 540 miles long, touches three of Canada's large provinces, and is roughly equal to the distance between Boston, Massachusetts, and Richmond, Virginia.

This huge state has only over three quarters of a million inhabitants, yielding a density of only 5.4 persons per square mile. Over 93% of this thin population is classified white, and only two tenths of one percent are classified as black. Over 5 % of the population is Native American.

Montana is a very special place. Much of it is still in the condition that other Rocky Mountain States were in prior to their widespread development. Some of the big, beautiful and empty mountain ranges and the small towns in valleys surrounded by snow capped peaks resemble what parts of Colorado must have looked like fifty or sixty years ago, before the postwar booms and migrations. Montana is more like Wyoming in terms of development, but more like Colorado in possessing large domains of beautiful scenery. Colorado and Montana also share a sharp division between plains in the eastern part of them and mountains in the western part.

The nicknames of Montana reflect its special unspoiled nature: It is called "The Last Best Place," "The Big Empty," and "The Big Open." It is also called the most Western part of the West.

Alas, even this relatively remote, cold and empty part of America has begun to fill up and develop, at least the mountainous western portion of it.

Part of the influx has been from celebrities who want to get away from the glitter and glitz of places like Aspen, Colorado, Jackson Hole, Wyoming, and Sun Valley, Idaho. Many wish to establish rustic hideaways where local people are likely to treat them as ordinary human beings and not lavish special attention on them and expose them to publicity, the kind of treatment that other places dispense too extravagantly. Here and there in faraway Montana, movie stars, well known authors, famous musicians and television personalities are staking claims to scenic spots where peace and quiet ought to prevail. They want to be where the cowboy bars are common and the autograph seekers are rare.

As in other Rocky Mountain States, the number of visitors constantly increases. In 1988 Montana had just over 800,000 residents but 4,500,000 people visited the state. Visitors are lured to Montana, tourist boosters declare, because an average square mile in the state holds only five people but has 3.3 deer; 1.2 elk or antelope, depending on the part of the state; and nearly 900 decent sized fish. There are also lures to induce urban-weary Americans to settle permanently: A good sized newer home on several acres still costs less than $100,000 in Montana.

Of course, the influx of newcomers has been controversial. Some close their newly bought lands to hunting and fishing,

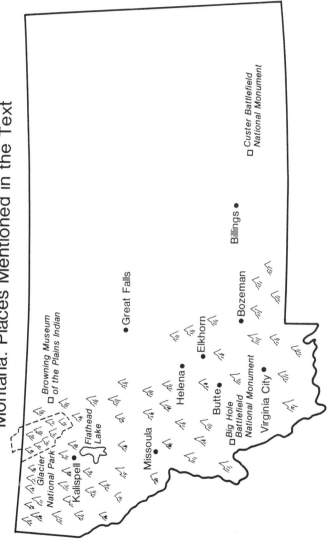

Montana: Places Mentioned in the Text

Custer Battlefield
National Monument

Billings ●

Great Falls ●

Browning Museum
of the Plains Indian

Glacier
National Park
Kalispell ●

Flathead
Lake

Missoula ●

Helena ●

Elkhorn
●

Bozeman
●

Butte ●

Big Hole
Battlefield
National Monument

Virginia City ●

thereby running the risk of taking away some of the favorite spots of old time residents. In addition to newcomers who flee urban pressures, a few strange sects have established themselves to the alarm of local residents. On the other hand, some welcome any economic growth for the increased land values and broader tax base growth brings.

Many of the rich and famous who have Montana hideaways live in the state for only part of the year, usually during the cool and lovely summer months or during autumn, which may be relatively mild until December. On the other hand, year-round residents complain that they experience nine months of winter and three months of visiting relatives.

Winter temperatures in Montana can be frightful: West Yellowstone often records temperatures of minus 30 to minus 40 Fahrenheit and the all time record cold for the continental United States, minus 70, was recorded near Helena. The eastern plains of Montana have the worst weather, sweltering in summer heat and taking the brunt of arctic blasts from Canada in the winter. A high of 117° Fahrenheit has been recorded on the plains. The plains are also drier, receiving only about 13 inches of precipitation while the mountainous western part of the state catches up to 18 inches.

The mountainous portion has relatively milder temperatures and more rain because it is often protected from Arctic air and subject to the flow of some moisture-laden pacific air. Despite some remarkably cold incidental Arctic blasts of cold, the mountainous region tends to enjoy much more moderate winters than the plains portion of the state. Snow melting Chinook winds flow up over the mountains from the Pacific for several days of each of the winter months.

Not only the weather divides the state between mountains and plains. The eastern three-fifths of the state is part of the high and dry Great Plains, consisting of high, rolling prairie land that is devoted to raising cattle and growing wheat. Montana's eastern plains are broken up somewhat near the long arms of the Missouri river and its tributaries, where some irrigated farms and some clumps of forests appear, as well as some rougher terrain cut by the rivers. Still, for the most part, this 60% of Montana is the land of dry farming and huge cattle ranches which has the most in common with the Dakotas to the east.

The western 40 % of the state contains 25 ranges of the Rockies. It is a heavily forested region with 13 million acres of timber west of the Continental Divide and nine million acres east of it.

Highlights of Montana's History, Politics and Economics

Since Montana has been called the "most Western part of the West," Montana's history can be expected to conform to classic patterns of traditional Western history. In fact, the patterns may appear to be clearer in Montana than anywhere else. Native Americans, explorers, fur trappers, miners, cowboys and cattle kings and copper barons fill the pages of Montana's history in succession.

For thousands of years Montana was the exclusive home of various tribes of Native Americans who collaborated and contended for the rich hunting grounds containing abundant fish, game and rolling seas of buffalo grass.

The first European people to see what became Montana were French. They arrived in the 1740's and gave the name of "Shining Mountains" to what they saw, although the state's name is actually derived from the Spanish word for mountains.

American incursion began with the famous Lewis and Clark expedition of 1804 to 1806, which went from St. Louis to Oregon and back under the direct sponsorship of President Thomas Jefferson, who wanted to discover just what the new American interior contained. Montanans take pride in the fact that the expedition spent more time and covered more miles in Montana than anywhere else. Every Montana schoolchild is taught something about the expedition's main personalities and the famous route provides geography lessons for them. Sacagawea, a 17 year old Shoshone Indian with an infant son, served as a guide for the expedition. She, along with a part-Indian scout and a slave who accompanied it, offers an apt demonstration today of the diversity of people who contributed to important events in American history.

Today ten states promote the Lewis and Clark Route for tourism, and Montana's portion, which goes up the Missouri to the Bitterroot Mountains, is the lengthiest section. Nevertheless, it was only a trail taken by these explorers, not a pathway that was followed later on by thousands of pioneers like the Oregon Trail. Lewis and Clark camped out on the High Plains at places where nothing important has happened since.

Mountain men and fur traders moved to what became Montana shortly thereafter. In fact, some fur traders went along for part of the Lewis and Clark expedition. Soon forts were established which depended on transportation along the Missouri River, including Fort Union, just over the border in North Dakota, where the Yellowstone joins the Missouri, and Fort Benton near Great Falls. Steamboat navigation was critical for this early exploitation of Montana's resources, especially the use of those shallow draft steam vessels declared capable of "floating on a damp sponge," and able to navigate around dangerous sandbars in the shifting Missouri.

The fur trade, under the increasingly dominant American Fur Company, which was run by John Jacob Astor, serves as an example of a recurring theme in Montana history, the use of Eastern corporate capital to exploit Western resources boldly and unscrupulously. Mining, railroad and power corporations continued this trend later on, leading Montana's settlers to have a feeling not unlike that of colonial people whose development depended essentially upon the opportunities for profit perceived by powerful and distant entrepreneurs.

Beaver and buffalo skins were the principal exploited items until gold was discovered during the Civil War. A rush occurred, bringing thousands of people and tons of cargo up the Missouri and overland to the goldfields of the western part of Montana. Another route was the newly created Bozeman trail which came up from the Oregon Trail at Fort Laramie to the boomtown of Virginia City. The Sioux Indians were understandably upset at this trail because it cut right through their hunting grounds.

Rough and tumble mining towns such as Bannack, Virginia City and Nevada City had their complement of notorious characters. Perhaps Sheriff Henry Plummer of Virginia City is the most notorious of them all. He doubled as the leader of a daring gang of thieves who robbed gold shipments. A vigorous vigilante movement resulted in Plummer's hanging, a fate shared by at least twenty members of his gang in 1864. Some of these boom towns have become ghost towns or partial ghost towns, such as Bannack and Virginia City, and others, such as Helena and Butte, have continued to be important cities, growing out and around the original sites of mineral strikes and boasting of great mansions owned by dozens of new millionaires.

The range cattle industry came to Montana on a large scale shortly after the rushes to the mining towns. The dominant era of the cattle barons was from the 1870's to the 1890's, as it was for other Western territories. Yet cattle ranching was more dramatic in Montana than elsewhere because there was so much broad landscape and big sky and harsh, cold weather. This was the stuff out of which cigarette advertisements would be made a hundred years later.

The Montana Stockgrowers' Association was created to control scattered animals and to deal with rustling. It went on to have a powerful influence over both the politics and development of the state.

In popular culture much has been made of the struggles between powerful cattlemen and the sheepherders, whose herds of despised "hoofed locusts" were supposed to spoil the range for cattle because their eating methods ripped plants up. Indeed, there was once a celebrated slaughter of over 2,000 sheep by masked men at Lame Deer, but highlighting these conflicts obscures the fact that many large operations in Montana ran sheep and cattle on the same ranges and used the same watering spots for both species.

Gold rushes and the replacement of buffalo with cattle on the open range had a disastrous effect on Native Americans. The economic base of indigenous tribes was shot away by buffalo hunters, some of them Indians, who were greedy for profit from buffalo robes and pickled buffalo tongues. These hunters, often blood splattered, filthy and lice-ridden, cleared the way for cattle and thereby made Native Americans desperate economically. The upshot was that one of the last chapters in the long struggle between Euro-Americans and Native Americans was fought out in Montana.

As elsewhere, Euro-Americans were able to find Native American allies because long and deadly tribal rivalries could be exploited. As elsewhere, confused whites sometimes slaughtered friendly Indians by mistake, as when over 170 men, women and children of the Piegan tribe were butchered in Montana in 1870. Also as elsewhere, solemn treaties to preserve tribal lands were ignored time and again as the lure of profit acted as a magnet to draw whites through or into areas that had been mutually agreed to be permanently assigned to one or another tribe.

The most well known event in the long history of Native American resistance took place in Montana, although what set the train of events in motion was the penetration of the Black Hills hunting grounds by gold seekers in the Dakotas. The end result was Custer's Last Stand at the Battle of Little Bighorn in southern Montana, a location enshrined as the Custer National Monument. This celebrated victory of Crazy Horse and Sitting Bull was followed one year later by the crushing of Sioux power in the region.

The conclusion of another dramatic chapter in the tragic history of the Indian Wars took place in Montana. Chief Joseph's long retreat was described in the chapter on Idaho. It ended in Montana, after the Indians crossed the Continental Divide. They were attacked at Big Hole, but were able to rally. This scene is commemorated by the Big Hole Battlefield National Monument. The place where they eventually surrendered is commemorated as the Chief Joseph Battleground of the Bear's Paw Mountain.

This was the last incident of the Indian Wars in Montana. The remaining Native Americans settled down on relatively small portions of their former hunting grounds which were set aside as reservations. They became dependent upon the Federal Government because the space and the animals that they needed to live their former way of life were now gone. To this day, Native Americans make up a small but significant portion of the state's population.

While gold and silver brought excited mobs of fortune seekers, it was copper that proved to be the most valuable mineral for Montana in the long run, providing up to two-thirds of the mineral wealth taken out. Copper also brought in one of the most powerful companies ever to exert influence over a region, the Anaconda Copper Company. It is ironic that the company has the name of a large python-like tropical reptile which crushes its prey. Those who unsuccessfully fought the influence of the company had reasons for grave reflections upon this irony.

Before Anaconda extended its power over the economy and politics of Montana, a colorful "War of the Copper Kings" pitted William A. Clark, a dour Presbyterian, against Marcus Daly, a gregarious Irishman. After a furious struggle between them to control the copper mines in the 1890's, a powerful subsidiary of Standard Oil took over. After the subsidiary was separated from Standard Oil it became the Anaconda Copper Mining Company, a giant corporation controlled by Wall Street. In its heyday, Anaconda produced nearly all of the state's copper, 90% of its silver, 80% of its gold, 75% of its zinc and 65% of its lead.

The feeling of being a colony of distant capitalists became strong in Montana when Anaconda dominated the economy. It was said for a long time that no one who crossed Anaconda could ever succeed in Montana politics. A popular saying was that without Anaconda's support, nobody could be elected dogcatcher.

In the early 20th century, Montanans displayed prejudices directed not only at Wall Street moguls but at Native Americans, Asians and members of left wing unions, particularly the

International Workers of the World. During World War One, Germans were added to this category. Nevertheless, Montana mounted a progressive movement, laying the foundation for the election, every now and then, of outstanding liberal Montanans to the Congress, such as Mike Mansfield.

One Missoula politician, Jeannette Rankin, deserves special mention. She was the first woman to sit in the United States House of Representatives, where she was noted for voting against America's entry into both World Wars.

Outside of such strong individuals, Montanans have generally sent conservatives to the legislature in Helena and to Congress. Nevertheless, there is always some grass roots support for liberal positions, particularly from the ranks of poorer people.

While Anaconda was booming in the western part of the state, homesteaders were staking claims on the plains and turning over more and more virgin soil with their plows. The opening of the Northern Pacific Railroad in 1883 meant not only that Montana's minerals and cattle could be shipped to the populous East but also that Great Plains grain could now be exported at competitive prices as well. Yet it was not easy to farm in a region subject to spells of dryness and periodic ravages of insect plagues. The old adage that dry farming succeeds in wet years proved to be very true. Farmers in eastern Montana flirt with depression to this day, although the key factor now tends to be the price that they can get for their products. Partly as a result of the hazards of farming, particularly without irrigation, Montana's population did not grow rapidly. In fact, in some periods, such as the 1920's and most recently, it actually declined while the United States' population rose significantly.

Incidentally, in the phohibition era, Montana's long Canadian border became the scene of smuggling. Fast cars raced across the border, laden with illegal alcoholic beverages.

By the 1950's, Anaconda had loosened its hold on the state. Anaconda divested itself of newspapers and distanced itself somewhat from its ally, Montana Power, which supplied electric power to its smelter operations. Because of circumstances affecting the copper industry outside of the United States, Anaconda actually closed its mines at Butte in 1983.

Montana's economy did not grow as rapidly as that of many other states after World War Two because it continued to be primarily a producer of raw materials rather than a processor of them. Distance from markets has been a perpetual retardant of Montana's growth. It is a long way to the cities of the Pacific Northwest or to Chicago and the Twin Cities. Big corporations have not relocated themselves or established themselves in Montana's cities the way they have in Salt Lake City, Boise, or Denver. A key reason is that no Montana city acts as a central hub the way these other cities do.

Oil and tourism have come to the rescue of Montana's economy. Also, after decades of plunder of the resources of the state, opposition to such practices has been exerted by a coalition of environmentalists, Native Americans and other Montanans who have backed legislators slapping closer regulations and heavy severance (extraction) taxes upon mining companies. While it is never too late to take such steps, evidence of the ravages in the past will always be in view.

Montana's people have tended to be conservative on social issues. Like Western people in many states, they have resented federal meddling in Montana's affairs until help is needed.

There are some bright spots for Montana's economy today. The Federal Government continues to spend more in Montana than it takes out in taxes. Federal funds flow from all sorts of projects from soil banks to dams to missile sites. Exports to Japan are lucrative also. Japan buys over 40 products from Montana, including cattle, grain, log homes, beef jerky (cut into smaller strips), jams, jellies and even Western wood carvings with clocks.

Some Scenic Highlights

MONTANA'S SCENIC HIGHWAYS

As mentioned earlier, there are probably more square miles of undeveloped, unexploited, impressive Western scenery in this state than in any other. The mountainous two fifths have some delightful highways going through remarkably undisturbed landscapes. Western Montana is a fine place to roam on two lane highways in the summer season, where delightful scenic and wildlife surprises are guaranteed on them. Specifically, U.S. Highway 93 is exceptional from the Idaho border in the south and straight up north to Kalispell. It goes through Missoula, past the National Bison Range and through the Flathead Indian Reservation and around the west side of clear and beautiful Flathead Lake. U.S. 2 from northern Idaho to Kalispell is also recommended. Even portions of western Interstate 90 as well as Interstate 15, just after it comes out of Idaho, are richly scenic.

The portion of U.S. 212 going from Red Lodge to Cook City has been cited as the most scenic mountain highway in the United States. Nevertheless, such a claim could be advanced for many other stretches of highway in this beautiful region.

GLACIER NATIONAL PARK

Montana's outstanding Glacier National Park lies along the Canadian border. Parkland crosses the border where it becomes Canada's Waterton Lakes National Park. Glacier's 1,600 square miles has over fifty small glaciers and hundreds of glacial lakes. It straddles the Continental Divide at an altitude that ranges from 3,154 to 10,448 feet above sea level.

The contrast between dark mountains and bright white slabs of glacier ice are particularly sharp in the summer season. One road goes all through the park. It is called "Going to the Sun Road" and was regarded as a marvel of engineering when it was completed in the 1930's. Its 50 miles of twists and turns make it an exhausting drive of 1½ to 3 hours, but an adventure rewarded by vistas of gorgeous scenery. Vehicles and combinations of vehicles over 30 feet long are expressly forbidden from July to August and those over 35 feet are forbidden in June, September and October.

The National Park Service provides very informative newsletters for visitors. Relations between visitors and bears create recurring problems. In addition to the more common black bears, a number of grizzly bears prowl through the park. The phone number for the National Park Headquarters is 406-888-5441.

Some Special Places in Montana

BROWNING MUSEUM OF THE PLAINS INDIAN

The Native American heritage in Montana is especially rich because the state was the scene of some of the most fierce and tragic battles of the Indian Wars and the place where a number of tribes were placed on reservations.

Just to the east of Glacier National Park is the Museum of the Plains Indian, located in the windy plains town of Browning. The artifacts on display include clothing, decorations and weapons. The museum emphasizes the importance of buffalo hunting to them. Various northern plains tribes are represented in what is essentially a big, square and rather old fashioned museum. Nearby Indian dances are performed from time to time during the tourist season. Call 406-338-2230 for more information.

BIG HOLE BATTLEFIELD NATIONAL MONUMENT

The Big Hole Battlefield National Monument is close to the Idaho border and the Continental Divide in southwestern Montana along route 43. It is the place where Chief Joseph's fleeing Nez Percé Indians thought they were safe, so safe that they erected their tepees and celebrated their deliverance from United States troops. It was premature. Before dawn, U.S. troops launched a surprise attack, shooting down all Indians in range, regardless of sex or age. Nonetheless, some Indians were able to scramble to defensive positions and fire at the troops with such deadly accuracy that the troops had to retreat. For a time they were even pinned down by the Indians' deadly fire while the main group of Nez Percé slipped away to continue their long odyssey.

Despite the Nez Percé victory, their losses were so severe that they decided to flee all the way to Canada for refuge, something they could not quite accomplish despite all of their desperate and heroic efforts.

Today there is a Visitor Center at the site to explain the Nez Percé War of 1877 and the Battle of the Big Hole. There are foot trails to the site of the Indian camp and to the place in the woods where the troops were pinned down.

The National Monument is open daily from Memorial Day through Labor Day from 8 a.m. to 8 p.m. From Labor Day through Memorial Day it is open from 8 a.m. to 5 p.m. Phone 406-689-3155 for further information.

CUSTER BATTLEFIELD NATIONAL MONUMENT

Presumably nearly all Americans know at least something about the Battle of Little Big Horn and the last stand of General Custer. Many Americans certainly know a great deal about it, down to the smallest detail. These are the people who keep this episode of American history alive by contributing to the many debates that still go on over the battle and the roles of its leaders. As a result of enduring interest, a steady flow of visitors comes to the grassy, windswept Custer Battlefield National Monument on the plains of southeastern Montana.

Over the years, the battle has stood for different things for different people. For some it was a heroic last stand comparable to that of the Spartans at Thermopylae or of the Jews at Mossada, or the Texans at the Alamo. This image of a heroic last stand was firmly lodged in the American historical consciousness by its constant reenactment in every Buffalo Bill Wild West Show. In fact, the earlier performances included some actual Native American survivors of the battle. Buffalo Bill himself had enlisted as a scout after the battle, during which time he managed to scalp an Indian before retiring to show business.

The first films, from 1912 on, reinforced this image. Custer was a martyr and the Indians were an evil, elemental, faceless force. Custer's death was a sad counterpoint to the glorious "winning of the West," but a loss that revealed how dangerous the west really was and, therefore, how heroic its conquest had to be. Carried to an extreme, Custer became, for some, a Jesus-like figure in his sacrifice.

From a contrary point of view, Custer and his men got what they deserved and it is too bad that this scenario was not repeated more often. From this vantage point, Custer's reputation is turned upside-down. Instead of making a brave sacrifice for a good cause, Custer is seen as a headstrong, predatory, racist villain, a man so consumed by ambition that he was foolhardy enough to charge right into the largest concentration of armed Indians off the reservations that had ever been mustered. Most recently, another negative image of Custer depicts him as fundamentally a vainglorious buffoon.

At least some facts about Custer can be agreed upon by all: He did graduate at the bottom of his class at West Point; he was a showman who wore unorthodox clothes and long, golden curls; and he was indeed brave and ambitious, judging by his Civil War record.

His attitudes towards Native Americans are more controversial. While he did have Crow allies, he also assumed responsibility for a massacre at an Indian village before the Big Horn campaign. His military skills have also been the subject of debate. Superior officers had difficulty reigning him in, and at Little Big Horn he was impulsively aggressive. What was worse, he divided his smaller forces in the face of a superior enemy, which is a grave violation of a basic canon of military science and, obviously, of common sense. The part of his forces under his direct command when he attacked an Indian encampment numbering 8,000 to 10,000 consisted of only 210 men! A total of between 1,500 and 2,000 warriors were sent against them.

Those who won the West in the end controlled the way the battle was portrayed, just as Texans have put their stamp on the display of the Alamo. For example, at the battlefield museum displays of the U.S. cavalry outnumber displays of the Indians by far. The very name commemorates the white loser instead of the Indian victors, among whom were two of the most famous Indian leaders in history, Sitting Bull, of the Sioux, and Crazy Horse, who led Indian cavalry to many tactically outstanding triumphs. What is more, the death places of the troops are marked by headstones, while to date only a painted board has marked Indian graves. There are also numerous sources which declare that the battle had "no survivors," thereby implying that the Indian survivors did not count. Much of what is known about the battle in fact comes from Indian survivors who gave accounts and painted pictures of it.

Lopsided treatment of the vanquished and the victors appears to be on the mend, due in large part to the appointment of Barbara Booker as Superintendent of the Custer Battlefield National Monument. She is a Native American who aims to erect monuments to the Indians and redress the imbalance of museum displays. Moreover, a Congressman who is a descendant of Sitting Bull has introduced a bill to change the name of the site to Little Big Horn National Battlefield. His proposal has the backing of the National Park Service, but it is strongly opposed by many in the region who are used to the old name and think that it draws tourists. Yet another skirmish must be fought on these hallowed grounds.

Simultaneously, objective historical scholarship continues to seek a balanced understanding of these events. Recently excavations revealed just how the bodies of the fallen troops were mutilated, but an explanation of why the Indians carried on this practice was also given. Indians had the view that their enemies had a less pleasant time in the spirit world if they arrived mutilated.

In a broader context, the clash of cultures was already decided when the Battle of Little Big Horn took place. Euro-American civilization was just too powerful for the Indians to ever have a chance to win their lands back. Nevertheless, the battle did give a rude shock to a nation celebrating its centennial in 1876. Thereafter the policy of putting Native Americans on reservations was followed vigorously and harshly. Sitting Bull was broken and Crazy Horse was killed in a scuffle after he came in to a reservation. So in the long run, Little Big Horn was truly a pyrrhic victory for the Indians.

The battlefield today also includes both the place where other detachments of Custer's command fought as well as the famous site of the last stand. It is a broad, sad, windswept terrain of rolling plains. There are guided tours by rangers and a museum in the Visitor Center. It is off of Route 90 on the Crow Indian Reservation, open daily from 8 a.m. to 4:30 p.m.,

October to May, and from 8 a.m. until 8 p.m., June through August. Telephone 406-638-2621 for further information.

TWO MONTANA GHOST TOWNS: ONE QUICK AND ONE ALMOST DEAD

Butte and Helena went on from their origins as frontier mining towns to become major cities. Many other places died quickly or very nearly died. Some such places have been resurrected as thriving entertainment centers for tourists, at least in the summers, and others are still deserted or decaying for the most part.

Virginia City, off of State Route 287 in southwestern Montana is one of the places that blossoms every summer, allowing tourists to browse through an assortment of shops that sell Western gear, clothes, and fast food on a long, narrow main street. Recreational vehicles parked everywhere on the side streets during the peak season, but in the winter the town is much quieter because its population dips to below 100.

Virginia City's original buildings from the 1860's and 1870's make the town something of an outdoor museum. Two indoor museums have many artifacts and much memorabilia from the days when over 10,000 people crowded along nearby Alder Gulch to exploit a gold bonanza.

Nevada City is a mile and a half from Virginia City and it, too, has several original buildings plus a number of old buildings that have been brought from considerable distances to be reassembled there.

Just to the west, on the old stage route from Virginia City to Bannock, near the town of Laurin on State Route 287. is a two-story structure of square hewn logs where notorious Sheriff

Henry Plummer and his gang were supposed to reside from time to time.

Perhaps the most striking ghost town in all of Montana is Elkhorn, just to the east of Boulder. The approach is on a winding gravel road where cattle may present an obstacle every so often. Nearly all of the remaining buildings are deserted, although here and there on the fringes a car motor or a lawn mower may be heard. A few hardy souls still live on the edges of this town which once held thousands.

Gold was discovered in the vicinity in 1870, and by the 1880's a railroad and a smelter had been established to serve the booming town. Today nearly all of it is privately owned, and nothing at all should be molested by any visitors. Elkhorn's brown, weather-beaten buildings are hulking wrecks that give the place a true ghost town atmosphere. The general silence, except for buzzing flies and occasional distant sounds, adds to the aura from the bygone past. While a trip to Elkhorn involves a long, slow trek over a dirt road, it is well worth the time and effort.

MONTANA'S CITIES

Montana's urban centers are somewhat different from those of other Rocky Mountain States. First of all, there is no dominant metropolis, such as Denver for Colorado or Salt Lake City for Utah, each of which absorbs half of the population of their respective states. Second, Montana is so large and its population is so spread out that even relatively small places are called cities. Even the major cities have populations which would place them in the second or third rank of urban areas if they were on either coast. Billings, Montana's largest city, has an estimated 1990 population of just over 80,000, and a metropolitan area of 116,400; next, Great Falls, has 54,600 with an estimated metropolitan area of 78,200. Missoula has under 43,000; Butte, 33,787; the capital, Helena, has only 24,449 and Bozeman has under 23,000. The next "city" on the list, Kalispell, has only 11,800.

The map shows that Montana's cities do not cluster and are, in fact, usually separated by great distances. With low populations, these Montana cities can offer something of the best of both worlds: urban culture, conveniences and a variety of goods and services as well as a personal, almost small town atmosphere. There are fewer and fewer places in the United States where such claims can be made.

Helena: Helena is an old gold mining boom town that became the state capital. Its most historic section is named "Last Chance Gulch" after the final attempt of down and out prospectors to take one last chance at striking it rich. They did so in 1864, and the city boomed in the usual rapid, roistering manner. Today Last Chance Gulch has become the Helena Historic District, where many substantial buildings from the late 19th century have been preserved. Nevertheless, new buildings jostle the few remaining old ones and all of the new concrete and plaster of refurbishing detract from an atmosphere that seems to need to be more old and seedy. Skateboarders appreciate the long, curvaceous concrete pedestrian mall that the main street has become. There are also rather heroic statues of miners and a mule driver that can perhaps be likened to the "new realism" statues so popular in the old Soviet Union.

Helena provides a "Last Chance Tour Train" to see the sights which departs from near the capital from June 1 to Labor Day. Another notable item is the Cathedral of St. Helena, whose architects drew upon southern German cathedrals for inspiration. There is also the Montana Historical Society Museum that houses a great variety of historical artifacts and materials from Indians, miners, and other early Montanans. There are also several hundred works by the famous Western artist, Charles Russell.

Butte and the World Museum of Mining and Hellroarin' Gulch: Butte is deeply scarred by its history of mining and still retains the atmosphere of a company town. Before Anaconda shut down, Butte was called "the company town to end all company towns." It was also described as "ugly as sin and steeped in it," a roistering, swaggering place, filled with tough, hardworking people.

Butte is built on what was claimed to be the richest hill in the world. A total of $3.5 billion in minerals, chiefly copper, have been taken from this hill over the years. Beneath Butte's streets are over 2,000 miles of tunnels for silver and copper mining. Above them are some of the grand old buildings of the town dating from the era of the "wars of the copper kings." They are huge, opulent private as well as public Victorian structures, either set dramatically on the hillsides or scattered along what have become drab streets. Butte has lasting character from its Victorian past, and it can be clearly distinguished from other Western cities.

Butte has a major attraction that draws directly from its rugged past, the World Museum of Mining and Hellroarin' Gulch, located in the northwest of town at the end of West Park and Granite Streets. It is the site of the Orphan Girl Mine, which once produced silver and zinc. The towering minehead frame lends a dramatic note to the adjacent museum, which contains equipment of all sorts. Anyone with an interest in mining will find it fascinating. People with no particular interest in the subject will find at least some remarkable items in this collection, if only to gain an appreciation of the ugliness, size and dangerous nature of some of the equipment.

Outside, in adjacent Hell Roarin' Gulch, mining buffs in particular and anyone in general will find the reconstructed mining town fascinating. It contains over two dozen buildings based on what a 1900 mining camp looked like, including a Chinese laundry and herb store; a funeral parlor and a sauerkraut factory. Like nearly all reconstructions, it is too neat, painted and well maintained, too devoid of mud or dust and stench and bustle to convey the true atmosphere of a mining town in 1900. A good imagination needs to be brought to bear when viewing this carefully constructed camp.

The museum complex is a departure point for the Neversweat and Washoe Railroad, a motorized railway that goes six miles through the mining district.

The World Museum of Mining is a non-profit educational corporation that is open from mid-June through Labor day from 9 a.m. to 9 p.m. daily and from 10 a.m. to 5 p.m. from September to late November, and April through mid-June, with the exceptions of Mondays, when it is closed. It is also closed from late November through March. Phone 406-723-7211 for more information.

Great Falls and the C.M. Russell Museum Complex: Great falls is a plains city on a bend of the Missouri but close to the mountainous part of the state, a proximity proclaimed by a huge smokestack from a copper smelter and wire mill. Nevertheless, wheat and livestock land surround the city and stretch for countless miles to the east. During the long winter, Great Falls is exceptionally cold and windy.

Today parts of Great Falls sprawl rather drably. In the midst of what is not a particularly attractive city is a gem of a museum for a very specialized art, the C. M. Russell Museum

Complex, which houses the most complete collection of the oils, watercolors, bronzes and illustrated letters of Charles M. Russell. He was that famous artist of the Old West whose work undoubtedly shaped the rest of the nation's visual impressions of the region in that era. He depicted cowboys, Indians and horses in scenes of high adventure, muscular grace or pathos. Charles M. Russell (1865-1926) lived as a herder and a range rider, and had a closeness with Indians. His vivid works are a romantic depiction of the Old West, accurate to the smallest detail.

Besides housing this rich and interesting collection, the C.M. Russell Museum Complex also displays his original log cabin studio and his two story home, furnished in styles from 1900 to 1926. It is open from 9 a.m. to 6 p.m. Monday through Saturday and from 1 p.m. to 5 p.m. on Sunday from May through September. From October through April it is open from 10 a.m. to 5 p.m., Tuesday through Saturday, and from 1 p.m. to 5 p.m. on Sunday. Phone 406-727-8787 for further information.

Billings and Missoula: Billings, Montana's largest city, is on the banks of the Yellowstone River. It is a modern, bustling plains city, the center for Montana's cattle and dry farming region. Refineries, feedlots and power plants make the city's atmosphere less than desirable. The newness of this part of the West is attested to by the age of Billings' historic district, which dates from the early 20th century. Billlings has a historic trail above the city and boasts of a colorful Boot Hill Cemetery.

Missoula is smaller, a city tucked in the mountains close to Montana's western border. Missoula is the home of the University of Montana and considerable new urban sprawl.

CHAPTER NINE

IDYLLIC IDAHO

What is Special About Idaho

Idaho's 83,557 square miles cover an odd-shaped state of forest and farm that has only a million or so people, which amounts to twelve per square mile. Idahoans are homogenous in broad ethnic categories: The population is over 97% white, only around 2% native American and less than ½ of 1% African American. On the ground, however, this seeming homogeneity breaks down into differing religions and differing regional loyalties.

An old witticism about the ungainly camel is that it is an animal that must have been designed by a committee. Judged by its geography, Idaho is the camel of states. It was in fact created by several committees, Congressional ones at that. They sliced both Montana and Wyoming away from what had been the original Texas sized Idaho territory, leaving an odd shaped entity with a long panhandle. Although Idaho is 500 miles long, north to south, and 300 miles wide at its widest span, the panhandle can be crossed by driving as little as 44 miles.

Idaho's unique shape encompasses an odd assortment of areas that do not fit together. The populous southern plains should be considered first. The Snake River flows through southern Idaho, moving from east to west on its way to the great Columbia River. The Snake provides irrigation water to southern Idaho's plains, making it a rich agricultural area, known everywhere for its potatoes. Without this irrigation water, all of southern Idaho would look more like Nevada or

Idaho: Places Mentioned in the Text

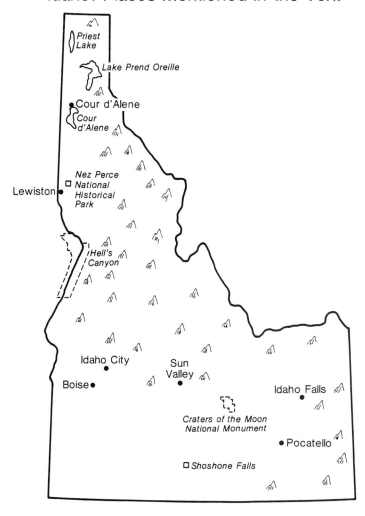

Priest Lake

Lake Prend Oreille

Cour d'Alene

Cour d'Alene

Nez Perce National Historical Park

Lewiston

Hell's Canyon

Idaho City

Boise

Sun Valley

Idaho Falls

Craters of the Moon National Monument

Pocatello

Shoshone Falls

northwestern Utah, places noted for their stark aridity. The unirrigated parts of southern Idaho do look barren, lonely and desolate, so much so that the United States Department of Energy chose southeastern Idaho for an important nuclear facility.

Railways and Interstate highways follow the great drooping curve of the Snake River through southern Idaho, linking the population centers which have naturally sprung up along the river. They are, from east to west, Idaho Falls, Pocatello, Twin Falls and Boise.

North of the plains is one of the most scenic, wild and little known parts of the whole United States, except for one highly publicized ski enclave, world famous Sun Valley. The rich and famous and ski buffs in general tend to fly in and fly out for ski vacations. Sun Valley is a very exceptional place because the rest of the area is not known for such posh development. Instead, wild wilderness prevails in most of the rest of the Sawtooth Mountains. Central Idaho has to this day only one major road going through it to link north an south, scenic U.S. 95. National forest after national forest and wilderness after wilderness take up most of central Idaho. No roads and only a scattering of remote airfields penetrate deeply into the wildest areas. It is here that the Salmon River, called by the Indians "the river of no return," winds its way into seemingly impass-able canyons.

Central and northern Idaho are sprinkled with lakes that are not the kind ordinarily found in the Rocky Mountain West. They are natural lakes, which means that they have trees growing right down to their soft shorelines, rich growths of aquatic plants, naturally sandy and pebbly bottoms and, above all, water as clear and beautiful as light blue glass. What a contrast such lakes make to the artificial human made bodies of water that serve as lakes in Colorado, Montana, Wyoming and

Utah. These human-made lakes are known for their rough, crude, bulldozer shaped shorelines which are nearly lifeless, bottoms filled with rocks and debris and water that is likely to be brown and muddy from the erosion of unnatural banks or from the roiling of muddy bottoms. The lakes of Idaho are doubly gorgeous in comparison.

Central and northern Idaho's crystal-clear lakes, dense, dark green forests and general lushness of vegetation are the products of a moisture flow that rises out the of the Pacific and flows eastwards. These parts of the state do not belong to the arid climatic zone that the rest of Idaho shares with the other Rocky Mountain States. Therefore climate serves to divide the state's regions.

The odd shaped panhandle, in part a wheat growing area, has the largest and most beautiful lakes, which draw tourists from eastern Washington. Moreover, Spokane, the large metropolis of eastern Washington, sells its newspapers to Idahoans living in the panhandle. For a long time, Spokane has dubbed itself the hub of an "eastern empire," and the panhandle of Idaho has been a part of it. At one time, Washingtonians in the Spokane area actually had a dream of uniting their part of Washington, Idaho's panhandle and western Montana into a new state, with either the name of Lincoln or Columbia. Today this "eastern empire" functions only in cultural and economic realms.

An old saying about Idaho is that it actually has three capitals. Since many Idahoans in the south are Mormons, they look to Salt Lake City for leadership. Since so many in the north are economically involved with the Spokane region, they look to that city more than Boise, the real capital of Idaho. Another factor is that the people in the north have a high population of Roman Catholics for whom the diocese of Spokane is of great importance. There is a political dimension as well. More of Idaho's liberals live in the north and the more populous south is the bastion of conservatism. It is widely believed that laws made in Boise, in particular restrictions on the use of alcohol, will be flaunted in the north and ignored in the southeast, because the Mormons do not use alcohol anyway.

Idaho is not a very well-known state. Americans might be aware of the fact that Idaho produces potatoes or that mining goes on or that Sun Valley is a ski mecca. Idaho was generally bypassed when money and people streamed into the Rocky Mountain region after World War Two. The rugged terrain of the central part of the state, including deep river chasms and formidable ranges, helped to keep growth down. So Idaho retains more of an undeveloped appearance and most Idahoans live a lifestyle that is both less advanced and less hectic than that experienced in most parts of the country. After all, America's last hand cranked telephones and gravity-feed gas pumps existed along the Snake River. Idaho still has the treasure of large, undeveloped wild tracts, an abundance of fish and game, and inhabitants who are genuinely open, friendly and easy going. Most Idahoans still tend to be close to the soil and close to the forests.

Being an outdoor type is much easier and much more natural in central and northern Idaho than in most places in the Rockies today. Understandably, many Idahoans do not want to have the pristine nature of the interior of their state advertised too widely for fear that it may fall, piece by piece, to the surveyors, the bulldozers, and those who pave everything over for the real estate developers. The fact that there is so much still untouched is what makes Idaho so special.

Highlights of Idaho's History, Economics and Politics

Idaho's history shares many similarities with other Rocky Mountain States. The Lewis and Clark expedition came through, struggling over what is now the high and rugged border between Idaho and Montana and then continuing through a particularly beautiful section of the panhandle along the Lochsa River. Their report noted that there were so many animals that they got in the way of each other. The Lewis and Clark Trail of 1805 can be followed along U.S. 12 today.

The first fur trading post was established at Pend Oreille Lake in northern Idaho in 1809. The fort which became the most important fur trading center, Fort Hall, was built by the Hudson's Bay Company in 1834 near present day Boise.

1860, the year before the outbreak of the American Civil War, was a big year in Idaho's history for two reasons: First, the earliest permanent English speaking settlement was established in the southeast by Mormons and, second, because placer gold was discovered in the north. Shortly thereafter more strikes were made in the vicinity of Boise. A remarkable feature of Idaho's gold and silver rush was that miners flocked in from west to east, that is, from California and Oregon, for the most part, instead of from an easterly direction. For a time the chance of striking it rich in Idaho was more attractive than staying with the newly established mines and farms of the West Coast.

Along the Snake agriculture developed to feed the growing mining communities. Meanwhile the Mormons in the southeast built town after town in their geometric patterns and irrigated

the fields with water from communal irrigation projects. At first
the Mormons mistakenly thought that they were in the Utah
territory, but even after they found out that they were not in
Utah they continued to look south to Salt Lake City for
direction.

Idaho gained territorial status in 1863, in the middle of the
Civil War. Farmers and miners continued to encroach on the
lands of Native Americans in the region, with the usual
disregard of treaties. Finally a good portion of one tribe, the
Nez Percé, who had been proud, generous and friendly in their
dealings with the Euro-Americans, refused to accept the treaty
which foreited most of their territory and fled to Montana in
1877. The saga of these Indians, led by the courageous, skilled
and legendary Chief Joseph, has become an epic of Native
American history. They were almost able to go from Idaho to
Montana to Canada in their search for a place to live in peace,
but they were caught and defeated just a few miles away from
the Canadian border. See the chapter on Montana for a more
detailed account.

Cattle grazing was introduced in the 1870's, but never as
massively as in some of the other states in the region because
farming irrigated land along the Snake proved to be more
profitable than raising cattle. This was especially the case after
the railroads were built across Idaho right along the course of
the Snake in the 1880's. Southern Idaho, including Pocatello,
built up quickly along the railroad tracks. Mining, farming and
grazing together brought enough people into Idaho to make
statehood possible in 1890.

Idaho, like Colorado, was the scene of some particularly
nasty labor disputes around the turn of the century. A violent
and bloody confrontation between miners and mine owners at
Cour d'Alene in 1899 led to martial law being imposed. Miners

had dynamited the mines and later the governor who called in the troops was assassinated.

The first of many federal reclamation projects began in 1904, shortly after the franchise was enlarged by including women (1894) and contracted somewhat by disenfranchising Mormons who were polygamous. Progressive legislation for this period gave the state control over water rights, prohibited child labor, provided boards of arbitration for labor disputes and spelled out the right to workmen's compensation.

In recent decades Idaho's history has been marked by tension between economic development on the one hand and the desire to preserve wilderness areas on the other. Liberals and conservatives have divided on these issues sharply, making a two party system viable. Early in the 20th century an influential liberal Republican, William E. Borah, served Idaho in the Senate, and later on similar stature was gained by a liberal Democrat, Frank Church. He was noted for taking strong stands against the war in Vietnam and for conservation despite powerful opposition from Idaho's hawkish logging, mining and grazing operators.

The power of Idaho's liberals has been in the north, in the rainy forest region where a higher proportion of Catholics and Democrats live, often employed in the lumbering and tourist industries. Ironically, this is also the part of Idaho that has garnered lurid headlines for harboring remote cells of white supremacists. The south has been the bastion of conservative and arch-conservative strength, as indicated by how the John Birch Society flourished in Pocatello and Boise in the 1960's. Masons, Mormons and Republicans tend to unite in this part of Idaho, leading to the passage of such items as a right-to-work constitutional amendment that restricts union activities in 1986 and an attempt to put restrictions on abortions in 1989.

Mining has continued to be an important segment of Idaho's economy, with most ores coming from an amazing ten-mile by thirty-mile strip of ore bearing timberland near Cour d'Alene. Idaho is first in silver, second in lead and third in zinc mining. Recently an immense deposit of phosphates has been discovered near Pocatello.

Environmentalists have been particularly pleased that random mining for gold and other minerals here and there has generally petered out. The ugly little slag heaps covered with weeds lie in stark contrast to their often beautiful surroundings. Nevertheless, quite a few small diggings for gems go on in widely scattered places. Idaho is known as the "gem state" and hobbyists called 'rockhounds' never tire of praising the state.

Many parts of the world wish to import Idaho's timber, and this demand has set the stage for a classic struggle between environmentalists in and outside of the forest service and those who own and work for the timber industry. Idaho has the nation's largest stand of white pine and a substantial supply of other desired types of trees, including Douglas fir, Engleman spruce, lodgepole pine and ponderosa pine.

Sheep grazing has been an occupation that has brought a very specialized and exotic type of worker to Idaho, the basque sheepherder. Many of these people from the rough country of northern Spain can be found in the desolate hills of central Idaho and in Boise. Those in the city compose a significant ethnic minority and have their own Basque Center, Basque Museum and Basque dancers. Those in the hills are still likely to follow the old dream of living simply, often in a colorful trailer, saving whatever can be saved from a low salary and going back to Spain someday to retire in a degree of comfort. The plunging dollar and strong economy of post-Franco Spain may ruin this dream for some of them.

Idaho's potato growing soil along the Snake River, rich, irrigated volcanic ash, continues to produce abundantly. Nowadays large companies do most of the growing and all of the processing. Large groups of Mexican and Indian workers are brought in to do much of the labor in the fields and local people take jobs in the plants. Approximately two thirds of America's processed potatoes come from Idaho.

Idaho's greatest resource in the next century will undoubtedly be its water. Of all the Mountain States, Idaho is unique in having an abundant supply. Consequently, it is estimated that Idaho has more land under irrigation than any other state except the large, populous states of California and Texas. By comparison, the Colorado River, which brings life giving water to so many areas in the region and outside of it, contains only one fifth of the water in Idaho's rivers. The abundance of Idaho's water is the direct result of the heavy flow of Pacific moisture that falls across Idaho's rugged north and central regions. Struggles over the control of it will undoubtedly enliven Idaho politics in the next century. California has already schemed for a diversion of some of it to supply its ever more thirsty cities.

Some Scenic Highlights

Idaho's name hints at its scenic splendor. It comes from an Indian word, 'eedahow' which means "light on the mountains." Central and northern Idaho have vast scenic stretches that offer access to wilderness areas by foot and horseback.

Several major highways have been designated as scenic routes and bear special names as such. The "Payette River

Scenic Route" goes north from Boise along State Route 55, while the "Ponderosa pine Scenic Route" follows State Route 21 out of Boise. The latter bisects two other scenic routes towards the middle part of the state, the "Sawtooth Scenic Route" and the "Salmon River Scenic Route." The latter follows the Salmon River north to the Continental Divide and western Montana. The Sawtooth Scenic Route connects the ski area of Sun Valley and Ketchum with Twin Falls and other cities along the populated belt following Interstate 84 across the bottom of the state. In the north there are other scenic routes, including the "Clearwater Canyons Scenic Route" on U.S. 12 which goes through to Nez Percé Indian reservation and the "White Pine Scenic Route" following State Routes 6 and 3. The way to get from the central scenic routes to the northern scenic route is U.S. 95, which is, as mentioned previously, the only highway connecting the northern and southern parts of the state.

All of these scenic routes more or less live up to their billing. Most of them follow rivers, which is both advantageous and disadvantageous. A river always seeks the path of least resistance as gravity draws its water out towards the ocean. While this guarantees some beautiful vistas along the way, it also means that driving will be hard and slow on account of all of the twists and turns required in a roadway that follows its natural, meandering pathway. Allow extra time for these Idaho scenic routes, particularly in the tourist season when somebody who is either enthralled or frightened by the curves and drop offs may be ahead in a big Winnebago. One advantage of scenic routes in Idaho is that they frequently provide "slow traffic turnouts.". Slower vehicles are expected to pull into them and allow swifter vehicles to zip past.

Signs frequently beckon drivers to "historic sites," to the extent of every few miles on some roads, such as route 30 in southeastern Idaho. Most "sites" only offer a plaque which might say something like: "Here was a particularly difficult place for the pioneers to ford this river," and then go on to tell how they did it in great detail. Many of these "sites" without any physical artifacts and commemorating rather thin historical circumstances are not worth a stop.

As mentioned previously, Idaho's lakes are gorgeous and there are over 2,000 of them of all sizes. The narrow panhandle has the greatest concentration of lakes in the Rocky Mountain Region, including three giant lakes, all set off by the dark forests surrounding them: Priest Lake, Lake Prend Oreille and Cour D'Alene Lake. Whatever anyone wants from them, solitude, excursions or lake side resorts, is abundantly available.

Idaho's Hell's Canyon is widely touted as the deepest chasm in North America, deeper at 9,300 feet than the Grand Canyon in Arizona. While its measurements do indeed confirm this claim, the irregular layers of pine-covered hills that climb up the sides of the chasm rob it of some of the grandeur and drama that the sheer walls of the Grand Canyon present. Nevertheless, the Hell's Canyon National Recreation area is one of the most remote stretches of river in the United States. Access on paved roadways is from U.S. 95 to State Highway 71 heading southwest out of Cambridge. Other access is by jet boat or unimproved roads. Authorities advise checking with the U.S. Forest Service for current information about access.

Another scenic place in Idaho that seeks to rival a famous site in another state is Shoshone Falls, the "Niagara of the West." Again the statistics give the Idaho attraction the edge because some of its water can plummet 52 feet further than Niagara, but there is a hitch. Much of the Snake River water is siphoned away for irrigation from April to October. In the off season, the falls can be seen in more magnificence. They are off of Interstate 84 near Twin Falls.

Idaho's greatest treasure may be its mountain wilderness areas, the Selway Bitterroot Wilderness, the Frank Church River of No Return Wilderness Area and the Sawtooth Wilderness Area. They are all in central Idaho from the Montana border down to just above the Sun Valley area. The designation of wilderness areas was not without major struggles against corporations adamant against seeing land "locked up" in them. Fortunately for Idaho, the struggles ended in putting large expanses aside, places where humans and their internal combustion engines do not dominate; places which can only be visited on foot or on horseback.

Some Special Places in Idaho

CENTRAL IDAHO AND THE CRATERS OF THE MOON NATIONAL MONUMENT

Central Idaho has some of the most barren, deserted land in the Rocky Mountain region. Barren hills, hardly covered with vegetation stretch down towards southeastern Idaho, where farmers have made the valleys bloom by using irrigation in the same manner that valleys in arid Utah have been brought into cultivation.

Central Idaho was barren enough for the Department of Energy and its bureaucratic predecessors to build nuclear reactors for years at the Idaho National Engineering Laboratory.

Route 20 from Idaho Falls heading west towards Boise traverses Idaho's badlands. Along the way is the Craters of the

Moon National Monument, the only national monument in the state. It consists of dark, twisted heaps of burnt out lava flows from ancient times. Those with an interest in geology will find the site fascinating, and all will find it grim, stark and barren.

SUN VALLEY

Sun Valley seems more like an enclave from the most prosperous part of Colorado. In fact, there is very little to distinguish the ski area of Sun Valley from Vail or Aspen. The towns of Sun Valley and Ketchum, only a mile from each other, sparkle with affluence. Chic shops selling the most fashionable and most expensive clothing line the streets, along with exotic coffee shops, bistros and stylish restaurants. Ordinary items, such as gasoline or frozen yogurt, cost considerably more than they do just a few miles south in the rather ordinary town of Hailey.

Vacationers fly in to Sun Valley from everywhere, many of them rich and famous. Those who purvey goods and services to them act the same way as Rocky Mountain merchants did towards the miners: they charge whatever they can get away with.

SOUTHEASTERN IDAHO'S MORMON AREA

Southeastern Idaho can be called Utah irredenta, a word defined in the dictionary as unredeemed territory, because it looks so much like part of that neighboring state. As it has been mentioned, the Mormons who first settled the area were convinced that they were still in Utah. Their settlements date back to the early 1860's, and many of these early Mormon pioneers in Idaho came from Britain originally. Roadside plaques commemorate their arrival and early challenges.

Towns in this part of Idaho have that big, square, clean, quiet look of Mormon settlements. Their large Victorian stone buildings and Mormon churches often look as if they were constructed for much larger communities than the ones that they adorn. Modern buildings seem to be few and far between in these towns. Those who remember America in the 1950's will find these towns in southeastern Utah capable of evoking considerable nostalgia for that era.

THE NEZ PERCÉ
NATIONAL HISTORICAL PARK

Close to Lewiston in northern Idaho is the 12,000 acre Nez Percé National Historical Park, located within a large Nez Percé Indian Reservation. The park has a museum at its Visitor Center containing excellent Nez Percé materials.

Among the Indian nations, the fate of the Nez Percé ranks as one of the most tragic. They were well known as friends of the first whites in the region, noted for providing guides and accepting missionaries. Even so, the usual territorial aggressiveness of Euro-Americans manifested itself when gold strikes were made in Nez Percé territories. Some bands of the tribe were persuaded to sell out to the whites, but other bands refused. Tense confrontations led to the outbreak of war, during which time a most remarkable Nez Percé leader exerted himself, Chief Joseph, who ranks with Crazy Horse and Sitting Bull as a skilled commander in the desperate and, in the long run, hopeless struggle against white encroachment. His strategy was to lead his people on a long retreat out of Idaho to Montana. His tactics of retreat, aimed at inflicting the smallest number of casualties possible on whatever whites his band encountered along the way, were brilliantly executed. In four months, he led his people over 1,700 miles on an epic retreat, fought many successful skirmishes and a few battles, only to be halted and captured just a few miles short of the Canadian border.

The scene of the first engagement of the Nez Percé was is the White Bird Battlefield on Route 95, 14 miles south of Grangeville. It was another overwhelming Indian victory but different from Little Big Horn because the Nez Percé deliberately let the surprised, defeated and confused federal troops escape after a third of them fell as casualties. The impressive battlefield site can be viewed easily from a convenient roadside visitor's display.

IDAHO CITY

Idaho City has character. It was once the largest and wildest gold rush town in the state. Its rugged and quaint old buildings, some of them still functioning and others shut down, have a genuine Old West appearance. The log exteriors of some and the plank sidewalks do not have that fresh look which so often reveals that these effects were slapped on to impress gullible tourists. Never mind that a rough hewn timber establishment called Killer's Saloon and Steak House has a sign declaring that it is air-conditioned.

Tourism is increasingly important to Idaho City, but the town and the area around it is still dependent, in a very Western way, on an extractive industry: timber. The classic battle between jobs and environment rages on in this town, dividing its inhabitants. Some work for the timber industry and some work for the National Forest Service. As in classic Western economies of boom and bust, the timber industry jostles the town with its cycles.

Local life is blessed with active, democratic, grass roots activity. Local people vigorously debate the virtues of various individuals or schemes for development. All of this is aided by an old local newspaper which enjoys the services of a very sharp editor.

Idaho City is a good jumping off place to visit some very dead and almost dead ghost towns. Centerville, Placerville and Pioneerville are some of the more notable ones. Make inquiries of local people. If it is open, stop in at the newspaper office on main street because it is a very helpful and friendly place.

BOISE

Idaho's only metropolitan area has approximately 200,000 people, 123,000 of whom live in the city proper. It is a spacious, open, clean, progressive metropolis. Perhaps it now resembles, in some ways at least, what Denver was decades ago.

Many corporations have their headquarters in Boise. The big lure for corporate executives is that the heart of the great outdoors is only an hour away, meaning that fishing, hunting, hiking and skiing are easily accessible. What is more, it is a good environment for families.

Many of Boise's corporations deal with Idaho's products, especially paper, potatoes and timber. This serves to dispel the old image of out-of-state giants colonizing and exploiting a Rocky Mountain state. In addition to these big corporations, light industry thrives, and the city serves as an important distribution hub for a wide area.

Boise derives its name from the French word for wooded place, "bois," and its present appearance certainly does retain this aspect. In addition to cherishing numerous trees, it is a city of wide streets, tasteful modern box-shaped buildings and some old, handsome buildings dating from the turn of the century. This architectural mix is set off against the stark, dry foothills of the Rockies.

Boise has the remains of Old Fort Boise, a remarkable Old Idaho Penitentiary, and the Idaho Historical Museum which features displays of exact interiors to recreate the past.

OTHER IDAHO CITIES

Pocatello and Idaho Falls are major southeastern cities based on agriculture. People in these cities look towards Utah for cultural and religious leadership because they are in that part of Idaho which is subject to Mormon influence.

The location of Pocatello was chosen for the first American fur trading post west of the Continental Divide, Fort Hall. Today a replica of it exists eleven miles away from the original site. Although it looks rather too spick-and-span for an old fur trading post, and despite the fact that its exhibits are rather cluttered, it is an earnest attempt at restoration.

Lewiston is the largest city in the panhandle. In the early years of the territory it served as the capital for a time. Recently Lewiston has become a busy, bustling inland port because the Columbia and the Snake inland waterway has been put into operation.

Utah: Places Mentioned in the Text

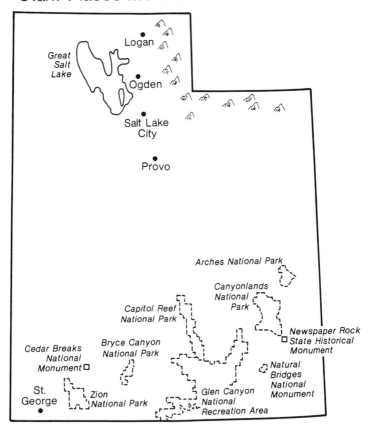

CHAPTER TEN

UNIQUE UTAH

What is Special About Utah

Utah is a unique state culturally and geographically. It is the center of the world for Mormons, who number seven out of every ten inhabitants and close to nine out of every ten members of the state legislature. While other locations in the United States have dominant religious groups, such as the Great Plains Lutherans, the New England Roman Catholics and the Southern Baptists, in none of these places is the percentage of the dominant group so overwhelming as it is in Utah.

Geographically Utah is divided into three regions: the Rocky Mountain region, the southwestern plateau and the basin of the western desert. That part of Utah which has snow-capped mountains and dark forests flanking a plain containing modern cities resembles Colorado's Front Range development. By contrast, the high, dry reddish Colorado Plateau stretching across southern Utah looks more like a part of Arizona with its flat-topped mountains, buttes, cliffs, deep canyons and rock formations of the most fantastic shapes and bright colors. The basin area is characteristically a hard, flat, monotonous desert stretching out westward to the Nevada border. Parts of it are put to use as a race course and a target range.

Utah's population is homogenous beyond the Mormon majority. Over 95% of the population is white and less than 1% is black. Utah's population is highly concentrated in the north central part, where three quarters of all Utahans live in a north-south belt 150 miles long and usually 10 to 25 miles wide. This population core mirrors that of Colorado, which is concentrated along the Front Range, but differs because Utah's mountains are to the east of its cities, whereas Colorado's mountains are to the west of its urban belt. The other Rocky Mountain states have their population centers hundreds of miles apart. St. George in the far southwest is the only substantial city outside of Utah's urban concentration. Although vast stretches of Utah are amazingly empty, the urban belt insures that the state's population density is just over 20 per square mile. The total population is under two million.

Perhaps the most well known of all of Utah's geographical features is the Great Salt Lake, which has varied in size over the years. It is fifteen miles west of the city named for it. Recently it has averaged 30 miles wide, 75 miles long and only 30 feet deep. Islands in the lake are populated with swarms of birds, but the salty waters only contain blue-green algae, diminutive brine shrimp and brine flies. Everything and everyone floats easily in it because of its extremely high salt content, which is six times that of ocean water. Great Salt Lake is noted as the second saltiest body of water in the world, with only the Sea of Galilee having a higher salt content. This comparison was not lost on the Mormons, who named the river flowing into Great Salt Lake the Jordan.

The Great Salt Lake of today is but a shrinking remnant of gigantic prehistoric Bonneville Lake which covered up to a quarter of Utah 50,000 or so years ago. The cities in the region are built on terraces of this ancient lake. Unfortunately its remnant is highly polluted today by industrial waste and sewage.

Another unique feature of Utah's geography are the Uintas Mountains, the only major range of mountains in the United States to proceed from east to west instead of north to south. The Uintas are in one of the most scenic and wild parts of the Rockies, although they are somewhat close to the urban belt. The Wasatch Mountains are even closer to the cities, and are easily accessible, thereby providing urbanites opportunities to escape from the heat of summer, to hunt in the fall and to enjoy winter sports in both winter and spring.

Utah's varied climate reflects its distinctly differing terrain. Some desert areas have less than five inches of precipitation per year, while more than 40 inches accumulate in the Wasatch Mountains. Although some fierce hailstorms and windstorms occasionally occur, and the winter can produce some blinding snowstorms, Utah's climate tends to be moderate and mild most of the time.

Utah's economy is varied. Grazing in most places requires one of the nation's highest ratios of land to livestock. Mining has been important from the time of the first discoveries in the 1860's. Less than 30 miles from Salt Lake City is North America's largest surface copper mine, where over 1,000 acres are excavated, producing an enormous crater half a mile deep that is over 1½ miles long and over one mile wide. Salt Lake City serves as a distribution center for West Coast products. In the urban belt surrounding this metropolis a considerable amount of new, light industry flourishes, and defense contracts are put into operation regularly. Utah takes pride in its well-educated, disciplined, and highly productive work force and hopes to bring more high tech industries to the state because of it, and because of the large number of young scientists Utah trains.

Utah's Dominant Mormons: Beliefs, History and Lifestyles

Utah's history and culture is inextricably interwoven with the Mormon faith. The minority of Utahans who do not adhere to this faith must nonetheless deal with it because it is so dominant. Likewise, visitors ought to be aware of this Mormon presence and know something about their beliefs as well as their history.

Mormons and non-Mormons, residents and visitors, can all find it difficult to be objective about this religion. For believers, Utah is the center of their earthly universe. For non-believers, the overwhelming numbers and power of the Mormons in Utah can seem oppressive at times or at least annoying. Utah is actually a good place for mainstream non-Mormon Americans to experience what it feels like to be a members of a minority for a change. In no other state are the Mormons a dominant group, although there are substantial numbers of them in other Rocky Mountain states. There are close to 200,000 Mormons in Idaho and tens of thousands of them in Colorado, Wyoming and Montana.

In some ways, the Mormon Church functions as a state within a state, much as the dominant Roman Catholic Church operates in Ireland. Its power can be felt everywhere, in politics, in economics, in cultural affairs and in society in general. Mormon dominance is not expressed in a harsh or cruel manner. Mormons are courteous, enthusiastic and always on the lookout to impress a potential convert. Their presence is marked by neat, solid homes, a surprisingly high level of social cohesion and activity, and a remarkable loyalty to their faith and to its leaders. They are usually supremely self-confident and forcefully public spirited.

BELIEFS

The theology of the Mormon Church can seem peculiar to outsiders. Their own name, The Church of Jesus Christ of Latter Day Saints, often abbreviated to just L.D.S., refers to a number of prophetic saintly leaders of the 19th and 20th centuries. Through them Biblical revelations have continued to come forth, the Mormons claim, producing, among other things, the Book of Mormon, a relatively modern adjunct or addition to the Bible.

The Book of Mormon is supposed to be based on the Prophet Joseph Smith's translation from buried golden tablets that an angel named Moroni led him to in Upstate New York, twenty miles east of Rochester, in the early 19th century. He was helped in his work of translation by utilizing two magic transparent stones that miraculously enabled him to read the "reformed Egyptian" writing of the gold plates. The story the tablets contained told of how Israelites came to the New World in 600 B.C., were visited by the resurrected Christ and were eventually slaughtered, except for Moroni, who was the son of Mormon, the last of the Israelite prophets, and who reappeared later as an angel. It was Joseph Smith's appointed task to publish the Book of Mormon and restore the original Church of Christ on earth with its hierarchy of apostles and councils. To aid him in his task, Smith was supposedly visited by God, Jesus, John the Baptist and many apostles.

Thereafter Joseph Smith became the prophet and First President of the Mormon Church. Once he had published the Book of Mormon in 1830, Moroni whisked the gold tablets away. The faith he founded became what has been called the most persecuted and the most successful of the 19th century's revivalistic-utopian religious movements. For many people, then and now, the L.D.S. movement looked like a captivating and therefore dangerous cult, one that demanded obedience to its hierarchy, conducted secret and mysterious ceremonies, and carried on sexual practices, namely polygamy, that violated community standards. To make matters worse for them, they proved to be an economically competitive group because of their industriousness. Moreover, after a time they organized their own armed defense forces. Above all, they invited opposition by displaying absolute confidence that they had the only true church.

For all of these reasons, the history of the expansion of the Mormon Church was tumultuous and sometimes violent. Faced with persecution, the Mormons fled from place to place, finally coming to a vast, dry, empty wasteland that they transformed into their homeland, their Zion, or promised land. They called it Deseret until Congress arbitrarily changed the name of the place to the Utah Territory.

HISTORY

Joseph Smith never lived to see Deseret. He was murdered in an Illinois jail in 1844 by an enraged mob. It was Brigham Young who led the increasing number of persecuted converts out West to their new promised land. He deliberately sought out the most isolated place in North America in explorers' books and concluded that it must be near the Great Salt Lake. The only people who ever visited this place from the outside before American explorers saw it were a few Franciscan Spanish priests and a few British and American fur trappers.

A very orderly Mormon migration to the Great Salt Lake began. Mormons set up rest camps with food, cabins and blacksmiths' shops along the way. Brigham Young first saw the valley of the Great Salt Lake in 1847, and, according to legend, he is supposed to have said, "This is the place." Today a monument commemorates the event from the vantage point where he first saw the valley.

The first settlers had to work prodigiously to make the harsh desert bloom. Under Brigham Young's able, forceful leadership, disciplined, obedient Mormons were able to dig an efficient system of irrigation ditches, the first irrigation project in the West. They planted trees and crops and fought off insects with a zealous determination to master the environment. At one critical juncture great swarms of crickets threatened their survival, but they were saved by the sudden appearance of flocks of seagulls, an event heralded as a sure sign of Divine Providence.

The discovery of mineral wealth in the West meant that Mormons' wishes to be left to themselves would be frustrated. At first they made money by selling supplies at exorbitant prices to people bound for the gold rush in California, but when precious metals were discovered in Utah itself it meant that non-Mormons would invade their promised land and some would stay there permanently. Mormons themselves disdained mining because it was not work that God's chosen people took up in the Bible.

Facing a need for more manpower, the Mormon community of Deseret sent out a stream of dedicated, devoted missionaries to bring converts to the blooming desert from the East Coast and from Europe, particularly from Britain and Scandinavia. Their appeal, like the original appeal of Joseph Smith, was among the poor and the dispossessed. Meanwhile, carefully planned and organized colonies of Mormons spread out between the Rockies and the Sierras, settling wherever a reliable water supply allowed irrigated farming. Where they established themselves, the Mormons maintained an active social and intellectual life centering upon their church. They were extremely dedicated, enthusiastic, active and cohesive. In an increasing number of locations, the desert yielded the riches of comfort, security, and devoted family lives.

When Utah became a United States Territory, it was much smaller than the Mormons expected it to be and it was not called by the name they desired, Deseret, which means honeybee, a reference to the Mormons' incomparable industriousness. Instead it was named for the region's Indians. Nevertheless, Brigham Young was appointed territorial governor.

Outsiders were deeply suspicious of the Mormons, who seemed to be immoral, fanatical eccentrics. Rumors flew that the Mormons were planning to massacre the non-Mormons in Utah. From a Mormon perspective, the outsiders, called gentiles, were likely to become persecuting bigots and plot with the forces of evil to destroy Mormonism. These antagonistic perspectives led to some severe clashes, the worst of which was the brief "Mormon War" of 1857.

Federal troops were sent against the Mormons who fought back with guerilla tactics and on one occasion joined up with Indians to perpetrate the notorious "Mountain Meadows

Massacre" of 1857. Brigham Young was replaced as governor of the territory and most of the issues were resolved.

One issue that was not resolved was that of polygamy. Congress went so far as to take away all of the property of the L.D.S. except for its churches and cemeteries to coerce the Mormons into giving up this practice. Statehood was denied to Utah seven times because of this deadlock. Eventually the L.D.S. officially renounced polygamy in 1890 and gave assurances that church and state would be kept separate.

Brigham Young was dead for thirteen years when these assurances were given. Young left 27 wives and 56 children behind him, not the only grounds for his claim to be the father of his state. Through his skilled, autocratic, charismatic leadership, Young was able to combine executive, legislative and judicial powers. Since he governed on the basis that he understood and applied Divine Will, Utah can be said to have had theocratic, or church government in his day. Even critics of his Utah had to admit that he was one of the most successful leaders of a frontier community in the history of the world.

THE MORMON LIFESTYLE

Mormons prefer to call themselves "the saints," and to call non-Mormons "gentiles." An irony of this terminology is that Jews in Utah have the unique opportunity of being called gentiles, a name that Jews have always used for non-Jews!

The saints continue to apply that remarkable social dynamism today. A sense of belonging and purpose seems to release their energies. They are noted for working hard, playing hard, studying hard and worshiping hard. Their church requires an extensive regimen of participation which takes them away from their homes on most nights, and when they do have what they call a "home night" it may be given over to family prayers, music and religious discussion. These activities are not supposed to be solemn tasks. On the contrary, they are intended to be full of zest and fun. Other important activities, especially making money and producing offspring, are also supposed to be carried on in a joyful atmosphere free from the dour Puritanism so pervasive in other parts of the United States.

At work or at play, Mormons appear to be well groomed, courteous, vigorous, and optimistic. Neat, well organized, solid communities have long been hallmarks of Mormon Utah. Mormon leadership is noted for conveying a strong sense of integrity and efficiency. Practicing Mormons must surrender a tithe, or 10% of their income before taxes, to the church. Practicing Mormons are drug free. Their prohibitions include tobacco, coffee, tea, soft drinks with caffeine and alcohol. Not all Mormons can maintain these standards or the rigorously fundamentalist beliefs. Those who backslide or drop out are called "Jack Mormons."

Various state controls over alcohol can lead Non-Mormons into some awkward situations over purchasing and imbibing drinks, and there have been complaints that restrictions on the free flow of drinks retards economic development because it discourages corporations contemplating relocation to Utah. Recently laws have been amended to loosen restrictions on drinking.

POLITICAL AND SOCIAL ISSUES

Since there is no professional clergy, almost every Mormon male is some sort of church official, functionary or missionary. Authority in the church is strong and flows downwards through a pyramid. At the top is the President, who alone is open to prophetic revelation. Beneath him is a group of twelve apostles who supervise spiritual affairs. Since the apostles hold their posts for life, this guarantees that older men will always be in charge of the L.D.S. Beneath the apostles are the bishops who preside over specific territories called stakes. They have that name because they are supposed to support the church the way stakes support a tent. The important churches in these territories are called stake houses. A classic story exists about gentiles who were invited by their Mormon neighbors to a stake house and who politely suffered the pangs of hunger while seemingly endless religious activities proceeded. Anyway, the stakes are further subdivided into wards, which resemble parishes.

Mormons facing economic hardship always have the material support of their church because an effective church welfare system operates. The L.D.S. is involved in the economy in other ways. It owns all sorts of businesses, including operations in farming and the media. Capital is poured into these enterprises, and when profits accrue they are siphoned off for social services and education, which is a major field of Mormon effort. Brigham Young University is specially well endowed by the church. The emphasis on education has enabled Utah to be one of the highest ranking states in per capita educational attainments.

One byproduct of Mormon beliefs is one of the best genealogical archives in the United States, which is housed in an underground vault in a canyon near Salt Lake City. Mormons organized it so that they can carry out proxy baptisms and marriages for their ancestors. They have done so with vigor. It is estimated that well over 30 million people have been vouched for a place in the Mormon's celestial eternity. Scholars of all backgrounds from all over come to Salt Lake City to use these detailed records of families that the church has created through its lavish investment in these records.

At one time politics in Utah involved a Mormon party and a non-Mormon party. To have their people adjust to American politics, Mormon leaders decreed that the saints should join both major national parties. Since then, Democrats and Republicans have enjoyed Mormon backing, although now Mormon Republicans predominate and the Democrats tend to draw voters from poorer Mormons and Jack Mormons. Ordinarily up to nine out of ten state legislators are Mormon and very few non-Mormons have ever been governors of Utah.

Non-Mormons tend to become exasperated over how much L.D.S. news is featured in newspapers and on television. Criticism has also been voiced about how ritualistic and male dominated the church seems. Feminists note how Mormon women are often expected to stay at home and concentrate on family, church charities, gardening and crafts. This is changing as more and more L.D.S. women are finding work outside the home. Problems of the larger society, including drugs, gangs, teenage pregnancy and A.I.D.S. have made some inroads in Utah, particularly among the non-Mormons and Jack Mormons, but also among some ostensibly practicing Mormons as well.

Mormons were sharply criticized in recent years for racial discrimination against African-Americans, but what has been declared to be recent Divine Revelation on the subject to Mormon Presidents has ameliorated that situation considerably because these prophesies have come down in remarkable accord with United States laws against discrimination.

Much more agonizing has been the ongoing struggle over the practice of polygamy. From 1852 until 1890 the L.D.S. church officially sanctioned plural marriages. Although guarantees of religious liberty under the United States Constitution seemed to preclude Congressional interference, anti-polygamy laws were passed and the Supreme Court upheld them. As a result, polygamous Mormons were subjected to a wave of federal persecution that included no-knock raids of suspects, jail terms for husbands and removal of children from parents.

Even after the L.D.S. church banned polygamy on the grounds that fresh divine revelation declared it detracted from the mission of the church, Utah legislators were slow and reluctant to apply anti-polygamy laws in their state. This approach was much like that of Abraham Lincoln decades before. In referring to polygamy, Lincoln said that when he found a stump in the field he plowed around it.

Polygamy continued on as part of the "shadow history" of the Rocky Mountain West. There has been an upsurge in the practice from Canada to Mexico since World War Two that some put as high as 500%. Isolated communities, some over the border in northern Arizona, quietly carry on with polygamous lifestyles today. While anti-polygamy laws are still on the books, they are not being applied. Unlike their Victorian forebears, most contemporary Americans seem to have little inclination to disturb the private lives of these people. One would think that the modern view that consenting adults may carry on a variety of sexual practices would apply to this old Mormon custom as well. As a matter of fact, the American Civil Liberties Union has taken this very position on polygamy in the Rocky Mountain West.

Some Scenic Highlights

SOUTHERN UTAH: ONE OF THE BEST TRAVEL DESTINATIONS IN AMERICA

Southern Utah has miles upon miles of wide open, sparsely populated, brilliantly colored and dramatically shaped and eroded terrain. Even the sights along major Interstate highways can be gorgeous during hours of hot, dry travel. Film directors and German tourists are noted for appreciating these vistas. Indiana Jones and countless cowboy epics play against backgrounds of southern Utah's grandeur. In the summer large, rented recreational vehicles disgorge platoons of enthusiastic Germans at every notable scenic wonder. In the swimming pools of commercial campgrounds more German is sometimes spoken than English. These tourists arrive for a very Western experience: the opportunity to view gorgeous scenery in a wide, vast, and empty terrain in blazing, dry desert heat.

Southeastern Utah has the richest scenery. The relatively dull Great Basin extends into the southwestern part of the state. The rough line of demarcation between the two sections of southern Utah is Interstate 15 itself, the main highway connecting the state from north to south.

EXPLORING UTAH'S NATIONAL PARKS

Everyone can be thankful that some of the best parts of scenic Utah have been preserved as National Parks and National Monuments. There are more of them in Utah than in most other states. While debates rage on about how they are to be preserved or developed, the presence of an increasing number of tourists is beginning to mar the sense of lonely, isolated, barren grandeur that was once the essence of these places.

Good starting points for exploring the National Parks and National Monuments are the towns of Moab in the east and St. George in the southwest. Moab can be reached south off of Interstate 70 and St. George is on Interstate 15. Roads are few and far between in southern Utah, but they are excellent for providing wide open, lonely spaces, the kinds of vistas that should be among the top priorities for vacationers in this part of the world. U.S. Highway 163 in and out of Moab is excellent, and so is State Route 95 which makes one of the very few crossings of Glen Canyon Reservoir. State Route 9 out of St. George and U.S. Highway 89 and State Routes 12 and 24 can also be cited for their attractions and lack of heavy traffic.

Arches National Park: Arches National Park, which is a few miles north of Moab, was established in 1971. Before that it was a National Monument. It has an area of 115 square miles in which hundreds of arches can be found. Sources vary about just how many arches it has, and just what can be considered to be a true arch. Regardless of the exact number, this is unquestionably the greatest concentration of them to be found in the world. This National Park has paved roads to many exciting sites and offers hiking, backpacking, four wheel drive opportunities and mountain biking.

Temperatures are moderate in the fall and spring, but in the summer the temperature can reach 110° Fahrenheit. Consequently rangers recommend that hiking take place in the mornings or evenings and urge that the absolute minimum of water carried by each adult be no less than one gallon.

There is a Visitor Center open all year which explains how the arches were formed. Phone 801-259-8161 for more information.

Canyonlands National Park: Recently a national network reported a controversy over whether or not to declare the Canyonlands of southwestern Utah a wilderness area. Although this part of the state is regarded as the last best unspoiled area in the Continental United States, opponents of this designation claim that jobs in mining, ranching and ancillary development will be lost if it becomes a wilderness area.

Fortunately a good portion is already protected in the Canyonlands National Park, whose 402 square miles may contain some of the most remote portions of any National Park outside Alaska. The scenery is grand, but it is so hot and dry that the warnings about taking enough water along while exploring must be heeded unequivocally.

Like ancient Gaul, Canyonlands National Park is divided into three parts. The Colorado River and the Green River have shaped the region, and both of these great rivers come together within the park forming a letter "y". The northern portion, above the confluence, is called the Island in the Sky. A paved road into it is accessible from secondary roads from the north and there are wide ranging jeep trails though its northern section. The southeastern section, called the Needles, has a concentration of arches, spines and canyons, as well as prehistoric Indian ruins and pictographs. It has a paved road accessible from the east. The section called the maze, west of the rivers, derives its name from its tangled maze of canyons. It is extremely remote and has no roads going through it at all. For information call 801-259-7164.

Capitol Reef National Park: Capitol Reef National Park is a long, narrow slice of land bisected by State Route 24. Its name comes from a barrier, or reef, of red stone that is shaped somewhat like the dome of the United States capital. The park follows a vertical escarpment, which is part of a hundred mile bulge in the earth's crust called Waterpocket fold.

Mormons settled in the area for a time, founding the town of Fruita, whose remains are situated within the park. Its old fashioned one room schoolhouse now serves as an exhibit, complete with an audiotape. The Mormons also planted orchards, and to this day bountiful harvests of fresh fruit, uncontaminated by pesticides, can be gathered by visitors to the park. The author attests to the fact that the park's warm, tree ripened cherries are simply superb! Apples, pears, peaches and apricots are also available in season. Another feature of the park is hiking to ancient petroglyphs, or prehistoric rock carvings. Call 801-425-3791 for further information.

Bryce Canyon National Park: Bryce Canyon has some of the best scenery and some of the worst commercialization of any national park. The canyon contains fantastically eroded reddish pink pinnacles, spires and hoodoos, a name for odd shaped rocks left standing by the forces of erosion. These panoramas vary with both sunlight and moonlight. Some foreign visitors go so far as to rate this eroded canyon as the very best natural sight in all of America, more spectacular than the Grand Canyon itself. The Indian name for it was actually a description: "Red rocks standing like men in a bowl-shaped canyon." A Mormon settler named Ebeneezer Bryce who tried to farm in the area gave his name to the canyon, although he referred to it simply as "a hell of a place to lose a cow." One special advantage of Bryce Canyon is its altitude of approximately 8,000 feet, which keeps it cooler in the summer than other parks in Utah.

Chain link fences protect observers from falling into the canyon at the most spectacular overlooks, which can be very crowded in the tourist season because paved roads bring in fleets of buses, cars and even large touring cars left over from the 1930's. Crowded vantage points are loud with conversations and there is a constant undertone of clicking and purring cameras. These spots are so busy that signs warn that valuables should not be left in cars and that pets must be kept on leashes. The best way to see the park is actually to go on some of the trails in order to avoid mob scenes.

The approaches to the park are worse. Western hype abounds to lure dollars from tourists in every conceivable way. Horses wait for riders in one field just as helicopters wait for them in an adjacent field. There are fake "old West" emporiums, hotels, motels and lodges galore. Signs announce that "chuckwagon" dinners will be delivered to groups riding off. Unfortunately, many large and busy concessions are allowed to operate within the park itself. Here is a good example of the struggle between natural beauty and development in which development has clearly won. For information on Bryce Canyon call 801-834-5322.

Zion National Park: Zion National Park protects yet another gorgeous portion of Utah. Zion Canyon is its main feature, a long, scenic corridor created by the crystal clear, cool flowing Virgin River. The rock formations are very varied in shape and color, displaying reds, pinks, whites and greys in abundance.

The park has an eastern entrance and a southern entrance. The former is quite dramatic, involving a ride through a mile long trail and over numerous switchbacks.

Trails in the park are particularly interesting, especially those leading along streams to pools and waterfalls. Mormon pioneers used Zion canyon as a place of retreat. Before them the prehistoric Anasazi Indians farmed in the area. For more information telephone 801-772-3256.

OTHER SCENIC ATTRACTIONS IN SOUTHERN UTAH

Glen Canyon National Recreation Area is a boater's delight, containing the largest artificial lake in North America, Lake Powell, which is 200 miles long and has 2,000 miles of shoreline. Dam water now reaches into spectacular canyons, creating a beautiful though partly artificial landscape. Very few bridges go over this paradise for boaters and fishermen. The huge Glen Canyon Dam that turned the Colorado River into this lake is actually across the border in Arizona.

On the way to Canyonlands National Park on State Route 211 is Newspaper Rock State Historical Monument. It consists of a crowded collection of hundreds of petroglyphs on a smooth rock. Debate goes on over which inscriptions are prehistoric and which were added by later Indians.

Natural Bridges National Monument is south of Canyonlands National Park and east of Lake Powell. A paved loop is at the very center of it, affording good views of these natural bridges, which are similar in appearance to the arches in some national parks.

Cedar Breaks National Monument is a high park at 10,000 feet, which insures summer temperatures of 60° to 70° Fahrenheit, cool for southern Utah. No facilities are available in the area and the campground is only open from June 15 to September 15. It is just north of Zion National Park and not far from Interstate 15. For further information call 801-586-9451.

Since so much of Utah is open and empty, very interesting attractions can be found along major highways. Cove Fort is right off of Interstate 15. It was built in 1867 to protect a Mormon telegraph line that ran from Logan to St. George from attacks by Indians. It had living quarters and places for traveling Mormons to stay.

Along little traveled State Route 95 there is an outstanding rest stop called "Mule Canyon River Interpretive Rest Stop." It has delicate ruins of prehistoric Anasazi Indians right by the rest rooms. It appears that the simple posted request to respect the ruins has been obeyed. It is a pity to think of how many other places in the United States would be desecrated if left to the mercies of the passing public in this manner.

Two attractions shared by Colorado and Utah, Hovenweep National Monument and Dinosaur National Monument, are in the chapter on Colorado.

Utah's Cities

SALT LAKE CITY

Salt Lake City is to the Mormons what Mecca is to Muslims and Jerusalem is to Jews. Nevertheless, a degree of diversity in lifestyles exists, along with a variety of economic activities, making this city with a metropolitan area of just over a million people show some signs of the problems encountered in any major American metropolis.

Salt Lake City is spacious and sunny, and although it is laid out on a very flat plain, it is quite close to its beautiful backdrop of the Wasatch Mountains. They loom over the city impressively, and are much closer to the city than Denver's mountains are to that metropolis. Downtown consists of a large number of substantial, unspectacular, uncluttered buildings set along spacious, wide, clean streets. Brigham Young directed that the streets be 132 feet wide, broad enough to turn a span of oxen around in them. A short trip east brings its inhabitants to some of the most luxurious mountain ski resorts in the United States.

Just as Rome has its Vatican, Salt Lake City has its Temple Square, a ten acre area of buildings and gardens shielded from the rest of the city by a fifteen foot wall. Here the grey stone, six-spired Mormon Temple rises 210 feet out of the square. It is only open to Mormons in good standing and its ceremonies are exclusively for Mormons. Such is not the case for the Tabernacle nearby, a magnificently engineered structure whose excellent acoustics have enhanced the performances of world famous Mormon Tabernacle Choir, which has been singing in the Tabernacle since the building was built in 1867.

Two interesting sculpted works are found in Temple Square. The Angel Moroni, covered in gold leaf, perches on top of the Temple. In the grounds is the Seagull Monument, commemorating the intervention of these birds to save an early and much needed harvest from ravenous crickets.

The Beehive House on south Temple Street was Brigham Young's home and official residence as well as the home of several church presidents. It was where important visiting dignitaries were housed. It has been restored to its original Victorian style. There are many other historic houses on South Temple Street and another historic area is the Marmalade District where many early pioneer homes can be found. The district gets its name from its street names, such as Quince, Apricot and Plum.

As one might expect, Salt Lake City has several large galleries and museums. Of particular interest is the Pioneer Memorial Museum on North Main Street, which has material from the first pioneers of the 1840's up to the turn of the century.

OTHER CITIES IN UTAH

Most of Utah's other cities are grouped close to Salt Lake City, which makes it possible for their citizens to zip into the capital on fast Interstate highways to attend a religious or cultural function.

Provo, 43 miles to the south, is a city of approximately 85,000 inhabitants. Brigham Young University, which is at least as significant to Mormons as Notre Dame is to Roman Catholics, is located here. Provo also has a steel plant, a rare enterprise in the West.

Ogden, 30 miles to the north, is a progressive city reputed to maintain a small town atmosphere nonetheless. Close by is Fort Buenaventura State Park, reconstructed by Utah Parks and Recreation on the basis of archaeological evidence. It was originally a trading post and now contains three reconstructed log buildings and a stockade. Ogden boomed as a railroad town, and now the 5th Street Historic District seeks to preserve some of the buildings from the later Victorian era.

Logan is to the northeast, 80 miles away from Salt Lake City. It is a university town of around 33,000 that has colder winters than other Utah cities because it is just a thousand feet short of being a mile above sea level. It has several notable Victorian buildings, including the Logan L.D.S. Temple. The Utah State University campus has much to offer in cultural activities.

Only one of Utah's notable cities is not in the northeastern corner of the state. St. George is in the southwestern corner of the state, the so-called "Dixie" of Utah, which is warm enough to grow cotton. St. George is drawing an increasing number of retirees seeking a place to resettle in the sun belt. It was here that various Mormon leaders from the Salt Lake City area, including Brigham Young, established winter homes. Today an increasing number of non-Mormons are moving in, producing a boomlet and changing the city's character. St. George has the oldest Western Mormon Temple, and the largest one in the state, a great white building that dominates the city's skyline.

Colorado: Places Mentioned in the Text

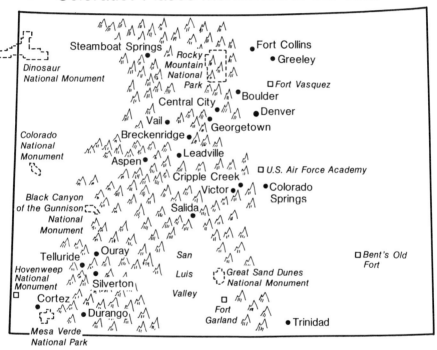

CHAPTER ELEVEN

COLORFUL COLORADO

What is Special
About Colorado

DIVERSITY OF DEVELOPMENT

Colorado is a truly unique state in the region because of
several important reasons. It is the most populous with over
three million people and a population density of over thirty
people per square mile, the highest in the region. It has a mini-
megalopolis stretching north to south down the Front Range,
a corridor of urban development right along the juncture of the
plains with the mountains where an estimated 80% of Coloradans live.

Growth along the Front Range has alarmed many Coloradans. In the 1970's it was three times the national average.
Places like Fort Collins and Colorado Springs have been noted
for growing at the rate of 50% in a single decade. Towns are
sprawling into each other and the haze from auto emissions and
other pollutants is beginning to obscure the wonderful views of
the mountains that lured so many people to the area in the first
place. Although some communities are seeking to control
growth by taking such steps as limiting the number of permit-
ted housing starts, rapid growth in the future is inevitable.
Desired lifestyles, the prospect of jobs, and the urge of so many

business people to encourage growth will continue to attract people to the state from all over. It is simply impossible to leave any of these Front Range cities for even a few months without coming back to see major changes in the form of either a new shopping center, or widened roads, or a new housing tract or the disappearance of old, familiar trees and farms.

Colorado is also the most developed Rocky Mountain state economically, with a more diversified economy than the others in the region. Mining, ranching and farming go on as in the past, but the newer components of the economy are the most profitable. These include new high tech industries, defense industries, government agencies and installations, and tourism. As a result of these diverse enterprises, Colorado has the highest per capita income of all the Rocky Mountain states.

Naturally, Colorado has not escaped the downside of modern economic development. Denver's "brown cloud" of pollution is famous. In recent decades, intense fears about the environment have centered on the Rocky Flats plant twenty miles northwest of Denver where the U.S. Department of Energy manufactures plutonium triggers for hydrogen bombs. Repeated government assurances that minimal amounts of hazardous material have escaped into the atmosphere fall short of consoling many people. Similar concern surrounds the Fort St. Vrain nuclear plant which generates electricity. It was built in an experimental manner most closely resembling the plant that melted down in the Soviet Union. Fortunately another threat to the environment was removed by the Federal Government some years ago. For a time a large quantity of poison gas was stored not far from the end of a runway at Denver's Stapleton International Airport!

While life along the Front Range may increasingly resemble life in California without an ocean, the mountains and the sparsely populated western part of the state offer the same kinds of outdoor adventures, wilderness areas, National Parks and National Monuments that are the hallmarks of the region. Colorado also has a rich concentration of historic mining towns, many of them within easy access of Denver. Ghost towns actually number in the thousands, clustering in great numbers around places like Central City and Aspen.

Another special feature of Colorado is the number of Victorian hotels that are still extant, some as museums and some still carrying on their old trade. It can be a treat to stay in some of these establishments savoring the past that they preserve so well. Among the more noteworthy old hotels are the excellent Strater in Durango, the very expensive Jerome in Aspen, the Hotel de Paris in Georgetown, the Vendome in Leadville, the Teller House in Central City, the Imperial at Cripple Creek, the Sheridan at Telluride and the Grand Imperial at Silverton.

Colorado's billion dollar ski industry is well known throughout the United States. Places like Vail, Beaver Creek, Breckenridge, Aspen, Telluride and Steamboat Springs have long been famous as winter playgrounds. What makes Colorado different from neighboring states is the number of ski resorts, the diverse geographical location of them and their appeal to varied tastes, ranging from the ordinary to the truly posh.

DIVERSITY OF POPULATION

Colorado can be considered either as a state belonging to the Rocky Mountain Region or to the Southwest. The Hispanic heritage of the state is a key reason for the latter designation.

Part of Colorado was originally explored and settled by Hispanic people, making it similar in that regard to Arizona and New Mexico. Hispanic connections continue to be an important factor because almost an eighth of the state's population is Hispanic today. The roots of some in Colorado go back centuries, long before settlers descended from northern Europe arrived. Others are very recent immigrants from Mexico, and undoubtedly there is an uncounted number of *illegales,* or illegal immigrants. Today Spanish can be heard in many places, Mexican food is as popular and widespread as Italian food, and Denver recently enjoyed the tenure of a popular Hispanic mayor.

Colorado's human diversity sets it off from the other Rocky Mountain States. There is a black population of 4%, not large compared to the over 12% in the nation, but the most substantial for the Rocky Mountain states. Denver elected its first black mayor in 1991, and there is an old, established black community in the city, middle class in lifestyle to a considerable extent.

Surprising ethnic enclaves show up here and there in the state. Many Coloradans whose family origins are in eastern Europe are descended from mine workers who were brought in as cheap labor. As any phone book reveals, a large number of people have German ancestry. Many of them are descendants of a vary particular ethnic group, the Germans from Russia. These people left Tsarist Russia in the early 20th century and established themselves along the Front Range where they became noted for growing sugar beets. Families of Japanese-American Coloradans were relocated from the Pacific shore during World War Two. Their descendants enjoy a complex in Denver called Sakura Square. Many Vietnamese came to Colorado during and after the long war in southeast Asia.

Human diversity can also be seen in the ranks of Coloradans who like to refer to themselves as "plain Americans," most of whom actually descended from settlers from the British Isles who may have come over as early as the 17th century. Some of them came from New England and the East Coast, some from the Midwest, particularly from neighboring Kansas and Nebraska, some have relocated to get away from economic constraints in Wyoming or social constraints in Utah. Some very rich and some poor people have come up from Texas and there has also been an influx of people who have had enough of California.

Colorado also has a Native American population, although the surviving members of the Cheyenne and Arapaho tribes which controlled most of the state were removed to distant reservations. Part of Colorado's Native American population lives in Denver and is of diverse tribal backgrounds, and tends to intermarry. Another part of the Native American population is of the Ute tribe, living in and around Colorado's only Indian reservation in the southwestern part of the state, the Ute Mountain Indian Reservation. Anglos and Hispanics are interspersed with the Utes, and there is concern that Ute culture is being eroded. The town of Ignacio in the reservation is a good place to observe this Anglo-Native American-Hispanic cultural mix.

The Utes maintain the Ute Mountain Tribal park on their reservation, which is dedicated to preserving the remains of the Anasazi, or the ancient Native Americans of the region.

A DIVERSE GEOGRAPHY

For some time it has been a commonplace to speak of the existence of several Colorados because the geography is so varied. The min-megalopolis of the Front Range from Fort Collins on the north to Pueblo on the south is certainly one geographic environment.

A second is found on the high, dry, tawny plains stretching east to Kansas and Nebraska, where both roads and population are scarce. Much of it looks as it did generations ago, a landscape of scattered wheat farms, ranches, and forlorn towns. The population of this last part of Colorado to be settled has been declining since 1920. Retired farmers and small businessmen have dominated the politics of these plains counties for a long time.

One new geographic feature for many places on the eastern plain is the appearance of huge center pivot irrigation systems to replace dry farming. From the air, great circles of green indicate where sorghum, wheat and corn are grown. The unfortunate aspect of this procedure is that the Ogallala aquifer is being depleted rapidly.

A few parts of the eastern plain are preserved as prairie, indicating how the whole region looked before submitting to the ravages of the plow and the ensuing dust storms. Both the Pawnee National Grassland on the northern part of the Colorado plains and the Comanche National Grassland on the southern part offer an expanse of prairie.

A third Colorado can be the Hispanic areas of the south, particularly the San Luis Valley, where Hispanics are still in the majority, but also including Trinidad and Pueblo, the old coal and iron belt of Colorado. Actually, when the southern border of Colorado was struck east to west as a straight line in 1861 it severed the single Hispanic cultural region centered in New Mexico.

These parts of Colorado belong to the Rio Grande basin area and include the "Sangre de Cristo" or "blood of Christ" mountains, named because of the bright reds that appear when struck in a certain way by the sun's rays. Today this is the least prosperous part of the state as well as of the Rocky Mountain region. Income is low, unemployment high and housing conditions are substandard. Recently a scandal erupted over residents poaching game, which came to reveal that many poor families needed the extra protein from wild animals.

Another Colorado consists of the high spine of mountains, filled with old mining towns, many of them continuing on as busy ski resorts and some of them lapsed into ghostly remains. There are also new ski resorts, built from scratch in the post-war era. This is the Colorado that lures millions of tourists each year, winter and summer, the part that contains its glittering names and draws the rich and famous who are likely to arrive in their private jets. It is also the part that is thronged with campers and recreational vehicles and people trying to make the most of their two or three week vacations.

The "western slope" is the name of yet another Colorado, a particular region that has long played an oppositional role in Colorado. It is in the westernmost part of the state, which is rather sparsely populated with ranchers and farmers. Life on the western slope is more simple and rural than anywhere else in the state. It is an area so resentful of the dominance of the eastern megalopolis that it has often grumbled about seceding and forming its own state. Western slope residents are wary of new developments emanating from Denver and dislike the siphoning off of western slope water by the thirstier eastern Colorado cities. The irony of all this, of course, is that the feelings of eastern and western Colorado about the use and development of resources mirrors the feelings of the Eastern and Western United States on the same subject historically.

Highlights of Colorado History

Since Colorado's history conforms in large measure to aspects of the history of the Rocky Mountain West detailed in previous chapters, only the highlights with a particular bearing on Colorado will be presented in this section.

While the eastern plains of Colorado were the home of shifting groups of Native Americans dependent upon the buffalo, the mountains were occupied by the Anasazi and Utes. The Anasazi or "the ancient ones" are believed to be the ancestors of Pueblo Indians to the south. Their mysterious disappearance from Colorado has been the subject of considerable speculation because they left such magnificent ruins behind, particularly at Mesa Verde National Park. The Utes hunted in the mountains and wintered in the river valleys, competing with the Anasazi for food and perhaps thereby helping to contribute to their decline. See the section on Mesa Verde for more details on the Anasazi.

Spanish and French expeditions explored Colorado long before English speakers arrived in the area. The Spanish were established for several hundred years in New Mexico and regarded the plains and mountains of Colorado as Indian territory that would not be worth the attempt to occupy, except for projections of New Mexico into southern Colorado in the upper Rio Grande basin in the San Luis Valley and the upper Arkansas valley.

American exploration in the region began with the expedition of 1805 led by a young lieutenant named Zebulon Pike. Although he could not climb the peak named for him, he continued on in the area until he was arrested by Spanish authorities. American title to the whole of the state's area came only after the Mexican War of 1846 to 1848.

There have been two revolutionary surges of development in Colorado: the first from mining precious metals and the second from growth forced by national demands during World War Two.

A small gold strike near what became Denver in 1858 brought a flood of prospectors in 1859, who were called the '59ers' in memory of the 49ers who rushed to California. Denver was laid out in anticipation of supplying a great rush. Many who went West to Colorado found only disappointment until the greater strikes high up in the mountains occurred. Claims along the rivers near Denver were never very productive, and in general placer mining and sluice mining gave out. The good ores tended to be in quartz rock, necessitating big operations to dislodge it.

Despite the tumult of acquisition, law and order and rudimentary government emerged quite quickly in the mining district. Violence was curtailed early. Simultaneously, with amazing speed, Denver established itself as a settled community geared to supplying distant miners.

The rush for riches was disturbed by the onset of the American Civil War. When Colorado became a territory just before its outbreak, President Lincoln appointed a union governor to preside over a territory that was clearly unionist in sentiment. An opportunity to participate in the struggle arrived when an army of Confederates set out to march far north from New Mexico in 1862 in the hope of controlling the new goldfields of Colorado. They were met by a force of mostly Colorado volunteers at La Glorietta pass in New Mexico, stopped and pushed into headlong retreat. Local pride heralded this relatively minor battle as the "Gettysburg of the West."

One of the commanders of the Colorado volunteers was Colonel John Chivington, a former minister whose name lives in infamy because of the Sand Creek Massacre of 1864. When regular troops departed for the Civil War campaigns to the east, Native Americans in the Colorado territories became restive, as they did elsewhere because of the incursions on their territories and the revisions of solemn treaties that occurred after precious metals were discovered. Their resentment led to disruptions of freight and mail along the overland trails leading to Colorado's mines as well as the theft of some livestock. More seriously, a few settlers were murdered.

On what is now a remote site near an unimproved road on the eastern plains of Colorado, one of the most brutal episodes in American military history took place, and event that ranks with the Mai Lai massacre in Vietnam. Arapaho and Cheyenne had come in from the plains to camp at their Sand Creek Reservation, believing that they were at peace with the Americans since they were following the instructions of authorities to segregate hostile Indians from non-hostile ones. Friendly Indians were supposed to be on the reservations. Chivington marched his forces all night and surprised the Indians at Sand Creek. His troopers got out of control and began a terrible slaughter of Indians of both sexes and all ages. One memorable image from this terrible tragedy is that of an old chief who simply stood before his quarters and sang a death song which declared that "nothing lives long except the earth and mountains." The survivors were those who escaped, because no prisoners were taken. Nobody knows for sure how many Indians were massacred. Estimates range from 100 to over 500.

Many of the troops who participated believed that Indians should be exterminated. But the American sense of justice would not be overcome by such racist sentiments. Congress investigated Chivington and his troops and condemned him and his forces for what came to be known forever as the Sand Creek Massacre.

Railroads and mining boomed after the Civil War. In fact, railroads made it possible for what were often high, remote mines to get their heavy ores out and their heavy equipment and supplies in. Every miner at work meant that several non-miners were at work in Colorado.

By the closing decades of the century people were coming to Colorado for reasons not connected to mining and the support services for mining. Some were tourists and some came to improve their health in the high, clean air. Some came to farm in cooperative colonies along the Front Range, in those places which became some of the cities of the megalopolis of a later age. Others came to work in expanding educational facilities.

In the 1860's and 1870's, gold was the most important mineral to mine, but in the 1880's silver replaced it as Leadville and Georgetown became the "Silver Queens" of the Rockies. Many workers of eastern European ethnicity came to work in the new silver mines, and then in the newly developed gold mines at Cripple Creek in the 1890's.

Colorado gained a reputation for fierce industrial strikes, particularly from 1894 to 1914. The fundamental issue at stake in the worst of them was the recognition of the unions' right to collective bargaining. The appearance of strike breakers often produced violence, which led companies to call in the state militia to restore order. Strikers came to regard the militia as a force on the side of the companies.

The worst clash was the famous "Ludlow Massacre" of 1914, when the tent city of striking coal miners was suppressed by the militia. Among the dead were some women and children. Before the militia arrived the miners themselves had been violent in the coalfields, even resorting to dynamite as a weapon.

Strife in the minefields was only part of the story. There was also romance, particularly of the rags to riches variety. The most famous of these involved Horace Tabor who started out as a storekeeper in Leadville and had the good fortune of grubstaking prospectors in exchange for a percentage of whatever mines they would discover. They were very lucky and Tabor became a multi-millionaire who added to his fortune by making a number of other fortunate deals over mines. Romance entered when Tabor left his faithful wife for an extraordinarily beautiful, ambitious and divorced waitress who was known thereafter as Baby Doe Tabor. Eventually Tabor built an Opera House and became a U.S. Senator. Yet the fates which had smiled on him began to frown. He overextended himself and lost his fortune. He died a ruined man, urging Baby Doe to cling to their last dormant mine. She did, to the extent that her old, malnourished, frozen body was found in a cabin on the site in 1935. Rags to riches to rags makes a compelling tale.

While the Tabors were building their fortune the cattle kingdoms expanded over the open range of the Colorado plains. What complicated ranching in the late 19th century in this state was the fact that the herds of sheep tended to be run by Hispanics, adding the element of ethnic hostility to the ordinary confrontations between cattlemen and sheepherders. Many sheep were "rimrocked," or driven over cliffs in this era.

On the western slope some mineral discoveries prompted a "Utes must go" movement to clear out the Indians. A massacre at an Indian agency in 1879, called the "Meeker massacre" after the agent, contributed to the movement. Eventually some of the Utes were settled in a fragment of their former territory.

At the beginning of the 20th century Colorado was strongly influenced by the populist movement and the drive to set aside lands for national parks and monuments. In 1894 Colorado became the second state to provide political equality between the sexes.

As irrigation became more of a critical issue, the state became more of a partner and patron in developing water resources. Sugar beet farming became increasingly important, but dependent upon irrigation and favorable tariff policies.

During World War One, strong agricultural prices led to rash plowing of the eastern plains, tearing up some prairie land that contributed to the Dust Bowl of the 1930's. Both dry farms and mines tended not to do well in the 1920's as well as during the Great Depression of the 1930's. Coloradans came to abandon farms on the plains when the dust storms began.

When Franklin D. Roosevelt inaugurated the New Deal, Coloradans and other Westerners profited from it to an exceptional degree on a per capita basis. Huge, federally sponsored water diversion projects brought jobs as well as water to parts of the state.

Between World War One and World War Two, the 1920's and 1930's, Colorado's population tended to be static. When World War Two began, both the population and the economy expanded at an unprecedented rate, an expansion which has never really stopped up to the present day. As in the great expansion of the 19th century mining era, rapid urban growth took place. Colorado came to supply all sorts of products and manufactures during the war. It was also a major training ground for the armed forces.

After the war, many ex-G.I.s returned to Colorado to live. Denver became the "second national capital" because of all the federal agencies which came to be located in the city. There were also booms in uranium mining and oil, and most recently in high tech and tourism. All of this has contributed to Colorado's diversity, strength and growing number of modern American problems.

Some Scenic Highlights

MOUNTAINS AND ROADS
IN COLORADO

Colorado is the state with the highest portion of the Rocky Mountains, higher than those in any of its neighboring states. There are 54 peaks over 14,000 feet, 830 peaks between 11,000 and 14,000 feet, a total of well over 1,000 mountains rising to

10,000 feet or more. Of the 75 highest peaks in the Continental United States, 57 are in Colorado. Colorado's mean elevation is 6,800 feet for the whole state which makes an interesting contrast with Montana's 3,400 feet. There are hundreds of mountain passes and dozens of roads that go over them, often with steep vertical ascents of thousands of feet.

In general, the most majestic mountains march from north to south down the center of the state on both sides of the Continental Divide. The Rocky Mountain National Park has some of the best peaks, but spectacular ranges also can be found in the southwestern part of the state as well. Far western Colorado merges into the high, dry, reddish Colorado plateau which goes on across a substantial part of Utah. Also, the south central part of Colorado has the high, flat San Luis valley.

Colorado's roads are admirably suited to bring visitors high into the mountains. For those wishing to cross the state from east to west, three good routes are available, one each across the north, central and southern part of the state. Most people use Interstate 70, which goes right up and over the center of the state, close to resorts and old mining towns. Most of it is quite scenic, with good views of the mountains and the Colorado River. The big advantage of taking I-70 is that it has four lanes, while the other two routes have two lanes almost all of the way.

There are actually two choices for the northern route, each of which leads to the ski resort of Steamboat Springs. State Route 14 goes through scenic Poudre Canyon and over Cameron Pass. U.S. 34 goes up and over Rocky Mountain National Park as Trail Ridge Road, which only opens around Memorial Day. Trail Ridge Road is famous for climbing above the timberline as the highest continuously paved highway in the United States.

A scenic southern route across the state is U.S. 160, which goes across from Walsenburg from I-25 to Durango and Cortez in the southwestern part of the state, climbing over dramatic Wolf Creek Pass on the way. Durango and Cortez are departure points for two spectacular roads. U.S. 550 goes north from Durango to Silverton and Ouray over what may be some of the most breathtaking, twisting, turning miles of road in the whole United States. Sheer drop offs loom frequently. Winter travel on this road is extremely hazardous, so it is closed frequently in that season. State route 145 going north from Cortez is a highly scenic road leading to Telluride, a city in a gorgeous setting.

Roads in Colorado are generally quite good and well maintained, but there is one exception that is so bizarre that it deserves being mentioned. Route 67, which goes to Cripple Creek, has a scary one lane tunnel. It resembles a ride in a carnival haunted house, except that daylight can be seen at a distance. It has narrow walls and is quite dark inside. The worst thing about it is the fear that a vehicle may be be coming the other way, in defiance of red and green stoplight that hangs over the tunnel on either side. When a long time resident of Cripple Creek was asked whether there were many fatal accidents because of the tunnel, he said that he could not remember any, but things had improved considerably since the stoplights were added! Here is a hint to ease anxiety about the tunnel: Drive slowly miles from it so that someone passes from behind. Then follow that car through.

ROCKY MOUNTAIN NATIONAL PARK

Although it is smaller than Yellowstone National Park, Rocky Mountain National Park offers its own unique landscape and rivals Yellowstone in drawing a large number of visitors each year. It is, in fact, the state's major tourist attraction, attracting over two and a half million visitors each year. The best time to visit may be in the fall, after the main tourist season and before the winter snows.

Rocky Mountain National Park offers unsurpassed views of some of the best snow covered peaks in Colorado, as well as icy lakes, high meadows, and wild, rock strewn moraine basins carved by retreating glaciers. The 412 square miles of the park contain 98 peaks over 10,000 feet. Long's Peak, at 14,256 feet, dominates its surroundings and is visible from a very considerable distance out on the eastern plains.

Trail Ridge Road goes over the Continental Divide at 12,183 feet and goes along for four miles above 12,000 feet. It rises fifteen miles above the timberline, which is the point where it becomes too cold for trees to grow. Trail Ridge Road makes it possible to have snowball fights in August and to observe carpets of miniature plants in actual Alpine tundra. At extremely high altitudes growing seasons are reduced to a few weeks and some slow growing plants may live for hundreds of years. As mentioned, Trail Ridge Road usually opens on Memorial Day, but when the weather is bad the opening may be postponed until early June. It usually closes for the winter in early November.

Animals are abundant in the park, especially mule deer and elk. Sometimes bighorn sheep can be seen as well. Unlike Yellowstone, bears are rare. There may only be around 35 black bears in the park because bears survive only marginally at high altitudes. For more information about the park, call 303-879-0080.

MESA VERDE NATIONAL PARK

Mesa Verde National Park has the most spectacular collection of prehistoric structures in the United States. There are more cliff dwellings here than anywhere else in the world. All told there are hundreds of cliff dwellings and thousands of sites, all well preserved by the dry air of the Southwest.

Mesa Verde, which means green tableland, is split by deep canyons. Although flat topped and without mountain peaks, Mesa Verde is quite high, ranging between 6,964 and 8,572 feet. Although the park only covers 81 square miles, it cannot be visited quickly. The roads are slow and twisting, and there are seemingly countless places to stop and observe ruins. The really spectacular ruins, the Cliff Palace in particular, are well marked on the maps provided at the Park entrance. Hiking is not encouraged, but there are very worthwhile conducted tours of the ruins from mid-May to mid-October.

The Native Americans who built these places as well as the many sites in the Hovenweep National Monument and other places in the vicinity are called the Anasazi. They are believed to be the ancestors of the Pueblo people of the Southwest. Anasazi means either "ancient ones" or "ancient enemy." They grew corn, beans and squash and supplemented their diet with game. Their extensive trading activity is clearly indicated by their caches of sea shells.

Anthropologists, archaeologists and historians have contemplated and debated the reasons for their mysterious departure hundreds of years ago. Was it a set of climatic changes, such as a long drought or a shift in seasonal rainfall patterns? Did lower temperatures result in shorter growing seasons? Did a virulent disease become widespread? Did the arrival of a warlike nomadic people make them flee? Were the resources for humans in the region simply used up, that is, was the soil eroded, the thin forests overcut, and the wildlife overhunted? Was it a combination of some of these reasons?

These questions become most intriguing while actually visiting the sites. Archaeologists have traced a dramatic evolution of their civilization through progressive stages, from hunter-gathering to settled agriculture, which was paralleled in their architecture. The Anasazi started with pit dwellings, went on to build pueblo style structures and finally reached their architectural heights with their famous cliff dwellings. Many of these buildings contain large Kivas, or underground religious chambers that are surprisingly well ventilated. One elaborate building, the Cliff Palace, had space for 400 people in a total of 200 rooms.

Some of the best sites were discovered accidentally by cowboys in the 1880's. Once known about, the ruins were subjected to looting by pot hunters and scavengers who took many artifacts. Serious expeditions also carted off treasures. One particular European expedition was responsible for the present appearance of hundreds of Mesa Verde artifacts in a museum in Finland! Preservation was imposed with the force of law when Mesa Verde became a National Park in 1906.

The beauty of these remains, the colors of the surroundings and crisp air all make Mesa Verde a very memorable place to visit. For more information, phone 303-529-4465.

NATIONAL MONUMENTS
IN COLORADO

Hovenweep National Monument: Not far from Mesa Verde is Hovenweep National Monument, which is partly in Colorado and partly in Utah. The Anasazi moved to this area 43 miles west of Cortez presumably to be near a permanent water supply. Six village sites can be observed in the National Monument, but to get to them it is necessary to drive on unpaved roads for the most part.

Dinosaur National Monument: Another National Monument shared by Utah and Colorado is the 326 square mile Dinosaur National Monument, which encompasses a large stretch of barren and rugged country, mostly in the northwest corner of Colorado. This particular spot has yielded an extremely ample number of diverse fossil remains. On display is a rather large dinosaur embedded in stone which serves to indicate the difficulties of retrieval and reassembly.

Black Canyon of the Gunnison National Monument Park: The Black Canyon of the Gunnison is in the western part of the state, near Monrose. The view offered of a deep, dark, narrow canyon is simply unforgettable. The park contains a twelve mile stretch of what may be one of the least accessible places in

North America. Visitors look down into it from the heights above.

Great Sand Dunes National Monument: One of the great curiosities of nature is the Great Sand Dunes National Monument in south central Colorado. Blowing sand has been uniquely trapped in a mountain valley, where it maintains its own undulating ecosystem. There are 55 square miles of Sahara-style 700 foot high ridges, making them the tallest sand dunes in North America. Their general position has not shifted for generations, and none of the scientists who have studied this formation can explain the phenomenon without fear of contradiction.

This place is a wonderful playground for children and adults. The great game is to scale the dunes or to tumble from the heights on hot sand.

Unfortunately a private water company wants to draw water out of the underground water table of the San Luis Valley. The National Park Service is alarmed at this prospect, fearing that the dunes, which are moist to a degree, will dry up and blow away if subterranean water is drawn off. Lawsuits are pending to keep the water company from drilling.

The Great Sand Dunes National Monument is between Walsenburg and Alamosa off of State Route 150.

The Colorado National Monument: The 20,445 acres of Colorado National Monument are located near large, sprawling city of Grand Junction in the central western part of the state. The canyons are exceptionally colorful, due in part to their elaborate sandstone configurations. The 23 mile long rim rock drive has grand overlooks. The atmosphere of this high, dry relatively treeless monument is not unlike parts of Utah.

Some Special Places in Colorado

ASPEN

Aspen is an expensive, well known and fashionable mountain town where the rich and famous cavort on the ski slopes and nightspots. It is also a place where important things happen in the realms of culture, art, education and politics. A recent significant event to transpire in Aspen was the meeting of then Prime Minister Margaret Thatcher with President George Bush which is supposed to have reinforced his resolve to handle Iraq with truly Churchillian resolve.

Aspen was the first of the old mining towns to capitalize on its old Victorian charm to draw tourists. One farsighted post World War Two developer, Walter Paepcke, is credited with resurrecting what was mostly a ghost town as a center for the arts and winter sports. Paepcke was a Chicago industrialist with a vision of what Aspen could become.

Famous people, particularly film stars, appreciate that in Aspen, for the most part, they are treated like normal people. Private planes fly them in and out, as well as the *nouveau riché*. As a result of Aspen's glamour, real estate prices in this once crumbling town have soared. An average vacation home now costs over a million, and it may be used for only a few weeks in the year. A room at a luxury hotel will go for $300 a night and a three bedroom apartment can rent for $3,000 per month. As in other prospering mountain towns, ordinary people and hired help have great difficulty in finding places to live.

Amenities are first class and, naturally, **very** expensive. Shopping and restaurants are as good as in major cities, and there are top of the line health clubs and night clubs. The level of education in Aspen is extremely high, said to be second in the nation. Here computers and fax machines go to mountaintops.

Aspen's music festival and institute are famous and draw world class creative persons to the mountains every year. Performances still go on in the Wheeler Opera House, built in 1889, and the Hotel Jerome, built in the same year, is the very center of Aspen's glittering social life. For the most part, this hotel still looks the way it did 100 years ago.

These old buildings and a year round resident population keeps Aspen from being a mere playground for the rich. Aspen is a year round organic community with old roots in the boom times of Colorado mining. It is a good place for a visit, but those on modest budgets need to make hotel arrangements out of town.

SOME OTHER FAMOUS SKI TOWNS

Colorado has a number of duly famous ski towns which offer summer recreation as well. Telluride in the southwestern part of the state, in the so-called Switzerland of Colorado, is booming to the extent that it may be on its way to becoming another Aspen. Rents are soaring and real estate developers are catering to a runaway building and buying craze.

Telluride has grown out of an old mining town. The same cannot be said for Vail and Beaver Creek, two posh ski resort areas along I-70. Vail tries to resemble a new Swiss ski resort with mixed success. Prices are high. Nevertheless, Vail has become the largest ski area in the United States.

Breckenridge is another old mining town that has become a popular ski resort. The old buildings blend with the new in this lively spot.

Steamboat Springs is headed towards continued expansion, although the town is already well supplied with recreational sites. A huge new billion dollar ski area is planned for all seasons. Condominiums and new subdivisions will be designed to service a million tourists per year. Opponents point out that this new expansion is not necessary, that ranchers and ordinary people will be driven away and that prices for everything will rise.

LEADVILLE

Once called "Cloud City" and "The Silver Queen," Leadville today is a stark, formidable city over 10,000 feet, high up in the Rockies. It has been the heart of the American mining industry for over a century.

A serious environmental problem from mountains of mineral tailings has earned it Superfund clean up designation for a 10 to 20 year project. Mining still goes on in the region. Nearby Climax and one other Colorado town are said to have more known deposits of steel strengthening molybdenum than the whole rest of the world put together. Recently a slump caused up to 3,000 workers to be laid off in Climax. Many of them had homes in Leadville.

Leadville has a raw climate and a raw history to match it. At one time it boasted 31 restaurants, 51 groceries and 120 saloons, as well as one of the most celebrated red light districts in the West. Fortunes came from silver mixed with lead, and the most famous fortune of all came to Horace Tabor.

Many of the old buildings remain, giving Leadville considerable character. Mines are all about the town, some of them offering tours. The Leadville Historic District contains the Tabor Opera House, once the most lavish theater between St. Louis and San Francisco. The Healy House and Dexter cabin, both elaborately furnished in the style of the late Victorian era, are among many other interesting buildings.

Leadville is a tough, organic community with a lot of character and historic atmosphere. It is well worth a visit.

GEORGETOWN

Georgetown does not have the cramped look of most old mining towns, nor does it feature the loud and cheap appeals to tourists that detract from other historic cities in the Rockies. Georgetown is more gracious and dignified, a characteristic noted early in its existence. An abundance of old Victorian buildings survive, in large measure because, unlike other important mining communities, Georgetown never had a major fire. Moreover, the substantial and stable appearance of the community can be traced to the fact that from the beginning Georgetown was populated with church going families.

Georgetown is an excellent place to walk around. Among the noteworthy sites are the Hamill House Museum which displays Victorian opulence and the Hotel de Paris, which evokes the boomtown years.

East of old Georgetown is a sprawl of new buildings, condos, gas stations and stores, fortunately segregated from the older parts of town.

Nearby is the Georgetown Loop Historic Mining and Railroad Park operated by the Colorado Historical Society. The Georgetown Loop is a restored stretch of exceptional narrow gage railroad engineering that connects Georgetown to Silver Plume, another old but smaller town. The Lebanon Mine and Mill is another attraction. The park is open from Memorial Day to Labor Day from 10 a.m. to 4:30 p.m. Train rides continue on weekends only in September. Telephone 303-279-6101 for more information.

CENTRAL CITY

Central City was once a rival of Denver in its boom town mining days, and it may be poised on another resurgence with the advent of legalized gambling in its precincts. The town lies in a narrow valley, along crooked, hilly, lively streets. It has similarities in physical layout to European towns.

Its two most famous buildings are the Central City Opera House and the Teller House, a large old hotel where President Grant stayed. Its famous "Face on the Barroom Floor" does not date from its mining heyday but is a portrait painted by a newspaper artist in 1936. Opera is still a major activity in Central City. Some of the world's stars are flown in for Central

City's summer season. Incidentally, Denver does not have an opera company or an opera house.

The town of Blackhawk is just a bit further on down the valley, and more or less blends in with Central City. In the tourist season both places tend to be congested and finding a convenient parking place close in can be a problem. Abundant free public parking does exist high up on a hill to the south of the main thoroughfare.

CRIPPLE CREEK

Cripple Creek has a lot left to evoke the spirit of the booming late Victorian mining town that it once was. At one time it housed 50,000 people, but until recently its population has been well under 1,000.

Cripple Creek's boom began late, in 1891, when a cowboy discovered gold nearby. The town gained its name from a local stream bed whose rugged contours lamed several cows. Devastating fires leveled the business district twice, but a solid town of brick and stone was erected in the early 20th century.

Cripple Creek is perched high up in the mountains with a magnificent snow capped range in the distance. It has an extensive museum, several streets of historic buildings and improved, steep side streets with quaint and diverse buildings scattered along them. From a distance and up close, Cripple Creek looks genuine.

VICTOR

The town of Victor is only a few miles south of Cripple Creek. Victor is smaller, less developed and more rundown and therefore may be more appealing than Cripple Creek for those who think that a degree of seediness and decay is necessary to give character to old mining towns.

Victor is framed dramatically by reminders of its days as a frontier mining town, slag heaps and mine shafts. They loom over a core of old streets and a typical scattering of diverse houses on steep dirt roads.

A large billboard near the fire station and city hall boldly announces the town's claims to fame: Jack Dempsey trained in the fire house and Lowell Thomas grew up there. The fact that young people are likely to ask who these people were may disconcert some middle aged folks.

SALIDA

Salida is an interesting old railroad town rather than a mining town, although it is close to mining regions and some ghost towns. Downtown has numerous old buildings and local people seem extremely friendly and energetically engaged in promoting the town's cultural and entertainment attributes. The Arkansas river runs through Salida and enables white water rafting businesses to flourish in July and August. Kayaking is another active sport. In the summer, a kayaker's obstacle course can be seen in the river.

ROYAL GORGE

Royal Gorge is advertised far and wide. It is just off of Route 50 between Pueblo and Salida. Before it was developed, it was a scene of impressive natural beauty, a deep and colorful canyon. Today it is a garish circus. Billboards and flags abound. A splashy theme park, other similar attractions and numerous fast food outlets give the place a hustle and bustle and "plastic Western" atmosphere. The big draw of the place is an expensive ride over the gorge on what is the world's highest suspension bridge, 1,053 feet above the Arkansas River and a quarter of a mile long. There is also the world's steepest incline railway that goes down to the canyon floor at a 45 degree angle and an aerial tramway that goes over the gorge. Yet all of the hoopla and hustling detracts from the natural beauty and makes Royal Gorge one of the most overrated tourist stops in the Rocky Mountain region.

DURANGO

Durango is a pleasant college town in the southwestern corner of Colorado that is an excellent jumping off spot to see many attractions in that part of the state. It was founded in 1880 as a railroad town and continues as such, only now the railroad carries tourists rather than ore wagons. Durango is the terminus for the Durango and Silverton Narrow Gauge Railroad described in another section of this book.

Durango is also the home of the Strater Hotel, a well maintained establishment with an elegant late Victorian decor. Downtown is lively and crowded in the summer tourist season.

BENT'S OLD FORT

Bent's Old Fort National Historical Park in southeastern Colorado is a neglected gem of historical reconstruction that recaptures the heyday of the Santa Fe Trail. It is neglected because it is out on the plains away from the big Interstate highways that funnel tourists to Colorado's mountains from the east and approximately 80 miles east of the major north to south route, I-25. As a result, most of Bent's Old Fort's visitors come from Oklahoma, Kansas, New Mexico and Texas, areas in relatively close proximity.

Bent's Old Fort was completed in the early 1830's and served as a major trading post and port of call between Missouri and Santa Fe on the famous Santa Fe Trail. It was along the Arkansas River and for a long time it was the last stop in United States territory, because Mexico and then the Republic of Texas claimed everything over the river. Trade at the fort was complex. United States goods went through from the east while Mexican and Navajo goods went in the opposite direction. Some goods were sold at the fort to resupply travellers and to serve the needs of local Indian tribes and some mountain men who exchanged buffalo robes and fur pelts for trade goods.

The fort was named for William Bent, who shared in a commercial empire that stretched from Missouri to New Mexico and maintained the fort as an important midpoint. these traders knew both Mexicans and Indians quite well. William Bent was noted for encouraging rival Indian tribes to meet and trade at the fort. He himself married the daughter of a powerful Cheyenne Indian leader.

During the Mexican War the fort became a base for the American invasion. Afterwards the fort turned into a smoldering ruin. Just how this came about remains a matter of spirited conjecture.

Today the fort rises suddenly and dramatically from the plain like a large oasis, looking just as it must have to thousands of early travelers who were undoubtedly overjoyed to see it after grinding over hundreds of miles of empty open country. Its high adobe walls encompass a large open square, and a great number of various rooms open on to this enclosed space, including those devoted to the craftsmen, such as blacksmiths, carpenters and coopers. The dining room was the largest of all. Throughout the furnishings are either antiques or reproductions.

Today costumed "historical interpreters" wander about, always ready to answer questions patiently and in whatever detail the questioner desires. Daily visitors may stay for as long as they like. Regular tours led by an interpreter take place no matter how few people assemble for them. Visitors to the fort who arrive during a rendezvous put on by a club of history buffs in costume will be treated to many of the sights and sounds of the fort in its heyday. While this is good fun, a strictness about historical accuracy is self-imposed by participants.

Those heading to the mountains are strongly advised to make a side trip through the stark southeastern plains to visit Bent's Old Fort. It is on Route 194, eight miles east of La Junta. From Memorial Day through Labor Day it is open from 8 a.m. to 6 p.m. daily. For more information phone 719-384-2596.

TRINIDAD

Trinidad is the southernmost city along the front range, one that looks to the southwest and has a very pronounced Hispanic influence from the time it was first settled by Mexican sheepherders. Trinidad was built along the mountainous branch of the Santa Fe Trail.

Today the Corazon (heart) de Trinidad National Historic District preserves several buildings of significance. The Baca House is restored to show how a prosperous Hispanic family lived in the Victorian era, mixing Anglo and Hispanic furnishings and items. A pioneer museum exhibits the history of ranching and early settlers. There is also an elaborate three story building that belonged to a prosperous banker known as the Bloom House.

FORT GARLAND AND FORT VASQUEZ

Those taking the southern route across Colorado, U.S. 160, may wish to stop off at Fort Garland on the stretch between Walsenburg and Alamosa. Fort Garland was built as a military fort to protect local residents from the Ute Indians. It operated from 1858 to 1883. Today Fort Garland has a museum and some recreations of military quarters from the period. It is not nearly as elaborately restored as Bent's Old Fort.

Even less restored is Fort Vasquez. Although it appears on road maps as an historic site, it has relatively little to offer. It is south of Greeley on Route 85, just north of Platteville. In fact, it is in a median between the north and south lanes of that highway. It has a visitor center with some exhibits open in the summer and archaeological digging at the site continues, but the old fort itself appears only as an adobe shell, which was actually a reconstruction of the Works Progress Administration in the Depression. While it was an important rendezvous point for the fur traders of the area and a place to stop for those rushing to find gold, Fort Vasquez as it appears today may not be worth a visitor's detour.

The Cities of the Front Range Mini-Megalopolis

DENVER

Denver is the largest metropolis in the whole Rocky Mountain region, with over 1,800,000 in its metropolitan area and nearly half a million in the city proper. The Salt Lake City metropolitan area, at just over a million, is its nearest rival for size in the Rocky Mountain states.

Greater Denver covers a large, sprawling area that has one cluster of ultra-modern skyscrapers and tens of thousands of acres of detached suburban homes, most of them landscaped with trees and lawns that would become a withered brown without irrigation, which is actually the appearance of the unirrigated plains and foothills around Denver for most of the year.

Denver has a ravenous thirst for gasoline as well as for water. Businesses and industries, shopping centers and civic centers, satellite city after satellite city are so spread across urbanscapes that active Denverites are required to do considerable driving on their elaborate system of multi-laned highways. Roads that radiate out towards the many suburbs pass by a sprawling, unplanned jungle of neon signs, parking lots, shopping malls, motels, car dealerships and miscellaneous businesses, most of them looking quite new. Rush hours, accidents and bad weather can sometimes cause gridlock reminiscent of California. Since the air flow over the mountains frequently sets up inversion conditions, meaning that foul cold air is held down by warmer air above it, pollutants, especially carbon monoxide from exhaust, gather at alarming rates. The air is often as bad as in Los Angeles, if not worse on some days. In recent years substantial improvements in air quality have been noted, thanks in large part to a vigorous civic clean air program.

This is the worst that can be said about Denver. Overall, it remains a very liveable city. Compared to other American cities it is quite informal and friendly. Its pace is not furious. Also, it is not nearly as dangerous as many other American cities. Very few sections have a reputation for a high crime rate, although recently reports have circulated that the drug trade has brought in some gang members from Los Angeles.

For many years Denver was a regional center for the importation of Eastern capital and influence and the exportation of raw materials. Although Denverites balk at the image of being a colonial capital or a big cow town, it still is a place where a person can wear a business suit with a stetson and boots and not be very conspicuous. When the Western Stock

Show is in town in mid-winter, Western dress is much more commonplace, as it was in the past.

Much else besides livestock and cowboys come to Denver regularly. Traveling shows going between the East and West Coasts frequently stop off to perform. Meanwhile the Denver Symphony struggles to survive and other arts are represented as well.

Downtown Denver has undergone an architectural renaissance. A cluster of metal and glass skyscrapers have replaced what were seedy rundown areas. The city has an appearance of cleanliness and spaciousness. A few surviving old buildings here and there, blend in with the new Denver nicely.

Suburban cities, such as Aurora, Arvada, Lakewood and Westminster, have been growing while Denver proper has not. Suburban cities surround Denver on all sides and engage in countless disputes with the city over funds and related matters. Nevertheless, Denver forsees a bright future. A new convention center, airport and baseball stadium are highlights of the city's improvements underway as the century draws to a close.

Denver has many places of interest. The Larmimer Square Historic District near downtown has numerous old brick structures that were restored in the 1960's to house various shops and restaurants. Close by is the Brown Palace Hotel, which is just as elegant and impressive as it was during the turn of the century. Nearly all the famous people who have ever come to Denver, including presidents, royalty and the leaders of society have stayed at the Brown Palace.

The Denver Art Museum has a representative collection from all locations and all eras. It is especially good for North American Indian art and African art. Denver also has a large and interesting Museum of Natural History, the largest between Chicago and the West Coast. It is particularly noted for displaying dinosaurs and dioramas of animals. The museums are open from 9 a.m. to 5 p.m. daily.

The Colorado History Museum is in a ultra-modern building and has many interesting exhibits, although the more modern attempts to depict Colorado history have resulted in some fearfully cluttered exhibits. The old fashioned dioramas of Native Americans and early settlers constructed as a public project during the Depression remain the most popular with many visitors, particularly children. The Colorado History Museum is open from 10 a.m. to 4:40 p.m. Monday through Saturday and from 12 to 4:40 on Sunday.

The late Victorian Molly Brown House Museum is named for the "Unsinkable" Molly Brown who survived the Titanic disaster of 1912. After making their fortune in Leadville mining, the Browns moved to Denver and made their home the scene of lavish entertainments. It has been restored and furnished as close to the style of its Edwardian heyday as possible. It is closed Mondays from September until May, but open from 10 a.m. to 4 p.m. on weekdays and 12 p.m. to 4 p.m. on Sundays.

Denver has other historic buildings open to the public. If interested, check with the Colorado Hospitality Center at 225 West Colfax Avenue for more information.

COLORADO SPRINGS

Colorado Springs is on its way to becoming a smaller version of Denver. With a metropolitan population of nearly 400,000, the Air Force Academy just a few miles up Interstate

25, a sizeable retirement community, especially for the military, and a large draw for tourism because of Pike's Peak, the Garden of the Gods and a dozen or so commercial operations, Colorado Springs is one of the thriving places in the region.

Undoubtedly the clean, spacious downtown area will continue to grow upwards and gain a closer resemblance to Denver's downtown. Nevertheless, the residential areas of Colorado Springs are made up of gracious, well-kept, well-landscaped older houses, the very habitations one would expect people like retired colonels to maintain.

Just outside of Colorado Springs is Old Colorado City, which is another attempt of modern business to infuse economic activity in an area of old, square brick buildings dating from the late 19th century and the early 20th century.

The huge, elegant, Italian Renaissance-style Broadmoor Hotel is below nearby Cheyenne Mountain. Actually underneath the mountain is the North American Defense Command and on top of it is the Cheyenne Mountain Zoo, which features a large number of giraffes at the highest altitudes this species must experience other than those on the slopes of Africa's Mount Kilimanjoro.

Downtown Colorado Springs has a pueblo style Fine Arts Center whose collections represent the diverse ethnic groups of the Old West. There are also a number of commercial enterprises catering to tourism, such as a wax museum, carriage museum and ersatz ghost towns. The McAllister House and Pioneer Museum are more noteworthy buildings, dating from the Victorian era and open to the public.

Colorado Springs has always maintained its strong connections with the military, partly because so many training operations have gone on in the vicinity. So it was fitting that the United States Air Force Academy was built north of the city.

The massive steel and concrete buildings, crowned by the dramatic, unique chapel, are indeed impressive. Visitors are welcomed.

BOULDER

Boulder is different from all of the other cities in Colorado. In a way the colorful, festive atmosphere of the 1960's has settled permanently in the place. In fact, an actual contingent of faded and now somewhat unpleasant leftover hip types still gathers and makes noise in public places. Boulder continues to draw drifters and romantics from all over. Unfortunately it has also been the headquarters of some drug dealers.

The ambience of Boulder is readily apparent along the famous Pearl Street Mall, now a pedestrian street. It offers old and new bookstores and restaurants with very varied cuisines, some of it from the Old World via the East Coast. What gives Boulder so much of its style is the University of Colorado, whose campus may be one of the most beautiful in the nation. The towering Flatirons Range rise up right behind the campus and the town most dramatically. Boulder is close to Denver and connected to the metropolis by good roads. Important high tech firms and scientific government agencies contribute to the notable affluence of the town's immediate vicinity. With an ocean, Boulder would belong in southern California.

GREELEY

Greeley is a pleasant small university city that is noted for its connections to the cattle industry. Large feedlot and meat packing operations are close by and Greeley sponsors some of the region's notable rodeos.

Greeley began as a colonized settlement, called the Union Colony. It was named for Horace Greeley, the famous New York Tribune journalist who was an ardent booster for the region. The colony fostered family life, education and temperance.

Of particular historical interest is the Centennial Village Museum. It gets its name from the year that it was created, 1976, which was both the nation's bicentennial and Colorado's centennial year. A number of interesting buildings are clustered on a five and a half acre site, serving to illustrate life in the region from the time of the first settlements until the early 20th century. There is an Indian tepee, a homesteader's house, a bunkhouse, a log cabin house, several well furnished and comfortable Victorian homes and a town depot. For further information call 303-350-9220.

FORT COLLINS

Fort Collins is a thriving and constantly expanding small city with a diverse economy whose strength is based upon some high tech industries and Colorado State University. A few moderate sized Victorian buildings survive from the 19th century, but nearly all of the town consists of ever expanding, ever sprawling suburban developments. Fort Collins has a restored historic district called Old Town with some interesting buildings, but renovators may have sapped much of the old atmosphere by applying too much new brick and concrete. Nearby are other old buildings not included in the restoration that are sadly in need of refurbishing. Fort Collins also has an interesting museum, housed in an old library building.

Fort Collins provided much inspiration for the section in a previous chapter entitled "Home, Home on the Front Range." Horsetooth Reservoir, the subject of a short treatise on the outdoors in the New West in the same chapter, is just to the west of the city.

A Closing Scene

Nearly a quarter of a century after first seeing the Rocky Mountains off in the distance, the author found himself riding towards them again in the gathering gloom of an evening on the drab eastern plains of Colorado. When I had first hurried towards the mountains they were strange to me, and now, after living within sight of them for decades, they have become a sign of home.

On this particular trip I had driven back after visiting the East Coast, where I noted how low the skies were and how bleak the urbanscapes seemed. I became disappointed as darkness grew, thinking that I had left Iowa (or was it Nebraska?) too late that morning to see the sunset on the Rockies. Instead, I would have to pitch and twist over the eroded high plains in the blackness of night before coming to the bright urban belt hugging the mountains from north to south.

Suddenly, as my car rose up over a barren slope I was transfixed by a sight in the distant west. There were the mountains, small and golden brown on the horizon, glowing like gems in the last rays of the afterglow of the sun that had set behind them. On the mountaintops was the brightest sparkling silver white I had ever seen. So even after a quarter of a century the Rockies can take my breath away. Dynamite!

Index